LEGEND  TRIPPING

WOLF'S CLOTHING

E.J. RUSSELL

RIPTIDE
PUBLISHING

Riptide Publishing
PO Box 1537
Burnsville, NC 28714
www.riptidepublishing.com

Wolf's Clothing

Cover art: L.C. Chase, lcchase.com/design.htm
Editor: Carole-ann Galloway
Layout: L.C. Chase, lcchase.com/design.htm

ISBN: 978-1-62649-411-4

First edition
October, 2016

Also available in ebook:
ISBN: 978-1-62649-410-7

LEGEND ✶ TRIPPING

WOLF'S CLOTHING

E.J. RUSSELL

RIPTIDE
PUBLISHING

For absent friends.

"*Wife, I become Bisclavret. I enter in the forest, and live on prey and roots, within the thickest of the wood.*"

After she had learned his secret, she prayed and entreated the more as to whether he ran in his raiment, or went spoiled of vesture.

"*Wife,*" *said he,* "*I go naked as a beast.*"

"*Tell me, for hope of grace, what you do with your clothing?*"

"*Fair wife, that will I never. If I should lose my raiment, or even be marked as I quit my vesture, then a Were-Wolf I must go for all the days of my life. Never again should I become man, save in that hour my clothing were given back to me. For this reason never will I show my lair.*"

—Marie de France, "The Lay of the Were-Wolf," circa 1160;
translated by Eugene Mason

TABLE OF
CONTENTS

CHAPTER
ONE

*S*unlight. Damn, it was awesome. After seven years living only the hour between midnight and 1 a.m., Trent Pielmeyer didn't think he'd ever get enough.

Every night since he'd gotten out of the private-care facility—*fuck, just call it what it is: a loony bin*—his recurring nightmare had driven him out of the house into the dark. He'd logged countless miles along the shore or through neighborhoods where houses stood shoulder to shoulder, but he always timed it so he'd catch the sunrise over the ocean. Then he'd run home with its warmth on his back and the streets of Newport brightening before him.

He slowed as he approached his family's estate. Shit. His timing was off this morning. The sun hadn't yet topped the evergreens that lined the property. The driveway was as murky as if it were still the middle of the night.

He jogged up and down in front of the gate, panting and sweaty.

Do it. Just do it. Sure, the shadows are really fricking dark, but they're only trees. Half a mile to the house. Piece of cake. Now!

He sprinted for the mouth of the drive, his Nikes crunching in the gravel, but as soon as he got to the shadow of the first tree, he stalled.

Jesus, why couldn't his inconsiderate ancestors have planted maples instead of evergreens?

He made two more abortive attempts, but it wasn't until the sun cleared the treetops that he was able to force himself to run down the driveway. How many miles had he clocked this time? Twelve? Thirteen? Hell, he could run a half marathon, but he couldn't sleep through the night without waking in a cold sweat, his throat raw from useless screams.

Trent slowed to a stop by the giant magnolia tree next to the koi pond. He could handle the magnolia—barely. *Not a fir tree. Good job, ancestors.* A few brown-edged petals clung to the chest-high canvas-shrouded object at the edge of the pond. He removed the stones weighing down the tarp and flipped it up, revealing the marble plinth underneath.

Trent McFadden Pielmeyer, Beloved Son,
May 14, 1990 - October 17, 2009

His tombstone.

Or was it technically a memorial, since his parents had had no body to bury?

Some people might wonder why his father hadn't removed it. After all, Beloved Son was home again. Not dead. Not missing. Still gay, but, hey, can't have everything.

Trent knew the truth, though. If his father had to spend money on something he considered outrageous—such as paying a crew for a whole day's work just to remove one piece of marble—he might keel over on the spot. Forrest Pielmeyer might have more money than God—including a lot that should have been Trent's by now—but he'd always be a frugal New England Yankee at heart. *Use it up, wear it out, make it do, or do without.*

How many times had Trent heard that when he was growing up? Every time he'd wanted to do something that didn't fit the Pielmeyer Way of Life—the perfect preppy image his father clung to like a life preserver from his yacht.

Trent peered at the sun. From the angle, he was late for breakfast. Again. He delayed another minute, closing his eyes and basking. *Lizards totally have the right idea.* Then he trudged up the vast slope of lawn and into the house.

The housekeeper, carrying the silver coffee service into the breakfast room, gave him her usual disapproving glare. *Yeah, yeah. Get in line, sweetheart.* Trent put on his best I-don't-give-a-shit attitude and followed.

He settled at the table across from his mother, the sunlight playing off the crystal and silver and bone china. She glanced at him and then away.

"You'll need to . . . freshen up soon, Trent. Deborah will arrive for your session at ten thirty."

Deborah was the last of the lineup of therapists who had tag-teamed him since his return to Newport. All of them agreed he was either repressing memories of a traumatic captivity, or suffering from Stockholm syndrome and trying to protect his alleged kidnapper.

Whatever.

He couldn't exactly confess what had really happened: *See, there was this ghost war, and I got sucked into it. I've been appearing—or should I say disappearing—nightly as Danford Balch, frontier murderer and first man hanged in Oregon, for the last seven years.*

That'd go over *outstandingly* well. They'd probably clap him back in the loony bin for life.

Other than the sheer unbelievability of the story, though, if he came clean about it, he'd implicate Logan Conner, his old roommate and best friend, who'd told Trent about the ghost war in the first place. Logan had been there that night, from slightly drunken beginning to horrifying end. But when the police had questioned Trent about his vanishing act, poking and prodding, looking for someone to pin the blame on, they'd never mentioned Logan as a "person of interest" in the case.

Trent hadn't had a chance to talk to Logan before the *Haunted to the Max* medic had bundled him off to the ambulance, or afterward, when his family had descended like a plague of perfectly groomed locusts. Somehow, though, Logan must have found a way to keep himself out of the whole shit-storm, and Trent intended to keep it that way. After all, Logan had tried his damnedest to talk Trent out of doing what he did. It wasn't his fault Trent had behaved like a fucking idiot.

Yeah, they were both better off with Trent insisting he couldn't remember his supposed ordeal. Too bad it wasn't true. How could he forget it when he relived it every fricking night in his dreams?

Trent sipped his coffee. Jesus, what he wouldn't give for a nice heavy ceramic mug instead of the delicate china. He wanted something he could hold on to. Something weighty, that could anchor him to the world. Not something this fragile, something that could break and send him floating, adrift.

"Trent." His father was apparently intent on smearing exactly one tablespoon of quince preserves on his toast. "It's a bit morbid, don't you think, to stare at your own headstone twice a day?"

Hunh. Guess dear ol' Dad paid more attention to him than he thought. "I couldn't see it if it wasn't there."

"It's in a private spot, and the tarp is there for a reason. The stone can't be seen, or wouldn't be if you didn't persist in uncovering it."

"You know, anyone who knows you will figure you're sparing the expense as usual. I mean, why undo something you'll just have to do again sometime in the next seventy years or so?"

His father heaved a too-familiar sigh. "How many times have we discussed economies of scale? It's inefficient to contract a single service of that sort. Better to wait until we have several similar tasks and put them out to bid at the same time."

"Aren't you afraid people might get the wrong idea—that you're keeping it because you wish me under it?"

"Don't be ridiculous. Nobody thinks anything of the kind."

I do. "Even if you can't bring yourself to remove it, could you maybe zap the date of death?"

"That would mar the marble unnecessarily."

"So what happens when I actually die? You gonna leave the 2009 date on there and add a fucking footnote?"

"That's enough, young man," his father boomed. "I will not have that sort of talk at the breakfast table."

"Right. We save the really knotty problems for *luncheon*."

His mother dropped her fork onto her plate with a clatter. "Excuse me. I have a . . ." She rose and left the room, her back as straight as the creases in her beige slacks.

His father balled up his napkin and threw it on the table. "See what you've done?"

"Me? You ever think leaving that memorial in place might bother Mom? It sure bothers the gardener. Every time he sees me, he makes the sign of the horns, like he's warding off the evil eye."

"He does no such thing." His father retrieved his napkin and shook it out, settling it on his lap before reaching for his egg cup.

"He so does."

Jesus, how much longer could he stand to live here? He'd remained holed up in the ancestral pile after he'd emerged from the loony bin because even though his parents didn't particularly like him, they were undeniably real. The housekeeper and the gardener might stare at him in contempt or fear, but at least they could *see* him. That none of them tried to hang him every night? *Bonus.*

Besides, he didn't have anywhere else to go.

He took a deep breath. Antagonizing his father, no matter how gratifying, wasn't a brilliant idea, considering he needed his cooperation. But as Deborah frequently pointed out—although in much more scientific and PC terms—his impulse control was for shit.

"So, Dad. Have the lawyers made any progress getting me declared undead yet?"

"It's a complicated process. The conditions your grandfather saw fit to impose—"

"What's the big deal? The trust would have been mine absolutely when I turned twenty-five anyway."

"Why are you in such a hurry?"

"Hurry?" Trent's voice slid up half an octave on the word. "It's been seven months. My birthday is this week, and I've got sh—stuff I want to do." *Like maybe move out of my ex-bedroom, aka the Blue Guest Room.*

His father squinted at him over a forkful of three-minute egg. "You have no need of your trust fund at the moment. You're living in this house. Eating our food." He nodded at Trent's T-shirt—yellow, with a sad-faced cartoon brontosaurus and the caption *All my friends are dead.* "The housekeeper bought a number of perfectly presentable outfits for you, so you have no need to continue dressing like a derelict."

"That's kind of my point. On this birthday, I'll officially be twenty-seven. Don't you think I'm a little old to have someone else dress me?" Trent had ignored the stack of junior executive outfits and chosen his own wardrobe from the thrift stores in North Providence, like any good ex-college student. "Isn't it time for me to rise above parental handouts?"

"What do you imagine trust fund income *is*?"

Trent put his toast down and clenched his hands together in his lap. "I think it was Grandfather's attempt to make sure I got an education that I chose for myself."

"Well you're not pursuing that at the moment, are you? As far as I can see, you're not pursuing anything except the best way to embarrass me and distress your mother."

"I'm trying to get it together." He was. He really was. But while he was unable to escape the recurring nightmares, the lack of sleep was a real handicap to rational thought. Maybe if he could tell someone about them, share the experience, he could—

No. Safer to keep the truth under wraps. Safer for Logan. Safer for himself, if he wanted to avoid mental health arrest.

If he had his trust fund, though, he'd leave. Go back to school, get the gen. ed. stuff out of the way while he decided whether he could ever face the stage again.

That was the worst part about the ghost war experience. Clueless asshole that he'd been, he'd leaped into the role of Danford Balch as if he'd been making his Broadway debut, without realizing the contract had no opt out. It had been horrible and dehumanizing and terrifying while it was happening, and continued to rob him of his sleep seven months after his rescue. Worst of all, like seven years of aversion therapy, it had also robbed him of the thing that he'd loved most in the world—acting. Now, the very idea of auditioning for another play was enough to send him scurrying back to the safety of the loony bin.

But he had to start somewhere.

"When I head to school this fall, I'll—"

"Where exactly were you planning to go?"

Trent blinked. "Uh . . . well I . . ." How stupid was it that he hadn't thought about it? "I guess I assumed Portland State would let me reenroll. I mean . . . unless their requirements have changed in the last seven years. I should—"

"Do you seriously imagine we'd allow you to return to Oregon after this whole escapade?"

Trent frowned. "'Escapade'? You make it sound like it's something I did for fun."

"Wasn't it? You refuse to divulge the details, name your accomplices—"

"'Accomplices'?" Dread pooled in Trent's belly. *Don't mention Logan, not when they're still searching for someone to blame.* "I told you, it was all me."

"You were obviously *somewhere*, Trent. And under the terms of your grandfather's trust, you're not owed a penny if you've committed any crime greater than a misdemeanor."

He'd been in Forest Park after hours—a violation of a city ordinance, but surely that wasn't enough to rob him of his inheritance. "I haven't—"

"Until the authorities are satisfied that you didn't engineer your own disappearance in an attempt to extort more money from this family, the trust will remain precisely where it is. Invested under my name."

Trent jumped to his feet, and his chair toppled over in a crash of oak on marble. "Did you ever get a ransom demand? A single *hint* that I was trying to scam you? Jesus *fuck*, Dad."

"Trent! If you can't moderate your language, you may leave the room."

"Excellent idea." *I'll leave the room. I'll leave the* house. *I'll leave the whole damned* state! He stalked out into the foyer and ran up the staircase, his father's voice echoing behind him.

"You want to know when I'll take down that memorial? When I'm convinced my son isn't dead to me!"

Trent stumbled on the last step. *Jesus.*

His therapist thought he was shielding his kidnapper; the police thought he was covering for an accomplice; and his own father thought he'd kidnapped *himself* for some never-demanded ransom.

The worst part was, he couldn't tell any of them the truth. How could he convince them that a cheesy paranormal investigation show had gotten it exactly right? Nobody would buy anything that unbelievable.

Except for one person. *Logan.*

Trent's birthday was on Friday—he wasn't sure if it counted as the twentieth or the twenty-seventh, and no way was he celebrating it alone except for his parents and one of the housekeeper's heavy cakes.

Damn it, he'd spend the day in Portland with Logan, the only person on the planet who knew he wasn't insane, hallucinatory, or a goddamn fucking criminal.

CHAPTER
TWO

hristophe Clavret studied his reflection in the full-length mirror. This new jacket wasn't quite what he'd imagined when he'd discussed it with his tailor. Was the cut a trifle too snug? The tailor his family had used since before he was born had retired, and the man who'd taken over the business had more modern notions of fashion than the old fellow had.

He rather liked this silhouette, though, and the suit had arrived with flattering speed, considering it'd had to be shipped from Vienna to Portland. One of the only acceptable benefits of being the heir to his family's import-export business, in his opinion, was the ability to navigate the intricacies of international shipping.

He turned and checked his back. Hmm, he'd have to get his shirts replaced—the old pattern was too bulky under the slim fit of the jacket, but he'd found a local tailor whose work he liked. His father would never approve, neither of the new suit style nor the blasphemy of using an American tailor.

All the more reason to order a half-dozen shirts from the local shop immediately. Perhaps the next suit from there as well. If he—

His doorbell chimed, and he frowned at his reflection. He wasn't expecting visitors, and he'd left orders with the front desk that he didn't wish to be disturbed. Acquainting himself with a new suit was not an activity to rush, nor was it one he wished to share with strangers. It was very unlike the security team to ignore his instructions. Since his family owned the condominium building, the staff was usually too deferential for his liking.

He strode down the hall into the entryway and peered through the spyhole. *Mother of God.* His father and brother. No wonder the guards had waved them through.

Christophe threw open the door. "Papa. Anton. What are you two doing in Portland?"

"Conversing with you in English, it appears." Anton chuckled as he escorted Henri into the flat with a hand under the old man's elbow. "If you bothered to read your emails, *mon frère*, you would know that we're in town for an international commerce symposium."

"Then English conversation is good practice for you." He closed the door and followed them into the living room.

"I see. So your refusal to speak French is entirely for *our* benefit. Very considerate." Anton settled Henri into the wingback chair Christophe kept just for him. "Was your absence from the opening day's events a gift to us as well, to give us practice in the American way of networking? Or could you simply not be bothered to open your messages?"

Christophe grinned at his brother. "Have you considered that perhaps I study my email very closely indeed? Those gatherings are nothing but pointless chatter, over things that matter little. I prefer to avoid them whenever possible. I advise you to do the same."

"That is no way to talk, *mon fils*." Henri rested his hands on the silver wolf's head handle of his cane. "You missed a very satisfying session. We've finessed a most favorable trade agreement with the Portuguese, despite interference from that impudent pup, Etienne Melion."

"If you had to deal with Etienne, I'm even more pleased I wasn't there."

"Bah. You cannot avoid him forever. Now that he's taken over Melion GmbH from his father, you'd best learn to handle him. Understanding the nuances of such negotiations will be critical when you assume control of our company from me."

Christophe winced inwardly. His father might not notice the tightening of Anton's jaw whenever Henri brought up the archaic succession plan for Clavret et Cie, but Christophe caught it. Every time.

Anton lived and breathed the business, but would never inherit it as long as Henri insisted on adhering to the outdated tradition that decreed the CEO must be a *true Clavret son*.

In other words, only a male who could transform into a wolf was allowed to captain the company.

Christophe carried the damned genetic mutation that meant he qualified. Anton did not. No matter that Anton was twenty times better at the corporate dance than Christophe; no matter that Christophe's vocation lay in another direction. In their father's eyes, their fates had been sealed at the moment of their conception.

"Papa, we've discussed this. Don't you think—"

Henri held up his hand, his golden eyes flashing even dimmed with age as they were. "I know you once had other dreams, *mon fils*, but I also know you will never disappoint me." He snapped his fingers. "Anton, give the files to Christophe?"

"Of course, Papa." Anton opened his briefcase and withdrew a tablet. He woke it with a swipe and handed it to Christophe.

Christophe stared at the screen, which displayed the pictures of several young women. "Surely these two are Gemma and Natalie Merrick? When I came to America, they hadn't left school for university yet. They appear to have done well." His lips twisted in disgust. "The Melion sisters, however . . ." Amazing how those three poisonous personalities were so accurately conveyed in a single image. The photographer must have cared for them as little as Christophe did.

"Your brother was not entirely accurate as to the reason for our visit. Since we have been unsuccessful in convincing you to quit America and assume your traditional responsibilities, we have brought your responsibilities to you."

"Papa, you know I prefer coordinating the American side of the business. I like it here."

Henri waved a hand. "*Bêtise*. Any underling can manage such things. You are to be CEO, *mon fils*. You should be back in Vienna, attending meetings with me, learning the details of our company. Or home in Nantes, where your comfort can be seen to much better than in this paltry place. You have spent so many years here that our rivals, our peers, do not know your face. You even begin to sound like an American."

"America is an important market."

Henri's shrewd eyes narrowed. "Yet that is not why you persist in remaining, is it? You think I don't monitor your expenses? You have been dabbling again. Biology. Genetics. Bah. There is nothing to learn that we haven't known for centuries.

11

We don't know how to fix ourselves. "Let us leave that conversation for another time. Tell me instead why I have a slate full of pictures of all the women from the Old Families save ours."

Henri chuckled. "Well you could hardly mate with one of your cousins."

"Mate?" Christophe's breath faltered. "I have no intention of—"

"Christophe. Enough. I have indulged your fancy since you left university, but the time has come for you to embrace your destiny. You need to return home. Assume your rightful place as my heir. Sire the next true Clavret son."

Christophe ran a shaking hand through his hair. "Even were I inclined to marry a woman—which I am not—I would never risk a child. And certainly not with any of these women, who have a much greater chance of carrying the defective gene."

His father bridled, thrusting his jaw out. "The gene is not defective. It is what makes us who we are."

"You are wrong, Papa. It made us who we *were*. But in today's world, the mutation is a disability. How many times has Anton had to step in for you because you were 'unavailable'—at the chateau, coursing through the woods in pursuit of a hare or a deer?"

"It should not have been Anton. It should have been you."

"What if the compulsion had taken us both at the same time? Modern business moves rapidly. It doesn't await the pleasure of the baron as feudal society did. It has already left us behind, and will leave us further if you persist in clinging to the old ways."

Henri's knuckles tightened on the head of his cane. "I will not hear this."

"You must. Anton is far more qualified to take over the company than I. Furthermore, he wishes to do so. I do not."

"Anton is not a true Clavret," Henri bellowed.

Christophe glanced at his brother, but Anton had turned his back, apparently busy with something in his briefcase. Christophe knew the tension in those shoulders, though. He'd witnessed it often enough throughout their lives when his father or uncle had given him, the younger son, preference over Anton, simply because Christophe was a damned throwback.

"Papa, we've discussed this. I've learned this much through my genetics studies. All male descendants carry the gene. The Y chromosome is passed unchanged from father to son. Anton is as likely to sire another mutant boy as I am." *For which reason, I hope he never marries.*

"Then why are not all sons true Clavrets? Why is Anton as mundane as any man not of our lineage?"

"I know it can be confusing, but remember the gene is what is called dose-dependent. It can only be expressed if the X chromosome of the mother also contains the gene. But X chromosomes recombine, unlike the Y, which is unchanged. Anton's mother did not pass it on to him. Mine did." *And she died for it.* "Our semen doesn't produce as many Y sperm, either." *Another present from our distant cursed ancestor.* "That is why so few sons are born in each generation. Why," he tapped the tablet's screen, "the Merricks have no male in this generation. Why my cousins are all female. Why even the Melions have only a single male."

"Enough about *X*s and *Y*s. Etienne may be an insolent *connard*, but he is aware of what is owed to his family. He is in negotiations with the Merrick family and expects to wed by the end of summer."

Christophe raised his eyebrows. "Gemma or Natalie?" Both women were intelligent, independent—or at least had been when they were younger and he'd seen them on a regular basis. Could one of them have had the ill luck to fall in love with that sadistic bastard?

Henri flicked his fingers. "It hardly matters. Whichever one is dutiful enough to accept her responsibility to our heritage."

"Mother of God, it's the twenty-first century. We shouldn't be bartering brides as if they were no more than brood mares."

"It is how we have always done it. How we protect our lines. The girls know what is due to their families. As should you."

"Even if I were attracted to women—"

"You had little trouble while you were at university."

"Yes, but I prefer men nowadays."

"Why should that matter? By nature, our kind are *bisexuels*. It is one of the ways we prove our worth, maintain our power."

"Once upon a time, perhaps. But we can hardly fuck a business rival into submission, Papa."

Henri's grin could only be described as wolfish. "So you say."

That is not something I want to know about my father. "Be that as it may, I will not marry one of these women." *Or any other. Who knows how far our ancestor's genetic defect has spread? Or the Merricks' or the Melions'?* "I can't understand why any of them would agree to such an arrangement in this day and age."

Anton snorted. "Not all are as fortunate as you, Christophe, with your mother's money at your back to give you independence. The other families are arranged exactly as ours is. The girls' inheritance is held in trust, only released to them if they mate with a man from the Old Families."

"And that compensates them for a one-in-ten risk of death in childbirth?"

"Who are you to judge if they choose those odds rather than a life of certain penury?"

"Hardly penury. They're as capable of earning their own way as anyone."

"It may seem a hardship, though, after a life of privilege. Besides, you've said it yourself. The world has changed. Science has advanced. The risks—"

"Remain." Christophe held his brother's gaze. "Anton, would you agree to such a match?"

Anton glanced down at his hands, bare of any rings—no wedding band, and no heavy gold signet such as Christophe wore, the badge of his role as the heir. "I don't have your prospects. None would have me, even if I chose. Not while you're available."

"But I'm not." *I never will be.*

Henri thumped the carpet with his cane. "*Mon fils*, please. I am old. I cannot continue to lead as I have in the past, and our company, our family will suffer. You must come home."

Ah God. The I'm old gambit. His father was extraordinarily adept at wielding filial blackmail. *If only I weren't so susceptible.* "Papa—"

"Not another word. You will return home. You will choose a bride. You will do your duty as each Clavret man has done since the first baron."

"But the American offices—"

"Anyone can do that. Anton can stay."

At Anton's flinch, Christophe clenched his fists. "Papa, Anton is not *anyone*. He's head of logistics."

"And you are the next CEO. But I—" He stood, hands braced on his cane, but with his spine straight, his shoulders thrown back. He looked Christophe square in the eyes—they were exactly the same height, several inches shorter than Anton. *Another gift from our ancestor. The stature of a medieval man.* "I am the current CEO, and I am reassigning you to the Vienna office. Permanently."

"Papa—"

"Enough, Christophe. If you do not obey, I will shut down the American operations."

Anton's head jerked up. "Papa, the revenues from this market count for over half our profits. You can't—"

"I can, and I will if I must. What are profits when our heritage is at stake? I'd rather liquidate the entire company than leave it in the hands of any but a true Clavret." Henri glared at Christophe. "So you see, if you persist in destroying our family, you risk destroying our business too. Is that the legacy you want?"

Christophe bit back a bitter retort. *Now is not the time for this fight.* "Of course not."

Henri nodded, a decisive jerk of his chin. "Good. The private jet is at the airport. We leave tomorrow at ten."

"No. My friend's wedding is on Saturday, and I intend to be there for him. Afterward—" He shared a glance with Anton. "Afterward, I will come home and do as you say." *At least for as long as you are with us.*

But the instant they laid Henri to his final rest, Christophe would turn everything over to his brother. In the meantime, he had less than a week of freedom. He intended to make the most of it.

"Very well. When—" Henri sniffed and Christophe froze. "When did you shift last?"

"A while ago. It is no matter."

"It is. You are depending too much on the suppressant. It is not good for you. It is not how we were meant to live."

"No. We were meant to live as wolves three days out of seven. Will you insist on that?"

"Don't be ridiculous, but one day out of fourteen is not excessive. How long has it been?"

Christophe stared at his hands, their tremor more noticeable now, the light winking off his signet. "Six weeks."

"Six *weeks*?" Henri rarely used his alpha voice, but now it rang in Christophe's brain, activating his submissive response. He ducked his head. "It's a wonder you can still think, let alone walk and talk. Nobody has ever gone six weeks before."

Nobody has ever wanted to before. Had I a choice, I would go forever without shifting. "It is nothing, Papa. The suppressant does its job."

"Where did you last shift?"

"I took a weekend off and flew up to the cabin in Fairbanks."

"Who went with you?"

"Nobody."

"Christophe. You know how dangerous that is. You must promise me to always take someone as guard. As backup."

The alpha timbre had returned to Henri's voice, compelling Christophe's obedience. "I . . . I promise, Papa."

"Good." Henri cast an appraising glance at Christophe's new jacket. "Is that a new suit?"

"Yes. Do you like it?"

Henri sniffed. "It won't do. I'll order another for you from Gottschalk."

"No, Papa." Christophe had the same alpha potential as his father, and he injected a bit of it in his response. He could at least be master of his own clothing. "I prefer this one. I shall keep it. In fact, I've decided to order several more in a similar style. From an American tailor."

Christophe held his breath, but Henri's eyes twinkled appreciatively. "So. You are capable of a challenge after all. Keep your suit, then, but I don't understand why the classic style won't do for you."

"Perhaps it's time for a new classic."

"We shall see. I expect you in the Vienna office on Monday."

"Wednesday."

Henri raised one silver eyebrow. "Christophe—"

"Riley's wedding party lasts the weekend. With travel and the time difference, I can't commit to earlier than that."

"Very well. Wednesday. Anton, forward Christophe the agenda." Henri squeezed Christophe's shoulder. "We have much to discuss."

CHAPTER
THREE

Trent stepped onto the escalator that led down to baggage claim at the Portland airport, his hands deep in the front pocket of the same PSU hoodie he'd worn the last time he'd been here—the same PSU hoodie he'd worn for seven years under his phantom pioneer costume. Any sane person would probably have burned the damn thing at the first opportunity, but it was all Trent had left from his old life and he clung to it like a toddler to a security blankie. Because seriously? Sometimes the real world was freakier than his supernatural prison, and by everyone's account, he and sanity weren't totally reacquainted.

For instance, now that he was sneakers-on-the-ground in Oregon, it occurred to him that he should have phoned Logan—or at least figured out how to find him—before jumping on the first plane out of Rhode Island.

Trent hoisted his backpack farther up his shoulder as he followed the rest of the crowd from his flight to their designated carousel. The week Trent'd checked into the loony bin, barely coherent and half-convinced he'd hallucinated the whole rescue, Logan had called the house and left a ton of messages, although Trent's family hadn't told him about them until months later. He'd wanted to call back. He'd thought about it every fricking day since. But whenever he mustered the courage to approach his father's assistant and ask for Logan's number, he'd remember the suspicion in the cops' eyes as they'd questioned him—none too gently—about where he'd been and who he'd been with. Even though the case was technically closed now that he'd returned, Trent didn't want to point attention at Logan, the only person who'd tried to contact him.

Nobody else had ever called. No one from high school. None of his old legend-tripping friends. Nobody he'd known in his short time at PSU.

Why should they? Seven years was a freaking long time when you were nineteen, when your life was measured in school-related blocks: four years in high school, four in undergrad, another two or three in graduate school. But once those little time boxes were blown open by graduation, the coincidental ties disintegrated.

Trent had jumped out of the PSU box before it had expired, so it was unlikely anyone would remember him—just another guy who'd bailed freshman year.

But Logan had called. So Trent hadn't called back. Unfortunately, the calls had been on the landline, so he had no idea what Logan's phone number was. Or where he lived. Where he worked. In fact, did he even *live* in Oregon anymore? Maybe Deborah-the-shrink was right. His impulse control was truly shit-tastic.

Trent fingered the new iPhone in his hoodie pocket, which he hadn't gotten the hang of—although he hadn't really tried. He'd held on to his old phone, a Nokia flip phone that had been the height of cool the year he became a ghost, because it was something he understood. But it had finally died as he was shoving clothes into his duffel in his desperate rush to escape the old homestead.

He'd had the cab stop at the nearest cell phone store on the way to the airport. The clerk had laughed at his old phone and called the other clerks over to poke at it and laugh some more. They'd insisted the latest model iPhone was what he wanted.

It wasn't. But if he didn't want to be a fossil forever, he needed to start somewhere. So he'd bought a new laptop too. Thank God and his father's image-consciousness for American Express Black, and the card he'd bestowed on Trent "for emergencies"—because if getting away from home wasn't an emergency, then Mount Hood was an anthill.

The red light over the baggage carousel flashed, accompanied by the harsh blare of an alarm, and the belt jerked into motion. Trent stood near the far end of its serpentine path, because what was the hurry? He had no fucking clue where he was going. Maybe he should go back upstairs and book a return flight to Rhode Island.

"Mr. Pielmeyer."

Trent whirled, clutching the straps of his backpack. *Fuck.* Bishop, the detective who'd questioned him in the hospital and later at police headquarters, was sauntering toward Trent, his hands in the pockets of his trench coat.

Trent plastered on a cheeky grin. "Detective Bishop. Fancy meeting you here."

"I could say the same for you."

"Is staking out airports new on your dance card? I don't recall ever seeing you outside of that lovely interrogation room. Oh, and on camera of course, costarring with my parents in all those awesome press conferences." Trent winked. "Love the new haircut too."

Bishop's dark skin didn't show a flush, but given the way his jaw tightened, Trent's old powers of irritation hadn't atrophied. It helped that he'd had so much practice with his father lately.

"On that account, I *can't* say the same for you."

"You don't like the new do?" Trent flicked his bangs with a finger. Actually, he hadn't had a haircut since he'd gotten out of the sanitarium. They'd shaved his head there, the bastards, with his father's permission. "I think I'll start a trend."

Come on, baggage handlers. How long can it take to unload the fucking luggage? Half the passengers on his flight had already snagged their bags and split, lucky devils. Where the hell was his duffel?

"What's lured you away from the comfort of your Newport mansion, Mr. Pielmeyer?" Bishop nodded at Trent's hoodie. "Your timing's a bit awkward for a visit to your old stomping grounds. Isn't the yachting season about to begin?"

Trent licked his lips and edged away. "I wouldn't know. Never got into that scene. Besides, the old man's yacht was a casualty of hurricane what's-her-name."

"Sandy?"

"If you say so. I'll check when I go back to Newport."

If he ever *went* back. Though he hadn't a clue what his next step should be, he'd felt as if a giant boulder had rolled off him as soon as the plane had lifted off the tarmac. He belonged here. Or at least he belonged *away* from there.

He glanced past Bishop's massive shoulders at the exit, and a shiver chased up his back. Was he ready to face *Portland* again?

Sure, he'd had a short, happy time here—but then the shit had kicked in. Should he have picked another destination? Hawaii, say, or Fiji, or Tierra del fucking Fuego.

But even as he considered other options, he axed them. None of those places held unfortunate memories, true, but they also didn't hold Logan.

Bishop took a step into his path, blocking his view. The fluorescent overhead lights gleamed on his shaven head. *Looks waaay better on him than it did on me. Kinda hot, actually, and—*

Shit. What am I thinking? Trent was here to reconnect with Logan, not perv on the detective who'd never believed a word of his story.

His overstuffed duffel finally emerged from under the rubber flaps onto the carousel, *Thank you baby Jesus.* "Oh look. There's my bag. As lovely as it was to see you, Detective, I really must be off."

"In so much of a hurry you can't spare me a few minutes?" Bishop's deep voice turned coaxing, and he neatly blocked Trent's access to the conveyer belt. "I'd like to chat."

"What's the point, Detective? Isn't the case closed if there's no victim anymore?"

"There's a victim, all right. You. And if your kidnapper did it once, he could do it again. Do you want anyone else to go through what you did? Some other college kid? A woman? A child?"

"Trust me. The same thing will never happen to anyone else."

"Why not? What do you know? Come on, Trent. I'm on your side."

"Is that so?" His duffel slid by and disappeared. *Crap.*

"Someone held you against your will. Hurt you." Bishop pointed to the rope welt scars at the hinge of Trent's jaw. "In my book, that's wrong."

Fucking great. Deliver me from righteous cops on a crusade. Snark-deflection worked much better against anger and suspicion than against concern. Trent hitched his sweatshirt hood higher to shield his scars, and broke out the assitude.

He tilted his chin and fluttered his eyelashes. "All this attention is very flattering, Detective. Are you sure you're not after my ass?"

Bishop barked a laugh. "Not the way you think. My boyfriend wouldn't stand for it." He took a step closer, the laughter disappearing from his eyes. "Not everyone comes back, Trent, but you did. After seven years. How?"

"I . . . Just lucky, I guess."

"I don't believe in luck. Something you did, or some quirk in your captors, made it possible for you to survive. To escape. I— We need to know everything. So the next time someone goes missing, we stand a better chance of finding him sooner. You can help us understand."

Bishop's voice was a caress now, his dark eyes intent, as if he were trying to hypnotize Trent into blurting his darkest secrets.

Trouble is, it was working.

Resist, damn it. Trent shook the hair out of his eyes. "How'd you know I was here? Last I checked, Rhode Island wasn't under the jurisdiction of the Portland Police Department."

"There are other ways to follow up, other connections I can tap. If a case interests me, I pay attention. Your case interests me."

"Obsesses, more like," Trent muttered.

Bishop's gaze shifted to the bags rolling by on the carousel—which included the second coming of Trent's duffel. "We could learn so much from you, like why they targeted you in the first place. Don't you want to help?"

Almost within reach. "I'd like to, but I can't. I really have to go."

Bishop rocked back on his heels, studying the reader board over the carousel as if *Delta Flight 289* was a coded message he had to decipher.

"Logan Conner."

Trent froze, his fists tightening on the straps of his backpack. "I beg your pardon?"

"The commissioner's kid. He was your roommate at the time, wasn't he? Other witnesses claimed he might be more. We thought he must at least be an accessory, maybe the perp himself, but his father swore up one side and down the other that the kid was with him the night you went missing."

So that's how Logan stayed off the radar. His father's political agenda was actually useful for once.

"His behavior changed radically after you disappeared. He turned transient, never sticking in one place for long. But he showed a hell of an interest in Forest Park. Visited that derelict building by Balch Creek every night for a year, and every anniversary after that."

"How do you know?"

"It was my case."

"It's closed. I'm back. The end."

"Is it? Kind of a coincidence Logan would be in the same spot when you showed up again."

Trent's palms were damp against the backpack straps. "Coincidences happen."

"Do they? You wouldn't be heading to Stumptown Spirits, would you?"

"I— What?" Trent let the duffel slide by. "What's that and why would I go there?"

Bishop pushed his trench coat aside and shoved his hands in the pockets of his slacks. "Stumptown Spirits, the bar owned by your old pal, Logan. Which he conveniently inherited after you showed up in Forest Park last October."

"I have no idea what you mean." Trent tried not to let the huge swell of relief that flooded his chest show on his face, although judging by Bishop's raised eyebrow, he wasn't particularly successful. But Jesus *fuck*. Bishop had just given him Logan's whereabouts. He didn't have to flail around trying to find him with an incomprehensible phone.

The duffel made another appearance on the conveyer belt, and this time Trent strolled over to meet it. He grabbed its strap and slung it over his shoulder. God, the thing weighed a ton. Should he have been a little more selective about packing? Nah. Too much work. He'd sort it out at the hotel.

Bishop caught up with him in two giant strides. "Come on, Trent, help me catch the guy who did this. Help me catch the next guy. You haven't told us the whole story. I can feel it."

With Bishop looming over him like the hangman who haunted his sleep every night, Trent's momentary relief faded. Sweat broke out along his hairline.

He couldn't hate Bishop for wanting to find an alleged kidnapper. If he really *had* been kidnapped, he'd probably kiss the guy's feet or fling himself against his massive chest. But Bishop was too smart, too good at his job, and too intent on seeing justice done. And he clearly wasn't about to give it a fucking rest until Trent gave up something.

Keep this guy far away from Logan. Bishop wanted the truth, but he was the last person in the world who'd believe it.

So maybe he's the only one I can actually tell it to.

Trent dropped the duffel and stood on top of it, so he was eye to eye with the giant detective. "You want a story? Here's one. Once upon a time, in a park in a city very like Portland, a whole cast of ghosts acted out the same story night after night. Betrayal. Murder. Capture. Punishment." He punctuated his words with pokes at Bishop's massive chest. "Every. Single. Night. Whether anybody could see them or not." The back of Trent's throat burned and his voice turned hoarse. *Hold it together, damn it.* "Then, this dumb-ass college kid got the brilliant idea to join the party—for kicks, for thrills, for adventure. Because he wanted to be the goddamn fucking star. Only problem was, he forgot to read the fine print. You can check in to the ghost war, but you can't check out. Not until someone takes your place. And who'd want to take the place of the guy who gets hanged? Every. Single. Night."

Bishop's frown was a scary thing. "Christ on a crutch, Pielmeyer, make up an original lie at least. You stole this one from that bogus TV show. The one that was filming in Forest Park when you returned."

Trent shrugged, trying to recapture his don't-give-a-shit act. "You asked for a story." He jumped off the duffel and hauled it across his shoulder. "That's the best I've got. See you around."

He turned away and headed for the exit, keeping his gait even and unhurried, although the panic welling in his chest was urging him to run, the way he ran every time his memories of the ghost war threatened to overwhelm him. But in the glass exit door's reflection, he could see Bishop watching. He couldn't afford to appear guilty, and he couldn't go directly to Logan's bar.

Hotel first. Shower. Dress like an adult. Then tonight he'd hit Stumptown Spirits. If Bishop's "connections" could find him in an airport, the bar was probably under surveillance too, so Trent would have to be sneaky. Trent flipped his hood over his head, the better to mask his face. A quick in-and-out—get Logan's digits and arrange a private meet up later.

Not too much later though, because he'd *dreamed* of this—of how Logan's familiar grin would dawn when their gazes met across the room. He'd laugh then. God, Trent had missed Logan's laugh. Trent would hold his arms open and Logan would rush across the bar and— *Whoa. Don't get ahead of yourself, Pielmeyer.* Logan had never gone in for PDAs—he'd always been terrified of pissing off his politico father.

Maybe that's changed too. Trent could only hope. Because nobody had touched him with real affection for over seven years, and the one thing he wanted more than anything was for someone to give him a fucking hug.

When Christophe arrived at Stumptown Spirits, the bar owned by Riley's fiancé, he apparently became part of a mob. The bar was packed, every table filled, every barstool occupied. He hesitated just inside the heavy front doors. Was there some peculiar festivity or sporting event today that he was unaware of? Even after years spent in the Pacific Northwest, he occasionally missed the specific triggers of herd behavior.

After all, he was a lone wolf himself.

He scanned the crowd until he caught the familiar glint of Riley's rectangular glasses. Riley was standing at the end of the bar, in earnest conversation with a tall woman with curly blond hair. Christophe edged through the crowd to stand behind Riley's shoulder, waiting for him to conclude his conversation.

"Logan *owes* me, Rile. If it weren't for him, I'd have touched a real ghost. A whole posse of real ghosts."

Riley shuddered visibly. "Trust me, touching a ghost isn't all that great."

"I don't care." The woman crossed her arms. If she didn't have such a determined jaw, Christophe would have classified her expression as a pout.

"God, Jules." Riley sighed. "You'll never let it go, will you?"

"Never. Unless the two of you agree to do the special. 'Witch's Castle: Where Are They Now?' It'll be great." She dropped her militant pose and her tone turned wheedling. "Please? Come on,

Rile, you know you can sweet-talk him into anything. If I can prove to the *Haunted to the Max* producers that I can deliver the same buzz as the first Witch's Castle episode, they've promised to listen to my next pitch. If you guys won't sign on, they'll make me use Max fucking Stone, and the show'll tank for sure."

"Don't pretend you can't wrangle Max into shape without breaking a sweat."

"That's beside the point. I'm trying to get *away* from that guy. It's bad enough you invited him to the wedding."

"Hey, that was Logan, not me."

She snorted. "Right. Logan hates Max."

"You'd think. But he says Max grows on you. Like mold."

"Then sign me up for mold remediation, stat. Because the show got way more traction with you and Logan front and center—hell, Logan's gotten traction too. I mean, he must be raking in the bucks. Last fall, you could throw a cat through the place and not hit anybody."

"I think he preferred it then."

"Bullshit. Look around you. How much fun is this?"

Riley followed her instructions, scanning the room. "Ask Heather. If Zack hits on her one more time—" Riley froze as his gaze met Christophe's, and his eyes widened.

Christophe grinned. "Hello, *cher.*"

"Chwistophe?"

Ah. Riley's charming little speech impediment still manifested when he was flustered then. It was one of the things that had attracted Christophe to him when they first met. He hugged Riley and kissed him on both cheeks.

By the time they disengaged, a wide smile had replaced Riley's astonished expression. "I didn't think you'd be able to make it."

"I would never miss your wedding. You look wonderful, *cher.* Incipient matrimony suits you."

Riley blushed furiously. "Well, you know. Happiness. What can I say?"

"You need say nothing, except perhaps to introduce me to your charming companion."

"Oh. Right. Christophe, this is Julie Ainsworth. She's my best . . . person, I guess you'd call her. Attendant. Witness. Whatever."

"Try *friend*, doofus." Julie held out her hand. "Pleased to meet you, Christophe . . . ?"

"Clavret. The pleasure is mine, I assure you."

Her handshake was firm, accompanied by an appreciative nod. "I like this guy, Rile. He's a lot more polite than dick-bag shit-bucket Logan."

Christophe's eyebrows shot up. "Indeed?"

"Jules," Riley growled. "Not now, okay?"

"Fine." She smiled at Christophe, the two of them nearly of a height. "So how do you know Riley?"

"We dated once upon a time, when I first arrived in America."

She buffeted Riley's shoulder. "Why didn't you ever tell me? See, the killer accent, the beard, the manners. Why couldn't you stick with him instead of—"

"Jules! Give it a rest. It wasn't that serious, right, Christophe?"

Christophe inclined his head, but couldn't resist casting a sly smile at Julie. "As you say."

Riley rolled his eyes. "Don't encourage her, please. She can't resist antagonizing Logan at every opportunity, and he's on edge enough about the wedding."

"Ah. So his feet are getting a trifle cold?"

Julie snorted. "Hardly. He barely lets Riley out of his sight."

"He's just stressed. The bar—"

"Keep telling yourself that. He's secretly afraid you'll come to your senses and dump him before the deal is sealed."

"Not going to happen. You know that and so does he."

She slanted a glance at Christophe from under her lashes. "As you say."

A flush chased up Riley's face, reddening his cheeks, forehead, and the tips of his ears, but before the poor man exploded, Christophe relented. "Don't worry, *mon ami*. It is the nature of grooms to experience prewedding jitters, and with two of them in the equation, the effect is bound to be magnified."

"I suppose." He glared at Julie. "My best *person* is supposed to be making this easier for me, not busting my chops every chance she gets."

Julie grinned. "I'm a full-service kind of best person. Plus I can multitask. Please, Rile. A 'Witch's Castle: Where Are They Now?' special. Just think about it, okay? It'll totally springboard my career."

"Whatever. Go rescue Heather from Zack, and remind him he's here to film the wedding, not harass Logan's best person."

Julie peered through the crowd, toward where a petite woman with a brown ponytail was maneuvering a laden tray past a bearded man in a flannel shirt. "I thought she was the assistant manager now. Why is she waiting tables?"

"Because one of the servers called in sick and the place is packed. Go. She doesn't have time for Zack's pathetic banter."

"Got it. Great to meet you, Christophe. See you at the wedding?"

"You may depend on it."

She threaded her way through the crowd. As she approached, Christophe noted that the other woman's face lit up like the August moon. "I fear the importunate Zack is, how do you say, shit out of luck?"

Riley grinned at him. "Don't pretend you don't speak English better than I do."

Christophe shrugged. "Sometimes it's amusing to play the part, no?"

"No." Riley frowned as he studied Julie and Heather. "What did you mean about Zack?"

"Haven't you noticed that little Heather has eyes only for your friend?"

Riley blinked and rose on his toes to get a better view. "Really? That's sorta cool . . . I think. I mean, Jules is bi, but she's pretty intense."

"Perhaps that is what Heather prefers. We like what we like, regardless of what others may think." *Or what is good for us.*

"Yeah." He grinned. "Isn't it great?"

Christophe laughed. "You, my friend, are in love."

Riley wrinkled his nose. "It shows?"

"It does. But never apologize for it. It's wonderful." Christophe's eyes prickled with heat. He had no such joy to anticipate himself, only the threat of a marriage with no more affection, passion, or trust than a corporate merger. He took a deep breath and glanced around the bar. The celebratory crowd hadn't thinned, and several people were standing inside the door, searching for seats. "What is the occasion? Is this connected to your wedding?"

"No." He heaved a sigh. "That stupid *Haunted to the Max* episode about the Witch's Castle and the ghost war in Forest Park aired again this week. Whenever it does, the bar gets an influx of customers, and the place is standing room only for about a week before the fuss dies back down."

"*Haunted to the Max*? That is the paranormal investigation show you work for?"

"Used to work for. I'm finishing up my degree right now. Oh God." Riley grabbed Christophe's forearm. "Please tell me you didn't see that episode, the one with me freaking out all over Portland because Julie made me do on-camera work?"

"Sadly, no. However I have seen the video of your fiancé's marriage proposal."

"Oh God. I think *everyone* must have seen it. I could throttle Jules for uploading it to YouTube."

"Surely, as your friend said, the exposure is good. Business is business after all."

Riley cocked an eyebrow. "How would you know? Don't you spend most of your time avoiding business?"

"You are correct; however, my days of freedom are coming to an end." Christophe's chest tightened. Soon, he'd be forced to attend to business whether he chose to or not.

"I'm sorry." Riley squeezed Christophe's arm. "I know you'd rather do something else with your life."

Christophe laid his own hand over Riley's. "You remember that, eh? Yes, but not everyone can be so lucky as you, to find passion in our work as well as our loves."

"What the hell is this?"

A tall man with dark hair and eyes the color and relative flexibility of slate crowded against Riley, glowering at the point where Christophe's hand rested on Riley's. Christophe recognized him from the viral video: Logan Conner, Riley's fiancé.

Riley tried to tug his hand away, but Christophe held on to it for an extra moment before he released it, merely to see the way Logan's jaw clenched.

"Oh. Logan, this is Christophe Clavret. He's . . . an old friend."

"That so?"

"Indeed." Christophe held out his hand. "You must be Riley's fiancé." When Logan hesitated for an instant before shaking, Christophe offered a bland smile. "I need not tell you what a lucky man you are."

Logan's expression softened as he gazed at Riley. "Nope. I've got that."

Riley blushed again, but he leaned against Logan, who placed one large hand at the small of Riley's back.

If it had been anyone but Riley, who might be distressed by his actions, Christophe would have enjoyed goading Logan a trifle more, because it was blatantly clear that if the man were a wolf, he'd be pissing on Riley's high-tops to mark his territory.

It takes an alpha to know an alpha, my friend.

"I was so pleased to receive an invitation to your wedding."

"You were." Logan gave Riley the side-eye. "Hunh."

"Don't be a jerk, Logan. You saw my guest list weeks ago. You probably didn't bother to read it because you were too busy obsessing about your own."

"I didn't obsess," Logan growled.

Riley peered at Christophe over his glasses. *Obsessed*, he mouthed.

"So." Logan crossed his arms. "How do you two know each other?"

"Well." Clearing his throat, Riley scuffed the floor with one toe. "A long time ago, way before I met you. My junior year at UO, before I even started graduate school. So you know. A *looong* time ago. We were, that is, we did—"

"We dated." Christophe flashed his teeth in his most wolfish smile. "For two months."

"Two months." Logan eyed Christophe as if he were measuring him for a body bag. "No shit. Funny you didn't mention that little detail, Riley."

"Oh no. Do *not* go there." Riley poked Logan in the chest. "This is not a competition, Logan, so can the alpha-hole crap right now."

Oh, cher, *how little you know of men like us.* Logan, however— if Christophe were any judge—had recognized a kindred soul immediately.

Christophe unbuttoned his jacket and tucked his thumbs under his belt on either side of his fly. His father would faint if he saw one of his sons in such a casual posture, but Christophe had so little time before he had to behave like a *true Clavret son*, that he intended to misbehave at every opportunity.

Logan's arm snaked around Riley's waist and pulled him in tight. "Riley. I need to show you something in the . . . uh . . . stockroom."

Riley frowned. "The stockroom? But what—"

"I'll *show* you. Come on." Logan practically dragged Riley across the bar.

Christophe chuckled as the two men disappeared down the hallway. He'd wager any amount of money that Riley was about to get fucked—or at the very least, spectacularly blown—in the stockroom. For Riley's sake, Christophe hoped Logan was adept enough to ensure the room had a sturdy lock.

He had a sudden urge to follow them. If he were to knock on a few doors, perhaps he could engage in the type of challenge that—

What the bloody hell are you thinking? Flaunting yourself, preening to provoke Riley's lover for sport? You are a man, not a wolf. Behave like one.

His hands trembled, fumbling the buttons as he set his suit to rights. *Mother of God.* He must truly be approaching the limits of the suppressant's efficacy to even have contemplated such a thing.

If he behaved so to a man he'd only just met, the wolf vying for dominance merely for amusement, didn't that prove he was right to insist the Old Families should allow the damned mutation to die out? It was one thing to confront a man like Logan, who had all the power on his side—his own place of business, a mate who clearly loved him, a supportive crowd at his back. But to exercise that same dominance where his opponent had no recourse would be unconscionable, no matter what his father believed.

He glanced at the empty hall doorway. In this case, however, he could excuse himself. His little contretemps with Logan could be an early wedding present to Riley, who had never been anything but sweet to him—not an exercise of Christophe's own power, or even Logan's, but rather to prove to Riley the extent of the power he held over his mate.

Congratulations, mon ami. *You have chosen well.*

And Logan was luckier than he would ever know. He'd found a partner who would do anything for him, challenge him when he deserved it, yet yield so sweetly when needed. Loyalty, caring, protectiveness—qualities in a mate that Christophe had no hope of finding for himself. The Clavrets, like all cursed families, had an unfortunate history of disloyal spouses. The progenitor of each line had been betrayed by his wife. Far better to avoid that threat.

Likewise far better for the wife. How could his father seriously think it right to ask any woman to risk death merely for wealth and the illusion of power? For despite the false glitter of the prize, any independence a woman believed would be hers was an illusion. The Old Families guarded their brood stock, and no matter how Christophe objected, he stood little chance of overruling them. The woman who agreed to marry him would be locked in a gilded cage of his family's making for life—at least until that life was taken from her by bearing a *true Clavret son.* How could he trust any woman who would make such a bargain?

Just as well his tastes ran more to men nowadays.

All at once, several parties left their tables and the people sitting at the bar were quick to occupy them. As the groups pushed their boisterous way out of the big wooden door, a man slipped in, his face shadowed by the hood of his sweatshirt.

Something about him piqued Christophe's interest. Was it how he squared his shoulders, with his fists clearly clenched in the kangaroo pocket of his sweatshirt? The defiant tilt of his chin as he surveyed the crowded bar? Whatever it was, it appealed to Christophe—his inner wolf, shifting restlessly so near the surface, recognized a kindred spirit.

You have a dark center too, don't you, pretty man?

He dove into the crowded bar as if breasting a wave, aiming for one of the newly vacant barstools. Christophe waited until the man took his seat.

Then he pounced.

CHAPTER
FOUR

*J*esus fuck, how could so many people fit in a bar no bigger than his dad's study? Granted, his dad's study was big, but shit. Trent clutched the edge of the bar counter, willing his heartbeat to settle. The last time he'd been in a crowd this large, the others had all been dead for a century and a half.

It hadn't turned out well.

The bartender stopped in front of him. "No one under twenty-one allowed."

Trent pulled out his wallet and tossed his Oregon license onto the bar. Thank God he'd still had it in his pocket when he'd tumbled out of the ghost war. Although he hadn't seen more than nineteen birthdays, according to this, he was twenty-six. Chronologically old enough to drink. Emotionally? God, did he ever need it.

The bartender checked his birthdate. "Guess you're older than you look. What'll it be?"

"You have Woodford Reserve?"

"Yep."

"Make it a double. Neat."

"Coming up."

Trent rested his elbows on the bar and bowed his head. *Breathe in through your nose; out through your mouth. Concentrate. Calm.* He'd gotten through the third round of Deborah's stupid meditation exercises—not exactly easy when the decibel level in the bar rivaled that of a punk-rock concert—when the stool next to him scraped on the floor. He opened his eyes. *Nice thighs.* His new neighbor sported dress slacks in a smooth gray wool. His father tried to force him into similar high-end suits on a regular basis whenever the family appeared in public, which was one of the reasons that Trent insisted on wearing his thrift-store wardrobe.

Not that he didn't appreciate high-end clothes, but it was the principle of the thing.

The bartender tossed a beer mat in front of Trent. *Stumptown Spirits* was printed on it in spiky letters, along with a logo of a ghost with staring red eyes drinking a beer. Trent shuddered and turned it over.

"Not a fan of nonrepresentational art?" His new neighbor's voice matched his pants—smooth, high-class, with a definite European flavor. French? Maybe, but it was slight.

The bartender set Trent's bourbon on the overturned beer mat without a blink. Trent shrugged and took a sip. "Don't like being watched." He stole a glance at the stranger in the mirror behind the bar.

He wasn't as sneaky as he'd hoped, because—*busted*—the guy met his gaze and a smile quirked his mouth.

Jesus *fuck*. Gorgeous. His chin-length hair was on the reddish side of brown, his close-trimmed beard a shade redder. His eyes were the same color as the liquor in Trent's glass, and his features were chiseled, something about them calling to mind the illustrations in Trent's nearly forgotten medieval history book. *Ascetic*? Was that the word? Like the face of a monk or a saint in mid-martyrdom.

Trent forced himself to stop staring. *What the hell are you doing, asshole? First Bishop, and now a random stranger? You're here to reconnect with Logan, to get your own life back on track. Eyes on the prize and tell your dick to keep its opinions to itself.*

"I'd offer to buy you a drink, but you appear to have one already. May I join you?"

"It's a free country."

The guy made a sound that would have been a snort from anyone less classy. "For some, perhaps." He caught the bartender's eye and pointed to Trent's glass before turning back. "Christophe Clavret."

Oh, what the hell. "Trent." They shook hands. Christophe's grip was firm, lingering long enough for Trent to recognize it as an invitation. In the old days, before he'd sort of hooked up with Logan, he'd have been totally down with the implied offer. Those days were behind him though. Weren't they? He ought to have grown out of them, but sometimes he didn't seem to have grown at all.

Christophe accepted his drink from the bartender and slid his credit card across the bar. Amex Black. *Cool.* Trent could let the guy pay for his drink without guilt.

With a sideways glance, Christophe turned his beer mat over to match Trent's.

Nice touch.

If Trent had been interested in a pickup, Christophe would have scored major points. But this wasn't a pickup. Trent was only killing time until Logan showed. So why did the idea of facing Logan suddenly fill his belly with lead, while sparring with Christophe sent a buzz through his veins like in his acting days, in those heady moments just before he'd stepped onstage?

Must be because one thing mattered and the other was just for fun. He'd always been better at blowing things off. He'd never taken anything seriously except acting, legend tripping, and Logan—and look where that had gotten him.

Was that the problem? Logan was part of the ordeal, snarled up in the Witch's Castle nightmare along with Trent. *He's still the only person who'll ever understand you. Stop fucking around.*

He swiveled on his barstool to face Christophe. "Let's get things straight. You're hot. I know it. You know it."

Christophe grinned. "Indeed? How gratifying."

"Doesn't mean we're gonna hook up."

A trick of the light made Christophe's eyes appear to flash molten gold. "Why is that?"

"I'm . . . well . . . kind of here to meet someone."

"You sound uncertain."

"Nothing's certain."

"Except death and taxes, no?"

"Don't be too sure about that." Trent had learned recently that death could be negotiable, and his father made it his life's work to prove taxes weren't a certainty either.

Christophe grinned. "You, my friend, are a man with issues."

"That a problem?"

"Not in the least." He leaned closer, his voice lowering to a suggestive growl. "I love a man with issues. Happy people are so boring. Who was it who said, 'All happy families are alike'? Tolstoy?"

"Don't ask me. I was a theater major."

"Ah. Then we can rest assured it wasn't Shakespeare. You are an actor, then?"

Trent's stomach clenched. "Not anymore."

"A student?"

"Nope. I more or less dropped out years ago."

"Years ago? You must have been a mere child."

"I was nineteen."

"How old are you now?"

Trent glanced at Christophe from under his lashes and took a deliberate sip of his bourbon. "Nineteen."

Christophe blinked, his eyebrows lifting. "I don't—"

"Or twenty-six. Maybe two hundred and five. Depends on who you ask." And whose skin he was in at the moment.

Christophe turned and leaned an elbow on the bar, his knee brushing Trent's leg. "What if I ask you?"

"Then I'd say I'm old enough to know a wolf in sheep's clothing when I see one."

This time, Christophe did a full-on double take that would have made Trent's old comedy teacher proud. *I should take notes. In case I can ever face an audience again.*

"You think you know so much about me, yet we've barely met."

Trent nodded at the credit card the bartender had returned. "Know you're not hurting for cash." Christophe inclined his head. "You're multilingual. I'm guessing . . . two, possibly three other languages besides English, but you learned them at the same time, and you've practiced. So your accent isn't heavy."

"Four. French, German, Italian, and Japanese."

Trent's eyebrows shot up. "Japanese? Doesn't fit into the Euro-aristocracy vibe."

"The aristocracy was far in the past. In today's world, the only ruling house is commerce. The Japanese are important trading partners, with strict notions of manners and protocol."

"Commerce, huh? So you're a captain of industry? You really like that?"

Christophe's gaze dropped to his drink. "No."

"Then why do it?"

"We cannot always indulge our own whims. Sometimes we must bow to a greater responsibility."

"Bullshit. Who benefits from that?"

He smiled wryly. "Commerce."

"Fuck commerce."

"I'd prefer a more congenial partner, thank you."

"Wouldn't we all?"

They drank in silence for a couple of minutes. "Latin," Christophe murmured.

"What?"

"I know Latin as well."

"Not much call for that in commerce, is there?"

"Not these days, no. However, that is not why I learned it."

"So?" Trent gestured with his glass. "Don't leave me hanging. Spill."

"I learned it for . . . medical purposes."

Trent laughed. "First time I've heard that Latin is good for the health."

Christophe joined in the laughter, but his had a rough edge. "No. I'm interested in medicine."

"That's what you want to do? Study medicine?"

"Yes. Genetics."

Trent couldn't say he saw the attraction, but he was more than familiar with pressure to follow a path not of his own choosing. He leaned in, shoulder to shoulder with Christophe. "Then do it. The world has enough salesmen. Be a geneticist."

"Perhaps I shall take your advice." Christophe clinked glasses with Trent, and held his gaze. "There is a flower that grows near my family's home in Brittany," he murmured. "Gentian. Your eyes are exactly that color."

Trent got lost for a moment, pinned by that amber regard, as if Christophe could see straight through him. It activated a quiver in the pit of his stomach and a tingle in his balls.

No, damn it. I'm here for Logan.

Trent broke the gaze and took another sip of bourbon, idly scanning the bar. "Is that your best line?"

Christophe chuckled. "Perhaps not my best, but the truth nonetheless." He followed Trent's line of sight, no doubt trying to figure out what was so damn fascinating about the walls and ceiling fans. "Stumptown Spirits is busy tonight. I'm lucky to have secured a seat at all, let alone one next to you."

"Nice recovery." Trent saluted with his glass. "Why is it so packed anyway? Do you know?"

"As I understand it, the place has become something of a tourist attraction, at least among those who watch certain occult programs."

Trent's hand wobbled, sloshing bourbon up the side of his glass. *Shit.* Had that damned show aired again? He'd watched it the first time, back in the hospital, and had relapsed so badly he'd been on double meds for a week. Would anyone recognize him?

He swiveled to face the bar and scoped out the crowd in the mirror. *Shit-damn-fuck-it-all.* Some of them were definitely familiar. The bear trying to attract the attention of the perky waitress, for instance. Had he been there that night? And the woman the waitress was flirting with, the tall blond with Bernadette Peters hair. Was she the one who'd spoken to Trent briefly as he'd been hustled off by the show's medic?

He hunched his shoulders. Would it draw anyone's attention if he pulled his hood up?

Christophe put a hand on Trent's thigh, and for some reason, instead of pissing him off, the uninvited intimacy calmed him the fuck down.

"You are not a fan of such television, I take it?"

"No." Trent took a gulp of his bourbon and winced as it burned its way to his belly. "That supernatural shit? Keep it away from me, that's all I've got to say. Either it's bullshit and you're a moron to believe in it, or it's real and you can't depend on anything. A door might not be a door. The ground might be quicksand. A man might be a monster. I prefer to avoid both the bullshit *and* the quicksand, thanks."

"The touch of the uncanny isn't necessary to turn most men to monsters. Each of us can manage that quite well on our own, given the right trigger." Christophe removed his hand from Trent's leg and gestured to the crowd. "I myself have little partiality for such entertainments, but apparently others have different tastes."

Trent immediately missed the warmth, the grounding of Christophe's touch. He took Christophe's hand and placed it back where it had been. *Just because his hand is on my thigh doesn't mean his dick will be in my mouth or up my ass.*

Did he believe that? Did he want to? Impulse control—God, he sucked at it. But while the way Christophe's eyes glinted when they held Trent's, his focus, and his self-assurance said *predator*, his mouth held no hint of cruelty. Not *predator*. *Protector*.

"Good thing the only two guys in the bar who don't give a fuck about the show found each other, am I right?"

Christophe grinned, a flash of white teeth with pronounced canines. "You are most assuredly correct."

Oddly, he felt safer with Christophe's hand steadying him than he'd felt since falling out of the ghost war in October. More, he felt *wanted*. This was what he'd been searching for. Why he'd come for Logan. Not that Christophe would understand—or believe—Trent's experiences. But Jesus fuck. He been so broken since he'd been back that he hadn't felt desirable until now.

Christophe didn't know about the broken. Didn't know anything about him really, and that was incredibly comforting. *Maybe what you need is a stranger after all.*

"Zack." The blond woman's voice cut through the bar chatter. Trent tore his gaze from Christophe's to watch her in the mirror. "Leave Heather alone. We need releases from everyone in the bar. Riley said we can't film without them, and we'll need the footage if the follow-up special gets green-lighted."

"On it." The bear—Zack—rose from his chair and turned toward the bar. His gaze landed on Trent and he frowned. Trent could almost hear his brain click. Oh shit. *Danger!* This guy was a cameraman? He was used to *seeing* things. If he recognized Trent—

"Excuse me. Gotta—"

Trent pushed away from the bar under Christophe's surprised stare, and bolted for the john.

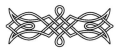

Christophe half rose from his stool, ready to follow Trent. Two things stopped him. The first was the cluster of bar patrons who were eyeing the empty stool with covetous intent. The second was that Trent might only need to use the facilities and wouldn't need an assistant. Christophe doubted this bar was the type—Logan and Riley's trip to the stockroom notwithstanding—to encourage sexual encounters in the restrooms.

Christophe hadn't abandoned the notion that he and Trent might yet find a way to their mutual release tonight. Although Trent's attitude toward the supernatural didn't bode well for a long-term relationship, Christophe didn't have time for one of those anyway. *Less than a week.* He'd have to make it count.

Zack paused behind Trent's empty barstool. "Hey, man. Did you see where the guy who was sitting here went?"

Ah. Perhaps that's why Trent left so suddenly. He was evading this man. I wonder why? Issues. Mother of God, but he loved a man with issues. "Sadly, I did not." A not-entirely-false statement. He could certainly extrapolate Trent's destination, but he hadn't actually *seen* where he'd ended up.

"Shit. I could have sworn . . . If he comes back, could you ask him to check in with us?" He fumbled a business card out of his shirt pocket and handed it over. "You might have heard of our show. *Haunted to the Max?*"

Christophe shook his head and shrugged. "*Je m'excuse.*" He studied the card. "This is, how do you say . . ." He let his accent thicken as if he'd never sweated for hours over his diction. "*Télé réalité?*"

"Little classier than that, but I guess we don't play well in the international markets." Zack grinned through his scruffy beard. "Listen, if this guy's who I think he is, we really want to talk to him about appearing in a special we're pitching. We've got an appointment across town, but we'll be back. So if he shows again?" He pointed at the card. "Ask him to wait?"

Christophe nodded. "I shall pass the word, although I can promise nothing."

"Right. Thanks, man. Later."

Zack returned to Julie and the two of them left, apparently to Heather's dismay, judging by the longing look she cast at Julie's retreating back. Their table was immediately captured by another group, this one made up of young women no older than Trent, who had an unfortunate tendency to giggle.

Trent. Yes, definitely intriguing. A brash young man, to be sure, unafraid of challenging Christophe, yet he seemed terrified—or at least reluctant—to speak to the television personnel.

The tingle in Christophe's hand from their contact hadn't faded. He'd been afraid he'd been too forward, overstepped. Trent had definitely been broadcasting mixed signals, one moment flirty, the next withdrawn.

Issues. Christophe longed to explore them, preferably naked and in bed. *Shite, where is my self-control?* Perhaps it would be better if Trent didn't return. Before a shift, Christophe's libido always spiked, perhaps to compensate for the fact he felt no sexual desire in his wolf form. He wasn't sure he could trust himself tonight.

A young woman approached, her gaze inquiring. "May I?" She indicated the stool.

"I am very sorry, *mademoiselle,* but this seat is taken. My companion will return momentarily."

Or so he fervently hoped.

Trent braced his hands against the cool tile of the stall. *Jesus, way to be subtle.* He should have stood his ground and fucking *lied* if the cameraman asked him if he was *that* Trent Pielmeyer.

It's not like any of the show's audience would recognize him. He'd been barely visible—nothing but a dark figure on the ground, while the cameras had been focused more on the ghosts and Riley and Logan. But freeze the frame and anyone who knew what he looked like might be able to pick him out, huddled in a pathetic lump in the mud.

He hadn't signed the release—he hadn't been in a state to sign anything at that point—and his father had made damn sure nobody on the show mentioned his name. He'd boasted about how he'd forced them to reshoot several of the background scenes to eliminate any reference to Trent.

Would Logan care that he'd been an asshole about that? Well technically his dad had been the asshole. Trent had been the basket case. *Apparently you're not out of those particular woods yet.*

He shuddered. *Don't think about woods.*

Instead, he needed to man up and *deal*—not enough to get cozy with the TV crew, but he could at least have a conversation with Logan. Maybe more than a conversation. Considering the way he'd nearly humped Christophe's leg based on a couple of admiring glances and a hand on his thigh, he really needed somebody to fricking *touch* him.

First step? Quit cowering by the toilet and get the hell out of this stall. As he washed his hands, he checked his reflection in the mirror—Jesus, he was the walking definition of freaked-the-hell-out. He tried to arrange his face to look less like a doomed teenager in a slasher flick and more like the guy who arrived in the nick of time, wielding dual chainsaws.

Raise the chin. Thrust the jaw out slightly—but not too much. I want determined, *not* belligerent. He narrowed his eyes so the whites weren't showing around his irises. *There.* Ready for his close-up.

Taking one last fortifying breath, he marched out of the restroom—and collided with a man carrying a stack of bar towels.

"Shit, man. Sorry." They both bent to retrieve the bundle at the same time, knocking their heads together. "Augh. Damn it."

"Nah, it's nothing. Don't worry—" The man's eyes widened. "You. You were there."

Fear staged a comeback, and his careful character work in front of the mirror went to hell. "I— Sorry, where?"

The man glanced up and down the hallway, then waited for a server to pass on her way to the bar, carrying two plates of burgers and fries. "In the park. The ghosts."

"I don't know what you—"

"'S all right. You don't want to talk about it. I understand, more than most, I expect."

Trent peered at the man in the dim light—he was familiar, yeah, but the clean-shaven face, the neat button-down shirt, and khakis seemed wrong. With a sudden jolt to his belly, Trent recognized those eyes—he'd locked gazes with them every night for seven years, just before The Drop. *He looks totally different without the spectral jawline beard and flat-brimmed hat.*

"You're the other one. You were trapped like me."

He nodded. "Joseph Geddes. You're— He called you Trent."

"Yeah."

"He—" Joseph swallowed. "He came back for you. And you had someone to come back for. Friends. A family."

"Friends, not so much, and the family isn't that great."

"But you came back to a world you could recognize. I'm . . ." He hugged the towels. "Sometimes I feel like I'm still a ghost."

"I know what you mean." Or did he? "How long were you in there?"

"I lost count of the years, but they tell me sixty-three."

Jesus. "Your family?"

Joseph dropped his gaze. "Gone."

Shit. Trent had *nothing* to complain about. All his moping around, whining, acting out. *What a giant entitled asshole.* "I'm sorry. I shouldn't— I mean, you had it so much worse—"

Joseph shook his head. "Don't apologize. I was trapped for longer, but I only had to watch." He tucked the towels under his arm. "You had to die."

With a final nod, he disappeared into the kitchen.

Trent ran a shaking hand through his hair. Nothing like a little perspective. Hell, if Joseph could face the world and carry on, Trent could hardly do less. *Face down the cameraman. Tell him to mind his own business, and you know, be cool about it if he doesn't.*

He squared his shoulders, marched down the hallway, and emerged into the bar. But his mini-pep talk had been pointless, because although the crowd hadn't thinned, the blond and her cameraman were gone. Still no sign of Logan though. Maybe the bar owner didn't have to show up every night. He really needed to plan his surprise visits so he wasn't always the one getting surprised.

At least Christophe hadn't split. He remained at the bar, Trent's unfinished bourbon at his elbow. He smiled and indicated the empty stool. *Amazing that the guy didn't take off.* He must either be desperate or else as nice as he seemed. *I'm opting for door number two. Because two desperate guys? Too fucking depressing.*

Trent threaded his way through the crowd and sat down. "Thanks for holding my seat. Sorry about the . . . you know. Vanishing act." He winced inwardly. Regardless of his resolution to cut back on the self-pity, he still didn't want to think about *vanishing*.

"It was no hardship. I take it, however, that you won't be interested in this."

Christophe passed Trent a business card. A *Haunted to the Max* business card. Anger flooded his chest. Shit, he hadn't considered a third option. *Entrapment*. How stupid was that, considering his recent face-off with Bishop. "You're one of *them*, aren't you? 'Commerce' my ass."

Christophe put his hand on Trent's arm, and sucker that he was, he calmed. "No. I've told you no less than the truth. The gentleman whom you . . . wished to avoid left it for you. I made no promises to him, so if you like, you may pretend you never saw it."

Fucking ironic that back when he was an aspiring actor, he'd have been all over this chance to make a Hollywood connection, even though he'd preferred stage work. Now, though, the last thing he wanted was to get caught in that public lens.

"Sounds like a plan to me." Trent ripped the card in two and tossed the pieces on the bar.

"I'm intrigued, though. If you have no interest in the show and are actively avoiding its staff, why pick this particular bar? There are others not as populated by fans, many with customers who might be closer to your, shall we say, demographic?"

You mean fucked-in-the-head morons with no impulse control? No, thanks. I can barely handle my own drama. "For that matter, why are you here? You're a little upscale for this joint, aren't you?"

"Ah, but I have a reason. I am in town for a friend's wedding. His fiancé owns this bar, and I stopped by to greet them."

Trent's insides turned to ice. "His fiancé? But I thought the owner was—"

"There they are now." Christophe nodded in the direction of the hallway. Trent turned, dread curdling his stomach.

Logan was standing there, the old shit-eating grin on his face, his arm around a nerdy guy in glasses. *Not just any random nerdy guy.* Trent recognized him. He was the one in the *Haunted to the Max* episode, the one who'd done the background scenes. *The scenes my father forced them to reshoot.*

Now, Nerdy Guy's rosy cheeks and swollen lips announced what the two of them had been up to. Add in Logan's possessive hand trailing down over the guy's ass and Trent's vision blurred, his heart taking a dive to his belly.

Clearly Logan hadn't been pining away while Trent had been appearing nightly in the thrilling melodrama of the Hanging of Danford Balch.

He'd been busy fucking the talent.

CHAPTER
FIVE

*J*ust as Christophe had expected, Logan had staked his claim. Riley had clearly been passionately kissed, and judging by the way he twitched when Logan's hand landed on his arse, probably fucked too.

Christophe glanced at Trent, and immediately his wolf went on alert. Trent's lips were parted, his eyes wide, and tremors were shaking his lean frame. Christophe laid a hand on his back. "Are you well?" He signaled the bartender. "Water, if you please."

Trent clenched his eyes shut, took a deep breath, then turned to Christophe with an obviously false smile. "Aces." He knocked back the last of his bourbon and slammed the glass on the bar. "Fuck the water. I need another drink."

"Perhaps you should wait for a moment. You—"

Trent's glare stopped Christophe midwarning. "You're not my mother, dude."

Christophe raised his hands, palms out. "I realize. But you appear to have sustained a shock. A moment to recover would be prudent."

"Fuck prudence and the horse she rode in on." He waved away the glass of water. "Another double."

The bartender hesitated, but Christophe gave a slight nod; the drink could be added to his tab. "At least allow me to introduce you to my friends." He gestured to the happy couple, who were chatting with a group in one of the booths that lined either wall.

Trent squinted at him. "You know them? Both of them?"

Christophe nodded. "It is their wedding I'm here for, although to be frank, I only met Logan this evening." He smiled as he caught

Logan's territorial hand drifting to Riley's arse again. "Riley and I used to date."

At the apparent urging of the people at the booth, Logan took Riley in his arms and soul-kissed him. The crowd cheered and began counting the seconds of the kiss. When they broke apart, Logan trailed one finger down Riley's face and Riley leaned his forehead against Logan's chest, his cheeks and the tips of his ears afire.

Trent took a large gulp of his fresh drink, and choked. "Is that so?" His voice rose, loud and rough, just as the noise in the bar faded for the first time that evening. "Logan and I used to fuck."

Christophe's eyebrows shot up. Logan's head snapped around, as did that of every other person in the bar, including Riley.

"Trent?" Logan took a step forward, his tone a mixture of anger and surprise.

Trent turned to Christophe, his face pale except for the flush on his cheekbones. "My hotel's three blocks away. If you want to cash in on all your lines, I'll be outside for another two minutes."

Pulling the hood of his sweatshirt up, Trent lurched off the barstool and barged through the murmuring crowd, head down.

Raising his hand, Christophe caught Riley's attention and indicated that he would follow Trent. Riley nodded and hooked his fingers in Logan's belt loops, tugging him back as the crowd began to boo.

Christophe quickly signed his check, paying for his and Trent's drinks and adding a generous tip. He wasn't taking Trent's offer seriously, but something was obviously amiss.

Ah, issues. Irresistible.

He made his way through the crowd—who were already chanting for another kiss—and out the door. Trent was standing on the sidewalk, his back braced against the brick wall beyond the Stumptown Spirits window.

"So. Wanna fuck?" Although his tone was gruff and his face hard, his eyes were bleak and his shoulders held none of his earlier confidence.

Christophe approached him slowly. "Whether I desire you is not in question, but I have no wish to be the bludgeon you use to punish anyone, whether that person is Logan or me or yourself. Perhaps you can tell me why you came here tonight. And why you decided to embarrass yourself and humiliate Riley only days before his wedding."

Trent's face crumpled. For a moment, Christophe was afraid he might weep, right there on the street. Another cheer erupted from inside, bleeding through the heavy doors and walls, and Trent seemed to shake himself, like a dog shedding water.

"I didn't mean to do that. Figures that the one time you could hear yourself think in that place had to be the time I was acting like a total douche bag. But . . ." He pushed himself off the wall and thrust his hands in the pocket of his sweatshirt. "I had this half-assed idea that Logan would be there for me, you know?"

"So you would give yourself to a chance-met stranger, just to prove to Logan that you don't need him? Why? From spite?"

"Not spite. Jesus, it's not like we'd pledged our undying devotion to one another. We weren't even boyfriends. And it's not as if I'd made any effort to find him since—or to return his calls."

"Yet it hurt you nonetheless. To see him with another."

"It's not even that—at least I don't think so. But you can tell, when you look at them, that they're solid. A unit. It's like . . . like you can almost see the connection between them." His shoulders rose with a deep breath. "It's not that I want Logan, exactly. But I want what they've got, you know? That trust. Someone who's always got your back and isn't afraid to show it."

Trent bowed his head, his face shadowed by his hood. The sound he made could have been a soft laugh, or perhaps a sob. It hardly mattered. Protectiveness surged through Christophe's chest.

"And you had no idea of their engagement?"

"No. I've been . . . out of touch. For a long time."

Christophe edged closer. "Perhaps it is time to touch again, yes?" He placed a gentle hand on Trent's arm.

Trent inhaled sharply. "God, *please*, yes." Christophe wrapped his arms around that lovely, lean body, and Trent laid his head on Christophe's shoulder, sighing into his neck. "Deep down, I must have known it was the wrong thing. Not only for Logan, but for me, you know? Because twice tonight I've had fuck-me thoughts about other men. I wouldn't have gone there if Logan had been, you know, *the* guy."

"Twice? Dare I hope one of those times was with me?"

Trent's lips curved against Christophe's neck. "Dare away."

"And the other?"

He pulled back, stepping out of Christophe's arms. "That one was a real pisser. The detective who's been on my ass since—" He rubbed his hands on his thighs. "Well, for a while."

"It is a very fine arse. How can one blame him?" Christophe stroked Trent's arm. "You needn't worry that I'll ask for more than you're willing to give. Every man has his secrets, no? Things in our lives we would rather not share. Things that might put us in a bad light, or burdens we wish we need not bear."

"You got that right."

"So." Christophe allowed himself to cup Trent's jaw with both hands. He waited, in case Trent wanted to pull away again, but instead Trent nestled his cheek against Christophe's palm. "Perhaps tonight we can share those burdens, even if we don't speak of them at all."

Christophe leaned in, closer, closer, until Trent's breath mingled with his own. Trent was slightly taller, so he had to tilt his head, draw Trent down to meet his lips.

Ah. Although he kept the kiss soft, inquiring, a tightness eased from between his shoulders and the back of his neck. *Lighten the burden indeed.* Nothing made your own travails seem trivial more than knowing others faced problems of their own.

Despite his precipitous exist from the bar, and his earlier hostility, the kiss Trent returned was just as sweet, just as tender and tentative. A heat kindled in Christophe's chest like a fire on a stony beach. He ended the kiss, unwilling to share this moment with passersby.

Trent leaned his forehead against Christophe's. "Besides, you're not."

"I'm not what?"

"A stranger. You're a friend of a friend of a friend. You could almost say Logan and Riley set us up on a blind date."

Christophe chuckled, smoothing Trent's hair. "Tell me what you want, *cher.*"

Trent sighed. "You. I want you."

"Then I am more than happy to oblige."

Jesus, he wanted—he wanted . . . Trent could barely say what it was he wanted, not with Christophe's arms holding him, loose enough to give the promise of choice, but close enough that he could feel the other man's heartbeat against his own chest, the other man's breath stir his hair, the other man's hands warm on his back.

This. This touch, this *belonging*. The last time he'd belonged was in that tiny dorm room years ago with Logan. That's what he'd missed. Not Logan per se, but feeling like he was worth the effort. Logan had gone with him, out into the cold, wet park at midnight because it had been something Trent had wanted, idiot that he'd been. To cheer Trent up after he'd lost that part in *Blithe Spirit*, Logan had taken him on a legend trip, even though Logan had thought it was a giant waste of time. It wasn't Logan's fault that Trent had ended up starring in a different ghost story for seven years. In fact, Logan had returned to rescue him.

With Riley. Shit, Trent had watched that fucking TV show. He should have remembered that Riley was the one who'd figured out the whole mess, even though it had been Logan who'd actually jacked him out of the ghost war.

Maybe someday he'd get the whole story from them. Someday when he could think about the whole ordeal without collapsing into a worthless shuddering heap.

Right now, though, this very fucking minute, he had someone willing to touch him, kiss him, *God please* maybe even fuck him. He'd think about that other shit later.

This was what he'd come to Portland for after all. To be touched. So he hadn't planned on the toucher being a drop-dead sexy foreign guy, but hey, the accent and the style? *Bonus.*

Christophe pulled away. *No. Come back.* He ran his hands down Trent's arms and laced their fingers together. "I have a flat in the Pearl District. We could go—"

"Too far. Told you. My hotel is a few blocks from here."

Christophe smiled. "So impatient."

"I've been waiting a long time for this." *You have no idea how long.* "I don't want to wait any more. Let's go."

Trent tugged Christophe's hand, unwilling to release him because *touching*. It was intoxicating. Better than the bourbon, although the alcohol buzz didn't hurt. It made it easier for him to ignore the glances from passersby, although by now, he should be used to the attention. People *looked* at him all the time. His father with disgust, Bishop and the other cops with suspicion, his therapists with that damned faintly inquiring expression. No matter what their priorities—his family, with their financial and social agenda; the cops, searching for someone to blame and punish; his therapists, for whom he was only a problem to solve—they all had that edge of fear, of uncertainty, as if they were afraid he'd explode at any moment, have a psychotic break, and disappear again.

But Christophe, with his steady gaze and unmistakable stand-up vibe, *saw* him. Was that a European thing? Supposedly men there didn't get skeeved out by meeting another man's eyes, so their gaze didn't shift away quickly, as if they had something to hide.

But Trent thought it was more than that. This was a man he could trust. He didn't know how or why, but he felt it, the way he'd always known in an improv when his scene partner was in the zone with him, living the part.

Savor this. You've got him for tonight, but you don't know his whole story. You're not guaranteed anything beyond this, so make it last.

He slowed them to a leisurely stroll, their shoulders pressed together, hands still linked. *If I had a real boyfriend, like Logan has Riley, this is what we'd do. We'd walk together, ignoring random judgmental assholes, because together, we'd be bigger than them, stronger than them.*

When they got to the hotel doors, he turned to Christophe, and *Jesus*, there it was again. That intensity. Trent's knees threatened to buckle. "Here we are. Still up for it?"

Christophe chuckled. Trent didn't know how he did it, but this time, the sound was sex-infused and dirty, and it went straight to his dick.

"I suspect both of us are most definitely up for it, yes?" Christophe angled his chin, claiming another kiss.

God-yes-more. "Absolutely."

"Then let us proceed." He waved the bellman away and held the door for Trent. "After you."

"Fuck that. We're in this together." He grabbed Christophe's hand and led him inside, across the lobby, past the wood-paneled reception area to the bank of elevators. A family with two little girls, each carrying Barbie and Ken dolls, entered the elevator with them, so Trent couldn't do anything other than hold Christophe's hand on the ride to their floor.

One of the girls, maybe six or seven, studied their clasped hands, her head tilted to one side. She turned to her sister and traded her Barbie for her sister's Ken, and cradled them in one arm, holding their hands together with her tiny fingers, her nails painted sparkly pink.

She grinned up at Trent, and he winked at her. Her parents shrugged and led the little girls off on their floor. *Guess we've made some progress in seven years. Good to know the next generation gets it.*

Trent pulled Christophe off the elevator on the next floor, toward his corner suite, and because he could, he kissed Christophe once before swiping his key card. He led the way inside.

God, his duffel looked like it had exploded all over the bed, and the clothes he'd shed before showering earlier were in a heap in the corner, a prelaundry habit Logan used to taunt him about when they were roommates.

"Yeah, um, sorry about the mess. Just a minute." He sprinted over to the bed, grabbed a double armful of clothes, and dumped them in the corner. Another armful, then he tossed the empty duffel across the room, leaving the lube and the condoms on the bed. "There. The important parts are clear anyway."

Christophe stalked over to him. The heat in his eyes sent Trent's pulse racing. "You are the only important part."

"Yeah?" He could barely get the word out. *Need to breathe if I want to talk.* "Pretty sure you've got some important parts yourself, hidden under those fancy clothes." Christophe wasn't wearing a tie, but Trent hooked his fingers under the placket of his dress shirt and tugged him close. "Want to show me?"

Christophe's smile glinted in the light. "What is it you Americans say? 'I'll show you mine if you show me yours?'"

"Hell yeah." Trent ripped his hoodie over his head. By the time his head was free of the fleece, Christophe was folding his own jacket and laying it carefully over the back of the chair. Trent balled up the sweatshirt and threw it on top of the pile of clothes. "Hold that thought."

Trent returned to the door and hung the Do Not Disturb sign on the outside doorknob, then threw the dead bolt and hooked the privacy chain. He had no idea what Christophe's agenda was in the morning, but he planned to stretch this out as long as he could. Who knew when he'd have another chance?

When he turned back, Christophe had removed his dress shoes and set them side by side under the desk, his socks folded neatly across the insteps. The sight of his bare feet—pale and narrow and arched—sent a fresh wake-up call to Trent's dick. *Jesus, I've never found feet sexy before. It's been way too long since I've been naked with someone.*

Christophe glanced up as Trent paced back across the room. Despite paying such ridiculous attention to his jacket—however nice it was—Christophe's breathing was short, shallow, and his pupils dilated as if he were already naked. Or as if Trent were. *Let's make both those things happen.*

Trent skinned off his T-shirt and sent it after the hoodie. Christophe took out his cuff links—*the guy wore cuff links to a bar, for fuck's sake*—and set them on the desk along with his TAG Heuer.

"Dude. At this rate, I'll be ready to get dressed again before you take off your pants."

Christophe smiled, a flash of those pronounced canines that sent a surprising shiver down Trent's spine. "I am in no hurry."

"Well I am." *Time to get a little skin on skin.* God. Gooseflesh rose on his arms and prickled his bare chest at the *idea* of that much touch. *Please soon.* He unzipped his fly.

Christophe unbuttoned the top button of his shirt.

God. This is gonna kill me. Trent toed off his Nikes and shucked his jeans down but left his boxer briefs on for the moment—because nothing said *not sexy* like a guy naked except for tube socks. He removed the socks and rocketed them into the corner, followed by the jeans.

Christophe unbuttoned the third shirt button.

"Okay, man. You seriously need to get with the program. I want to see your skin." *I want to feel your skin.* Trent put on his best brash attitude to hide his uncontrollable shivering. "And if we're gonna make it there before morning . . ."

He tried to bat Christophe's hands out of the way, but Christophe caught his wrists in a near-painful grip. Trent flinched, and Christophe let go immediately. "I am sorry. Reflex. Please continue." He lifted his arms to the side, offering Trent total access. *Yes!*

Trent moved in and fumbled with the next button. Jesus, his hands were trembling so much, it might have been faster to let Christophe continue his slo-mo strip tease. He finally got the last button undone and slipped the shirt off Christophe's shoulders.

He was wearing an undershirt, damn it.

Christophe caught his shirt before it fell and folded it like a fricking Nordstrom clerk before he laid it on top of his jacket.

"You know, man, I get that your clothes are high-end—"

"Bespoke tailoring. It's a family tradition."

"Whatever, but seriously? We're trying to have sex here. Could you be a little less Jeeves about this?"

"Sorry. It is . . . a habit."

"Time to break it." Trent took hold of the hem of the stupid fucking undershirt and skinned it off over Christophe's head. He tossed it into the corner where it could commune with Trent's clothes pile.

Christophe laughed, unbuckling his belt. "Perhaps you're right." After he unzipped his trousers and let them fall to the floor, he stared at them, pooled around his ankles for a moment, and his cock hard inside the—*Jesus, monogrammed?*—boxer briefs.

"Don't you feel compelled to fold them like a good little soldier?"

He stepped out of his pants and kicked them behind him. "I'm not a soldier."

"No?"

"*I* am the commander."

"Think you can command me?"

"I suspect, *cher*, that you would be a most insubordinate officer. Have you ever done as you were told?"

"Not if I can help it." *Yeah, and look where that landed me.* "But maybe we can try something different this time. Only no—no bondage, okay? Restraints are not cool."

"That has never been my game." Christophe's eyes glowed like fire in the lamplight. "I don't want an underling, a submissive. I want an equal. Someone with power in their own right."

"You think I have power?"

"At this moment, it is yours entirely. We do nothing you do not want."

"Does that mean we'll do anything I *do* want?"

Christophe smiled and captured Trent's hand, pressed a kiss to his palm. "Within reason, *cher*. There are some lines I will not cross, even for you."

"So we've both got boundaries. We'll deal."

"Then," Christophe ran his hands down Trent's bare back and under the waistband of his briefs, cupping his ass in hands that were surprisingly large considering Christophe was shorter than Trent, "you must be sure to tell me if I encroach on any of yours."

Trent closed his eyes, and let the tremors take him. "You're not remotely close."

"Excellent. Let us see if we can push them a trifle, shall we?"

"God yes." He grabbed both sides of Christophe's face and dove in for a kiss—lips, tongue, teeth, the whole nine, everything they hadn't done on the street. Christophe growled into Trent's mouth and drew him closer, chest to chest, hip to hip, cock to cock.

The skin. God, Christophe's skin was fire against his own, not the clammy, chilled skin of a quick club hookup, or the sweaty sheen of a shared summer jerk-off under the bleachers. Hot and smooth and perfect. Trent snaked a hand between them, and tangled his fingers in Christophe's rufous treasure trail, the only hair visible below his beard.

He pulled away from Christophe's mouth. "I want everything." Trent sucked on the skin of Christophe's shoulder. "The underwear must die."

"Consider it dead."

Christophe pushed Trent's briefs down until Trent could kick them into the clothes pile. His own he shucked and added to the puddle of his pants.

"Don't you feel compelled to fold them all nice and neat?"

"Not even one iota, thank you."

"What about the signet? You stripped your other bling."
"I never remove it. On the bed, if you please. Now."
Trent grinned. "Thought you'd never ask."

CHAPTER
SIX

For Christophe, the act of removing his clothing in front of a new lover never failed to thrill. But despite the many partners his father had so deplored, he'd never allowed anyone to *undress him* before. When Trent put his hands on Christophe's shirt . . . when he'd actually stripped off his undershirt? *Mother of God.* Christophe had nearly spent in his briefs, with no touch on his cock at all.

But now, naked and wanton and willing, Trent was so breathtaking that Christophe was glad he'd managed to hold on to his control. Because that body, that *man*, deserved to be worshipped slowly and thoroughly.

"You . . ." Christophe ghosted his fingers along Trent's skin—collarbone, shoulders, the length of his arms—fascinated by the way Trent's breath caught and released. ". . . are stunning." He circled Trent slowly, his hands trailing across the smooth skin of belly and hip and flank.

Trent moaned. "Jesus, Christophe. You—"

"Shhh. I'm busy."

He stepped close, his front to Trent's back, his cock nestled in the cleft of Trent's ass—and this time he was the one who moaned. *Jesu*, the way Trent trembled against him, pushing back as if to invite more. Christophe buried his nose in Trent's hair and inhaled. *Exquisite.* He splayed his hands across Trent's chest. *I swear I hear the blood rushing in his veins, his heart beating in sync with my own.*

"Christophe?" Trent's voice wobbled as he laced his fingers with Christophe's.

"Hmm?" He stroked Trent's chest, adding a slight scrape of his nails.

"Can we *please* go to bed now?"

Christophe chuckled and cupped Trent's balls, to a very satisfactory gasp. "So importunate."

"Fuck yeah. You have no idea how long I've waited for this."

"Very well." Christophe released Trent and stepped back. "I am at your disposal."

"Excellent." Trent climbed on the bed, kneeling to face Christophe, the expression on his face the very definition of *come-hither*. Christophe had no desire to resist. He stalked forward, his nerves sparking with desire.

Trent must carry most of his height in his long, elegant legs, because his current position put his head lower than Christophe's for the first time since they'd met. Trent wrapped his arms around Christophe and nuzzled his chest, flicking one nipple with his tongue, then kissing a path to the other and sucking it into his mouth with a moan.

Christophe growled and threw his head back, his cock leaking against his belly, and buried his hands in Trent's hair. When Trent added teeth, Christophe's fingertips began to tingle and burn.

Shite, no! He couldn't shift. Not here. Not now. *Control.* He took a deep breath and pulled Trent's head away from his chest, kissing him softly, as befit a man, not a wolf. "Lie down. I want to make love to you."

Trent's eyes widened. "Awesome." He scrambled backward and collapsed onto the pillows. He met Christophe's gaze, held it, nudging the lube and condoms toward him, then raised his knees to his chest, holding his thighs with both hands. So open, so trusting. Awaiting Christophe's touch, his passion, his *possession*.

Christophe's teeth ached as his canines tried to descend, and pain flared in the base of his spine as if his tail was beginning to sprout.

He clenched his eyes shut, breathing deep and steady, willing his other nature to stand down. *Who do you think to protect him from? Yourself?* Perhaps his wolf was not so far off the mark. Christophe wanted nothing as badly as he wanted to be inside Trent. But this close to the edge, with his wolf barely contained, he couldn't risk it, couldn't risk Trent. *Papa and Anton were right. I should never have postponed the shift for so long.* But how could he have known he'd meet someone like Trent, who spoke to both the man and the wolf?

Slowly, the warning signs receded, until nothing but a slight tingling remained in his fingertips, like the memory of touching a hot iron. He opened his eyes.

Uncertainty clouded Trent's face, and he released his legs, his erection starting to flag. "Too much. It's too much, I'm sorry, I—"

"Shhh." Christophe crawled onto the bed and stretched out on his side next to Trent. "You are the most beautiful thing I've ever seen, and how you offered yourself to me—" He kissed Trent on the temple, the cheek, the lips. "I am honored and humbled. But—" he nipped at Trent's jaw "—as I told you, I am in no hurry. This first time, let us learn what we can of one another. Taste." He kissed Trent again, urging him with the touch of his tongue to open, the taste of bourbon still in Trent's mouth, smoky and intoxicating, although perhaps that was Trent himself. "Touch." He stroked Trent's chest, down his ribs, across his flat stomach, enjoying the tremors that followed his fingers, the hitch of Trent's breath, his barely voiced moan. "Scent." He buried his nose in Trent's hair and inhaled. *Intoxicating indeed.* He trailed kisses down until he reached Trent's ear, but when he nuzzled there, where neck met jaw, Trent jerked away.

Christophe rose up on his elbow. "I am sorry. Did I hurt you?"

Trent shook his head and turned on his side to face Christophe. "No. But remember those boundaries we talked about? You just hit one."

"You dislike me scenting you?"

"No. That's fine, and by the way, you smell fricking great. It's . . . that spot. I'm a little sensitive around the neck."

"Duly noted." Christophe flicked one of Trent's nipples, as he'd done to Christophe earlier. "How about here?"

"No. That's—" He inhaled on a hiss as Christophe pinched and plucked each nipple in turn. "That's fucking awesome."

"And here?" He moved one hand down to cup Trent's balls, playing them across his fingers.

"That's good too. Jesus." Trent closed his eyes, and his long, lovely cock bounced on his belly, once again fully on board.

"I'm sure you'd object to this, however." He grasped that tempting cock and squeezed, pumping once and then stopping as the tingle returned to his fingers. *Control, damn it. I am a man, not a beast.*

Trent glared at him. "Now you're being a dick for the hell of it."

Not for the hell of it, cher. *For you.* His wolf's notion of possession was different than the man's—driven to cherish, to defend, to mark as its own. The wolf clearly wanted Trent. *He cannot have him.*

Christophe rolled Trent onto his back once more and sat between his spread legs. He pulled Trent up to face him. "Show me the error of my ways, then." He leaned back, bracing himself on his hand, and raised an eyebrow.

Trent didn't disappoint. He wrapped his hand around their cocks—and squeezed once, grinning. "You're not the only one with dick moves."

Christophe laughed, and his wolf backed off a bit more. "Noted."

"Then get with the program. You can't expect me to do all the work."

Christophe carefully laid his other hand over Trent's. *Will the wolf allow it?* Trent set the pace, stroke and pressure increasing, sending sparks skating along Christophe's skin. *I can't . . .* He gripped harder, changing the rhythm, pushing them both toward release—only to have the telltale burn start in fingers, teeth, and tailbone.

Shite. He let Trent take over again, and with him in charge, the wolf backed down. *Extraordinary.*

Everything about this evening was extraordinary. *Jesu,* had his bifurcated soul at last found the key to wholeness? His balls tightened with a different, exquisite tingling. *Ah yes.*

Trent's eyes clenched shut, and he gasped, an expression on his face as if he wasn't sure whether to cry or scream or shout. *Exactly. That's exactly what's building in my chest.*

"Christophe. I'm going to— Jesus *fuck*." His back arched and his cock spurted, coating their joined hands, splattering their bodies.

Jesu. The salty musk of the scent, the warmth on his hands, his belly, his groin. *This. This is what I've craved. Not any man, but this one.*

Trent opened his eyes. "Your turn," he whispered.

At the wicked grin on his face, the wolf whimpered in submission and withdrew. *He has mastered us both.* Christophe tilted his chin up, baring his own throat. Trent accepted the invitation, diving forward to kiss Christophe's neck, lighting a fuse that burned through his blood until, with an expert twist of his wrist, Trent ignited him in one brilliant blaze.

He gritted his teeth as he spent, ropes of his own seed joining with Trent's between their bodies.

Trent sagged against his shoulder. "Mmm."

Christophe kissed his temple, his breath still running apace with his heart. "You're painted with semen."

"I don't care." Trent rubbed his chest against Christophe's, smearing them both with it. "What's a little jizz between friends?"

He nuzzled Christophe's neck and sighed, clearly the type of man who fell asleep after orgasm. Christophe was not, but no matter. It gave him the opportunity to care for his partner. How he wished he could say *his lover*, but their time together was so short. Christophe breathed him in again, the scent enough to make his cock throb one more time.

What if their liaison didn't need to be short? Trent might be the incentive Christophe needed to stand up to his father. He had no intention of impregnating some mercenary woman with a death wish. That sort of bargain could never spawn a happy marriage, even if Christophe didn't prefer men.

Personally, I prefer this *man.* The one currently snoring softly against his shoulder.

Chuckling, Christophe eased Trent back onto the pillows and padded to the bathroom. He cleaned himself off, then took a fresh washcloth to the bed and sponged Trent's chest, belly, and groin. Trent smiled in his sleep and nestled into the pillows. Christophe pulled the duvet over him, and as he was tucking it round his shoulders, he saw them.

Scars.

He hadn't noticed them in the low lamplight before, and Trent's shaggy hair had hidden them somewhat, but Trent had inch-wide red welts running under his jaw behind his ears. Christophe's stomach clenched, and his fists tightened on the duvet. Someone had hurt Trent—badly—and from the look of the scars, recently. *How dare they?* He would find who had done this—find them and make them pay. He would marshal the full resources of Clavret et Cie. *Finally, a reason for my influence.*

Christophe's vision sharpened, colors fading as his wolf howled inwardly in agreement. The burning returned to his teeth and back and hands, the urge to drop onto all fours nearly overwhelming him. The signet ring—the last alert before he crossed beyond the point of no return—constricted Christophe's finger as his hands began to change.

Mother of God, no! He scrambled away from the bed and staggered to the chair where he'd left his clothes. *Please let me have another dose of the suppressant with me.*

He flung his shirt down on the puddle of his pants and dug the tiny pill bottle out of his jacket's inner pocket. Only one left. *Enough to get me through the night, God and the devil willing.* Because Trent must be protected. His terror, should he awake and find himself confronted by a wolf— *No. I won't allow it. I refuse, regardless of the cost.* He stumbled to the bathroom and locked the door behind him.

The suppressant—that vile, blessed concoction—made it possible for him to live with passable normalcy, without the need to skulk through the woods as a wolf three days out of every seven as his ancestors had.

But the side effects as it took hold were hideous. Cramps, nausea, blinding headache for an hour at minimum. *Very attractive, that.* But the alternative was worse. An uncontrolled change, in front of a virtual stranger, who loathed any thought of the supernatural, and might perish of shock when faced with incontrovertible proof.

His hands shook as he fought the bottle's damned childproof lid. Bloody hell, how were you supposed to pull and push at the same time? All of a sudden, the lid gave way and the tiny pill flew out into the sink.

"No. No-no-no." Christophe scrabbled in the sink, trying to capture the little oval, but it escaped his trembling hands and disappeared down the drain.

He sank to the floor, the tile chill against his bare arse, and hugged his knees to his chest. Rocking there, head down, hair tumbled forward, he willed his wolf to recede. *Go back. It is not time. I promise I—*

What could he promise, precisely? He'd never willingly accept the change. He'd fight it every day of his life. *This* was the reason he had to defy his father and abdicate his position as CEO-apparent. If only he could pursue his genetics studies, search for a gene therapy, a more effective—or at least less debilitating—palliative. But he'd never find it if he toed the family line and bred the next generation of monsters.

Finally able to see almost normally again, he levered himself to his feet. He turned out the light in the bathroom, and the desk lamp, dressing in the dark by guesswork. Disoriented, exhausted, and on the razor's edge of transition, he didn't bother to put on his underwear or his socks, just shoved them in the pocket of his jacket and slipped his shoes on his bare feet. His father would be appalled, but Christophe could scarcely hold the wolf in check as it was. The bare minimum trappings of humanity would have to do. He needed the feel of the clothing against his skin, the essence of himself as a man imbued in the fabric, holding the beast at bay, but taking the time and effort for sartorial perfection was beyond him.

He gazed at Trent in the moonlight spilling in from the window, his blond hair fanned across the white pillowcase, his hands tucked under his cheek like a child. *So beautiful. So troubled.* A man with issues.

Exactly Christophe's type.

Perhaps I should leave a note? But even if his eyes weren't still blurry, if his hands weren't trembling so hard that he'd doubtless drop the pen, he wasn't sure what to say. *Best think of it later, when my thoughts are clearer, when I can explain to myself as well as to him.*

He dropped a kiss on Trent's cheek and slipped out the door.

Faces. So many faces. Angry. Accusing. Anguished.

Hands, so many hands. *Can't break free. Can't breathe.*

This scene isn't— Can't the director see— Those actors, don't they understand? "Method" doesn't mean burying yourself in the part so far you hurt the other performers.

Cut. Cut! Please yell cut.

A huge man cornered him, the rope in his hands. *No. I'm not wearing the harness. I'm not ready for this stunt.* If the man put the rope around his neck, he'd—

"*No!*"

Trent bolted upright in bed, throat aching, neck burning, heart pounding like a jackhammer.

Just a nightmare. It's okay. It's over. But Jesus, when would he get free of the fucking things? Every night at the same time, his brain insisted on a rerun. Except, *shit.* This time he wasn't alone.

Would Christophe think he was a total freak? Not far off the truth. Trent was half-afraid to glance at the other side of the bed, but he was a firm believer in *Fake it till you make it.* That was what acting was all about, right?

Forcing a smile on his face in case he'd actually screamed, he turned.

He was alone.

Fucking awesome. *So much for round two.*

Trent switched on the bedside light, threw back the covers, and sat up, bracing his hands on the mattress, trying to calm his galloping breath. His own clothes were in their usual jumble in the corner, but Christophe's were gone. He rose, his legs shaky from the adrenaline crash after the dream.

If he weren't in a strange hotel room with a view of the Willamette and the lights of the Hawthorne Bridge outside his window, he'd be tempted to think Christophe—in fact his whole bolt to Oregon—had been a dream too.

Trent's stomach and chest were clean, Christophe's presence erased from his body. If only they'd fucked instead of frotting. At least Trent would be able to feel it in his ass now and know it had been real.

Someone had touched him. Kissed him. Held him as if he made a difference, as if he wasn't an inconvenience to be eliminated or a problem to be solved.

Someone had *seen* him.

He pressed a fist to his chest, just below his sternum, to ease the sudden hollowness. *He didn't owe me anything. I've got no right to feel betrayed.* The decision to hook up with Christophe had been an impulse anyway, a second choice, born out of his shock over Logan's engagement. Was he—what was it Deborah called it?—projecting? Assigning to Christophe's abandonment the feeling he'd had when he realized Logan had moved on?

Screw it. He'd had enough people fucking with his head, trying to analyze his feelings. He didn't need to do it to himself.

He stumbled to the bathroom and flipped on the light. Ha! There. Evidence of Christophe at last—the washcloth he'd obviously used for postsex cleanup was draped over the side of the bathtub, and the towel folded with military precision over the shower rod.

He used the john and splashed water on his face. When he emerged from the bathroom, the clock read just past midnight. Naturally. The ghosts haunting his subconscious were nothing if not punctual. Trent picked up his iPhone. Damn it, the thing was supposed to have a weather—what did they call it? An app. *Jesus, check out of reality for a measly seven years and the whole tech terminology changes.*

He poked at the screen. The freaky female voice said, "What can I help you with?"

Hell no. He had enough trouble with disembodied . . . well . . . bodies, he refused to talk to an imaginary person on his phone. Siri could go fuck herself.

Who cared about the stupid app? It was May in Portland. Rain was a distinct possibility, but if it was raining, no big. He'd get wet. He needed to run, and tonight he had more to run from than usual. Although he didn't have the shoreline of Newport to remind him he wasn't trapped, he could make do with Waterfront Park and the Willamette. As long as he kept away from fucking Forest Park, he should be okay.

He pawed through his clothes until he found his running shorts and a relatively clean T-shirt. It was the *All my friends are dead* dinosaur shirt that had offended his father so much.

Perfect.

He dressed and shoved his feet into his Nikes. As he left the room, he stuck his key card in the pocket of his shorts. If he put five miles or so behind him, he might be able to sleep again.

Yet even as he strode through the lobby and onto the street, a part of him wondered whether he'd have been able to make it through the whole night if only Christophe had stayed.

CHAPTER
SEVEN

By the time Christophe had walked back to his flat—he hadn't trusted himself in a cab or public transportation, or even with his own driver—it was well past midnight. When he opened the door, however, the living room lights were on.

He froze in the doorway. Surely he'd turned them off—he never left any light burning.

Easing the door closed, he removed his cell phone from his pocket, ready to call 911 if an intruder were present. Although given how close to the surface Christophe's wolf still prowled, the intruder rather than Christophe might require the assistance.

He toed off his shoes as he'd seen Trent do with his trainers and stole down the hallway, where light spilled from the open door of his study, and peered around the doorjamb.

His brother was sitting at the desk, frowning at the computer monitor.

"Anton?"

Anton startled, rearing back in the chair. "Shite, Christo. Could you move less silently? You nearly gave me a heart attack."

"Well it is my flat. I can move in it as I like. How did you get in?"

Anton held up a key ring with the Clavret crest. "You gave me a key."

"Of course. Forgive me." Christophe tucked his phone in his jacket pocket. "I fear my thinking is not entirely clear."

Anton frowned. "You look like bloody hell. Are you all right?"

Christophe sank down in the chair across the desk from his brother. "Not in the least. I nearly shifted tonight. Downtown. When I was with—"

He glanced at Anton. He and his brother had shared everything from the time they'd been boys, Anton showing remarkable patience with a brother four years his junior. However, Christophe wasn't willing to share his experience with Trent. That was too private, too precious.

Anton chuckled. "No need to go into details. I know how you like to kick over the traces whenever Papa issues an ultimatum, and this one is bigger than most."

Let him think that; it is not so far off the truth after all.

"As you say. Why have you chosen such an awkward time for a visit?"

"Finalizing that Portuguese deal." Anton gestured at the monitor. "Papa spent a bit too much time trying to outmaneuver Etienne Melion and not enough tying up details with the client. We would have lost a minimum of—"

Christophe heaved himself to his feet, nearly stumbling when his head swam sickeningly. "Forgive me. I must—"

Anton's brows drew together. "Christo?"

"You may tell me all about it later, but at the moment I urgently need a dose of the suppressant."

Anton surged out of the chair and took Christophe's elbow, leading him from the room and down the hall to the bedroom. "That bad, is it?"

"It could be worse."

Christophe turned toward the en suite bathroom, but Anton steered him toward the bed instead. "I'll get it. You lie down. You'll need to be in bed anyway, considering what that damn poison does to you."

Christophe didn't fight him. He let Anton take his jacket and hang it in the closet while he lay back and closed his eyes. Mother of God, but he was tired, and ached in every joint. The last time he'd pushed himself this close to his limits, though, he'd huddled for days in a darkened room, unable to eat, wincing at every sound. All things considered, he felt better than he had any right to expect.

For that, he gave Trent complete credit. For his wolf, who needed to protect as well as challenge, Trent was the perfect mate.

Mate? Where had that notion come from?

Anton returned with a glass of water, the suppressant-pill bottle, and a large basin. *My poor brother has trod this path with me too often.*

"Thank you." Christophe took the water. "Would you mind opening the bottle for me? I had a spot of trouble with it earlier, which is why I'm in this state."

Anton frowned, but did as he'd been asked. "This isn't good for you."

Christophe downed the pill, chasing it with half the water. "How can you think such a thing, *mon frère*? A potion first brewed by a half-literate herbalist in the fifteenth century, who was later burned as a witch for his trouble, thanks to evidence laid by one of our ancestors? How could it possibly not be the very pinnacle of modern medical science?"

For that matter, Christophe wouldn't have put it past the fellow to have made the cure as bad as the disease on purpose because he suspected the baron of duplicity.

Right on schedule, the cramps hit his stomach, and he curled on his side. He started to shake uncontrollably and, yes, there was the headache—blinding, pounding, making him want to drill a hole in his skull if only to release the pressure. The cure wasn't quite as bad as the disease, but it came damned close.

"Christo. Let me—"

"There's nothing you can do." Another wave of cramps hit, and nausea rolled through his belly. He swallowed against the urge to spew. "Mother of God, this doesn't work as well as it used to."

"That's because you expect too much of it. That baron only wanted a fail-safe, a way to delay the shift for a bit because he suspected his liege men planned to revolt."

Christophe's stomach tried to stage its own revolt. He gritted his teeth until the urge receded. "He should have asked for a cure. Back then, close enough to the original curse, he might have had a chance to spare his descendants this misery. *Jesu!*" He rolled over and spewed into the basin as Anton held his hair back from his face.

When his stomach stopped heaving, he rolled to his back. Anton handed him a warm washcloth without a word.

"When did you get this?"

"You blacked out for a moment after you stopped retching. I got it when I cleaned the basin. It's here if you need it."

"I trust I won't, but the side effects are definitely getting worse. I have to find a better solution."

"If you would only shift—"

"I have no place to safely do so here in the city, and no time to jaunt off to Alaska or Canada before the wedding. Afterward. Ah, shite. Mother of *God*." The nausea receded, but as it waned, the joint pain doubled and the headache worsened.

"You shouldn't wait until Wednesday."

Christophe closed his eyes, because even the low light of the bedside lamp pierced his brain like hot knives. "Wednesday?"

"Yes. You told Papa that you'd be back in Vienna by Wednesday. Leave directly after this ceremony of yours instead and go to Nantes for three days first. I'll alert the staff at the chateau—"

"No. I'll be fine."

"Christo, you are so far from fine that it's not remotely amusing."

Christophe reached out blindly and Anton took his hand. "I am so glad you escaped this blight. I wouldn't wish it on my worst enemy."

Anton squeezed his hand. "No? You'd wish Etienne Melion free of it, then?"

Christophe chuckled, but stopped when it hurt his strained stomach muscles. "He nearly deserves it, the sadistic bastard. But yes, him too, even though he's as much a bully in business as he ever was at school." *And now he's contracting for a wife to torment until she dies. Mother of God, we must stop this madness. This bloody curse needs to end.*

"I have your itinerary for the next few days. Are you able to listen while you rest?"

Christophe nodded, but kept his eyes closed. "My ears are possibly the only things that don't hurt at the moment." Even his nose betrayed him after a dose, bollixing up his sense of smell for a good twelve hours or more. "Do your worst."

Anton released his hand. "Let me get the files and my tablet. One moment."

"Take your time." Christophe concentrated on his breathing, and pinched the webbing between his left thumb and forefinger, an acupressure trick he'd picked up to temporarily alleviate these headaches, enough to enable him to think. The only problem with the trick was that it only masked the pain while maintaining the pressure on his hand—which was its own brand of pain.

Anton's steps returned and he settled in the chair with a rustle of paper.

"From the sound of things, you haven't convinced Papa to go paperless yet."

Anton chuckled. "Sadly for the environment, no. Papa is a traditionalist in every sense of the word. If he can't study the fine print on paper, even if he must wear trifocals to do it, he doesn't believe the deal is valid."

"He needs to accept that change is necessary if he wants the business to remain afloat."

"The business is perfectly healthy, I assure you." Anton's tone was decidedly tart now, as well it might be.

"Yes. Through none of my doing." He held out his hand and Anton took it again. "Thank you for that, *mon frère*. You deserve more credit for our successes than either Papa or me. You deserve to run the company."

Anton's hand jerked in Christophe's grip. "Don't. You know it's not possible."

"It is only impossible if we allow Papa to cling to his traditions. Perhaps it is time to force his hand."

"What do you mean?"

"I will not choose a bride from among the Old Families. Hell and damnation, Anton, the Merrick girls are like sisters to us, and as for the Melion women, I wouldn't touch one with a barge pole. They're as like their brother as makes no difference."

"Christo—"

"No. Hear me out. I will not do it, and neither should you."

"Me? I'm not the matrimonial prize that you are."

"You mean the matrimonial millstone. But, Anton, as far as fathering male children goes, there's no difference between us. You have the same Y chromosome as I do—"

"Don't start on genetics again, Christo. You know Papa doesn't believe any of that."

"You must listen. The danger of siring a cursed child is equally as great for you as for me, if your wife is one of the Old Families, a Merrick or Melion or Clavret. Marry where you love, not where you're forced, and your chances of normal children, a happy marriage, are so much better."

Christophe opened his eyes, pain be damned. He couldn't sit up, not yet, but he needed his brother to see, to understand. "In feudal times, men, especially noblemen, cast their seed far and wide, so you might, through ill luck, run into a distant cousin with the gene. But the odds are substantially less. Please, Anton. I want you to be happy."

Anton's face turned wooden. "You don't value your gift as you ought. You've never had to wonder what would have been different if my mother had—"

"Don't. Are you saying that if Papa asked it of you, you would go through with such a travesty of a marriage?"

"Why not? Our family, our money, our influence—how can anyone ignore such things, or fail to take advantage of them?" Anton stared at his hands. "All relationships are business transactions in the end."

"You can't mean that. Don't you dream of love? Of a true partnership?"

"No. I do not." He straightened and met Christophe's eyes. "And if you do, I fear you will be doomed to disappointment."

When had his brother turned so cynical, so hopeless? Had he fallen in love, only to be rejected because *he* wasn't the chosen Clavret heir? "Anton, you know I would give you—"

"Leave it, Christo. The discussion is pointless." He pulled his tablet from beneath the stack of paper contracts. "Now, as for your itinerary, I've emailed you the plane tickets. You're leaving on Tuesday morning, flying commercial, since Papa is taking the company jet back on Sunday. I still think you should go early. Give yourself time to shift before reporting to the Vienna offices."

"I will not."

Anton huffed out a sigh. "You are one stubborn bastard. That being the case, on Wednesday morning—"

"You misunderstand. I will not go back at all."

Anton gaped at him. "But you cannot mean it. If you don't return, Papa will—"

"Papa will have to come to terms with the fact that this mutation, this *birth defect*, has outlived its usefulness—if it ever was useful, which I take leave to doubt. Perhaps the first baron, when not being betrayed by his faithless wife, found his wolf nature helpful in governing his lands, keeping his vassals in line, but even so. Today, we may as well be dinosaurs."

"You speak of yourself?"

"I speak of the Old Families, every one of us, with our ludicrous archaic traditions. A company whose management team is selected based on a genetic anomaly cannot hope to survive in the modern world. The company doesn't need me, Anton. It needs you."

"Christo—"

"The only way Papa will finally realize that is if I refuse to go along with his schemes. If *you* refuse too, he will have to listen. Please. Promise me."

"I cannot promise anything now. Papa can be . . . difficult, as you know, but he is still our father, and he's proud of our family, our business, our accomplishments. What you're suggesting amounts to a mutiny, a hostile takeover."

Christophe smiled, although his skin felt too tight. "More like a hostile retreat."

"You heard him yesterday. He's willing to liquidate the company if you don't yield. Everything we've built over the years, gone. Could you live with that?"

"I'm not certain I can live with the alternative. Besides, I don't believe Papa was serious. To dismantle the business would be admitting defeat, relinquishing control. He's an alpha. He would never do it."

"But to take the chance—"

"He's bluffing, Anton. Trust me. And trust me to find a way to make it right with him. But my life is a shambles enough. I'd like to see if I can salvage some of it." Christophe's headache hadn't disappeared, but it was marginally bearable. "At least consider what I've said."

"Very well. But I promise you that my mind will not change."

Christophe smiled weakly. "Even if it means that you'll become a happily married CEO?"

Anton shrugged, a smile lifting one corner of his mouth. "Even so."

Christophe attempted to sit up, but a wave of nausea overtook him, and Anton handed him the basin. He pushed it away. "It's not that bad."

"Are you lying for my benefit? Because it's obviously that bad, and likely worse." Anton leaned forward, taking both Christophe's hands. "Where is this wedding of yours?"

"It is not my wedding." Although now that he had seen how Riley and Logan connected—and now that he had met Trent—he dared hope for his own someday. A wedding that didn't involve signing himself into stud service for the next generation of Clavret shifters. "It's at the Copper Dell Resort, northwest of Mount Hood."

Anton swiped the screen of his tablet and tapped out some commands. "It's inside the Mount Hood National Forest. Good. Here's what we'll do. I'll book two rooms at the resort for the day before the wedding. Then I can take you out into the forest so you'll be able to shift."

"Absolutely not. It's too risky."

"With me at your back, the risk isn't so outrageous. Oregon has begun introducing wolves into the wild, so if anyone sees you, they won't find it remarkable."

"You mean not as newsworthy as when Etienne Melion was sighted in France by that group of tourists?"

Anton's laugh had a sharp edge to it. "Indeed. You won't be a unicorn, the only wolf in France in nearly a century."

"Still, I don't know . . ."

"Think about how you feel right now. When was your last dose?"

Christophe averted his eyes. "Day before yesterday."

"My God, Christo. You're only supposed to ingest that shite once a week, if that."

"I know. It wears off sooner now."

"It wears off because it has too much to fight. Do yourself, and your friends, and their wedding guests a favor. Shift the night before the wedding and be comfortable."

"If you had ever experienced the shift, you wouldn't speak to me of comfort. You think the suppressant side effects are bad? The transition pains, both in and out, make this look like a bloody holiday."

"But at least they don't last as long."

"Only if you don't count the time as a wolf."

"You need this. Matings always stir the instincts, or so I'm told. You don't want to suddenly rip your clothes off in the middle of the ceremony, do you?"

"No. That would indeed be unfortunate."

"So. It's sorted, then. I'll book the rooms."

"Thank you, *mon frère*. What would I do without you?"

"Much the same as you do now, I'll wager," Anton grumbled. "You never did listen to anyone but yourself."

Christophe chuckled, grateful that this time his stomach didn't rebel. "Perhaps not. Even if Papa refuses to acknowledge your contributions, never doubt that I appreciate what you do for me, for him, for our company. And if you doubt all else, never doubt that I love you."

Two hours, nine miles, and three bridges later, Trent returned to the hotel. This late, he had to swipe his key card to get into the lobby, but when he entered, he discovered that the security measures didn't keep everyone out.

Logan was sitting in the lobby, and rose when Trent walked in. Still breathing hard and sweaty from his run, Trent nevertheless had a moment of panic when he considered running straight back out again. *Shit, am I about to get my ass kicked?*

Logan strode toward him, his expression serious, but not murderous. *That's good, right?* Trent put on as much of his old swagger as he could scare up after a run that had left him wrung out.

"Hey, Logan. Kind of late for a visit, isn't it?"

Logan stopped in front of him. "We need to talk."

Trent's shoulders drooped. "Yeah. I was afraid of that. Let's go upstairs."

Trent led the way to the elevators, Logan's presence at his heels making him walk faster than he wanted. "How'd you know where I was staying?"

"Followed you last night after you left."

Trent froze with his hand on the call button. "Uh . . . you did?"

"Yup." Logan smirked, and that familiar expression, even on a rugged face atop a man's solid body, took Trent right back to their dorm room, when both of them had barely had enough muscles between them to make one decent-sized guy. "Looked like you were busy, though. Didn't want to interrupt. Besides, I had to finish up at the bar."

"Thanks for that." They stepped into the elevator and the doors slid closed.

"Hey. Suited me. I'd rather that guy stayed away from Riley." Logan's scowl, its reflection distorted by the polished metal elevator doors, was more than a little freaky.

Trent glanced at him sidelong. "Why? Is there something wrong with Christophe?" Although it was a bit late now to worry about it, especially since the guy had bailed without a word. Trent wanted to check on his instincts though—the ones that had told him he could trust Christophe.

"No, and that's what's wrong with him." Logan ran a hand through his hair. "I mean, did you see that guy?"

"Uh . . . hello? You're the one who followed us, dude." The elevator pinged as it arrived at Trent's floor.

"Right. Stupid question. But he's like the perfect fantasy fuck. He's got the looks, the clothes, the money . . ."

Trent stopped halfway out the elevator doors, the light dawning. "Logan, are you *jealous* of Christophe because he used to date Riley?"

Logan's scowl deepened, and he stormed past Trent and down the hall. "No."

Trent put his fingers in his mouth and whistled. *Oops. Two in the morning is probably not the best time to make noise in the hallway.* It did the trick though. Logan turned, and Trent jerked his thumb in the other direction. "My room's over here, Mr. Green-Eyed Monster."

Logan stalked toward him. "I. Am not. Jealous."

Trent led the way to his room and keyed open the door, gesturing Logan inside. "What do you call it, then?"

"Due diligence. My responsibility as his— Ah, Christ." He sighed and rubbed the back of his neck. "I still don't know why Riley chose me. I mean, I don't have any of that shit."

"Is that why you came up here, to get premarital advice from me?" Trent shook his head. "Not your brightest move, and you pulled some pretty boneheaded stunts in our dorm days."

Logan snorted and checked out the room—from the bed with its mangled covers to the pile of clothes in the corner. "I see your housekeeping is about the same."

"What can I say? Not a lot of opportunity to beef that up in the alternate dimension."

Logan winced. "Shit. I'm sorry. I didn't come here to be a dick."

"Why did you come, then?"

"I wanted to . . . well . . . check on you. They hauled you out of the park so fast last October. Didn't let me visit your hospital room, and then shuttled you onto a jet to Rhode Island before the dust settled." Logan shrugged. "I was worried. I mean, I saw the news coverage about your return, at least the local stuff. But once you went back to Newport, there wasn't a lot available."

"You didn't miss much. My dad acting like a blowhard asshole and my mom like a society princess with an icicle for a spine. Nothing new about that."

"Why didn't you return my calls?" Jesus, did Logan sound hurt? "I left a ton of messages with whoever answers your phone 24-7."

"That would be Vance, dad's personal assistant. He functions as a sort of terminally constipated second sphincter for the old man."

"You mean he never gave them to you?"

Trent toyed with the notion of lying to Logan for about fifteen seconds, but didn't see the point. He and Logan had no future beyond Trent's desperate imagination, and a relationship probably would have been disastrous if Logan *had* been free. "I got them. Eventually. But for the first six months, I was checked in to a private psychiatric clinic. The loony bin didn't allow outside contact except for immediate family."

"What?" Logan's face paled. "They *institutionalized* you? Christ, Trent, if I had known—"

"Hey hey hey." Trent grabbed those big shoulders and squeezed. "No worries. It was my idea, okay?"

Logan nodded, his throat working. "Yeah. Sure. Okay."

"Good." Trent patted Logan and stepped into the bathroom to grab a washcloth. The one Christophe had left was still hanging from the tub. *Of course it is. It's the middle of the night, and housekeeping isn't likely to intrude, even if you didn't have the DND sign up.* He turned to stand in the doorway. "I needed some time to . . . process, I guess. They say I've got PTSD, which is a better diagnosis than batshit crazy."

Logan surged toward him. "Trent—"

Trent flapped the washcloth, one hand on the doorknob. "Do you mind if I take a quick shower before we talk more? I stink."

"I—" Shoving his hands in his pockets, Logan backed off. "Sure. No problem."

"Riley's not going to wonder where you are, is he?"

"He knows. He's the one who told me to come tonight. I think he saw Christophe walking past the bar a couple of hours ago, so he knew you'd be alone. I came over as soon as I closed up."

"I'll be quick anyway."

He was, but then realized that he'd forgotten to bring in any clean clothes. *Smooth.* He opened the door, a towel around his waist. "Don't take this as a come-on, but I need to get some clothes."

Logan was at the desk, fiddling with the iPhone. He barely glanced up as Trent scampered by in the almost altogether. "You know you need to charge this, right?"

"I know that." Trent located a pair of briefs and pulled them on under the towel. "Back in my day, we had to plug our stone cell phones into the fire every night too." He put on a pair of sleep pants and a T-shirt and hopped on the bed, sitting tailor-fashion, the way he had so many times in their dorm. "The damn thing is so . . . bare. I only got it this morning before I got on the plane. I was using my old Nokia before that. At least it had an actual keypad, not this weird onscreen touchy-feely shit."

Logan set the phone down and sat in the desk chair, facing Trent. "Is it hard? Getting used to the changes?"

"Some. I have to pace myself, you know? Too much too soon and my head might explode."

"Riley warned me about that last October, before we rescued you. He said we couldn't know what you might want or feel or do. That we couldn't know what you'd been through."

Trent picked the flannel fuzz off his pants. "Yeah. Not exactly a SparkNotes for *What to do when your friend returns from the dead.*"

"You weren't dead."

"Wasn't I? I can't say I was alive, not if being alive means you age and grow and change. I mean, look at me. Look at you. You're a man now. In love. About to get married. Me? I'm no different than that asshole kid back in the dorm." Trent met Logan's gaze. "It's my birthday on Friday, and I don't even know which one it is. How do you count birthdays anyway? By the number of days you're boots-on-the-ground, consciously in this world? Or is it just arithmetic? The magic of subtraction from today's date to the date on your birth certificate."

Logan stared at the floor, the desk, the ceiling—everywhere but at Trent. "Riley was afraid you'd be so freaked when you got out of the ghost war, you'd . . . you know . . . throw me under the bus. To take the pressure off yourself."

Trent's throat tightened, his hands clenched on his knees. *Seriously? After all the shit I've gone through* not *to implicate Logan?* He took a deep breath. What had Riley known about him then? *Not much more than he knows now.* "I would never do that."

"That's what I told him." Logan picked up the phone again, turning it over in his hand for a moment before raising his head to meet Trent's gaze. "I have to ask—are you, you know, okay with me and Riley?"

"What, you mean because you had the unmitigated gall to fall in love with somebody while I was checked out in the Twilight Zone?" Trent clutched his chest with one hand. "You dickhead, how could you?"

"Be serious. I mean, when you showed up at the bar tonight, you didn't expect to see what you did, did you?"

Trent canned the fake melodrama. What was the point? "No. I had some idea that you were the only person in the universe who'd understand me. Who I wouldn't have to lie to about the ghost war and Danford Balch."

"You're right about that. You can tell me anything, anytime. But Riley's right too. I don't know what you went through, and I have a feeling that me getting married this week isn't exactly going to help you on the road to recovery."

"Maybe not. But that doesn't mean I begrudge you your happiness. We were friends. You came back for me. That counts for a lot."

"You say we 'were' friends. Do you think we could be friends again?"

"I don't know. Can we? The thing I've noticed about couples is that there's not always a lot of room for third wheels."

"Screw that. I'm not about to cut you out of my life now."

"Okay. But don't push it, okay? Not for me, and not for you either. That honeymoon bed'll be a little crowded with three, know what I'm saying?"

Logan chuckled. "True that."

"How the hell did you end up owning a bar anyway? Aren't you an architect?"

"I dropped out after you disappeared. Spent the next seven years trying to figure out how to rescue you."

Trent's jaw dropped. "Seriously? Jesus *fuck*, Logan, I'm not worth that."

Logan set down the iPhone and grabbed Trent's foot. "You are. Absolutely. So don't give me that shit." When Trent wiggled his toes, Logan let go. "Besides, the bar's not my only problem. I own the whole fucking building. I inherited it."

"Inherited it? Wait, did your dad die? Dude, I'm sorry. I didn't know."

"No, not from him. And he's still alive and a pain in my ass, thanks. Did I ever mention my old neighbor, Bert Johnson, to you?" Trent shook his head. "Well, he owned the building, ran the bar. I was bartending for him just before we got you back. Turns out he was Cuthbert fucking Stump. He got displaced by—"

"Joseph Geddes," they both said at once.

"Right." Logan leaned forward, propping his elbows on his knees. "When he took Cuthbert's place, my grandfather took Cuthbert in for a few days. Gave him a start, a leg up, made it possible for him to live as Bert Johnson. Turns out, Bert willed the building to Granddad."

"But your grandparents have been dead for years. Wouldn't the building have gone to your father?"

"It would have, but my grandmother removed him from her will after Dad was such an asshole about Granddad's experiences. I'm the fucking heir."

Trent snorted. "Our grandfathers would have gotten along great. They both had dickhead sons and awesome grandsons. So now you're an enlightened slumlord?"

"No. Well, sort of. The building has a couple of apartments. I've been living in one, but Riley and I are moving to a place in Northwest after we get back from the honeymoon, so it's due to be gutted. Joseph lives in the other one." Logan carded his hands through his hair. "I've got a business I don't want hanging around my neck, and I need to unload it before I start school again in the fall. I want to give the whole damn thing to Joseph, but he won't let me. Says he doesn't know enough about this world to manage anything, let alone the bar."

"I know how he feels," Trent muttered.

"But I'm determined to give it to him." Logan grinned. "Heather, the bar manager, is my best person at the wedding, so we're leaving Joseph in charge for the weekend. He'll get the hang of it."

"Probably."

"So. The wedding. It's at this resort in the national forest out by Mount Hood, and I'd really love it if . . . well . . . Will you come?"

Trent's belly clenched. *Forest. Why'd it have to be in the forest?* "I don't know if I can . . ."

"Look, if you can't, no problem. But I'd like you to meet Riley. He's . . ." The smile that ambushed Logan's face was positively goofy. "He's amazing. He's the one who figured out how to get you back."

"Thank him for me, yeah?"

"You could thank him yourself if you—"

"Don't push, Logan, okay? I've got to take things a day at a time."

"Right. Well, if you change your mind, or need me for anything, I'm living in one of the apartments over the bar until the wedding." He picked up the phone and handed it to Trent. "Here. I programmed my number in there. Just say 'Call Logan' and Siri will do the rest."

"In my day, phones didn't talk to you unless you talked first," Trent grumbled.

"Yes, Grandpa."

"Fuck you."

Logan grinned. "I missed you too, man. It's good to have you back."

CHAPTER
EIGHT

The next morning, Christophe had nearly returned to normal—or as normal as he ever felt after a dose of suppressant. In other words, as if he'd just awoken from a nine-day bender that had involved a turn-up with at least half a dozen masked bravos.

He'd managed to feign recovery sufficiently last night to get Anton to leave—no point in his brother being forced to keep watch at his bedside.

After downing a couple of ibuprofen with a bottle of Vitaminwater, he took the hottest shower his sensitized skin would tolerate. As he dressed afterward, with each familiar article of clothing—briefs, undershirt, shirt, pants, socks, shoes—his humanity settled over him, bit by bit. By the time he donned another of the new jackets, he felt civilized enough to greet the day—and face his mistakes from yesterday.

He needed to contact his father soon, to start the conversation about his decision to leave the company. For that, he needed fortification. Not only nutritional, but emotional.

Trent.

Christophe paused in the act of mixing his morning protein shake. Why would his first thought for moral support fly to Trent? *Because last night, you felt it—the connection.* Something about Trent resonated inside Christophe, like the strike of a tuning fork, their inner shadows vibrating with the same frequency. *We could understand each other, I'm sure of it.*

But how could Christophe force the knowledge of his curse on another? It was difficult enough for him to bear alone. *But wouldn't sharing the burden with someone—with Trent—lessen it? I could share his as well.*

Attraction was a complicated knot—he'd learned as much in his abbreviated genetics studies. The markers for what someone would crave or avoid—why kissing one person thrilled but the mere thought of touching another revolted—were buried deep in each individual's DNA.

This was the first time Christophe had experienced such a strong, intuitive pull toward someone else. The only thing he could compare it to was its inverse—his instinctive revulsion for Etienne Melion, the only other male shifter of his generation.

Whatever the cause, he intended to explore it, provided Trent could be persuaded to speak to him after his unconscionable exit last night.

Anton had left a hard copy of the conference itinerary on his breakfast bar, so Christophe studied it as he drank his shake. A nine o'clock meeting with the CEOs of Merrick Industries, Melion GmbH, and of course, Clavret et Cie.

Best begin as he meant to go on, and let his father get used to his absence.

He texted Anton.

I don't feel equal to meetings today.

Do you need anything? I could come by.

No. But could you cover for me?

Naturally. Have you spoken to Papa yet?

No, but please give him my regrets and let him know I have much to discuss with him after the weekend.

As you wish.

So. His schedule was now free. He knew exactly how he wanted to fill it, but the question remained whether Trent would agree to the plan.

His cell phone rang. The caller ID surprised him.

"Riley? Good morning, *mon ami.*"

"Hey, Christophe. Are you . . . I mean, is this a good time? I know it's a little early."

He chuckled. "Do you mean, am I alone?"

Riley laughed. "Not exactly, but yeah, I guess."

"Sadly, yes. But I hope to rectify that soon."

"I wanted to warn you. Logan sort of . . . followed you and Trent back to his hotel last night."

Christophe's vision shifted, the green of the ficus tree fading to gray. "Indeed. That was rather presumptuous of him."

Riley snorted. "Tell me about it. But Trent was his best friend once, and he hadn't seen him since October. I think he wanted to make sure he was okay, you know?"

"Understandable." Christophe had wanted the same thing.

"He didn't stay. I mean, he wasn't staking the place out. Nothing stalkerish. But later, I saw you walking past the bar again. He went back and talked to Trent then."

"Was he—" Christophe swallowed. "Did he seem well?"

"We . . . ah . . . didn't go into it much. But I wanted to tell you that if you thought he might be hung up on Logan or anything? He's not. Or at least Logan doesn't think so."

"Do you think he's only telling you what you want to hear, *cher*?"

"No. I can tell when he's lying. He really sucks at it."

Excellent. The field was clear for Christophe to pursue Trent, if Trent would allow it. His vision returned to human-normal. "I hope for your sake that his sucking abilities are spectacular."

"Chwistophe!"

Christophe chuckled. He'd never imagined he could detect a blush over the phone, but judging by Riley's tone, he was probably as pink as a Paris sunset.

Another voice rumbled behind Riley's splutter. "Gimme that."

"Logan, no, I was—"

Judging by the grunts, gasps, and occasional squawk, Riley and his lover were engaging in a rather X-rated version of keep-away with the cell phone. Given Logan's size, however, Christophe wasn't surprised that his voice was next on the line.

"Hey."

"Mr. Conner. A pleasure."

"Yeah. Don't bother. I've got one thing to say to you."

"Indeed? I'm pleased we have this opportunity to speak. I believe I must request a favor."

"If it has anything to do with Riley—"

"I do not poach, especially when it is clear that you two were meant for one another."

"Oh. Good."

"But if you would be so kind as to give me Trent's cell phone number?" Perhaps he should ask for his last name too, but he had no wish for Logan to think the connection between them had been so slight Trent hadn't even trusted him with his name.

Logan hesitated. "I don't know . . ."

"If he doesn't want to speak with me, he can always decline the call or block my number. But like you, I want to make sure he is well."

"It's not that. I mean, he can use friends. He . . . Oh hell." He rattled off the number and Christophe noted it on the margin of the useless itinerary. "Trent's in a weird place right now. He's been a little . . . out of touch."

"Certainly with you, it seems."

"With everybody. He needs—"

"Don't you think it's a bit patriarchal of you to assume you know what he needs?"

Logan practically growled. If Christophe were in his wolf form, his hackles would have risen in response to the challenge. "Just don't fuck with him, okay?"

"'With'? Ah, your English prepositions," Christophe drawled in his most urbane tone. "So confusing, don't you agree, when one is not a native English speaker? One never knows exactly how to use them. Or when."

"Listen—"

"*Au revoir*, Mr. Conner."

As soon as he disconnected the call, he immediately tried Trent's number. It rang, but eventually went to a generic voice mailbox. Christophe frowned, tapping the counter. Trent didn't know Christophe's number yet, so he couldn't be refusing the call on purpose. Unless he was declining calls from any unknown number.

Whatever the cause, Christophe had no intention of abandoning the hunt so easily. He knew Trent's whereabouts. Unless he'd checked out of his hotel already, he'd be there at some point today. If Christophe wanted to be welcome, however, he needed to arrive bearing gifts.

Considering Trent's apparent youth, and his general unfamiliarity with Portland, Christophe decided to go with the standard treats. He refused to trust his transportation to chance as he had the previous evening, though, so he texted his driver to meet him downstairs in ten minutes.

Consequently, when he arrived at Trent's door an hour later, he carried the signature pink Voodoo Doughnuts box and a personal carafe of Peet's coffee. The Do Not Disturb sign was still in place and the sounds of the television bled through the door.

Excellent. Trent was in, unless he was the type to leave his appliances on when he left the premises. Christophe juggled his offerings and knocked. There was enough of a pause that he feared the second option might be true, but before he could knock again, the door opened and Trent stood there, tousled and beautiful in a pair of plaid flannel sleep pants and a blue T-shirt.

"You know," he said, crossing his arms over his chest, "when I put the DND sign up, I didn't mean for it to apply to you. You could have woken me up before you bailed."

"Yes. I am sorry. I should have said good-bye, but I had a sudden emergency and didn't want to trouble you."

"Nice story."

"True, nonetheless. But as you see," Christophe held up the pink box, "I've come bearing conciliatory gifts."

Trent eyed the box. "Is there a maple bacon bar in there?"

"Two."

"All right. You can come in." He stood aside. "You're still on probation though."

"I shall do my best to comply with the terms."

The instant Christophe set the doughnut box on the desk, Trent lifted the lid. He didn't grab a pastry, however. He simply closed his eyes and inhaled deeply.

"Jesus, these smell amazing. You don't know how I've missed this."

"They don't have such things where you are from?" Christophe kept his inquiry light, in case Trent was leery of sharing too much personal information.

Trent smirked at him. "Fishing for data much?"

Christophe shrugged. "Whatever works, as they say."

"'They' say a hell of a lot that doesn't make any sense. Is that *coffee*?"

"It is." He pulled the little bag of sugar and cream packets from his jacket pocket. "With all the necessities except cups."

"Got it covered." Trent retrieved two heavy white ceramic mugs from the hotel's complimentary coffee service tray. Christophe poured them both a cup. He was interested to note that Trent took his coffee black. Unusual for young American men these days.

Christophe pulled a wad of folded napkins from his other pocket. "Please help yourself." Lord, his tailor would never forgive him for the abuse he was heaping on his poor new jacket. The man complained constantly about how storing bulky objects in the pockets ruined the line of the coat.

Dropping his guarded look for the first time since opening the door, Trent grinned. "Thought you'd never ask." He captured one of the maple bacon bars, licking a stray bit of icing off his fingers in a way that made Christophe sorry that his pants fit quite as well as they did—they were now a half size too tight in the groin.

Given Logan's warning about Trent's supposed fragility, though, he shouldn't rush into intimacy. So to get his mind off Trent's mouth, he nodded at the television. "What are you watching?"

For some reason, that caused Trent's face to shut down again. "Just catching up on movies. Got a lot in my TBW pile. Hotel has free on-demand." He shrugged. "No-brainer."

"You haven't stayed abreast of the latest films? And you a theater major."

"I was stage, not screen."

"Nevertheless—"

"Can you please drop it? I haven't seen the fucking movies. Now I'm watching them, okay?"

Christophe inclined his head. "Of course. I meant no offense. I myself have little time for movies or television." He offered his best ingratiating smile. "One of the reasons I've never watched Riley's show."

Trent peered at him, chewing and swallowing a mouthful of doughnut. "Seriously? You haven't seen *any* of the episodes? Not even the one Riley was in?"

Christophe shook his head. "No. We weren't seeing each other at the time. I saw an announcement of sorts." The video of Logan's proposal, in fact. "However, I have never managed to catch the show itself."

Oddly, this news made Trent's shoulders lift, his back straighten. He took a sip of coffee and grinned. "So. Want to watch a movie with me?"

Just knowing that Christophe hadn't seen the *Haunted to the Max* episode in which he'd made an unintended cameo made Trent feel almost normal. *If nobody knows about your freaky-ass shit, they can't judge you for it.*

So keep it secret. Yeah, that was the ticket. If he kept his mouth shut about the ghost war, maybe Christophe would stick around long enough for more sex. *Because, Jesus, I need more touching.*

He moved the Voodoo Doughnut box to the coffee table, in easy reach of the suite's love seat, and patted the cushion next to him. Christophe brought the coffee pot over—*coffee* and *doughnuts; I think I'm in love*—and settled next to Trent, their shoulders brushing. *Thank God for hotels that don't spring for full-sized sofas.*

Christophe took a bite of his own maple bacon bar—a bare nibble of the corner as opposed to the way Trent had practically inhaled his own. *Guess you learn how to eat like an adult between nineteen and twenty-six.* Not that he was deficient in theoretical education when it came to manners. He'd been to the fucking etiquette classes, suffered through the cotillion lessons along with the other kids in his parents' social strata. But fuck rules when Voodoo Doughnuts were on the table.

Anyway, he'd shed that shit when he'd opted for the theater crowd rather than the golf-and-tennis set. The theater kids had tended to be scholarship students from North Providence and Pawtucket. They'd been a hell of a lot more fun to hang with—and they'd introduced him to legend tripping. Not that he wanted to think about that now.

But the taste of maple icing mingled with coffee made him wistful for the old days, when he could chase down the thrills and screw the consequences. The promise of the unknown, the possibility that it might be true, had been way better than finding the one that really *had been* true and having it kick his ass.

Kind of like the difference between the anticipation of Christmas and the letdown afterward, when the holiday, for all the endless hype about family and togetherness and *yada yada yada*, ended up being another day of disappointment and disapproval.

Christophe topped off their coffees, frowning at the big-ass TV. "Is such a large screen necessary for a room this size?"

"Hey, don't dis the amenities. This place doesn't scrimp on the important stuff." The bed was awesome too. Trent cast a sidelong glance at Christophe. Was he up for giving the bed another try later? He hadn't made a move since he'd arrived, but hey, he'd brought peace offerings.

That had to be a good sign—a sign Christophe didn't consider Trent a total waste of time and effort. Trent hadn't wanted to admit how hollow he'd felt when he'd woken up alone last night.

Alone. He'd had enough of that, since he'd essentially been in solitary confinement for seven years. It's not like the ghosts had ever become his pals, or listened to his pleas, or even varied their own actions by so much as a different hand movement. He'd been stuck in a hologram with sight and sound, but no taste, virtually no smell, and the only touch that of the rough hands dragging him to his fate. And the rope. *Let's not forget that.* Always the fucking rope.

No, damn it. Let's totally forget the fucking rope. Christophe was here—with scents and tastes and the promise of touch. For now, that was enough.

Christophe sipped his coffee. "What is this movie?"

"*X-Men: Days of Future Past.* You know, from the Marvel comics."

Christophe looked blank.

"Hunh. Guess you have a different frame of reference than I do."

"Perhaps. The movies I'm accustomed to tend to be rather less . . . emphatic."

Trent grinned and reached for another doughnut. "Foreign stuff or indie art films, am I right? I can get into those too. But sometimes, you're in the mood to blow shit up, know what I mean?"

"Indeed. I assume by the peculiar costume choices, however, that this is not intended to be taken seriously." Christophe smiled, and at the sight of those sharp canines a thrill jolted Trent from throat to balls. He gulped some coffee to chase away the shiver.

"The hard-core fans take it plenty seriously, believe me. Most of 'em know the characters better than they know half their family, which makes it easy on the filmmakers. They don't have to introduce the characters or spend a lot of time on character exposition. Everyone knows who Wolverine is and what he can do. Everyone knows Storm controls weather and that Magneto is essentially unstoppable if there's any metal around and he's wearing that stupid-ass hat."

"I see." He frowned at the screen.

"Yeah." Trent sighed happily. "I love superhero movies."

"Superheroes." Christophe's tone was tinged with disgust. "Yet their behavior is not always admirable, let alone heroic."

"Well, okay. Technically, they're mutants, not superheroes."

"Mutants?" Christophe spilled coffee on the table. "Shite. I'm sorry. So clumsy."

"Hey. No worries." Trent tossed a bunch of napkins on the spill. "See, they've all got a random genetic mutation that gives 'em special abilities." He nodded at the screen. "That's Mystique. She has the best powers."

Christophe watched Jennifer Lawrence take down a room full of military dudes. "So. She is a . . . a shape-shifter?"

"Yeah. And like her feet are almost as useful as her hands when she's kicking some guy's ass."

"The way she transforms. It is not in the least credible." Frowning, he pointed to the screen. "She changes her bone structure, her mass, her size, even her clothing. Yet she shows not the slightest discomfort, and can do it in an instant. No. That sort of change—" He leaned back, his arms crossed. "It must have a cost."

"You act like this stuff is real."

"Who's to say it is not?"

"Seriously? Mutants with superpowers?" Trent rubbed his hands on his thighs with a burble of nervous laughter. "Might as well believe in ghosts."

"I do."

"What?"

"I find it more expedient to believe in everything until it's proven false than to disbelieve everything until it's proven true."

"Either you're really open-minded or totally nuts."

Christophe chuckled. "Not the latter, I trust. But if we assume impossibility, we risk missing out on the extraordinary. Don't you find the notion of a world that holds nothing new incredibly dreary?"

"I . . ." Trent swallowed against a lump in his throat. "I suppose."

I used to feel that way. Exactly. In that visit to Forest Park with Logan, anticipating the ghost war. Shit, *seeing* the ghost war. It had been unbelievably thrilling. Even when he'd first entered it, taken the part of Danford Balch, the excitement in his chest had felt like a short-fused cherry bomb about to explode. Right up to the moment he'd played his part too well and shot poor Mortimer Stump in the face.

Of all the things he'd have preferred to smell in that hellish world—mud, rain, even horse shit—he'd been able to smell nothing but Mortimer's blood.

"Trent. Trent!" Christophe shook his arm gently. "What is wrong?"

Shit, did I just space out? "I— Nothing. I'm tired of this movie. Let's watch something else."

"Whatever you'd like."

"You don't have to be somewhere?"

Christophe smiled. "I am exactly where I want to be." He stroked a strand of Trent's hair back, and the gentle touch eased Trent's nerves.

I'm not trapped anymore. I'm here with someone who touches me with gentleness, who brings me coffee and doughnuts that I can eat and drink and taste and smell.

He gazed into Christophe's eyes, and the heat there chased the last of his chills away. He leaned forward, inviting a kiss, and Christophe accepted, pressing his lips to Trent's in a maple-and-coffee-flavored mating of tongues.

After a thankfully long moment, they separated and grinned at each other. Then Trent nestled against Christophe's side and Christophe wrapped an arm around Trent's shoulder, holding him close.

Oh yeah. Maybe he could make it through this movie after all.

CHAPTER
NINE

As perplexing as the ridiculous mutant film was, Christophe enjoyed it because of the company. In the past, when he had merely sought sexual release from any encounter, he hadn't taken the time for cuddling. He'd never before had an opportunity to simply hold a man close for pure companionship.

Nor had he wanted one, truthfully. His previous liaisons had been either a duel for domination, or a quid pro quo. Even if money hadn't changed hands, there had always been an agenda involved.

It was one of the reasons why he'd been so promiscuous at university. He'd been searching for something he'd never found—until now. He was more than content to remain with Trent nestled against him, as the first movie ended and they embarked on a second, then a third. At least the latter ones involved characters who derived their powers from science and technology, not inescapable genetic deviation.

As the credits rolled on the final film, Trent clicked a button on the remote and switched off the television. "So you've had your dose of the Marvel universe and survived."

"Barely." He gestured toward the empty doughnut box. "However I believe I may soon expire from hunger. Your ability to consume pastries rivals that of the best Frenchman I've ever known."

"The nineteen-year-old metabolism has its benefits."

"I thought you were twenty-six."

Trent shrugged. "Like I said, depends on who you ask. It'll change on Friday anyway."

"Why is that?"

"It's my birthday."

"Really? Which one?"

Trent's smile was sly. "Twenty. Or twenty-seven. You pick."

"You must allow me to join in celebrating your birthday."

Trent's face lit up, and for an instant, Christophe could see the joy and energy that must have delighted his audiences when Trent was still an actor. If he could project that joy and energy, that charisma, beyond the footlights, then he must have been mesmerizing as a performer. That he wasn't any longer was a travesty.

Also a mystery, which Christophe intended to solve.

"That would be awesome. What do you have in mind?" Trent waggled his eyebrows and stared pointedly at the bed.

Christophe laughed and kissed him. "You have the libido of a teenager."

"That's because I am one. Sort of."

"Let us say that that may be part of our agenda, but it will assuredly not be the only line item. I want to make the night special for you in as many ways as I'm able. I'm guessing you may not have had the opportunity for special festivities of late?"

Trent's light extinguished as if some inner connection had been severed, and Christophe immediately regretted his words. He also steeled himself for the obvious question—how could Christophe know about Trent's dearth of celebrations—and then he'd have to confess learning about his emotional state from Logan.

Would Trent resent that? In his place, Christophe certainly would. He despised knowing that his future, both professional and personal, was discussed in a boardroom as if he were nothing better than a poorly performing company to be acquired and managed.

He pulled Trent into the circle of his arm. "It's nearly four o'clock. A trifle late for lunch, but allow me to take you out for an early dinner."

"Dinner . . . would be good. I'll ditch the pajamas, but I don't have a lot of clothing options, if you know what I mean."

Christophe eyed the pile of clothes in the corner, which seemed to have grown—or at least gotten more tangled—since last night. "You needn't worry. The place I have in mind is quite casual."

"I think," Trent cocked an eyebrow at Christophe's suit, "your definition of casual may be different than mine. I mean, do you even own a pair of jeans?"

"You wear jeans and T-shirts because you find them comfortable, yes?"

Trent nodded. "That, plus they can stand a lot of abuse."

"Clearly." Christophe grinned, and although at first Trent appeared insulted, he soon laughed.

"Fair cop. But I gotta tell you, back home I've got some classier duds. They just weren't on my radar when I was packing."

"Understood. You packed for comfort. I do too. My manner of dress is a habit, a family tradition ingrained in me from childhood, so these are the clothes I feel most comfortable in." *The ones that protect me best from my unfortunate nature.* "So these are the clothes I wear."

"All right."

Trent stood and stretched, his pants riding low on his hips, accentuating the curve of his arse and the cut of his hip bones. He glanced down and caught Christophe staring. Mother of God, his tongue was practically hanging out, and judging by Trent's smirk, he knew precisely what effect he was provoking.

He sashayed over to his disreputable clothes pile—truly, no man should treat his clothing with so little care and respect, although considering the style Trent preferred, perhaps no respect was due. But then he bent over, keeping his legs straight and his arse elevated, and Christophe's mouth went dry. *Bloody hell, he's as flexible as a ballet dancer.*

He peered at Christophe from between his legs. "Sure you don't want to . . . assist?"

"You, *cher*, are a cheeky little bastard." Trent shot him an upside-down grin and wiggled his arse. "However, if I succumb to your tempting invitation, we shall never get our dinner. You may have the grazing instincts of a university student, but I need more than pastries to get me through the day."

"Killjoy. Fine." He jerked his pants to his ankles in a swift movement, and stepped out of them without bothering to stand upright. Faced with Trent's bare arse as he rummaged through his clothing, Christophe was intensely grateful for his own elaborate layers. His alpha nature demanded that he pounce on that delectable body, grip Trent's neck gently in his teeth, and fuck him until he'd never dare to want any other partner again.

Christophe's civilized veneer was near to cracking, but he held on to his disintegrating control, if only because Trent's neck was off-limits. He should thank Anton for suggesting a way for him to shift soon, because if this continued, he'd never be able to safely bed Trent again without his wolf howling for release.

And he intended to bed Trent again. Without question. And without his wolf attempting to run the show.

For now, he gritted his teeth and texted his driver to be ready in five minutes, then leaned back on the sofa, stretching his arms along its back so he could grip the cushions.

Trent stood up and stripped off his T-shirt. Totally naked, the sunlight from the window gilding his body in liquid gold, he faced Christophe and tossed the shirt over his shoulder. "What do you think? Should I go for briefs, or straight commando?"

"Ah . . ." Christophe attempted to find his voice when he wanted nothing more than to growl.

Trent grinned. "I'll let you guess." He squatted and rummaged in his disreputable pile. Once he'd gathered an armful of clothes, he stood and walked toward the bathroom. "Be right out."

"Take—" Christophe swallowed in an attempt to moisten his dry mouth. "Take what time you need. I'm going nowhere."

"Counting on it." Trent disappeared into the bathroom and closed the door.

Christophe let his head *thunk* against the wall. "*Jesu*, give me strength."

The door opened and Trent poked his head out. "We don't need like a reservation or something, do we?"

Jerking upright, Christophe struggled to appear collected. "This place doesn't do such things. We must arrive and take our chances, like everyone else."

"Okay, then. Won't be long, I promise. I showered earlier so—"

"I noticed. You smell divine."

Trent grinned, his cheeks pinkening. "You're confusing me with the doughnuts."

"I assure you, I would never confuse your scent with anything else."

"All righty, then. I'll be—" He jerked his thumb over his shoulder. "Yeah. Well. A minute."

Trent was true to his word, or nearly. In only a couple of minutes, he emerged, fully dressed. *Commando?* Christophe could only hope. "Let me grab my wallet and phone and stuff and we can go."

Christophe rose and joined Trent by the desk, unable to resist taking another deep breath of Trent's scent. "When you didn't take my call earlier, I thought perhaps you didn't want to see me again."

Trent glanced up in surprise. "You called? I mean that was you? Jesus, I have no idea how to use this fricking phone. I only got it yesterday morning."

"Really? I'm gratified it wasn't a personal rejection, then. But how can you live in the world of millennials and not be an expert at mobile communications?"

Trent ducked his head, apparently intent on shoving his wallet and card key in his jeans pockets. "Like I said. I haven't had a lot of opportunity to do that kind of shit lately."

Christophe frowned, another notion arising as he considered Trent's downscale wardrobe, his apparent unfamiliarity with recent entertainment and technology. He was such a contradiction. He had a new phone—apparently brand-new—and a laptop that still had the protective film on it, its cables wrapped in twist ties. His clothing was certainly well-worn—which could be nothing more than a fashion statement. He'd mentioned other wardrobe choices at home, though. Was he— Could he have come by his funds recently, perhaps by unscrupulous means? Or could Trent have been hired by the Clavret family—or worse, his family's rivals—to entrap Christophe in some way?

He dismissed the idea at once. For one thing, what would be the point? It wasn't as if he were planning to exercise a business coup against a rival. For another, he didn't believe he could be so wrong about Trent. No one who had ill intent could avoid giving off the sour scent of guilt. Before his wolf senses had been blunted by last night's suppressant, he'd detected an odd and appealing tang to Trent's scent, but no stench of regret or reek of evil.

Besides, Trent wasn't an unknown. He was Logan's long-time friend. Indeed, he had arrived in town for Logan, not for Christophe, and they were chance-met.

Enough. Not only were Christophe's nerves on edge from putting off the change, but now he was seeing conspiracies when likely nothing more sinister than a formerly tight budget was at fault.

"Perhaps during dinner I could give you a few pointers. The next time I phone you, I'd prefer you to accept my call."

"Shit, everyone wants to teach me to use my damn phone."

Christophe's wolf growled, a rumble in his chest. "Everyone?"

"Dude. Chill. Logan was over last night. He gave me shit about it too."

"Very well. If *Logan* says you should learn, then it must be true." He stalked across the room and held the door open. "Come. My driver is waiting downstairs."

"A driver? Cool. Come along, Marshmont, old chap." Trent shifted to a posh English accent. "We mustn't keep him waiting."

Trent grinned like a lunatic all the way down the elevator. When Christophe had had the same jealous reaction about Trent that Logan had about Riley, Trent had wanted to spike the damn phone like a football in the end zone, and screw the cost of replacement. Christophe cared enough to feel possessive. How fucking cool was that?

He bumped shoulders with Christophe when they got to the lobby. "Come on. You know Logan can't see anybody but Riley." He laced his fingers with Christophe's. "Although I totally dig the get-away-from-my-bone act."

Christophe's lips twitched, although he didn't quite smile, rocking that upper-crust dignity that Trent had never been able to master—or rather that he didn't get the point of mastering. He could totally walk the walk if he needed to—he was an actor after all—but with the stuck-up assholes at his parents' country club, it had been way more fun to play the grunge role to the hilt and watch them squirm.

Christophe squeezed Trent's hand, though, and held on to it across the lobby and out the doors, where— *Holy shit!*

"When you said your driver was waiting, I thought you meant a cab, not a fucking town car."

This time, the pointed-tooth smile made an appearance. "I wanted to impress you, but I thought the stretch limo might be a tad over the top."

"Dude. You had me at Voodoo Doughnuts. No further effort required." Trent grinned. "But hey, I'll take it."

The driver held the rear door and Trent slid in onto the wide leather seat.

Christophe exchanged a few words with the driver in French, then joined Trent. "Thank you for agreeing to accompany me."

The car, with its heavily tinted windows and privacy screen between them and the driver, underlined the difference between Christophe's obvious wealth and his own lack of visible means. "You realize we look like a mob boss and a rentboy." He pointed to his jeans, the thighs worn nearly white, and the knees nothing but threads. "A low-end rentboy at that."

"Does what others think matter so much to you, then?"

Did it? "In some ways, yeah. I mean, one of the reasons I dress like this is to piss off my dad."

"Does it work?"

"Hell yeah. But I think I piss him off just by existing." *He was a lot happier when I was conveniently missing, so he could have the appearance of caring about me without the inconvenience of my actual presence.* Trent's rib cage seemed to shrink two sizes. "He didn't take well to me coming out."

Christophe took his hand again and drew him across the seat to nestle against his side. Immediately, the tightness eased. "I am sorry you had a difficult time. But he must have reconciled himself to the fact, yes?"

"Uh . . . no. Not so much."

Christophe's hand tightened on his, and under Trent's cheek, his chest rose in a gigantic breath. "Did he disown you? Kick you out?"

"Technically, no. This was right before I graduated from high school, and I was practically living with a friend in Pawtucket by then. I was already eighteen, because my father made me wait an extra year before starting school so I'd be bigger for sports." Trent glanced up at Christophe and attempted a snarky grin. "That didn't work out so great for him."

"You didn't get bigger?"

"Oh I got bigger, but I hated sports. *Hated* them. He made me go out for them anyway."

"*Bâtard.* Why must parents insist on making their children live the lives they wished for themselves?"

"Funny thing about that. The coaches for competitive sports teams expect their players to *want* to win, and maybe show a little aptitude. It's amazing how *bad* you can be at sports if you really try."

Christophe chuckled. "Is that what you did?"

"Hell yeah. In fourth grade, we had this outreach program come in from this children's theater program in Providence. One of the guys in it was this brilliant physical comedian. The actors did a workshop afterward, and he taught me how to take a pratfall. Best lesson I ever learned."

"Is that when you decided to become an actor?"

Trent snuggled closer. "Oh, I knew way earlier. When I was about six, I used to pose in front of my mirror with a shoe for a microphone. I begged for voice lessons, dance lessons, acting lessons. No dice." Those things weren't befitting the *true Pielmeyer lifestyle.* Of course, *the true Pielmeyer lifestyle* had gotten blown out of the water, yacht and all, by his sexual orientation. "It's weird. My mom sits on the board of a ballet company, a symphony, and two chamber orchestras, but when it came to a son in the arts?" He shrugged.

"Why did she not support you?"

"My mother hates confrontation. She goes with whatever the party line is, as long as she doesn't have to take a stand. Why? Does your mother love you unconditionally, like all mothers are supposed to do?"

Christophe's breath stilled and his face turned bleak. "My mother died giving birth to me."

Trent scrambled upright. "Jesus. I'm sorry. I'm so used to being an asshole about parents that I forget—"

"It is scarcely your fault." Christophe placed his hands carefully on his knees, glancing from his shoes to the blank window of the privacy shield, his throat working.

Ah, shit. Trent had used those same mannerisms when he'd played Macbeth in acting class. "You think it's yours though, don't you?"

Christophe shook his head. "What I think doesn't change the past."

"Nobody could blame you for an event that happened before you could even *breathe*."

"Perhaps not. But my father . . . he knew the risks, yet chose to ignore them."

"Yeah. Fathers. What can you do?"

"You clearly did something."

"Yeah. I moved across the country and went to school in Portland."

"But . . . you said you were no longer in school. And you live in a hotel."

"That was before. Just lately I came from the ol' homestead in Rhode Island. I bailed when I found out my father—" Trent dropped his gaze. *Secrets, remember? He doesn't need to know your father wants to get you arrested for your own kidnapping so he has an excuse to keep your money.* "Well, let's say I decided it was a good time for a visit to Portland."

"But—"

The driver's voice spoke over the intercom. "We have arrived, *Monsieur* Clavret."

Saved by the chauffeur. Trent scooted across the seat. "Am I allowed to open my own door?"

"Of course. François opens it from courtesy, but he will not be outraged if you take matters into your own hands."

"Right, then. Let's see what kind of joint you think is worthy of our valuable patronage."

He jumped out of the car and . . . immediately wanted to jump back in, as his stomach took a quick ride to his feet. They weren't in the city anymore. They were parked in the tiny lot of a diner at a crossroads, woods marching along the edge of the streets on three sides, a sign for a gated community on the fourth.

Trent fought the urge to run, far and fast. "You didn't tell me we were going into the fucking forest. I don't—"

Christophe caught him by the shoulders. "*Cher,* forgive me. I didn't realize you had such a strong preference for the city."

Breathe, damn it. Fake it till you make it. He forced a laugh. "If you're that ashamed to be seen with me that you have to take me to a dive in the middle of nowhere—"

"I am proud to be seen with you anywhere, and we are hardly in the middle of nowhere. Downtown Portland is but a few minutes away. This place," he gestured to the sign, "I have long wanted to try it."

"Seriously? The Skyline Restaurant?"

Christophe smoothed Trent's hair back from his forehead. "I will tell you a secret. I am passionately fond of hamburgers. But I prefer them rare. These days, few restaurants will consent to prepare them as I like. This place will."

"Fancy restaurants in Europe won't fix you a burger the way you want? If you wave money at them, I'm sure they'd overcome their scruples."

"I think perhaps you are a snob." Christophe smiled at him, showing his canines. "You can find perfectly wonderful meals at places far less ostentatious. Besides, James Beard himself commended the burgers in this place."

"He did, huh?"

"However, if you'd prefer someplace more—"

"No. You want to go here." *And once we're inside, I won't feel like the trees are creeping up on me.* "Let's see if James Beard knew what the fuck he was talking about."

CHAPTER
TEN

W hen Christophe's wolf was this close to the surface, his craving for raw meat intensified. Satisfying that craving was another way for him to appease the wolf, coax it into remaining quiescent. As he'd hoped, after an exceptional burger prepared exactly as he liked it, Christophe felt much less on edge.

During their dinner, Trent seemed to regain the confidence he'd lost for some reason in the parking lot. *Another mystery, my troubled young man.* He'd enthusiastically consumed his own meal and now, once again in the car, he collapsed against Christophe's shoulder, rubbing his belly.

"Dude. Those were seriously intense burgers. And the milkshakes? Awesome."

Christophe chuckled and hit the intercom to give François the signal to go. "I am glad you approve. What would you like to do next?"

Trent gazed up at him and ran a finger along the beard at Christophe's jawline. "You did promise that we'd have time to try out the bed later."

"Don't you wish to recover from your meal a bit first?"

"Hey. I've got the metabolism of a nineteen-year-old."

"Or twenty-six-year-old. But I, sadly, have the metabolism of a twenty-five-year-old."

"Seriously? You're only twenty-five? You seem older."

Christophe pressed the back of his wrist against his forehead in a theatrical gesture. "Oh the humiliation. I fondly imagined I carried my age so well. I shall have to invest in a walker next, and perhaps learn to play shuffleboard or horseshoes."

Trent laughed. "That's not what I mean. You're so confident, like you have no questions about how you fit in your own skin. Usually guys in their midtwenties haven't hit that stride yet."

"My father has been grooming me to take over for him practically since I was born. I have had a great deal of practice in appearing confident and in control."

"Because of that captain-of-industry shit?"

"Captain of commerce, certainly. Our family business is import and export, not manufacturing, but the concept is similar."

"But—" Trent struggled upright, and Christophe immediately missed his warmth. "Last night—Jesus, was it only last night we met? It feels like we've known each other forever. Last night you said you wanted to study medicine. Genetics, right?"

"Yes. However, in my family, the tradition has always been for the sons to follow in the footsteps of the father. I—"

"Bullshit. You shouldn't let your father control your life."

"No? But isn't that what you do yourself?"

Trent frowned. "I flew across the country—twice—to get away from him, so no."

"Yet when you allow your feelings for him, his actions, to control what you do and where you go, you grant him the same sort of power."

"But at least I'm trying to find a way to do my own thing—once I figure out what the hell it is. You *know* what you want to do, but you're not doing it."

"I was bred for this position." *More literally than you can know.* "Choosing another path is not as simple as you make it seem."

"Well it should be. I think you should do what you want."

"What I want . . ." He took Trent's hand and drew him back. "What I want is to take you to my flat where we, after a suitable recovery period, will try out *my* bed."

"*Yes!*" Trent grinned. "Is this like waiting an hour after eating before you go swimming?"

"Something like that."

Trent grabbed Christophe's face and dove in for a quick but thorough kiss. "Then we can—" He jolted back, eyes widening as he stared out the window beyond Christophe's shoulder. "Where— God, where are we?"

Christophe glanced outside. "On Cornell, near the Audubon Society, I believe. My flat is in the Pearl District, so this is the most direct route."

Forest Park. No. Not here. Not now. Trent plastered himself against the door, his eyes like saucers, whites visible around the blue. "Please. Go back. This is— I can't— We have to—"

Christophe smacked the intercom with his fist. "François. Pull over!" The car slowed as François turned into the Audubon parking lot. Christophe inched toward Trent, holding his hands palms out. "Easy, *cher*. Whatever it is, we will fix it, I promise. Let me—"

Trent flung himself into Christophe's arms. "Jesus *fuck*."

Christophe gathered Trent close, petting his hair, kissing his temple. "Shhh. What do you need? I have water here." Liquor too. Was liquor ever prescribed for a panic attack? He couldn't remember. "Whatever you want, whatever you need, I will get or be or do."

Trent heaved a shuddering breath. "This. Just . . . hold me. You make it better. I don't know why, but you do. When you hold me, I can think again."

"Then I shall hold you forever."

His laugh was bitter. "Might be inconvenient. For both of us. François too. Hope the poor guy at least had lunch."

"Yes. He had a Skyline burger as well."

"Good."

"But we must talk about you, not François." Christophe leaned back until he could gaze into Trent's eyes. "*Cher*, you must tell me what is wrong. I am happy to do what I can to help, but if I don't know the triggers, I might inadvertently cause you distress."

"It's fucked up. You don't need to deal with my shit."

"Everyone has, as you say, shit to deal with. I told you, I adore a man with issues, and there is nothing you could say that would make me betray your trust."

"Not even if I'm a total fricking basket case?"

Christophe captured Trent's flailing hand and laced their fingers together. "I doubt your situation is so dire."

"Easy for you to say. Your issues are ordinary corporate daddy issues. Mine are totally whacked out."

Oh, cher, *you have no idea.* "I promise I won't judge you. You will be the same man after you tell me. I will simply know you better, and that cannot be bad."

"That's what you think," Trent muttered.

"What are you afraid of?"

Trent's face mirrored the terror he was clearly attempting to hold at bay. Christophe recognized the expression—he'd worn it himself only last night.

"That you'll think I'm crazy. That I'm broken."

"I promise, I will not."

His smile was crooked. "If that's how you negotiate your contracts, you won't have to worry about taking over from your father. He'll fire you before you run the company into the ground. *Always* check the fine print before you sign on the dotted line."

"I trust my instincts. And my instincts tell me that you are as sane as I am. A bit impulsive perhaps."

Trent snorted. "You think?"

"But that is not necessarily a bad thing. I rather enjoy spontaneity. So much of my life has been ordered, regimented, planned from the moment I was born." He kissed Trent softly. "Never fear, *cher.* I won't let you down."

Trent's chest felt as if it were being crushed by a giant vise. He should have told François to keep driving, fast, to get back to the city where the trees wouldn't menace him, enclose him. Where he could run away if the nightmare got too close.

But Christophe had promised, and Jesus *fuck,* he needed someone he could talk to. That was why he'd flown across the whole fricking country, wasn't it? To see if having someone he could talk to about his ordeal would make it easier to handle? If it would stop the nightly replay?

He had no idea why he felt safe with Christophe, even safer than with Logan, who'd been there at the beginning. *Maybe you still blame Logan for not saving you in the first place, or not saving you sooner.* Which was fucking nuts.

But nobody'd ever accused him of being logical.

He burrowed closer to Christophe. "This morning, when you said you'd believe anything until it was proved false—did you mean it?"

"I wouldn't have said it otherwise."

"Then . . ." Trent took a deep breath. It was only six thirty. They had a few more hours of daylight. He could handle the park in the daylight—he hoped. "Will you take a walk with me?"

Christophe's eyebrows drew together. "Certainly. When we get to my flat—"

"No. I mean here. Now."

Christophe peered out the window. "On this road? It seems a trifle dangerous."

"No. Into the—the park. It's about a mile, and the path is steep in places and might be muddy." He checked Christophe's shoes—handmade Italian, if he knew anything about them, and he did. "Never mind. Your shoes—"

"Are immaterial. However, as it happens, I have a pair of boots in the trunk that will do nicely for a hike."

"Okay, then." Trent blew out a breath. "Let's get this the hell over with."

When Christophe got out of the car to retrieve his boots, Trent's panic returned, and he started to hyperventilate, his vision darkening around the edges. *Jesus, not here. Not now. Hold it together.*

Christophe returned and sat on the end of the seat. "I haven't worn these in—" He glanced at Trent and dropped the boots. "Trent. What is it?"

Trent held out his hand. "Touch me, please. When you're too far away, it all comes back."

"Very well. Although putting on boots one-handed may be beyond my current skill set."

Trent scooted closer until he pressed against Christophe—legs, hips, and shoulders—and he could breathe again. "This'll do. Go for it. It's the contact, you know? The touching."

"Whatever you need, *cher*. Whatever you need."

CHAPTER
ELEVEN

Trent's description of the trail as steep and rough was rather an understatement, and as they made their way deeper into the park, Christophe wished his boots had sturdier soles. Although he had vast experience navigating forest tracks, that experience was with four feet, not two.

The ground was muddy in spots from recent rain, but the going wasn't impossible. Since the evening was fair, they passed other hikers occasionally, some of whom gave them odd looks, although they seemed more focused on Christophe's inappropriate hiking clothing than on the fact that he and Trent were holding hands, despite the narrow path.

Trent slowed down when they came to a small clearing where their trail intersected with another one—the left-hand fork heading up into the hills, the right-hand one following the creek. At the back of the clearing, abutting the hillside, stood a derelict two-story stone building, roofless, mossy, and defaced with graffiti on most of its intact walls.

Trent clutched Christophe's hand more tightly. "Funny. The first time I saw this place, I said I'd expected it to be bigger. Since then, though, it's gotten so enormous in my memory that it's a shock at how small it really is."

"What is this place?"

"Its nickname, at least in paranormal circles, is the Witch's Castle."

Christophe raised his eyebrows. "A witch lived here?"

"Nah. The WPA built it sometime in the thirties. I think it was a rest station or a john or something. But this area, a lot of Forest Park for that matter, was originally the homestead of Danford Balch, the first man legally hanged in Oregon."

"You are a student of local history, then?"

"No. I'm the moron who got so carried away by a ghost story that he— Well, never mind." Trent squared his shoulders. "Come on. Let's get closer."

Trent stayed glued to Christophe's side. When they were halfway across the clearing, a head with flyaway blond hair popped up over the wall on the upper level.

Trent backpedaled. "Jesus *fuck*."

"Easy, *cher*. It is only a little girl."

"Welcome to the Stone House," the child piped. "Welcome to the Stone House."

"Annie, sit down and drink your juice," a woman's exasperated voice rose from behind the wall.

Trent returned to Christophe's side. "Guess it's not responsible parenting to tell your kid you're having a picnic at the Witch's Castle. Not unless you're into tough love and aversion therapy."

"I imagine it would depend on the child. For some, particularly teenaged boys, I suspect the notion would be an incentive rather than a deterrent."

Trent barked a laugh. "You got that right. Jesus, do you ever. Come on." He led Christophe into a shallow alcove on the first floor, under where the hidden family continued their meal. He glanced at Christophe's trousers and grimaced. "Shit. If you sit down, you'll ruin your pants. Here." He stripped off his sweatshirt and spread it on the ground. "Sit on this."

"You don't need to do that. You'll get cold."

"No, I won't. I'm planning to wear you."

Christophe raised an eyebrow. "We're hardly alone."

As he'd hoped, Trent grinned. "Mind out of the gutter, Clavret. Sit. I'm using you as a backrest."

Christophe sat on the sweatshirt, the cold cement of the floor seeping through to chill his arse. Trent sat in front of him, between his legs. Christophe settled him against his chest. "Are you comfortable, *cher*?"

"Yeah. I—I'm actually okay at the moment."

"Excellent."

Trent's hand closed on Christophe's knee. "Not quite, but—" He swallowed audibly. "Okay. Here goes. Seven years ago last October, Logan and I sneaked into the park after hours."

"Was this one of those so-famous fraternity pranks?"

"You mean hazing? Nah. Neither of us were in a frat anyway. I'd just lost the lead in a play, and Logan was trying to cheer me up. Back then, I was totally into legend tripping."

"Legend tripping?" Christophe shifted uneasily against the rough stones. "What is that?"

"You visit the site of some urban legend or paranormal event, and try to re-create it. It's about the adventure, the thrill and chills. Cemeteries were *very* big with my legend-tripping group."

"Indeed."

"Yeah. Nuts, right? Anyway, Logan knew about this ghost war, a feud between Balch's family and the Stumps, the family of his son-in-law, the guy he murdered in front of practically the whole town."

"*Jesu.*"

"No shit. But as it happens, this legend was true. We saw the ghost war." Trent began to tremble, and Christophe wrapped his arms around him. "In fact, I joined it."

"You what?"

"Yeah. That's exactly what Logan said. He tried to stop me, but I was so into it, you know?"

"Trent—"

"How many days are there in seven years?"

"I did not realize our hike came with a mathematics test."

"That's how many times I've been hanged. How many times I've died. I took Danford Balch's place in the ghost war, and I was stuck there for seven fucking years. I'd still be there if Logan and the *Haunted to the Max* people hadn't sprung me from the Phantom Zone."

"Are you saying—"

Trent twisted in his arms, his glare accusatory. "You promised you'd believe me."

"Easy, *cher.*" Christophe kissed his forehead. "I am only trying to understand. So when you say you are either nineteen or twenty-six—"

"It's because I've been hanging out in limbo for seven years. How do you count that time? I don't look any different, but sometimes I feel older than dirt. And twice as lonely."

"Who else knows of this?"

"Logan, of course. Riley too. I guess he's the one who figured out how to spring me, but they had help from others, including the ex-ghost of Danford Balch, although apparently he was a tough sell. Have you really never watched the show?"

"No. Perhaps I should. I seem to be woefully uninformed."

"Hell, I wish *I* was. I checked into a private psych-treatment center to try and deal with it, you know? But it's not like I could tell them the truth. They'd have locked me up faster than you could say *schizophrenic*, and I'd have spent the rest of my days in a rubber room or drugged to the gills." He leaned his head on Christophe's shoulder. "And sometimes, that sounds like a fucking awesome idea."

"Wouldn't anyone who watched the episode know the story?"

"Mostly, but they kept my name out of it. My father insisted." Trent sighed. "Remember I told you my father wasn't cool with me coming out? Well when I disappeared, he had a PR field day. He got to play the bereaved father, offered a reward, the whole nine. Parading his fake grief on the news for as long as he could milk it."

"Shite."

"Then I showed up again. He can hardly disown me after making such a huge stink about wanting his dear son back. He's fucked himself good, and now he's doing his level best to fuck me too."

"How so?"

"When they declared me dead, the trust fund my grandfather set up for me reverted to my father. It should have come to me when I turned twenty-five, but I was busy getting hanged on my birthday, so that didn't happen."

"Trent—"

"Now he's trying to prove I engineered my own disappearance to extort money from him, because of teenage rebellion or some shit."

"Surely you have legal recourse—"

"The lawyer's my father's golf buddy. You tell me how this is gonna shake down."

Christophe's arms tightened, holding Trent closer. "You don't need to face them alone. I have access to a stable of excellent lawyers. We'll take your father to court—"

"Well, well, well." A shadow fell across their feet. "Mr. Pielmeyer and Mr. Con— Oh."

An extremely large African American man, dappled sunlight gleaming on the smooth skin of his head, blinked at them, his bewildered expression completely at odds with his aggressive stance.

Whoever he was, he'd given Christophe the gift of Trent's surname—*Pielmeyer*—so Christophe was inclined to feel charitable toward him.

It seemed Trent, however, was not. He scrambled to his feet. "Bishop. Shit, dude, are you stalking me?"

Bishop recovered his composure quickly, tucking his hands in his pants pockets in a way that would have made Christophe's tailor clutch his hair in outrage. "If I were, it wouldn't be difficult. You're not great at covering your tracks." He leaned against the wall. "But in this case, no. It's a public park, and as it happens, I come here often."

Trent's scowl deepened, but to prevent the conversation from devolving into something less civil, Christophe rose. He tucked one hand under Trent's elbow and offered the other to Bishop.

"Christophe Clavret, of Clavret et Cie. You are?"

Trent jerked his elbow out of Christophe's grasp. "He's the detective who's been on my ass since October." He snatched his sweatshirt off the ground and pulled it over his head. "Funny that he never seems to have anything better to do than follow me around."

"No need to exaggerate, Mr. Pielmeyer. This is only the second time I've spoken to you since you left Oregon."

"Yeah? Well, I still think you have way too much time on your hands."

Bishop's gaze slid off to the left, toward the creek. "No more than anyone."

Christophe glanced between Bishop and Trent. "Were you expecting to find someone else here, Detective?"

"As a matter of fact . . ." Bishop returned his attention to them. "Whenever there's a break in Mr. Pielmeyer's behavior patterns, Mr. Conner is usually involved."

"Indeed?"

"Case in point—last night. He left the airport and went straight to Stumptown Spirits."

"I didn't. Not straight there. I— You— Shit," Trent muttered.

"But instead of Conner, you got extremely friendly with someone else. Someone nobody would have thought to look at." Bishop ran a hand across his head. "Christ on a soda cracker, Trent. Please tell me this wasn't just some con. That you didn't spend all that time kicking around Europe with another goddamned overprivileged adolescent."

Trent's mouth fell open. "What?" he croaked. Where the hell had that come from?

Christophe stepped up to the plate, though. Despite Bishop topping him by a good foot, he managed to look down his nose at him, with the perfect *this insect is so beneath me* attitude that Trent had worked like hell to perfect for a role once. He'd never succeeded to his own satisfaction, because he couldn't help making it ironic. But Christophe's was awesome. Trent wanted to kiss him. *Later. Lots of that later.*

"Are you referring to me? Mr. Pielmeyer and I didn't meet until last night."

"Easy to say."

"Jesus, Bishop. You act like I'm a personal insult to you. What the fuck, dude?"

"'The fuck' is that people don't just vanish off the face of the earth." Bishop took a step forward, fists clenched at his sides. "They leave tracks. Traces. But you left nothing."

Trent eased closer to Christophe, away from Bishop's intent gaze. "Told you. Nothing to leave."

"Seven years! Seven years without anything but Logan Conner's annual pilgrimage and suddenly he's on deck when you come stumbling back into the same place where you disappeared. There's a connection. There has to be." Bishop's voice dropped to a desperate whisper on his last words.

Trent frowned. Desperate? Not a word he'd ever thought he'd apply to Bishop. Whatever. He didn't want the apparent desperation taken out on him, or Logan, or Christophe. Bishop needed to get over it. Trent opened his mouth to say so, but Christophe squeezed his elbow meaningfully.

"I believe we must take our leave. If Detective . . . Bishop, is it? If the detective wishes to interrogate you formally, he may make an appointment. Good day."

Christophe almost dragged him back up the path while Trent glared over his shoulder. Bishop stared after them, his eyes narrowed, until the little blond girl popped up again.

"Welcome to the Stone House!"

Bishop whirled and crouched. When the girl waved at him, he stood up and ran his hand over his head, as if to say *I meant to do that,* then stalked off down the opposite trail. Trent snorted a laugh. Guess the guy wasn't so put-together after all.

Maybe he should send the dear detective a thank-you note. He'd helped Trent dampen the emotions he'd associated with the Witch's Castle for more than seven years—tempering his old terror and despair with a huge dose of annoyance and a pinch of absurdity.

"That asshole. Between him and my father, they're trying to turn me into the criminal, not the victim. And he had the fucking nerve to accuse *you.*" He kicked a rock into the creek. "Know what the pisser is? I told Bishop the whole story when he ambushed me at the airport yesterday, but he thought I was only being a smart-ass."

He glanced at Christophe. *Shit.* His mouth was pressed into a line, and his eyebrows were lowered so far Trent was surprised he could see where he was going. "Christophe? You believe me? Right?"

Christophe glanced up at him, his expression lightening in surprise. "Naturally."

Trent stopped in the middle of the path. "Why?"

Christophe pulled him aside, out of the way of a couple of hikers. "Because, *cher,* you told me it was the truth. And I have seen far more implausible things in my life than this."

Trent's eyebrows shot up. "No shit? The import/export business must be a lot weirder than I thought."

Christophe laughed and drew Trent in for a kiss. "You would be surprised, I assure you."

When he reluctantly broke the kiss, Trent could still see a corner of the Witch's Castle over Christophe's shoulder. He swallowed. *Now or never.* "I—I want to try something."

Christophe smiled, baring those sexy canines. "Perhaps we should wait until we get back to the car."

Trent rolled his eyes. "I'm not that much of a show-off." *At least not anymore.* "No. This is something . . . Well, stay here, okay?"

Christophe's face grew serious. "Of course."

Trent inhaled and took a step away, letting go of Christophe's hand. A tiny frisson crept across the back of his neck. Freaky, but bearable. He retreated another couple of yards, Christophe watching him with a quizzical lift of his brows. The prickles traveled farther down his spine, and his breathing sped up a bit. *Still not too bad.*

"Let's try something different." Trent moved toward Christophe. With every step, his nerves eased further. When he got within touching distance, Christophe reached out and stroked his cheek.

Ah. There. It all goes away. But what exactly was "all"? He had no illusion that he was cured, but—

He edged past Christophe toward the Witch's Castle until he could see the whole front wall. It wasn't like breasting the ocean anymore, the way it had been earlier, even with Christophe's hand in his. Trent prodded that place in his mind, the one that usually sent him into a spiral of panic, and the spot wasn't as tender, the response not as severe. He kept imagining Bishop's face when the little blond girl popped up and piped, *"Welcome to the Stone House!"*

It's not a witch's castle. It's just a stone house. Nothing spooky about that, right?

He had no desire to sit around picnicking at the damn place, but he could stand there and not want to leap into the creek.

When he turned his back on the clearing, though, the same feeling of lurking danger returned. Heart pounding, he speed-walked back to Christophe and took his hand. Immediately, Trent's pulse slowed. *Safe.*

Christophe smiled. "Conducting experiments?"

"You could say that." Trent glanced overhead, where the trees' mossy branches were laced together like bony fingers. "One more, okay?"

"I am at your disposal."

Witch's Castle was out of sight behind them now. "When I tell you, could you walk up the path, around that bend, so I can't see you?"

Christophe squeezed his hand. "Give the word."

"Now."

With every step that Christophe trod up the path, Trent's anxiety crept farther up his back. When he disappeared around a bend, Trent's stomach clenched and he fought the urge to hunker down and cover his head.

It's the goddamned trees. It's not the Witch's Castle at all, not anymore.

He hurried up the path until he caught up with Christophe. Once he'd taken his hand—*touch*—he could breathe again. *I wonder if I'd have the same reaction with anybody?* Maybe it was being alone in the forest that sparked his panic attacks. Maybe anyone would do—Christophe just happened to be the one available. He'd save that experiment for another day, say in another fifty years or so.

"You must think I'm totally lame."

"On the contrary, after what you've been through, I think you're incredibly brave. You have a great deal of fortitude and loyalty too, denying Logan's involvement."

"It wasn't his fault. He tried to stop me. He saved me."

"Indeed. You know how to repay a debt." Christophe pulled Trent off the path into a cluster of tree stumps, his eyes seeming to glow like amber lights. "But I must say, *cher*, the way you defended me to your detective—"

"He's not my detective."

"Yet he appears quite fixated. I found your defense quite . . . arousing."

Trent grinned. "Yeah?"

"Assuredly. Also, his interest in you was quite annoying. I find I want no one paying you such attentions. I want that to be my purview only."

God, someone who wants me for a change. "Tell me more."

"Come back to my flat with me. I think it's time for me to make love to you as you deserve."

Trent shivered. *Not dread. Anticipation. The good kind of shiver.* "I am *so* down with that." He tugged Christophe up the path. "Let's get the hell away from these fucking trees."

CHAPTER
TWELVE

Once back in the car and on the way to Christophe's flat, Christophe restrained himself, keeping his elation tamped down to a low burn. He'd been certain Trent transcended the ordinary, although at first he'd thought it was mere physical compatibility, the promise of a challenge given and accepted. But it went far beyond that. Trent had been touched by the uncanny, had been a part of it, for years. Surely someone who'd had direct experience with the paranormal would be more likely to accept Christophe's disability.

He glanced down at Trent, where he nestled against Christophe's shoulder, staring half-fearfully at the woods as they passed. *Would he accept it, or would he be as terrified, as traumatized, as resentful of me as he obviously is of his ghosts?*

If Christophe followed his current plan, left the company, resettled in America to resume his studies—*broke my father's heart*—perhaps over time Trent could be reconciled to Christophe's dual nature. A willingness to believe in the impossible was the first step toward accepting it.

Also, Christophe's presence seemed to calm Trent, kept some of his demons at bay. *Even such demons as his quail in the presence of a true monster.*

The car pulled up outside Christophe's building. "Here we are."

Trent peered out the window and his shoulders visibly relaxed. "Whoa. Not bad. I mean, seven years ago, the Pearl was trendy, but now—" He shot a fair approximation of his usual cheeky grin at Christophe. "You really must be loaded."

The reference to his wealth cast a pall on Christophe's mood. Was that part of the reason for Trent's interest? He'd had a trust fund once, but no longer. Now that Christophe had a last name, he could research Trent's family and—

No.

Trust had to begin somewhere. *Let it begin with me.*

He escorted Trent up to his penthouse flat and led him inside. Trent raised his eyebrows at the expanse of cream-colored carpet in the living room, then toed off his muddy trainers on the mat in the tiled entry way.

As Christophe wrestled off his boots, Trent wandered over to the bank of windows overlooking the city and whistled. "Nice." He turned around. "But that's not the view for me."

Christophe's suspicions receded. "Is that so? And what would you like to see?"

Trent grinned. "What do you think? Your bed. Your skin." He sauntered across the room, leading with his hips. "Your dick. In me."

At that notion, Christophe's wolf perked up, but with the suppressant swimming in his veins, and a meal of nearly-raw meat so recently in his past, he had no fear of losing control.

"So importunate."

"It's the curse of being nineteen or twenty-six."

Christophe chuckled. "Just so. But we need not rush. I have no other engagements today. Do you?"

"Me? I'm the slacker who hasn't even reenrolled in school, remember?"

Again that niggle of doubt. *Is he in this for his own gain?* "Then let us take our time. I believe you wanted to inspect the bed? It's this way."

Christophe led Trent down the hallway to his bedroom. He employed a cleaning service, so unlike Trent's untidy hotel suite, the room was pristine—the gray duvet wrinkle-free, the carpet immaculate, and the silver stripes in the wallpaper glowing softly in the sunlight spilling in from the windows.

"Dude. Where did you get a bed this size?"

"It is custom-made."

"Yeah? How many guys can you fit in it at once?"

"I fear I've never tested its capacity. It's held no one but me." Christophe had never allowed any of his casual sex partners into his home—not that there'd been many since his promiscuous university days.

Trent turned toward him, the teasing lust he'd displayed in the living room vanishing behind the uncertainty in his impossibly blue eyes. "You know, I don't get that. You're . . . well, perfect. You're gorgeous. Kind. Sexy. Dress better than any ten runway models. Obviously aren't hurting for cash. Why the hell are you single?"

Christophe shrugged. "Duties. Family obligations."

"Dude, that totally sucks. You deserve way more. I may not be all that—"

"Stop. You are incredible."

Trent shook his head. "I'm not. I'm a hot mess. But with you, I think I'm better." He captured Christophe's head in both hands. "You make me better." Trent kissed him, urging Christophe's mouth open with a gentle probe of his tongue.

Christophe grabbed Trent's hips and pulled him close, groin to groin, and opened wide, swiping his own tongue into Trent's mouth, tasting him, that little tang that he now recognized as a touch of the supernatural, of *other*. Trent moaned into his mouth, then disengaged.

"We need to be naked. Are you gonna spend a half hour taking off your clothes and folding them into fashion origami?"

Christophe inhaled to prevent himself from panting like a desperate hound. Could he wait that long? *I think not.* "I've learned one or two things from you." He yanked off his jacket and flung it across the room.

Trent laughed. "Now that's what I'm talking about." He ripped the sweatshirt over his head and sent it after Christophe's jacket. "Race you."

"Unfair. You're wearing only a T-shirt and jeans. I have—"

"Hey. Your clothes. Your choice. But I'll give you a fighting chance." Trent went to his knees in front of Christophe, peering up at him through the fringe of his hair. "I won't take the rest off until you're down to your underwear. But in the meantime . . ." He unbuckled Christophe's belt and unbuttoned his pants. Unzipped his fly.

Christophe shuddered as he fumbled with his cufflinks. "What—what are you doing?"

"I need something to keep me occupied." Trent peeled Christophe's briefs down and hooked the waistband behind his bollocks. "You know us nineteen-or-twenty-six-year-olds have crap attention spans."

"Does that mean you'll lose interest halfway—" Trent engulfed the head of Christophe's cock. "Mother of *God*."

As Trent bobbed down the shaft, Christophe lost hold of his cuff link and it fell onto the carpet, bouncing under the bed. *Who cares?* He ripped his shirt open, heedless of the buttons, and stripped it off, followed by his undershirt.

Trent hummed around Christophe's cock, the vibration resonating in every nerve. He hollowed his cheeks and pulled all the way up slowly, with a flick of his tongue on the frenulum and a slight graze of teeth on the hood. He grinned, his lips red and shiny. "Good work. But you're not done yet." He dove forward and nuzzled Christophe's bollocks, sucking one into his mouth while rolling the other across his fingers.

Christophe's knees wobbled. "*Jesu*, Trent. I can't—if you don't stop, I'll either come or collapse."

Trent released Christophe's bollocks with one last lick. "Can't have that. This time, I want you to fuck me, and I'm not taking no for an answer."

Christophe's vision shifted, the grays in the wallpaper flattening, but no telltale burn flared in his fingers or back. With man and wolf in complete agreement about what they wanted, he had no need to fight his nature.

He shucked his pants and briefs down to his ankles in one swift movement and kicked them beneath the bed. "I believe I win."

Trent shook his head. "Socks, dude. I'll still win." He shed his T-shirt, sending it flying, unzipped his jeans and shoved them over his arse, while Christophe was yet wrestling with his last sock.

Of course, it didn't help that he was distracted by the expanse of Trent's skin, and his lovely cock, hard and straining. "That's scarcely sporting. You're not wearing underwear."

"Your clothes. Your choice." He sat back, propping himself on his hands, with his long elegant legs stretched out in front of him, crossed at the ankles. "What was that you said about winning?"

"Shite." Christophe removed his second sock, balled it up, and shot it into the corner. "I don't believe we bothered to set the stakes. What is it that you've won?"

Trent rose in one lithe move and stepped close. They were near enough to one another now for Christophe to feel the heat of Trent's skin, for his erect nipples to barely brush Christophe's chest. Their cocks tapped together, a wordless, wanton greeting. "Your dick in my ass."

"That's what I intended to claim as forfeit if I had won."

Trent kissed Christophe with open-mouthed fervor, although he kept his body—other than his cock—out of reach. He ended the kiss and grinned. "That, my friend, is what we call a win-win."

Christophe's grin was that feral baring of teeth that zinged straight through Trent's balls. What was that about? He had no idea, only that it made him want to lay back and give the man everything. Which was totally weird, because he'd never wanted that before—he wasn't a submissive guy.

Guess people can change. For the right person.

"On the bed, *cher*. Let us both claim our prize."

God yes. Finally.

He scrambled onto the bed. Shit, the comforter must be like a billion thread count. He couldn't imagine what it cost, so no way was he covering it with jizz. He flung it off, exposing the matching sheets. *Those'll have to take their chances.*

Rolling to his knees, he tossed the pillows aside too, then rested his forehead on his arms. He arched his back, his ass in the air, quivering for the first touch of skin on skin. He'd teased Christophe— and himself too, to be honest—delaying that first full-body touch. But now—*Jesus, Christophe, please move*—he didn't know how much longer he could wait.

It's been over seven years since I've been fucked. I might as well be a fricking virgin.

"Trent." Christophe's voice was steel velvet. "As beautiful as you are this way, it will not do."

Trent glanced fearfully over his shoulder. Shit, Christophe wasn't about to bail again, was he?

"I—"

"Turn over. I want to see your face while we make love."

Trent lowered his ass until he was huddled on the sheets, his face hidden in his arms. Christophe had seen him at his freaked-out worst and hadn't bolted. But for some reason, now that Christophe knew the truth, Trent felt ten times as vulnerable than when they'd been nothing but a bar hookup. How much could he bear to reveal? "I don't know if I can—"

"You can. You opened yourself to me so sweetly last night." Christophe moved closer and laid one hand on the small of Trent's back, then trailed it up his spine with the bare scrape of close-trimmed nails. Trent shivered. "Please. For me."

Trent took a breath and shifted onto his side. "What about this?"

Christophe chuckled. "Now you're being stubborn. Let me do this for you, *cher*. Let me show you that you are no longer alone."

Trent's throat thickened, and he blinked. *How did he know?* "Okay."

He rolled onto his back and raised his knees, keeping his feet flat on the mattress. Christophe gazed at him, his eyes molten gold in the westering sun. "You are exquisite, do you know?" He ran a hand over Trent's pecs and down his abs. "Absolutely exquisite."

"Pretty sure that's an exaggeration, but—" He gasped as Christophe pinched one nipple. "I'll take it."

"Yes. You will. All of it. Everything I choose to give." Christophe opened a drawer in the bedside table and pulled out condoms and lube. "Trust me. Let me care for you."

He squirted a dollop of lube onto his palm and covered it with his other hand as he knee-walked across the bed to kneel between Trent's legs. "Lift your hips, *cher*. Put them here, in my lap."

God. This was . . . He was . . . Trent's breath hitchhiked up his chest, and his dick leaked onto his belly. He raised himself and planted his ass on Christophe's spread thighs, with his feet on either side of Christophe's hips.

"So beautiful." Christophe coated his fingers with lube and trailed them across Trent's balls and behind, across his taint and around his hole. "I don't want to hurt you. I know it has been a long time."

Trent clenched his eyes shut at the gentle probing. "I don't care. Just do it. Please. I need to—need to feel." *To know I'm here. That you're here. That we're both real, that no supernatural shit-storm is raging overhead.*

"But—"

Trent bore down on Christophe's fingers and *God, there.* The burn of the invasion was as sweet as sin. "Now. Please. I need you."

Christophe growled. Seriously? Did he actually growl? Trent opened his eyes and *Jesus.* Christophe's face—so intense, so possessive—sent Trent's heart tumbling. *Does he really feel like that about me? Nobody ever has before.*

Christophe pumped his fingers in and out, one finger, then two. He turned them and curled them, brushing Trent's gland, and Trent's hips came up off Christophe's knees as black and white fireworks exploded in his vision. "God, Christophe, please. I need you now. Inside."

"You are not ready."

"I've been ready for seven fucking years. Please. Just fuck me now before I go insane."

"I want this more than you can know, but if I hurt you—"

"You won't. Trust me. I can take it." *Even pain is better than nothingness.*

Christophe ripped open the condom and rolled it over his dick—long, slender, uncut. He slathered it with lube, then thrust his arms under Trent's legs and lifted Trent's hips in his still-slick hands.

Trent couldn't look away as Christophe finally positioned his dick at Trent's hole and pushed. *Yes! This. Now. Please.* Trent's stupid traitorous sphincter fought back of course, but instead of forcing himself past the resistance, Christophe stopped.

No!

Teeth bared in frustration, Trent tried to shove downward and impale himself, but Christophe's hands tightened on his hips, holding him in place.

"Shhh, my darling. Are you so anxious to be done, then?"

"N-n-no." *He called me darling. Not Trent. Not cher. Darling.* Tears prickled the corners of his eyes—nobody had ever said that before. Not to him.

"Then allow me to take you as you deserve."

Trent nodded and closed his eyes. He took a deep, shuddering breath, trying to relax though his nerves were pinging like firecrackers. Then he felt himself give and Christophe pushed further . . . further . . . *there*. The head popped through the ring of muscle, and Trent wanted to shout, scream, cry, laugh—all of the above, because *God*, it was *glorious*, the stretch and the burn and the—*Yes!*—pleasure as Christophe worked his way inside with smooth, careful thrusts.

Then he lifted Trent's hips another inch, changed his angle, and—*zing*. Trent nearly levitated off the bed.

"Yeah. Oh, Jesus, right there!"

"As you wish."

Christophe picked up speed, nailing Trent's gland. Every. Fucking. Time. *God!*

As eager as he'd been for Christophe to start, now he didn't want this to end, because *touch*. Touch *everywhere*. Outside, as Christophe's fingers dug into Trent's hip bones. Inside, as he pumped into Trent's ass. *Touch. All the way to my heart.*

"Trent." Christophe's voice at once cajoled and commanded. "Look at me."

No. What if he mistakes the tears? Thinks he's being too rough? He might stop, and Trent couldn't bear that. Yet he obeyed—to the command or the persuasion, he couldn't be sure. "Mmm?"

"*Jesu*, with those eyes you could see down to my very soul."

Christophe's rhythm slowed, every slide of his dick lighting Trent up inside as if he'd swallowed a star. How had he lived without this, without someone in him, around him, through him? Had it been like this before? Ever? Even with Logan? He couldn't remember. Couldn't think. Only feel. He whimpered, and Christophe leaned forward to kiss him, slow and deep and hot.

"So beautiful. Come for me, my darling."

Darling. Trent's balls tightened as the star in his chest went supernova, blinding him with the explosion of inner light. *This. I want this. Now. Always.* He came, gasping, jizz painting his belly and chest in sticky heat.

As his vision cleared, he made out Christophe's face above him, so gorgeous, so intense, so *real*. Trent reached up, despite arms as limp as his spent dick, and touched Christophe's cheek. "Now you."

"Mother of God," Christophe moaned, "How can I—" He threw his head back, teeth clenched. Trent felt every single pulse of Christophe's cock. *Jesus fuck, it's like he gets bigger when he comes.*

How freaking hot was that?

Christophe lowered Trent's legs with shaking hands, cradling his hips between his thighs once again, and slowly pulled out. When Trent winced, Christophe froze. "I'm sorry. Did I hurt you?"

"No. But the exit's always an issue, right?"

Christophe chuckled and tied off the condom, dropping it into a waste basket next to the bed. He crawled up Trent's body, bracing his hands near Trent's shoulders and lowered himself for an open-mouthed kiss, a languorous mating of tongues and lips that Trent could fully get behind now that his behind had gotten what it—and he—had wanted.

Christophe fumbled with his bedside table and pulled out a handful of—what the hell, were those baby wipes? "Allow me." He dabbed at Trent's chest, and Trent's belly muscles jumped.

"Holy shit, those are cold."

"Sorry."

"I'd think that in a high-end joint like this one, you'd warm your jizz wipes."

Christophe's brows drew together and he suddenly seemed very interested in cleaning every drop of semen off of Trent's skin. "Perhaps this is not as high-end as you imagine."

"Dude. It totally is. But even if it wasn't—" Trent pulled him down into another kiss. "It'd be okay, as long as you were here. Now . . ." He yawned. "Do we have time for a nap before we go for round two?"

Christophe grinned. "I don't see why not."

Trent glanced at the window—twilight, and usually the nightmares didn't hit until around midnight. But if Trent got his wish and they were still in bed together by then? He didn't want Christophe to get freaked out because Trent was a bigger nutcase than he'd already revealed.

"I should warn you. I have . . . um . . . nightmares."

"About the ghost war?"

"Yeah."

"How often?"

Trent glanced away. "Every night."

"*Jesu.* Trent, have you—"

"Yeah, I've seen a therapist, and no, it hasn't helped. Usually the dreams don't hit until midnight, right around the time the instant replay used to start up. Didn't want you to get sideswiped by me moaning and shouting, or you know, screaming and crying."

"Is that why your scars seem so fresh?"

Trent startled, blinking up at Christophe. Usually people avoided looking at his scars, let alone mentioning them—a sort of anti-stare that made their attention more obvious rather than less. Christophe was the first person ever who'd addressed them matter-of-factly.

"I don't know. Maybe."

Christophe nodded, stroking Trent's face. "In a way, dreams are their own alternate reality. If our minds choose to make us walk those paths, we have little choice but to obey."

"At least we can wake up."

"Can we? Sometimes I am not so sure." He smoothed Trent's hair and dropped a kiss on his forehead. "But never fear, *cher.* I shall guard you from the dreams. They wouldn't dare trouble you when I am by."

"You think dreams are intimidated by captains of industry?"

His mouth quirked up on one side. "Perhaps not. But I have other resources. Sleep. You are safe with me."

CHAPTER
THIRTEEN

When Trent fell asleep, Christophe fully expected to stay awake, on guard as it were. But he'd surprised himself by dropping off soon after Trent.

When he awoke, the window was dark, the room lit by the dim glow of the bedside lamp. He raised himself on an elbow and checked the clock: nearly one.

He studied Trent, who was breathing slowly and calmly. He had a slight smile on his face, so apparently wasn't being troubled by his arcane dreams. *As I thought. What demons would dare approach him when he is guarded by a monster?* If Christophe's curse was worth nothing else, it was worth this.

He spooned closer, wrapping an arm across Trent's chest and capturing one long-fingered hand. Could he risk telling him the truth? After Trent's own extraordinary experiences, surely he could accept the existence of other supernatural gateways, though Christophe's opened within his own body and soul.

I'll do it. When he wakes, I'll tell him.

And then what? Anton believed the Clavret wealth and influence distorted every relationship, turning what should be personal and intimate into nothing but a business negotiation. Trent had made more than one comment about Christophe's lifestyle. Was he only out for what he could get?

But what had that been so far? A couple of drinks, a box of doughnuts, a hamburger dinner. Not exactly diamonds and caviar, yet Trent seemed content with them. Content to spend time with Christophe without demanding money or gifts.

The only thing he asked was for me to fuck him.

That was hardly the action of a man who viewed their relationship in only monetary terms.

Trent stirred against him, peeking at him through his tousled bangs. "What time is it?"

"Nearly one."

Trent's eyes widened. "No shit? I don't fucking believe it." He tossed the duvet aside and rushed to the window, staring out into the dark. "I slept through midnight," he murmured. Suddenly his knees buckled and he dropped onto his arse.

"Trent!" Christophe scrambled out of bed and kneeled next to him, putting an arm around Trent's shaking shoulders. "What's wrong?"

"Wrong?" He lifted his head, and instead of weeping as Christophe had feared, he was laughing, though tears glittered in his eyes. "Not a goddamn thing. Do you realize this is the first night in over seven years that I haven't had to shoot a teenager in the face?"

Christophe blinked. "Well. That's . . . gratifying."

"It's not gratifying, dude. It's a fucking miracle." He turned in Christophe's arms and tackled him, bearing them both to the floor. "This has been the best day ever."

He threaded his fingers through Christophe's hair and dove in for a kiss—hot, deep, and flavored with laughter. When he raised his head, he was grinning, and the joy that shone in his eyes took Christophe's breath away.

Mother of God, that inner light could banish even my shadows.

"Do you think, by revisiting the place—"

Trent's eyebrows drew together. "Let's not go there, yeah? I want to put it as far in my rearview as I can. Never going legend tripping again, that's for damn sure. Never going anywhere near a haunted cemetery or a Sasquatch sighting or any of that shit. I'm done. Nothing but mundane life for me from here on out."

"But now you know such things are possible—"

Trent pushed himself off of Christophe and kneeled next to the bed. "I'd rather forget it all." He shuddered, frowning. "Seriously. I don't think I could survive another trip to Oz, you know what I'm saying?"

Christophe's heart sank. *So much for sharing the truth of my nature.* Despite Trent's adamant opposition to another supernatural incursion, however, perhaps if Christophe remained in Portland, they might occasionally date. *Although you don't know if he plans to remain or not. He lives on the other side of the country, after all.*

"Trent." Christophe sat up and looped an arm around Trent's waist. "What are your plans?"

Trent glanced at Christophe and his smile faltered. "Why? Do you need me to get out of here?"

Christophe chuckled. "I meant nothing so immediate. You arrived in town with the intention of seeing Logan. But what did you intend to do afterward?"

"You know, I hadn't gotten that far. I just needed someone I could talk to about what really happened. Someone who'd touch me." He smiled and trailed a teasing finger up the length of Christophe's cock. "I guess I found that—just not where I expected."

"I'm glad."

"But afterward? With my dad being a douche bag about my trust fund, and not likely to foot the bill for my interrupted education— especially if I decide to stay in theater, well . . . who knows?"

"Are you uncertain about returning to your acting studies?"

"I—" He swallowed, hunching forward. "Every time I think about auditioning for something, I choke. After all, my last role had a seven-year run with no opt-out clause. It's kinda put me off my game, you know?"

"But it is where your heart is."

"My heart may need to find another fucking job, because nobody outside the A-list gets cast without an audition. If I can't deal with those, acting is pretty much a washout. Whatever. Maybe Logan will give me a job in Stumptown Spirits."

A growl rumbled in Christophe's chest at the thought of Trent anywhere near Logan. Ridiculous, really—Logan had no designs on Trent. *That you're aware of.* Riley might not know everything there was to know about his fiancé. Could Logan be the type to want a bit on the side, even after he was married?

Stop. This is your wolf talking, seeing threats where there are none.

Yet it would be for all their benefits—Trent's, Riley's, Logan's, and certainly Christophe's—if Trent were able to close the door on whatever hopes had brought him to Portland so impulsively.

Christophe frowned as he considered his options. Trent clearly needed to build up his confidence. If visiting the Witch's Castle today had helped slay some of his demons, perhaps he needed to close the door on the others as well in order to move on.

"Trent, I believe we should talk about—"

"Uh-uh." Trent cupped Christophe's jaw and kissed him again. "Talk later. For now, I've got other ideas." He jerked his chin at the bed. "Better climb back on board. Wouldn't want you to get rug burns on your ass while I give you the blowjob of the century."

"Trent—"

But then Trent dove for Christophe's lap, and when his mouth closed around Christophe's cock, any hope of coherent thought fled.

When Trent opened his eyes again, the sky was barely pink with dawn. *Happy birthday to me and halle-fucking-lujah.* For the first time since he'd staggered out of Forest Park, he'd gotten an uninterrupted night's sleep. Well, except for the sex. He grinned. *Some interruptions are totally awesome.*

He stretched, his side brushing against Christophe's. *Hell yeah.* Not sleeping alone. He was a definite fan. Maybe that was the key to keeping the ghosts at bay.

On the other hand, maybe Christophe was the key, like a spiritual nightlight or comfort blanket. Trent gazed at the man sleeping beside him. In the pale early light, Christophe's face was regal and austere and a little sad, like Trent imagined Richard III had looked when his life was falling apart—Shakespeare's Tudor-inspired revisionist history notwithstanding.

Trent suddenly felt like a complete and total dickhead. *He's got problems too. It's not all about me.* He'd bombarded Christophe with his own shit ever since they'd met—had it only been two days ago? Seemed like a lot longer.

But just because Trent had been an entitled asshole most of his life, didn't mean he couldn't be a good friend when he tried. *Or maybe a boyfriend?*

He snorted silently. Logan's wedding must have jacked happily-ever-after into his subconscious. He'd sure never wanted that before he went into the ghost war. Maybe this was the twenty-six-year-old side of him, trying to find a landing spot in his brain.

As reluctant as he was to leave the warmth and comfort under the blankets, he needed to pee, so he eased out from under the covers and padded across the carpet to the bathroom.

"Whoa." And he'd thought the rest of the condo was high-end. The bathroom put the best five-star hotel to shame. Christophe's interior decorator obviously believed in unifying color schemes—silver and gray seemed to be a theme around here, with wall-to-wall gray marble tile with silver veins. Hadn't stinted on the amenities either: a skylight, a tub, *and* a shower—Jesus, how many showerheads did one guy need?

Trent found a half a dozen packaged toothbrushes in the vanity drawer. He wondered if François or some other minion handled this little detail. Kinda hard to imagine Christophe cruising the aisles at Walgreens or Costco. *And why exactly does he need so many toothbrushes? Obsessive dental hygiene?*

Christophe had said he hadn't had any sleepovers, but that didn't mean sex hadn't occurred elsewhere. The carpet was certainly plush enough. The idea of someone else here with Christophe—in *Trent's* place—caused him to rip the toothbrush open with unnecessary force.

He glared at himself in the mirror—bedhead, pillow welts, and of course the ever-popular scars on his neck. Yeah, some prize he was. Why should Christophe want anything to do with him?

But I feel better when I'm with him. He makes *me better.*

It wasn't Christophe's job to fix him, though, any more than it was his family's, or his therapist's, or Logan's.

Okay, it actually was his therapist's job. He paid her for it. But nobody else had signed on to repair his broken ass. What had his reappearance meant to the other people in his life?

He would like to think his father had felt something when they'd declared him dead, if only grief for the son he'd wished he'd had rather than the one he'd gotten. Seven years was a reasonable amount of time for someone to move beyond grief—especially if they'd never felt any.

It was human nature to forget. To live through loss. But once the bereaved had reforged their lives, filling in the holes with new people, new experiences, new loves, trying to fit that old person into the new life must be like . . . like expecting someone used to the new fucking iPhone to give it up and go back to Trent's old Nokia. Possible, maybe even desired, but still inconvenient and bewildering and sometimes downright maddening.

Maybe reappearing practically on Logan's wedding day had been the most douche-baggish thing he could have done. Maybe the best present he could give Logan and Riley, Logan's invitation notwithstanding, would be to stay far away from the ceremony.

Maybe he needed to stay dead.

He stared at a love bite on his pec, above his right nipple. *Or maybe I need to find a different way to live.*

"Jesus *fuck*," he muttered, squirting toothpaste on the brush. "Guess that philosophy class I dropped made an impression after all."

After he brushed his teeth and splashed water on his face, he made an unsuccessful attempt to tame his hair. He eyed the shower and its many-splendored nozzles. Did he dare? Christophe hadn't woken yet, so why the hell not?

He was rinsing his hair when the door opened and Christophe walked in. Trent could see him through the steamy glass of the shower enclosure, taking a piss, brushing his teeth. Would he join Trent in the shower? That could be fun.

But instead, Christophe turned on the taps in the bathtub. How awesome was it that the water pressure in the shower didn't even budge? Yeah, money had its advantages. Nobody knew that better than he did, now that he didn't have any of his own.

Trent turned off the water and dried off with about an acre of fluffy towel. He wiped the steam off the glass shower wall. Christophe smiled at him over his shoulder.

"Good morning. Or should I say happy birthday?"

"Guess you should."

"Have you decided whether you will be twenty or twenty-seven?"

"The jury's still out."

"Let me know if you decide. I'd like to know whether I've debauched a younger man or am merely your boy toy."

Trent laughed and stepped onto the bath mat. "We can be versatile, right?"

"True. I suddenly find defying expectations quite exhilarating."

Trent dropped his towel and sauntered across the room to pull Christophe against him. "Did anyone ever tell you that you talk like a Regency dictionary?"

Christophe chuckled and kissed Trent's collarbone. "The disadvantages of an overly formal English teacher at boarding school. I think he might have been born in the Regency, come to think of it. He certainly seemed old enough."

He kissed Trent on the mouth once quickly, then stooped to turn off the bath water. *Nice view.* The tub was so long that when Christophe eased himself into the water and lay back, his feet didn't reach the other end, although Trent's might. Hmm. *Maybe we should try that out.*

"So. What are your plans for the day, other than loafing around in the bath like a Euroslacker?"

"Well, I was hoping to convince you to allow me to treat you for your birthday."

"Yeah? Will the treat involve fucking?"

Christophe laughed and splashed Trent. "You have a one-track mind."

"Guess I must be twenty, then."

"I can tell you, that as an official twenty-five-year-old, thoughts of sex don't diminish appreciably."

Trent sat on the edge of the tub. "No? Then the treat *will* involve fucking."

"Most assuredly." He grinned, and Trent noted that his dick had thickened under the water. *Maybe we'll try out bathtub sex after all.* "However, I intend for it to involve much more. I . . ." Christophe suddenly got very interested in his soap and washcloth. "I was hoping to convince you to go away with me for the weekend."

"Dude. How much convincing do you think I'll need? I mean, you promised me birthday sex. Get real."

"I have an obligation this afternoon, but afterward, I'd like you to join me at a resort near Mount Hood. Quite picturesque, I understand, and highly rated."

A resort at Mount Hood meant forests. Trent hunched his shoulders, his dick withering a little. Jesus, he couldn't hide his phobias while he was naked. *Must make a note of that.* "Do we have to go outside?"

"Not unless you wish it."

"Maybe I'll—" Trent frowned, something Logan had mentioned niggling at his brain. Mount Hood. This weekend. *Shit.* He bolted to his feet. "Logan's wedding. You want me to come with you to the wedding."

"Would that be so bad? He is your friend."

"Yeah, but—" Trees and regret? "I'm not sure I'm up for that."

Christophe sat forward in a slosh of bathwater and held out a soapy hand. "*Cher*, please think about it. Yesterday you faced one of your deepest fears and came away stronger for it."

Trent stared at Christophe's extended hand, the desire to take it overwhelming. "Did I?" *Or did I just find another crutch?*

"This is an unresolved issue from your past. Don't you think that watching Logan move into the next phase of his life, happily, will help you do the same? You can find closure—"

Trent stepped back, snatching the towel off the floor and holding it in front of himself. "Hold it. Are you trying to *fix* me?"

"No. I am only trying to help."

"Yeah, that's nothing but another word for *fix*."

"I think it would do you good—"

"Stop. So what you said in the park was a lie? You *do* think I'm broken."

"No more than I am, or anybody else, but—"

"Yeah, *but*. I get that a lot. Well, no, thanks." He'd seriously thought that he'd found someone that *got* him. Someone who'd let him move at his own pace, fix *himself*.

But Christophe wasn't content to hang with Trent as he was. He wanted someone different. Someone whole. Someone who wouldn't disgrace his fancy apartment by traipsing around it in holey jeans and an *All my friends are dead* T-shirt.

"I thought you were different. Guess it's same-ol', same-ol' after all." He ripped open the bathroom door. "Thanks for the awesome fuck. See you."

CHAPTER
FOURTEEN

other of God, how stupid am I? Christophe struggled to his feet, bathwater sluicing off his body, and fumbled for his towel, only to drop it in the tub. *Shite.* The only other dry towel was across the room. *No time.* He stepped onto the mat and hurried out the bathroom door, dripping on the Berber carpet, which was guaranteed to bring the ire of his housekeeper down on him.

Trent wasn't in the bedroom. *Curse his easy-on/easy-off clothing.* Christophe hurried down the hallway, gooseflesh rising on his arms and legs as the cooler air hit his wet body.

Trent was sitting on the floor by the front door, putting on his trainers.

"Trent. Please don't go. I didn't mean it how it sounded."

"Know what? Maybe you should have."

"What?"

"I need to quit depending on other people to clean up my shit, Christophe. But if I stop expecting them to be my training wheels, they can't expect blind obedience from me." He stood. "I've been in treatment for seven months. I've got the tools. Today I'm twenty or twenty-seven. It's time I learned how to deal on my own."

He opened the door, and Christophe darted across the room, heedless of his nakedness.

"I know you're capable. But you shouldn't have to do this alone. No one should."

Trent bowed his head, leaning his forehead against the doorjamb. "Yeah, well, know what I've learned? Life sucks, and then you die. And die. And die. Then you come back, and life still sucks. Guess I need to get over it."

Trent strode into the hallway. At once, the burn started in Christophe's fingertips, in his jaw, as his wolf objected. *He shouldn't leave. He should stay here. Stop him. Bite his neck. Claim him! He belongs to you. To us.*

Christophe clutched the edge of the door, breathing deeply as color faded from his vision. *Stop it. Back down.* Shite, he'd already bollixed up the morning. *Remain civilized. Or at least human.* "Please, Trent. Let me drive you to your hotel."

"No need. I'll run."

"But—"

"It's what I do. But you know what? Maybe I ought to stop. See you." He punched the elevator and cast a glance at Christophe over his shoulder. "So will everyone else at this rate. Go inside, Christophe, and put on all seventy-two layers of your clothing."

Trent pulled the hood of his sweatshirt up and shoved his hands in his pockets as the doors slid open. He disappeared inside the elevator, sidestepping another man who emerged carrying a takeaway coffee cup and a bag from the downstairs bakery.

The burn intensified, shooting down Christophe's spine to his tailbone. His nose twitched—*the other . . . his scent . . . familiar?* Irrelevant. Another male near his mate? Almost *touching* his mate? Intolerable! The hair on his neck rose, and he bared his teeth in a snarl.

The man stopped in the middle of the hallway, the bag falling from his hand. "Holy Mother."

Christophe bared his teeth. *Attack the intruder for his insolence?* He poised himself to spring, but caught whiff of something else. A different challenge. *Must protect my territory.*

He whirled and strode back inside, deep into his lair, where the scent of his mate lingered. He prowled the room, touching each place his mate had lain, sniffing the air, seeking the threat.

Danger. He was sure of it. To him, to his mate. But what? Where?

The agony in his spine—he could scarcely remain upright. But why would he? *Not natural.* His hands. His feet. *Pain.* Tendons stretching. Bones stressed to near breaking. And there. The band of metal, winking gold, cutting into his flesh, as if his paw were caught in a trap. *Take it off. Bite it off.*

Suddenly cold water drenched him from head to foot. He howled and shook his head, spattering drops across the walls.

"Christophe Augustin Bonfils Clavret. *Arrête!*"

Christophe blinked the water from his eyes as the pain in his back receded slightly, the burn in his extremities easing. "Anton?" he croaked.

"Put this on." Anton flung a white cloth at him, and Christophe caught it reflexively. *Undershirt.* With shaking hands, he pulled it over his head. At once, the pain diminished further.

What had he done? His wolf had nearly overpowered him—not only his body but his *consciousness*, and that *never* happened. The mind of the man was always dominant over the wolf. Always.

Until now. Until Trent.

Anton tossed him a pair of briefs. "And these." Then a shirt. Pants. With every piece of clothing he donned, his humanity returned. *Mother of God, I almost shifted. Here. In my own home. I was within seconds of attacking my brother, for nothing more than proximity to a man who may no longer wish to speak to me.*

Christophe knees gave way and he dropped to the floor, his back to the bed and his face in his hands.

"Merciful God, Christo, what happened? Did that man do something to set you off?"

"Yes." *But not in a way I can explain.*

"If you troll for sex outside our echelon, you must expect unpleasantness. But there are agencies that specialize in such things. I can—"

"Stop." His muscles clenched, the burn starting in his fingers again, firing the *danger* signals in his brain. *He's insulting my mate.* "I don't need you to pimp for me."

"I—I didn't mean—"

Christophe raised his head. *Shite.* Anton's face held the same expression it had when their father belittled him. *What is wrong with me? Are my instincts so cross-wired by this delayed shift that they violate everything I know?*

He held out a hand to his brother. "*Jesu*, Anton. I am so very sorry."

Anton smiled grimly and pulled Christophe to his feet. "If this doesn't prove how necessary it is for you to shift this evening, I don't know what will do it. You've never gone for me before. Was it because I didn't bring you a coffee?"

Christophe shook his head. "No. I've made a mistake, that's all. One I intend to rectify at my first opportunity."

"You'll need to table it, I'm afraid. I've arranged with François that we'll be leaving for the resort shortly. You need to pack. Prepare to shut up the flat since you won't be coming back—"

"Anton. We discussed this. I do not intend to return to Vienna. I'm staying in Portland."

Anton set his coffee on the counter carefully, more carefully than need be unless he was trying to avoid slamming it down. "I'm not convinced this is the best course, Christo, either for the company, or our family, or for you."

"That is your privilege. However, my mind is set on this."

"Nevertheless, you owe it to Papa to have the conversation at home. Not over the phone, and not here."

Christophe retrieved a towel from the bathroom and dried his hair. His clothes were clammy against his skin from Anton's cold-water treatment. "I told you—"

Anton's shoulders lifted and fell in a sigh. "Have it your way. You always do."

Poor man. Between Christophe and their father, he had much to put up with. "You're too good to me."

"Enough." Anton straightened. "Go lie down. Rest. I'll pack for you."

"You needn't do that. I can—"

"Give over, Christo. You're a bloody wreck. Or do you doubt I know your preferences?" Anton ticked off on his fingers. "At least five suits, fresh from the cleaners, enough underwear for your entire university rowing club on a two-week tour, all the—"

Christophe laughed shakily. "You've made your point. And I admit that a rest would be welcome." He twisted the towel in his hands. "But while you're doing that, I have an errand that I must run."

"Be quick. François will be here to pick up the luggage soon."

"No. I have another task for François. You and I shall rent a car and drive ourselves."

Anton frowned. "Are you serious? You know how I hate American roads."

"Don't worry. I'll drive."

"In your state? That's the most worrisome notion of all." Anton muttered in French as he walked away down the hall.

Christophe picked up his jacket from the floor in the corner—really, what must his brother have thought of the state of his clothing?—and retrieved his cell phone from the pocket. He retreated to his study, allowing Anton free run of the bedroom and closet.

After texting his instructions to François, and leaving a very specific message for his tailor, he called Trent.

Voice mail. Only to be expected. Trent was either still running, or had learned enough about his phone to refuse Christophe's call.

"Trent. I know you're angry with me, and I don't blame you. I expressed myself poorly, and what I said was not what I meant. You are strong, and brave, and everything I could want in a lover exactly as you are. I would dearly love to have your company at the resort this weekend. We could spend time together, even should you choose not to attend the wedding. I've left instructions with François to drive you there, if, as I hope, you change your mind. I'll leave a key for you at the reception desk, since I may not arrive until late tonight. However," he lowered his voice to a more suggestive register, "I hope to find you in my bed when I arrive."

There. Now he could do nothing but hope.

Almost as soon as he hit the street, Trent regretted his over-the-top exit. *Jesus fuck, once a drama queen, always a drama queen.*

He needed to decompress before he shut himself back in his hotel room, so despite how his jeans chafed his thighs, he headed to Waterfront Park and ran along the river.

Had he overreacted? Maybe. Christophe had seemed to be spouting the old party line—*Get over it, Trent.* He'd gotten the same message, in hints from his mother, suggestions from his therapist, and flat-out orders from his father. He should be used to it by now.

Yeah, just like I got used to the noose, and the snap of my neck bones every night.

He slowed down under the Hawthorne Bridge and stretched out, any benefit from his earlier shower gone. He was a mess, stank like a locker room, and was seriously in need of food. He should have stopped for something before he turned himself into a sweat monster.

He jogged up to Second, where a little pod of early-opening food carts was doing a brisk trade, and bought himself a falafel sandwich. Not exactly breakfast food, but technically it was nearly lunchtime, so what the hell. He took it down by the river and sat on a bench while the Canada geese stalked past him on the grass like masked storm troopers.

What was he supposed to do with his life? Go back to Rhode Island and try to make peace with his dad? *Not gonna work. The only reason he tolerates you in the house is because of the PR disaster it'd cause if he didn't play the formerly bereaved father.*

So that wasn't happening. Besides, as he watched a dragon boat crew stroke by on the Willamette, he realized he'd missed Portland. He'd chosen PSU at random from schools that met two basic requirements: good value for his education dollars; minimum safe distance from his father. *Dad's not the only frugal Yankee in the family.* But then he'd fallen in love with the city.

If he had a choice, he'd stay here again. See about getting readmitted to school, although the idea of stepping onstage made fresh sweat bead his forehead. If he didn't get the trust fund money, though, that might be tougher.

Maybe his flippant remark to Christophe about begging a job from Logan hadn't been that far-fetched. *I've got at least one friend in town. That can't be bad.*

He took a moment to mourn the loss of his other contact— Christophe. He'd really felt like they'd had a chance. A real connection. But damn Christophe for going all paternalistic on his ass. That was *not* what he needed.

He tossed his trash in a nearby can and walked the couple of blocks to his hotel. When he arrived at his room, the DND sign was still hanging on his door, so the place was exactly as he'd left it. He stripped immediately, tossing his clothes in the pile, and then hit the shower. After he got cleaned up, he'd go see Logan. Maybe check on the employment possibilities.

Probably not the best move today. It's the night before his wedding.

Trent froze in the act of scrubbing his chest. The night before Logan's wedding. His own birthday, and here he was, spending it alone again, with no better prospect than another Marvel movie binge and room-service pizza.

"Happy fucking birthday to me."

Once he'd dried off and dressed, he wrestled his cell phone out of the pocket of the filthy PSU hoodie and saw he'd missed a call. The message light on the hotel phone was blinking too. Birthday wishes from the management? *Not likely.* They could wait.

He sat on the bed, tailor-fashion, and tried to remember how to retrieve the messages from the fricking iPhone. If he poked that icon and this button then— "Abracadabra alakazam." Ah. There.

The first message . . . God, from Christophe. He listened, his chest tightening. If he intended to crush his new plan, he needed to stay strong. Resist. Otherwise, how could he remake himself? *New, improved, self-sufficient Trent! Sixty-two percent less pathetic and seventy-nine point nine percent less batshit crazy!* Well, maybe only thirty-seven point two percent, because if he'd really thought he had a chance with someone like Christophe, he needed to check back into the psych ward, stat.

The temptation to respond to Christophe's message with a *hell fucking yeah* was undeniable, though, nearly overwhelming. Being with him—the closeness, the acceptance, the *touch*—had felt so good. Maybe too good. Was wanting something this badly a reason *not* to do it?

No way. That was his Puritan New England ancestors and their whacked-out self-denial talking, not Trent Pielmeyer, hedonistic once and future college student. But hashing out whatever their relationship was in the sparkly glow of Logan's happily-ever-after? No, thank you. He'd wait until Christophe got back to town. Then they'd talk.

Who are you kidding? You don't want to talk. You want to fuck.

Well, true on both points. But though he didn't *want* to talk, he *should*.

And if he intended to earn his twenty-seven-year-old cred, he'd better fricking do it. *I can be responsible. I can have serious conversations. I can . . . do laundry?*

He stared at the mound of clothes in the corner, which was threatening to take on a life of its own. But God he hated Laundromats. Maybe the hotel had a service, although for the size of Trent's laundry monster, they'd probably charge as much as a semester's tuition. Laundromat it was. But first, he'd be a mature adult and listen to his messages.

He peered at the instructions on the desk phone—which were a hell of a lot more straightforward than the iPhone, and not an *icon* or *app* in sight.

The message, though, was enough to freeze his balls off.

"Mr. Pielmeyer, this is the hotel manager. I regret to inform you that your credit card has been declined. Although your father has settled your bill, if you can't provide another method of payment, we must ask you to check out by noon today."

Goddamnitmotherfucker. His dad had stopped his credit card? Now there was a fricking awesome birthday gift. He'd worried about Bishop monitoring his purchases, but he'd forgotten his father could do the same thing. More easily too, since the account was in his fucking name.

He checked his wallet. Thirty-seven dollars and some change. Not enough to do squat, and with his only connections on the way out of town for the weekend, he had zero couch-surfing options.

Wait. He had one. He could take Christophe up on his offer. Call François. Be on the way to Mount Hood—*Gah! Trees! Don't think about them*—before the management arrived to toss him out on his ear.

Jesus fuck, it was eleven forty-nine. He slung his duffel on the bed and stuffed armfuls of clothes, clean and dirty, into the thing, stuffing them down when they threatened to spill over. He'd sort them out later. He shoved his laptop in his backpack, checked under the bed— oops, underwear—and in the drawers for any last-minute stuff.

He called the number from Christophe's message. "Hey, François. It's Trent Pielmeyer. I . . . uh . . . I've decided to accept Christophe's invitation. Could you pick me up at the hotel, like, now?"

"*Oui, monsieur.* I will be there within the half hour."

"Awesome. Thanks."

He grabbed his backpack and slung his duffel over his shoulder. As he let the door close behind him, the last thing he saw in the room was the clock. Eleven fifty-nine.

Hot damn. Nobody could say Trent Pielmeyer didn't know how to time his exits.

CHAPTER FIFTEEN

After nearly an hour on the road, Christophe's clothes were irritating him so much that his skin had to be raw beneath them. His fingers cramped from clutching the steering wheel, and his jaw ached from clenching his teeth. *Soon. We'll be there soon.*

"Christo."

"What?" His voice was as raw as his skin.

"Leaning forward over the steering wheel will not get us there any faster." Anton's tone was laced with amusement. "You should remember, too, that this car is calibrated for miles, not kilometers."

Christophe glanced at the speedometer. *Ninety.* Shite. "Forgive me." He eased up on the gas pedal.

"However, I believe I should take the wheel. I can tell by the way you're fidgeting that you're fighting your nature."

"But you don't want to drive."

"No. I said I preferred to let François do it, since that is his job. But unlike you, I am capable of getting us to the lodge without actually achieving liftoff. Please. Pull over."

"Very well." Christophe did as Anton asked. Truth be told, he was so twitchy that when he'd spotted a deer in the trees earlier, he'd nearly swerved to chase it.

He climbed out of the driver's seat and circled the car. Pausing with his hand on the passenger door, he closed his eyes and sniffed the cool breeze that whispered through the trees, carrying the smells of the wild—damp bark, loam, sun-warmed rock. *Prey.*

"Christo." Anton's voice, less amused now, startled him out of his reverie. "Perhaps you should get in the car. We have another hour to travel, and we need to make as good a time as possible."

"Yes, of course. You're right." But when he returned to the car, Christophe cracked his window open and let the scents flow over him.

"It must be glorious."

Christophe turned to his brother, so serious behind the wheel. "What?"

"The freedom. To be master of the forest."

"Is that what you think?"

"Naturally. You look as if you could see heaven now."

"No." Christophe sighed. "I see only the woods."

"But—"

"I was near to snapping at the flat this morning. What man wants to be so at the mercy of his nature?"

Anton chuckled. "Isn't every man at the mercy of his nature?"

"All men don't have a beast inside them."

"I know some women who would argue that point."

"Anton, you imagine that the wolf makes me stronger. He does not."

"You speak as if you and the wolf are two different beings."

"We are." Christophe gripped his knees to hide the tremor in his hands. "At war with one another within the same body."

"You must find something about it good. The power—"

"The power is an illusion, whatever Papa says. When you are not master of your own destiny, when you are forced to relinquish your humanity, how can that be power? If Papa, or Etienne Melion, or I were to lose control in the midst of a board meeting or trade negotiation, how much power do you think we could retain from inside a prison or a zoo or a laboratory?" He squeezed Anton's arm. "Be glad you escaped the blight. I am certainly glad for you."

Anton smiled wryly. "I appreciate the sentiment." He jerked his chin toward the rear seat. "You'll find water in the bag behind me, if it will help."

"Thank you, *mon frère*. You are too good to me."

Christophe downed half a bottle, then leaned back against the headrest.

The next thing he knew, the car was slowing. He opened his eyes as Anton pulled into a long, narrow parking lot edged on three sides with towering firs. At the far end, set among the trees, stood a rambling three-story building, all red wood and glass.

The tires crunched on gravel as Anton pulled the car to a stop and set the brake. "As well as the central lodge, the resort has detached cabins. I've booked one for each of us, although it wasn't easy. Your friend's wedding guests are taking up most of the place."

"Thank you." The additional privacy was definitely convenient, not only to keep his own comings and goings discreet, but for Trent. Should he take Christophe's invitation, he could avoid the wedding party if he liked.

"I'll go check us in."

"No. I will come too."

"Are you sure?"

"Yes. There are certain . . . arrangements I wish to make." Just the notion of Trent once again in his space, in his arms, in his bed—*Jesu.* While the wolf might huff his approval, the heat in his chest and groin belonged solely to the man.

"As you wish." Anton didn't sound happy though. Did he imagine Christophe couldn't behave in a civilized manner in public now? Perhaps, given this morning's near-disaster, such fears weren't entirely unjustified.

The lobby was fronted with floor-to-ceiling windows that faced the forest, with a glimpse of Mount Hood's peak above the trees. A huge fireplace dominated one wall, the reception area opposite. Christophe strode toward the front desk.

"Good afternoon. Clavret is the name. I believe we have two cabins reserved?"

The young woman behind the counter tapped away at her computer terminal. "Yes. I'm afraid I couldn't place you near each other. One of the cabins is on the south slope and the other north, near the creek."

"I'm sure both will be lovely." He turned to his brother. "Do you have a preference?" Anton shrugged.

She glanced between them, clearly admiring Anton's chiseled profile. "They're very similar, although the one on the south has a fireplace inside and the north cabin has an enclosed fire pit on the deck."

A fireplace would be quite romantic. Flame and shadow dancing across Trent's skin? *Breathtaking.* "I'll take the south cabin, then, if you have no objection, Anton?"

"None."

She tapped her keyboard again, then handed them each keys and a map. "The trails are marked here and here. You can get to either cabin from the parking lot or from the lodge deck. There's a road to the north cabin, but not the south. Sorry, I should have mentioned that."

"Don't be concerned. It's fine." Christophe pocketed his key. "Anton, why don't you bring the car round to the door here, and I'll retrieve my luggage. Then you can drive over to your cabin."

"Are you sure? I can help carry your bags."

Christophe chuckled. "I'm capable of that much."

"If you like," the young woman said, "our bellmen can help with luggage transportation. You can leave everything here and they'll take it down for you."

"You see?" He took Anton's arm and drew him away "You need not monitor me quite this closely."

"Christo, you couldn't see your face at the flat, or in the car. You—"

He patted Anton's arm. "I am well, I assure you. Leave my bags with the bellman and come meet me at my cabin when you've unpacked."

"If you're certain—"

"I am. I'll see you shortly."

Anton crossed the lobby with only one dubious glance at Christophe before he exited into the parking area. Christophe turned back to the concierge.

"I am expecting a guest to join me, but business calls me away until later this evening. May I leave a second key for him?"

"Of course, sir. What name?"

"Pielmeyer. Trent. Although you should list it under Clavret too, as he might ask for it under my name rather than his own."

"Certainly, sir. And if there's anything we can do to make your stay more enjoyable, do let us know."

"Thank you." He offered his most charming smile—although by the way she blinked, perhaps his feral side was yet too prominent.

He walked out onto the wide deck overlooking the forest and the mountain. As a man, he could appreciate the view, the beauty of the trees, and sky dotted with puffy clouds. In a few hours, he would care for nothing except the best path through the underbrush.

Best not to think of that. Think of Trent.

He checked his phone for messages, which he'd been unable to do with the spotty reception on the drive.

Ah. Several messages from François. His finger trembled over the screen. Would it be good news, or was he doomed to disappointment? He tapped the icon.

Suit ready.

That was good. His gift for Trent had been a last-minute impulse, because he knew Trent hadn't any dress clothes with him. Christophe still harbored the hope that Trent would overcome his reluctance and attend the wedding, but he might hesitate if he had nothing appropriate to wear. Luckily, his tailor—who was most accommodating, given the correct monetary incentive—had had an appropriate suit on the rack, and Christophe had a very clear idea of Trent's size.

He could map the man in his mind whenever he closed his eyes.

Another message popped up.

T called for pick up. Leaving at noon.

Christophe's knees gave way, and he sat with a *thump* on one of the benches lining the deck. *Thank God.* Now he had incentive to get his shift over with as soon as possible, so he could spend as much time with Trent as he could.

Without the bloody wolf interfering.

After hauling ass downstairs, Trent huddled under the hotel's front awning, suffering from a sudden attack of beggar's remorse. *Fitting.* Because in his ratty clothes, with luggage bulging as if he'd swiped all his towels and bedding, he looked like an actual beggar too.

The bell captain stationed at the door obviously thought so—he'd been giving Trent the side-eye for the last fifteen minutes.

Fucking terrific. After his big talk about self-sufficiency, here he was again, depending on the kindness of strangers. If he wanted to prove he wasn't broken, he'd picked the wrong way to do it.

Shame curdled his belly, and he nearly bolted for the street as the sleek black town car pulled up. But he didn't have much choice, so he sighed and shouldered the duffel as François got out.

The bell captain shooed Trent aside, clearing his own path to the car. "Don't block the doors for the paying guests." He hustled to the curb as François popped the trunk.

François walked past him and touched the brim of his cap at Trent. "*Bonjour, Monsieur* Pielmeyer."

"Uh . . . hi."

The bellman approached, but François held up a gloved hand. "Allow me."

François collected Trent's duffel and stowed it in the trunk as if it were a matched set of Louis Vuitton. Then he inclined his head at the scowling bell captain, smiled, and *whoa.* The string of French profanity that François unloaded would have earned him major points with the guys in Trent's prep school French classes. The oblivious bell captain smiled back.

Well, boy howdy. There's more to François than a chauffeur's uniform.

For some reason, that little glimpse of kick-ass humanity spiked Trent's regret. François was a real person. *Christophe* was a real person. Neither one of them deserved being imposed on because Trent's father was a dickhead.

Guess that makes you Son of Dickhead, because you're gonna do it anyway.

But he pulled his hood forward and slid into the backseat when François held the door, pretending he hadn't understood a word. *Nothing like a language barrier to make it easier to hide.*

Safe behind the privacy shield while François navigated out of Portland, Trent huddled in the corner of the seat, poking at his phone. At least his father hadn't stopped his cell service, although he hadn't left Trent any messages either.

It's not like Trent had to get in tune with the infinite to figure out that the old man was pissed: *Spirit, I sense you are angry. Stop one credit card for yes, evict your son from the hotel for a hell yes.*

But a few extra deets would help. Not like he could come home without *any freaking way to pay for the plane ticket.* Maybe this was a kick-the-gay-kid-out-of-your-life move. With Trent on the other side of the country, the country-club set would never know.

Unless his father intended to turn this into a PR win: *We gave him everything, but he ran anyway.* More affecting TV footage. Cue the sobbing violin soundtrack.

Jesus, he'd probably played right into dear ol' Dad's avaricious hands.

About half an hour later, François voice spoke through the intercom, startling Trent out of an Angry Birds game.

"Lunch, *Monsieur* Pielmeyer?"

Trent peered through the tinted glass. They'd stopped at a strip mall, in front of a mom-and-pop diner with a Walgreens on one side and a RadioShack on the other. Trent's stomach rumbled. *God, yes.* But hello nearly empty wallet.

"No. I'm good."

"*Vous misunderstand. Monsieur* Clavret treats."

Great. *Son of Dickhead strikes again.* "Sure. Thanks. But you have to join me."

"*Très bien.*"

During lunch, Trent regretted his decision to hide his nearly fluent French from François. If he came out with *Surprise! I can understand you perfectly!*, he'd seem like an asshole. But the pretense made conversation awkward. Poor François had to work way too hard.

Then Trent remembered the translation app he'd randomly downloaded yesterday when he'd been making a serious effort to get to know his phone. For the rest of the meal, the two of them used it to triangulate their conversation. Although considering some of the peculiar French-to-English syntax, the thing needed a serious upgrade.

It was kind of like the old Monty Python skit about the bogus Hungarian phrase book. While François paid the bill, Trent waited by the door and typed in *My hovercraft is full of eels* to see what the app would make of it.

When he showed the translation to François, he laughed so much his hat nearly fell off. *Score.*

Trent grinned and pointed at the front passenger seat. "I call shotgun!"

CHAPTER
SIXTEEN

hristophe took his time unpacking, grateful that the resort didn't stint on drawer space or hangers. Had he overpacked? Of course he had. He always did. As he hung his shirts, his suit for the wedding, and his half-dozen other jackets, he smiled, remembering Trent's annoyance at how long it had taken him to undress. *Ah, cher, haven't you heard? Clothes make the man—and for me, that is literally the case.*

When he finished arranging the last of his socks in the drawer, he wandered into the main room and saw that he'd missed several more messages from François.

Stalling, as requested. Lunch. Store.

And then *Lube,* accompanied by an evil grin emoticon, the cheeky devil.

Christophe chuckled, astonished at the lightness of his heart. The usual dread that filled his belly whenever he faced a shift was tempered today by the anticipation of being with his lover again tonight. *Nothing like a carrot to make getting beaten bloody with the stick easier to bear.* He laughed, imagining what Trent's response would have been to that particular thought. No doubt he would have made a rude joke. Trent's carefree lack of deference was one of his most appealing qualities.

If he were to tell Trent the truth, would that change? *Time enough to test that later, after we've had the chance to cement what we have.* He could afford no complications tonight, so after he returned to himself and was as human as he ever was, he'd do everything—short of telling the whole truth—to convince Trent they belonged together.

He sat at the desk to write a note for Trent—apologies for not being there when he arrived, carte blanche to the hotel's amenities and entertainment options.

Entertainment.

A jolt of heat rocked his balls, and his cock rose as he wrote a few instructions that he hoped Trent would follow. *Jesu,* that would get Christophe through this evening with better grace than usual, although he definitely wouldn't be tarrying in the forest.

A brief knock fell on the door and Anton walked in, checking his watch. "I apologize for the delay. I had to sort out an issue for the company."

"The Portuguese deal again?"

"Something like that. Ready?"

"Just now."

Anton glanced around the room, his lips pursed. "I hoped perhaps your room might be less . . . rustic than mine."

"Really? I find it rather charming."

"Ah well. Log cabins have never been my preference."

"No," Christophe teased as he slipped his jacket on, "you prefer St. Moritz and Monaco."

Anton shrugged. "You can't blame me. What is wealth for, if you can't enjoy it?"

Christophe gestured for Anton to precede him outside and pocketed his key. "Perhaps for doing a bit of good?"

"Always the crusader, Christo. Are you ready to go? The sooner we leave, the sooner you'll be able to relax."

Christophe grinned. "Lead on. I can't wait."

"Is that so?" Anton's eyebrows rose. "That's . . . certainly a new attitude for you. Come. I parked the car on a service road."

"Trust you to find the most expedient way to get the job done."

"I have a lot of practice," Anton said dryly.

"That must be why you're so good at it." Christophe draped an arm across Anton's shoulders and gave him a half hug.

"Ah, give over, Christo, do." Anton batted him away.

Christophe laughed and climbed into the passenger seat. "If you insist on being so helpful, you must learn to take thanks for it and accept the honors that you're due."

Anton backed the car down the unpaved road. "That's usually not a problem with Papa."

Christophe's elation dimmed a little. "You must give Papa time."

"He's had my whole life."

"I mean after I tell him of my decision. Then he'll be forced to recognize what you've done for him, for the company, and you'll be rewarded as you deserve."

"That will be a landmark day for certain."

"It will. For each of us. A new era for Clavret et Cie. A new future for your children."

"Mmmhph."

Christophe let it be. No doubt their father would take some convincing, but Anton's record was exemplary. Papa would be a fool not to give him in title what he'd been doing in practice for years. He gazed out the window at the passing forest. "How far?"

"Several miles. We can't drive all the way to the spot I've got in mind. But we should be there within half an hour."

"A hike, eh? I should have worn different shoes."

Anton glanced down at Christophe's Italian loafers. "I'm surprised you didn't wear your boots."

"They needed to be cleaned, and I didn't have time. Foolish of me not to realize we wouldn't simply be able to drive up to the wilderness and park, eh?"

"Well, it's not like you can't afford new shoes."

"Yes, but these are my favorites."

"I'm sure they'll be as much use to you afterward as they are now." He pulled the car over. "We walk from here."

Christophe followed Anton up a steep path, winding through the trees, skirting a small clearing that was scattered with boulders as if a giant child had tired of his blocks and flung them to the ground. The path was damp but not muddy, and the going not difficult, although Christophe's smooth-soled shoes slipped on the steeper areas. At the foot of a rocky outcropping, Anton stopped.

"Up there. There's a cave where you can undress and shift."

Christophe eyed the nearly vertical hillside with its thickets of blackberry brambles. "Mother of God, Anton. How did you find this place?"

"Do you imagine that I'd have difficulty locating a simple cave? I handle the logistics for our entire firm. Besides, you can find anything on the internet these days."

"Ah. Of course. But you are truly challenging me today. I think I'd have an easier time scaling this mountain in bare feet than with these shoes."

"Don't exaggerate. It's a little incline. On the other side, it's an easier ascent, almost like a staircase."

"A staircase with a thorn hedge."

Anton glared at him. "Do *you* want to scout out a different location?"

"No. Forgive me." He picked his way up the hill, the brambles catching at his clothing. When he reached the ledge, however, he conceded that Anton had chosen perfectly. The spot had a greater than one-hundred-eighty-degree view, since this hillock broke the tree line for over a hundred yards. The vista spread across a gully into the forest, the mountain rearing behind it, and on the other side, a wide swath of pasture beyond the trees. "What's that? It looks man-maintained."

"More like sheep-maintained. It's a ranch."

Christophe shot a glance at Anton. "So near? Isn't that dangerous?"

"Why, do you have a taste for mutton?"

"Not for the sheep, you arse. I would never kill domestic livestock. But Oregon ranchers aren't proscribed from shooting wolves who they suspect of predation, now that wolves aren't on the endangered list in the state anymore."

"As long as you stay within the bounds of the forest, you'll be fine. Go south and west, not north and east."

"Understood." He hoped his wolf would remember. *I'll make it remember. For such a short time, surely the mind of the man could retain ascendency over the mind of the wolf.*

He ducked into the cave at the back of the ledge. It was shallow, its mouth wide so light filtered in from outside. Anton had clearly been here earlier, because he'd already laid a tarp out for Christophe's clothes.

As he took off his jacket, he marveled anew at his brother's efficiency. *He's wasted as logistics officer. He should be CEO.* Though even CEO was a poor match, nothing but negotiations and meetings.

Anton knew how to get things *done*. Chief operating officer. That was a better fit. Christophe must remember to mention that to his father when they had their little . . . chat.

He finished undressing, folding his clothes neatly atop the tarp. As he removed his watch, he smiled, thinking again of Trent and his likely reaction to the pristine pile. Perhaps he should have flung his clothes about instead. But that would make returning to human difficult. The more articles of clothing he could make contact with, the more readily he'd be able to launch the transition. Not to mention Anton would probably feel compelled to straighten up after him. *My brother has spent too much of his life cleaning up for me. That stops soon. After the wedding. After the weekend with Trent. Then I'll get it sorted.*

He drew off his signet ring—traditionally the last item removed before a shift—and held it in his palm for a moment. What had his long-ago ancestor done to bring this curse down on himself and his family? Perhaps he'd chosen it freely. They'd never know for certain. Their stories, their legends, didn't contain any of the *why*, only the *what* and the *how*, along with the cautionary tales of marital infidelity and betrayal.

He placed the ring on the top of the pile, more convinced than ever that he was making the right decision to end their line with him.

Once the ring was off his hand, he moved away from the tarp and hunkered down, head bowed. He breathed deeply, letting the scents of the woods, the sounds of the myriad lives that teemed beneath the notice of humans fill his senses.

This was always the point he hated the most: when he had nothing between himself and the transition, no reason for control other than his soul-deep hatred of what he was. Knowing what awaited, he had to force himself to let go of his human sensibilities, to allow the wolf dominance for long enough to transform.

Tonight, however, he wanted the change to take him quickly, the sooner to get it behind him. He tensed, though, anticipating the pain to come.

Let it go. Yes, it hurts. Yes, it's humiliating to be reduced from man to beast. But tonight you have a reason to get it done.

As soon as he thought about that reason—Trent, naked and willing—the burn in his fingertips and spine welled and spiked.

This time, he didn't fight it, huddling on hands and knees, panting through the agony as his spine reformed. His scream morphed into a yelp as his larynx warped, his jaw distending and narrowing, teeth popping out of his gums where none had been. He whined helplessly as the bones in his hands contorted into paws, as his ears lengthened and reoriented, at the million flares of pain as fur burst through his skin. Then his tail sprouted, and he howled until his breath gave out.

When it was finally over, he lay on his side in the dirt, whimpers vibrating his throat. As the pain receded, it was replaced by unease. *Something is not right.* His hackles rose and he rolled to his paws, sniffing the air. *Mice. Raccoons. Voles.* He paced to the mouth of the cave.

Rabbit. Deer. Wait. *Was that . . . wolf?*

A growl rumbled in his chest, and he lifted his nose, casting for the scent, but it was faint, like a memory.

"Christo."

He whirled, crouching. *Man. Brother. Safe.* He circled Anton, sniffing at his trousers. Was the wolf memory here? He started to lift his leg, to mark his territory so the other wolf wouldn't dare to—

Anton clapped his hands. "Oi. Don't even think of it."

Christophe huffed, but the maddening scent lingered. He growled again and shoved his nose against Anton's leg.

"Shite, Christo. What's the— Oh. You're scenting Melion, aren't you? I wore these pants yesterday, in the meeting with him and the Merricks."

Christophe bared his teeth. His wolf hated Etienne's wolf as much as Christophe hated the man.

"Go. Run. I'll take care of your clothing."

Christophe shook himself. Yes, he needed to get this over with, but had he remembered to tell Anton he wanted to be back at the resort by nine? He must have. Anton never forgot to verify such details.

Christophe turned and leaped down the hill in two bounds. *For some things, the wolf is far more suited than the man.* He raced off into the trees.

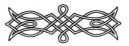

Trent was proud that he hadn't freaked the fuck out when François pulled into the parking lot of the resort. Bad enough that the trees had loomed on either side of the road for the last gajillion miles, but seriously—this parking lot? It was only one car deep, just a narrow strip of gravel keeping the trees at bay. Trent had seen a special on TV once about how quickly nature would take over again if humans suddenly vanished from the planet. This parking lot would be the first to go.

François stopped the car in front of the lodge doors. "*Monsieur* Clavret has left for you a key."

"Cool. I can handle it from here. Thanks a lot, François, for the lunch and the company and, you know, picking me up off the street."

"The pleasure was mine." He popped the trunk and trotted to the rear of the car.

Trent grabbed his backpack and followed. A bellman approached from the lodge doors, and François handed him Trent's overstuffed duffel. Then he removed a garment bag and handed it over too.

"Wait. That's not mine. Is it for Christophe?"

"No, *monsieur*. For you. *Un cadeau.* From *Monsieur* Clavret." He touched the brim of his cap. "*Bon anniversaires.*"

"Thanks." For a moment, Trent was annoyed that Christophe would think he couldn't afford his own suit, but then— *Oh yeah. At the moment, I can't.* Besides, considering his wardrobe choices while they'd been together, Christophe would be totally justified in thinking Trent didn't own anything without holes or a graphic.

"Well. Thanks again. See you around?"

"*Certainement. Au revoir.*"

"Yeah. You too."

Trent followed the bellman into the lobby. *Nice.* Lumberjack chic done right. He approached the desk and smiled at the clerk. "Hey."

"Good afternoon. Are you here for the wedding?"

Shit. Probably the first time of many that I'll get hit with that question. Probably more than once by Christophe. "Uh, no. But you've got a key for me." He panicked for a moment. Under whose name? Then he snorted. How hard could it be? They had a choice of two. "Either Pielmeyer or Clavret. Or maybe both."

She smiled brightly. "Oh yes. Here you are." She handed him a key and nodded to the bellman. "Jeremy will take you down to the cabin. Please enjoy your stay."

"Do my best. Thanks."

He turned to follow Jeremy and came face-to-face with Logan. *Shit.*

Logan's grin threatened to meet his ears. "You came." He grabbed Trent in a hug that nearly squeezed the breath out of him. "I can't believe it. I'm so glad."

"Yeah, well, thing is, I might—"

"Hey, I want to introduce you to Riley. You still haven't met him, right?" Logan let go of Trent and peered around the lobby. "He was here a minute ago, but Julie may have run off with him." He faced Trent again. "You remember Julie from last October, don't you?"

Trent swallowed, expecting the usual surge of panic that swamped him whenever he thought about that night, but surprisingly, it wasn't bad. "Yeah. She's with that show. The ghost one."

"Yeah, but she's trying to break out on her own as a producer. I think she's practicing on us. She's Riley's best-man equivalent, and she's got a mile-long list of things we're supposed to do or not do because of wedding traditions." Logan scowled. "That woman is a menace with a clipboard."

"I . . . um . . . have to go."

"Can't you hang out for a minute? Maybe get a drink?"

Trent waved vaguely in the direction of the waiting bellman. "Gotta pee. And you know, unpack. All that shit."

Logan's face fell, and Trent immediately felt like a douche bag. "Got it."

He clasped Logan's biceps. *Jesus, those hadn't been this big seven years ago.* "Listen. I'm happy for you, yeah? We'll catch up sometime this weekend. Promise." *Liar, liar.*

"Sure. Glad you could make it."

Trent saluted and headed for the staircase in the middle of the lobby.

"Ah, sir?" Jeremy gestured to the terrace doors. "Your cabin is this way."

Damn it, Jeremy led him out onto the deck, with a stellar view of more fucking forest than Trent ever wanted to see in his entire life. Then down a path that some idiot had laid out to make it appear as if the woods hadn't been disturbed. *Disturb them, damn it, and get them the hell away from me.*

He pulled his hood up and hunched his shoulders, hands shoved in his hoodie pocket, and dogged Jeremy down the path, wincing when the guy apologized for Trent stepping on his heels.

"Here you go. You're lucky. These private cabins are hard to book. Everyone wants them because you really feel like you're alone here in the woods."

"Yeah," Trent muttered. "Terrific." He opened the door and Jeremy followed him inside. *Shit. I need to tip the guy. I should have insisted on carrying my own damn luggage.*

He fumbled with his wallet. Two ones was too cheap, but he only had thirty-seven dollars to his name. Gulping, he pulled out a five and handed it over.

Jeremy tucked the bill discreetly into the pocket of his uniform. "Thank you, sir. Please enjoy your stay, and if you need anything, dial seventeen on the house phone."

Not fricking likely. "Sure. Thanks."

He left, and Trent stared thoughtfully at the door for a moment. A five-dollar tip for toting a couple of bags down a trail. Maybe he could get a job at a hotel. He shuddered. *Not out here, though. God no. Give me a nice, safe city.*

He hauled his bags into the bedroom and hung his suit in the closet, chuckling when he saw how many clothes Christophe thought were necessary for a three-day stay. Then, because it was his birthday, goddamn it, he unzipped the garment bag.

Holy shit. This suit was *awesome.* He pulled the pants off their hanger and held them up. Should he try them on, check out the length? Nah. He'd gone commando again, so he didn't feel up to the standard of the suit—not until he put on some underwear. And showered about three times.

He hung the pants back up carefully, in a way that would do Christophe proud, then eyed the jacket. *Should I? Oh why the hell not?* He lost the hoodie, dropping it by his feet, then carefully removed the jacket from its padded hanger. He pulled it on and it fit perfectly—across his shoulders, the length of the sleeves. *Sweet.* And it was cut close to his body too, not like the last suit he'd bought for his cousin's debutante ball, back before he left for college. He slipped it off and hung it up reverently. Wait. There was a shirt in there too. No, *two* shirts. With French cuffs.

For a minute, he was a little insulted. Was Christophe trying to bring him up to scratch, so he wouldn't feel embarrassed to be seen with him? *Hello, sow's ear. Meet silk purse.*

Or maybe he'd only wanted to do something nice for Trent's birthday, exactly as he'd said. *Stop being so damn suspicious.* Christophe had gone above and beyond in the short time they'd known one another, in ways that trumped the tangible shit. He'd encouraged Trent to put his own freaking issues aside long enough to share his only friend's wedding day. No judgment. No pressure. Just options. Trent appreciated the choice more than anything. After seven years of having no choice whatsoever, it was nice. No, way beyond nice. *Incredible.*

Maybe Christophe had been a stranger three days ago, but now he was rapidly approaching being Trent's favorite person ever. And not because he gave expensive gifts, but because he really *thought* about what Trent would need, what he would like. This wasn't a guy who'd leave a headstone in place after his son returned from the dead, just because it was inconvenient to remove it.

Who among his family and erstwhile friends had made this much of an effort lately? Hell, who had *ever* made this much effort for him? Only his grandfather, who'd had his son's number from birth, probably. He'd made sure to funnel a large part of his own fortune into Trent's trust fund.

No wonder Dad doesn't want to part with it. He always resented Grandfather for giving away an inheritance he'd counted as his own.

Suddenly, Trent's ragged hoodie seemed disrespectful in these surroundings, especially given Christophe's world-class thoughtfulness. He snatched it off the floor to stow it, but when he unzipped his duffel, its contents erupted like a clothes volcano. Jesus, he needed to do laundry, or at least sort out what was clean and what wasn't.

Later.

He wandered into the other room. The French doors opposite the fireplace opened onto a flagstone patio and beyond that ... woods. *Of course.* He closed the curtains.

A skylight over the kitchenette let in enough light for him to see the note propped against the phone. He'd thought it was some random welcome message from the resort, but the envelope had his name on it, in handwriting nearly as fancy as calligraphy.

Shit, what had they taught at that boarding school of Christophe's besides every language in the world and apparently how to illuminate your own manuscripts? He opened the envelope.

Trent, mon cher.

You have made me so very happy by accepting my invitation. I am sorry I cannot be here for your arrival, but I trust François took excellent care of you on your journey. Please make yourself at home. If you're hungry, order room service and charge it to the room. Also, I believe the resort entertainment center can provide a number of the type of films you enjoy.

I hope you liked your gift. Although it isn't a bespoke suit, it's nevertheless an excellent one, and the color will suit you admirably. Check in the desk drawer for two final gifts—one for you and one, if you permit, for me.

Trent opened the drawer. The little box tied with a dark-blue bow had a card that read *Trent.* He opened it. Cuff links in gold, set with lapis. He stroked the dark-blue stones. *Gorgeous.* He never thought he'd be interested in something this old-fashioned. *Guess I was wrong.*

The other thing in the drawer was a bag from Walgreens. He recognized it—François had tucked it discreetly under the driver's seat when he'd returned to the car after lunch. How had he gotten into the cabin—and ahead of Trent, for that matter? *Don't question Oz, the Great and Powerful.* The dude had skills, no doubt about it.

Trent checked the bag to see what rated François's stealth mission, and barked out a laugh.

Lube and condoms.

Dude, that's sooo *a present for me too.* He turned back to the note.

I expect to return by nine o'clock. If you would like to present my gift to me appropriately, be waiting in bed, naked, ready for me. Because I assure you, by the time I arrive, I shall be positively ravenous for you.

Yours,

C

Trent grinned and folded the note. Nine was a long way away, but he had a plan now. A movie. Dinner. Then a really long bath—maybe two. One before dinner and one after.

I'll be ready. Oh hell yeah, will I be ready.

CHAPTER
SEVENTEEN

Although the moon had never emerged from the clouds, Christophe's wolf time-sense told him that it must be approaching nine o'clock. Although he normally ran himself to exhaustion, the better to extend the span between transformations, tonight he'd held back, preserving energy.

For Trent.

Trent mustn't suspect how Christophe had spent his evening. *Although who would suspect anything as outlandish as the truth?*

He'd loped in a wide circle over the last few hours, keeping well inside the forest. Now he followed a creek back to where Anton would be waiting. Anticipation thrummed in his veins, and he sped up. *Soon. Soon I will be a man once more. Soon I will be with my mate. Not much further. Just past that thicket of— Shite!*

Christophe tried to stop his headlong rush, his paws scrabbling in the dirt and fir mulch, but to no avail. He crashed into a huge patch of Scotch broom, and pollen from the yellow flowers rained down on him like poisonous fairy dust.

He sneezed and sneezed again. He pawed at his nose, which was already clogging. His sense of smell would be bollixed completely until he could rid his fur of contamination. *Shower. Yes.* Thank God the man was less sensitive to the vile powder than the wolf.

Still sneezing, he bounded up the side of the hill to the rocky ledge and paced into the cave.

Empty.

No Anton, and what was more alarming, no clothing.

The fur on Christophe's spine rose. Unless he could lie down on at least one article of clothing that held the essence of himself as a man—sweat, tears, semen, even something as elusive as a fresh, untainted scent—he'd be unable to change back.

He lowered his nose to the ground and investigated the cave. The dirt floor showed signs of a scuffle. *Damn it to hell.* He could barely smell a thing. Was that Anton's scent? Was it overlaid with the taint of fear? He couldn't tell. A growl took him, nearly vibrating his bones. *If some intruder has hurt my brother . . .*

Exactly what could he do? Without his clothing, he was trapped in his wolf form, and if Anton had run afoul of someone— *No. Don't think of that. Think instead of options.*

Since Anton had driven him here, he had no scent to guide him back to the resort. Even when he found his way, how was he to get into his cabin without hands? He whined. *Trent. Trent is there.* He couldn't bear to frighten him, but if Anton was in trouble—

Think of that later. For now, act.

Despite an impaired sense of smell, his wolf had a better notion of direction than he did as a human. He cast about until he oriented himself. *There. North.* He took off, racing flat out through the trees. His brother's life could be at stake.

Whoever had dared to threaten him would pay.

Trent awoke on a scream, his throat raw and his neck aching from the rope. He sat up, drawing his knees to his chest, panting in the aftermath of the nightmare. *What the fuck?* After last night, he'd hoped he was free of it. Anyway, the nightmare never hit until midnight and it was—

Midnight, according to the bloody red digits on the bedside clock.

Shit. He'd fallen asleep after his second bath, feeling so decadent and naughty, naked between the sheets waiting for Christophe to return.

Yeah, how stupid does it feel to use that much lube and then not need it?

His hands still trembled; his breath continued to stutter. He wanted Christophe *now*, to make it better, to make it go away with his touch. Where the hell was he? Could something have happened to him? He hadn't said what he was doing, after all. What if there'd been an accident? Would anyone know to tell Trent if there had been? Shit, the only person who knew he and Christophe were acquainted, let alone fucking, was Logan, and it wasn't like anyone would notify *him*. He barely knew Christophe.

Trent struggled out of bed, the sheets having tangled around his legs as he'd thrashed in the throes of his nightmare. He flipped on the lights, blinking in the glare. Maybe Christophe had called or left a message and Trent hadn't heard it.

He hurried into the other room where he'd left his cell phone on the desk. It was dead. Just freaking fabulous—he'd forgotten to charge it. He ran back to the bedroom, pawed through his backpack for the charger, and plugged it in next to the bed.

Since whatever the trouble was, he didn't want to meet it naked, he grabbed the first reasonably clean T-shirt from his overflowing duffel and yanked it over his head. He snagged his jeans from earlier out of the bathroom and pulled them on—commando, because locating clean underwear was not on his timeline.

"Come on, come on, you fucking phone. Charge." He fairly danced in place, his arms wrapped across his stomach. Damn it, it was fucking *cold* in here. He pulled on his previously scorned PSU hoodie. Jesus, it stank. He *really* needed to do laundry, or else buy a new sweatshirt.

Finally, the phone let him power it on, although he was tethered to the wall by the cord. He punched in Christophe's number. It rang six times and went to voice mail.

"Damn it." Trent hung up and dialed a second time. Same deal. He dialed again. And again. Fuck leaving a message. He needed to hear Christophe's *real* voice. To know he was safe. He punched the number a fifth time, and on the fourth ring, it picked up.

Oh thank fuck. "Chr—"

"What is it? Why do you keep calling?"

The voice, deeper than Christophe's and angry, stopped Trent's breath.

"I— Sorry. Wrong number."

He disconnected the call and threw the phone on the floor as if it was a snake. *He hooked up with someone else. He knew I was waiting, and he fucking hooked up with someone else.*

Trent had a sudden horrifying thought. He checked the corners of the room for the telltale blink of video-camera lights, for the flash of camera lenses. Shit, he had no clue how to check for electronic surveillance shit. Could all of this—Christophe's attention to him, luring him out here, lulling him with gifts and luxuries, be nothing but an elaborate sting, an attempt by Bishop to get him to confess to his own kidnapping? Or by his father to find grounds to keep Trent's money?

Shit, he'd confessed the truth to Christophe, every fucking detail. That'd be enough to get him involuntarily committed—he'd be declared non compos mentis and be at his father's mercy for good. *Trapped again. No choice. No way out.*

His heart hammered so that he couldn't hear himself think. But Christophe . . . he wouldn't. Would he? Shit, what did he really know about the guy? Just because Trent had found Christophe's touch comforting and arousing in equal measure, didn't mean Christophe thought of Trent as anything more than a slacker ex-student with a wardrobe one step away from the dumpster.

He couldn't risk it. He had to get out. Now.

He smooshed everything back into his duffel and fought the zipper closed. The phone had a sliver of a charge. Too bad. He couldn't hang around to let it finish. As he slung the duffel over his shoulder and grabbed his backpack, his gaze snagged on the garment bag, half-hidden among all Christophe's clothes.

Fuck it. If he brought me out here to stiff me, I'm taking the damn suit. Payment for services rendered.

He draped the bag over his arm and hurried into the living room. When he opened the door, though, he heard footsteps on the path, the murmur of voices. He eased the door closed. Whoever was out there might not be here for him, but he couldn't take the chance. That left . . .

The patio.

Damn it, he'd have to go out under the trees. But given the choice between a night in the forest and a lifetime locked in the loony bin permanently, he picked the fucking trees.

He flipped on the rear light—he didn't care if someone was outside the front door, he refused to step straight out into the dark—opened the curtains, unlocked the French doors, and slipped outside. As soon as the door latched, he realized two things—he had no way to get back to Portland, and he'd left his key card inside the room.

Fucking. Perfect.

CHAPTER
EIGHTEEN

What felt like hours later, but was probably only slightly past midnight, Christophe finally arrived at the resort, half-lame from his desperate race through the forest. He crouched down in the underbrush at the edge of the parking lot, which held far more cars than when he and Anton had arrived earlier. Loud voices, music, and the occasional burst of raucous laughter wafted from the main deck.

He'd shaken much of the pollen off his fur during his run, so his sense of smell was returning. *There.* Not Anton, but Trent, his scent tinged with distress. Christophe's hackles rose. *Trent needs me. How can I help him though, trapped as I am, and with Anton in trouble?*

But if he was to help his brother, he'd need assistance of his own. Trent was the only person other than Anton who knew he was here. Therefore, he had to find a way to communicate with Trent, even if it set their relationship back when Trent found out about Christophe's supernatural disability.

Two women crunched across the gravel toward his hiding place. Afraid to move lest they spot him and became terrified, he remained as motionless as possible. One of them was tall, the moon that had finally emerged from the clouds backlighting her curly hair. He recognized her scent from Stumptown Spirits. *Julie.* Riley's friend.

He recognized the other woman too, the server from the bar. *Heather.* Judging by their scents, the two would be engaging in sexual congress with one another soon. But hopefully not in the parking lot.

"The resort has poker chips. Couldn't we use those?" Heather first smoothed her hair, then tossed her ponytail, causing her to veer closer to Julie until their arms brushed. Neither woman moved away.

"Hell no. This is a themed party, and when I produce something, I produce the *shit* out of it. Generic stuff won't do. I've got Logan-and-Riley branded supplies for everything. But we need to hurry. The strip poker game is scheduled immediately after the Jell-O shots, before pin the dick on the porn star."

Heather giggled. "Where did you get a life-sized full-frontal cutout of Logan?"

Julie nudged her. "Don't question my superpowers. Just be glad I use them for evil, not good."

"Did you see his face when he realized the picture didn't have a dick?"

"Are you kidding? I had Zack film it in close-up. It's going in the wedding video. I'm thinking we'll have an entire YouTube channel devoted to the footage from the party. What do you think?"

"I think we better hurry up or Logan will have burned the cutout in the fire pit."

"Good point. Grab those beer mats. I'll get the feather boas and the tiaras."

The two women rummaged around in the back of a van, juggling several boxes. Christophe noticed with interest that they were reaching across each other for their targets rather than simply switching places for efficiency.

"I think that's everything." Heather pushed a stray strand of hair off her forehead as a roar rose from the lodge deck. "Oh no. Do you think they've started the drag queen race without us?"

"They can't. We've got the stilettos. Grab that box?"

They fumbled around, Julie trying to close the rear door with her elbow.

"Hold on, Julie. Your vest is caught on the latch." Heather propped her box against the van with one hip and fussed with something. "There." She patted Julie's fleece vest back into place, then seemed to realize that her hand was resting on the other woman's hip. "Oh. Um. Sorry." She clutched her box again.

"Not me. If my hands weren't full, I'd—" She kissed Heather softly on the lips, causing Heather to lose her grip on the box. It tipped, scattering a few small, flat objects on the gravel, but the two women didn't notice.

Another roar rose from the deck, and they broke apart. Heather sighed. "Wish we didn't have to—"

"Me too." Julie's smile glinted in the moonlight. "But later, okay?"

Heather nodded, and the two turned, strolling back toward the lodge shoulder to shoulder.

Once they were safely out of range, Christophe crept forward, investigating what they'd left behind. If he was to convince Trent of his identity, he needed to do something so out of character for a wild wolf that Trent would understand what he was trying to say. He nudged one of the squares of cardboard with his paw. It was a beer mat from Stumptown Spirits, the same kind that he and Trent had played their game with on the night they met.

He trapped it between his paws until he could pick it up in his teeth.

This would do. It must. Anton's life might depend on it.

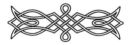

Once the people on the path had passed by harmlessly, Trent built himself a fortress on the patio with a pair of Adirondack chairs and a wrought iron table. He jammed his duffel between the chairs and sat on it, his back to the wall, his backpack in his lap, and the garment bag draped over the chair arms like a half tent. His cell phone lay on the table, plugged into the outside outlet. The resort's guests must insist on staying connected while they commune with goddamn fucking nature. At least there was free wi-fi, although with this tree coverage, Trent had no idea how they managed it. Maybe they pinged the signal off the bats that swooped under the trees.

The battery indicator had finally inched into amber, although it had seemed to take for-fucking-ever.

Why do you care how long it takes? It's not like you have anywhere to go or any way to get there.

The party up at the lodge was getting even more raucous, with no sign of winding down. He could go up there. See if he could snag a minute or two alone with Logan. Maybe float enough of a loan to return to Portland.

And then what? Camp out in Stumptown Spirits until he's back from his honeymoon?

As he thought about it, maybe it wasn't such a stupid idea after all. Joseph Geddes was in charge. If anyone knew what Trent was going through, it would be him.

We're in the same boat now. No family. No money. No future.

Except Joseph had one up on Trent. He had a job. A place to live. A future as a business owner, once Logan made good on his plan to sign over the bar.

Wait. Logan lived above the bar. He'd said so. Maybe Trent could crash there while Logan and Riley were off God-knows-where, basking in the wedding afterglow. Except—shit—he'd said it was being gutted while they were on their honeymoon, hadn't he? If he wanted to find out for sure, he'd have to dare the path and the lodge.

But interrupt Logan's prewedding party? Face the undoubtedly drunken guests, half of whom were probably from *Haunted to the Max*, which meant they'd seen Trent at his sniveling, basket-case worst?

No, thank you.

He'd figure something else out. He wasn't sure how, but—

The underbrush at the edge of the patio rustled, and Trent dropped his phone in his lap. *Was that a big rustle or a little rustle? Why does there have to be a rustle at all?* He tugged at the chairs, trying to angle them so they formed more of a barricade, but the things weighed a fucking ton. He hunched down to make himself as small a target as he could, pulling his hoodie up around his neck.

You're gonna feel damn stupid if it's a bunny rabbit or a squirrel.

Unfortunately, the less alarming things probably weren't active at night. Raccoons, now those bastards were vicious. And opossums? Just weird.

The rustle came again, getting closer.

He clutched his backpack and held it in front of him like a shield. *Like that'll help if it's a bear or a mountain lion or a chupacabra or some shit.* He couldn't believe that he'd used to court thrills like this on purpose. That he'd staked out empty graveyards and lonely crossroads, actually *wanting* a creepy-ass creature to appear.

Yeah, learned your lesson about that one, didn't you?

He stared at the bushes.

Something. Stared. Back.

Why couldn't it have been a bunny rabbit, damn it? But no, this thing was *big*, judging by the placement of the golden eyes glinting in the patio light.

Shit-shit-shit. The thing didn't move. Just kept staring at him. *Trying to decide if I'd be better with sriracha or guacamole? Maybe a little ranch dressing?*

He pressed his back against the wall until the logs nearly became one with his spine.

The thing came closer.

"Oh God." He clenched his eyes shut. This wasn't exactly what he'd had in mind when he'd hoped for another way out.

The rustling started again, then stopped, followed by a soft flap and the scrabbling of claws on stone. *Claws. It has claws. They* scrabble*!* If they could scrabble on stone, what would they do to his skin?

He braced himself, hands over his head, but nothing happened and nothing happened and nothing happened, except an owl hooted nearby.

Finally he peeked out from under his hood.

Wolf. There is a fucking wolf on the patio. And it was definitely a wolf. He remembered Logan mocking him that night in their dorm room when he'd told him about the legend trippers in France who'd seen a wolf—and that it must have been a werewolf because there were no wolves in France.

". . . it was somebody's German shepherd."

No way could you mistake this for anything but a wolf. For one thing, its head was huge. Its fur was gray and brown brindle on its face and back, but shaded to cream on its chest and paws—which were nearly as big as Trent's feet.

It was lying on its belly on the patio, those ginormous paws stretched in front of it like it was giving thanks to the god of easy prey. There was something flat and brown between them, something about the size of a maple leaf. *Where could it have found a maple tree? The whole damn forest is full of evergreens.* Trent squinted, trying to make the thing out. Squarish. Rounded corners. Too regular for a leaf. *Holy fucking shit.*

A beer mat.

What kind of wolf carried a beer mat? *A party animal, har har har.* He pinched the bridge of his nose. Even faced with death-by-fang-and-claw, he couldn't shake his assitude.

He peered at the beer mat more closely and made out the logo on one side. *Stumptown Spirits.*

"How...?"

The wolf held his gaze for another maybe ten seconds—which was a hella long time to get stared down by an animal the size of a MINI Cooper—then it nudged the mat with its nose, first tilting it one way, so the logo was visible. Another stare-down. Then, in what seemed a calculated move—could wolves calculate?—it nudged it the other way and shifted its paws so the mat fell logo-side down.

What the fuck?

The wolf raised its head, holding Trent's gaze again, and this time Trent *looked* at its eyes. Dark amber, like Woodford's Reserve, last seen in a glass at Stumptown Spirits, when he and Christophe had flirted with the beer mats.

He gulped and pushed his hood back. God, this was in-fucking-sane, but then, wasn't he the guy who'd spent seven years in ghostly limbo? Weird shit was totally in his wheelhouse, whether he wanted it to be or not. "C-C-Christophe?"

CHAPTER
NINETEEN

Christophe was so relieved when Trent recognized him that he whined.

How embarrassing.

He crept forward, keeping his belly low to the ground, watching carefully to make sure Trent wasn't too frightened.

"No. No, no, no. I knew I shouldn't have come. I should have deleted the damn voice mail. If I'd had any other choice, anyplace else to go, I wouldn't have . . ." Trent pressed the heels of his hands against his eyes. "God, a werewolf? Are you fucking kidding me?"

Christophe whined again and hunkered down, lowering his head to his paws.

Trent dropped his hands, eyes blazing in the dim light as if he were the wolf. "Dude. Couldn't you have maybe *mentioned* this? Like in passing? 'Hey, I've got this other gig. I'm a *freaking werewolf.*" Trent's head fell back against the cabin wall. "Jesus *fuck.*"

Christophe crept forward another few inches, stopping when Trent glared at him. Christophe's ears pricked up, then flattened when he saw the sheen of tears in Trent's eyes. *Ah, no, cher. I am sorry. Please do not cry.*

"I don't want to know this. I was done with legend tripping for good. Didn't I already pay seven years' worth of dues? Why won't legends leave me the fuck alone?" He drew his knees to his chest and rested his forehead on them. "The only live person who's wanted to touch me since 2009 is less normal than the fricking ghosts. At least they were human once."

Christophe's chest constricted. *Inhuman.* Trent saw him as a monster, precisely as Christophe knew himself to be.

"Why can't we go back to the way we were before?"

Trent's voice cracked on the last word, and Christophe wanted to howl. Instead he closed the last few inches and nosed Trent's ankle. "Don't."

Christophe did it once more, adding a soft whine.

"I said don't. Aw shit." He raised his head. "Do you know how crazy I look, talking to a wolf?"

No crazier than I'd have looked had I confessed to becoming one.

Christophe eased his head under Trent's hand. Trent snatched it away, then hesitantly extended it again. Christophe remained absolutely immobile.

"If I'm wrong about this, I'm about to get mauled, but what the hell. It's not like I could outrun you." He laid his hand on Christophe's withers and Christophe closed his eyes in bliss. No one had ever touched him while he was in his wolf form. Not even Anton or his father. He'd had no idea of the wave of comfort it would send coursing through him, settling him, calming him.

Perhaps the touch of any friend would have done the same, but he suspected that Trent's touch was extraordinary. Christophe's reaction wasn't sexual—he never felt that brand of desire while in wolf form—but protective and possessive nonetheless.

"Hey, your fur is really thick. Not soft, but wow." Trent dug his fingers through the fur at Christophe's crest. "*Really* thick. But it's soft down at the bottom."

Trent set his backpack aside and scooted closer. Christophe inhaled his scent: clean and a little spicy, as if he'd used a scented soap. Also . . . lube. Trent had done it. *He followed the instructions. He was waiting for me.*

If Christophe's possessive instincts hadn't fired before, they did now, on every possible circuit. This man was *his*, and woe to anyone who tried to harm him. He leaned his head against Trent's knee for a moment.

Trent put a trembling hand on his head and stroked. Christophe closed his eyes again and huffed. *Comfort. Belonging. Not only does he belong to me, but I belong to him, although he may not know it yet.*

As much as he'd prefer to revel longer in this new knowledge, this connection, Christophe had a mission. Recognition was only the first hurdle. He had to find a way to convey the need to locate Anton.

He raised his head and Trent reared back. "Whoa. Sorry. Didn't mean to—"

Christophe whined once more—*humiliating, but for Trent, I'll gladly sacrifice my pride*—and nudged Trent's leg with his nose. Then he slowly rose to his full height, Trent's eyes growing wider with each inch.

"Jesus fuck, dude, you are *huge*. Are real wolves this big?" Trent stood, holding up his palms. "No offense, I mean, not that you're not a real wolf, or whatever, but you're as tall as my fucking *hip*."

Christophe trotted off the patio. Once he'd cleared the shrubbery, he glanced back. Trent remained on the terrace, his hands thrust into the pocket of his sweatshirt.

Christophe took two deliberate steps forward, then stared over his shoulder, holding Trent's gaze. Trent still didn't move, although his shoulders hunched and his mouth turned down. The sight pierced Christophe's heart.

He yipped and jerked his nose at the woods, trying to entice Trent off the terrace.

Trent hunched further. "Yeah, I get it. Timmy's down the well."

What? Christophe yipped again.

"It's— I didn't tell you before, but being under the trees really wigs me out. Can't you just, I don't know, do whatever it is here?"

Shite, how can I communicate what I need? But he had no alternative. Staying here would do no good—the cabin held nothing that would solve his problem. He recalled Anton's half-mocking words when his brother had volunteered to pack for him. There would be nothing inside that hadn't been freshly laundered or cleaned. Christophe himself had insisted on that. Although he'd brought at least half a dozen pairs of shoes, they were leather—the skin of a prey animal. Useless.

Jesu, how idiotic could he be?

Yet he *had* to know that Anton was safe and well. Just the sight of him would be enough. Ordinarily, he'd have remained on guard over Christophe's clothing, but occasionally in the past he'd been called away. *That must be what happened. An emergency. Perhaps a call from Papa.* Then somehow he'd been delayed, and must be frantic wondering if Christophe was all right.

But there was that scuffed dirt in the cave. What if the delay was more sinister?

He paced back onto the terrace, approaching Trent slowly. He took the hem of that disreputable sweatshirt gently in his teeth and tugged.

Trent sighed. "Fine. But you've got a fuck-ton of explaining to do, Mr. Wolf, once you've shed the fur coat."

When the wolf—Christophe—trotted off the patio again, Trent followed. But Christophe didn't head for the path to the lodge—which would have been bad enough—no, he dove directly into the forest.

Oh shit. This is not gonna be good.

Trent made it right up to the edge of the clearing, under the canopy of fir branches, and then stalled.

Can't do it. Too much. Too soon.

The wolf—he still couldn't tag it as Christophe—poked its nose out of the underbrush and yipped, an odd, almost breathless sound, as if he wasn't accustomed to making it.

"Sorry. I—I can't."

The wolf bounded out of the woods in a rustle of leaves, and Trent couldn't help it. He flinched, stumbling back as his heart jumped into overdrive. He clenched his eyes shut and willed his anxiety to back the fuck off, but it continued to bloom in his chest, paralyzing his lungs.

Then something big and warm and *alive* pressed against his side, and suddenly Trent could breathe again, the contact derailing his panic attack. He cracked open his eyelids. *Yep. That's still a wolf—a wolf for Chrissake!* Trent ought to be freaking out *more*, not wanting to hug it like it was an animate teddy bear.

But it—*he*—wasn't just a wolf. *He's Christophe. I'm not alone. Remember that, asshole.*

Christophe-the-wolf nudged Trent's fist where it was clenched at his side, insinuating his head under it and wiggling forward until Trent's hand was in the ruff of fur around his neck. Trent took the hint and grabbed a handful. *God. Even better.*

When Christophe paced forward, Trent took a deep breath and let himself be pulled along.

Surprisingly, if he didn't count the fact Christophe seemed determined to lead him through every patch of blackberry brambles on the north side of Mount Hood, it wasn't too bad. After all, what could hurt him when he had a wolf on his side?

Other than, you know, the *wolf*. Jesus *fuck*, he was seriously disturbed.

Christophe led him in a wide arc around the lodge terrace where the party continued in full swing. Trent shuddered. If he compared being up there, with a so-happy-he's-stupid Logan and a bunch of drunken paranormal investigators, with being down here amid the fucking trees accompanied by a wolf-who-used-to-be-a-guy, he preferred where he was.

Seriously disturbed. But what the fuck.

Another blackberry vine scored a line across the back of his hand. "Dude. There's a perfectly good path not thirty feet away. Do we have to play wilderness trek? Is that some kind of wolf thing?"

"Hey," someone called from up the hill. "Is somebody there? The manager told us not to piss in the woods, man."

Christophe cocked his head at Trent. "Okay," Trent whispered. "I get it."

They stayed still—difficult, because Trent was *positive* something was creeping up his back—until the partygoer staggered past on the trail and up the steps of the deck.

Only then did Christophe huff and continue, with Trent glommed onto his side like a leech. No way was he letting Christophe out of his sight while he was stuck in the middle of all this . . . foliage.

As far as Trent was concerned, the resort had done *too* good a job keeping the landscape undisturbed. Aside from an occasional drift of laughter from the lodge, or the glimmer of light between the trees from another one of the secluded cabins, Trent and Christophe might as well be in the Forest Primeval.

Once they'd gotten far enough from the lodge that the noise had faded completely, Christophe led them up onto a narrow dirt road. *Finally.*

He put his nose in the air and sniffed, then plunged into the woods on the other side. *Damn it!*

But at least this time they didn't have far to go. Christophe was padding silently toward the unmistakable flickering glow of a fire.

What the fuck? A forest fire? *So* not good. It was early enough in the season that the forest wasn't dry, but seriously? Open flames plus trees were never a brilliant idea.

Once they'd gotten closer, though, Trent saw that the fire was contained in one of those enclosed outdoor fireplaces on the patio of another cabin. Christophe halted while they were still screened by the trees, fairly vibrating under Trent's hand.

Guess this must be the place.

Trent shifted from foot to foot. Someone was obviously home, unless they were an idiot who'd been careless enough to leave a fire burning. *Nobody's that stupid. Even I know better than that, and I've probably got the brain of a nineteen-year-old.* Make that a twenty-year-old. His birthday was well and truly past.

The French doors opened and a man emerged, a tarp-wrapped bundle in his arms, and left the door ajar. Trent frowned. Something about the guy's attitude didn't feel right. *I've seen him before too. But where?*

Christophe's muscles bunched under Trent's hand, as if he were about to leap out of the trees, but Trent hunkered down, draping his arm across Christophe's back, and whispered into his furry ear. "Shhh. Wait."

When the stranger turned his head, Trent got a good look at his profile, and then he remembered. *The elevator outside Christophe's condo.* He squinted, studying the guy's face. His nose had the same aristocratic slope as Christophe's. A relative, then.

The guy glanced back at the door and set the tarp bundle on an Adirondack chair. He unfolded the tarp and lifted something, giving it a sharp shake, like the crack of a gunshot in the silent woods.

Even in the flickering light of the fire, Trent recognized it.

Christophe's jacket. *What the ever-loving fuck?*

Christophe tried to surge forward again, but Trent threw his other arm around him, tightening his hold. "Wait. This doesn't feel right. Just wait." Although Christophe trembled, he didn't break away. "Good dog."

Christophe stared at Trent and his canine eyebrow canted in what was obviously the wolf equivalent of *Really, dude?*

Patio Guy checked the jacket pockets, pulling an object out and holding it in his palm for a moment before enclosing it in his fist. He held the jacket up, studying it in the light.

Then he threw it in the fire.

Christophe jerked in Trent's grasp, his chest vibrating.

"I know what you mean," Trent whispered. "I loved that jacket."

The guy watched the jacket burn for a minute, the light flaring and highlighting the satisfied smile on his face. Then he uncurled his fingers and held up the thing he'd taken from the pocket. It glinted gold in the glow from the fire. He smiled again and slipped it onto his left pinky.

He retrieved something else from the bundle—something white and less bulky than the jacket. *Undershirt.* He balled it up and shot it into the fire after the jacket.

"Good-bye, *mon frère*," he said with a vicious lilt to the last words. "And good riddance."

CHAPTER
TWENTY

Christophe trembled in Trent's embrace, half in anger, half in despair. Trent stared at him, eyes wide, and mouthed *Brother? WTF?*

Yes. My brother. His friend, his companion, his *hero.* Betraying him in this way. How could he do it? What had Christophe done to deserve this? For Anton knew what it meant to destroy Christophe's clothing, his only means of returning to his human form.

Anton intended for him to remain a wolf forever.

The signet now circling Anton's finger told its own tale, didn't it? Anton wanted to be the heir. He had claimed to be so worried about their father's response to Christophe's decision to abdicate—what did he think *this* would do to the man?

Christophe quivered, and Trent's arms tightened around him, centering him, until the jagged red urge to leap onto the terrace and take Anton's throat in his jaws receded.

You didn't need to do this. I would have given it all to you. I told you so.

It might not yet be too late. Anton hadn't burned his shirt or pants yet, let alone his socks. Christophe needed only a single article of clothing and he could return to himself. He could reason with Anton, discover why he'd chosen this path. Christophe would never trust him again—at least not with his clothes—but this needn't end with Christophe locked permanently in a form he loathed.

The door behind Anton opened, and Christophe nearly launched himself out of the woods despite Trent's restraining hold when Etienne Melion emerged. Christophe hadn't been imagining his scent; the bastard was here in the flesh. Had he threatened Anton in some way? Christophe wouldn't have put it past him. He'd always been an evil-minded, sadistic shite, as far back as their first childhood meeting, when Christophe had discovered him torturing a wren.

Melion strolled over to stand next to the fire. "Really, Anton. Isn't this a trifle melodramatic, even for you?"

"I could have sent them out for dry cleaning, but where's the satisfaction in that?" Anton lifted Christophe's shirt from the bundle and held it up in the light. "Do you know how much he spent with his tailor? Even Papa buys his shirts off the rack." He took out his pocket knife, *snicked* it open, and slit the shirt from the back of the collar to hem. "Not that this one will help him now."

Etienne chuckled. "So vindictive. I knew I liked you better than your prig of a brother." He picked up Christophe's pants and shook them as if he were enticing a puppy to play. "Feel the urge to savage these a bit before you incinerate them?"

"No." He snatched the pants from Etienne and flung them into the fire along with the shirt. Christophe's belly clenched when Anton wadded up the remaining clothes and hurled them into the flames. "Now I wish it over and done."

"Were those the last?"

"Only what he wore this evening. I'll clear out his room later. All of those are clean, however, so they're no use to him."

"Excellent." Etienne stroked the back of Anton's head and neck. "I was pleased to get your call. Overdue to my mind."

"Mine too."

"I can give you what you want. But you understand trade agreements, Anton. What price do you place on control of Clavret et Cie, unencumbered by your hide-bound sire or your short-sighted brother? With you at the helm, but with a werewolf in the wings to enforce your claim? Hmm?" He gripped Anton's neck and shook him slightly. "What price would you pay for your dream?"

Anton's spine was rigid. "I told you on the phone."

"Tell me again."

"Anything. Anything you want."

"Then let us proceed." Etienne inhaled, long and slow, his nostrils flaring. "I can smell him on you, you know." His eyes flashed yellow in the firelight. "Down."

Anton clenched his teeth. "Etienne."

"Consider this your first lesson in how the Old Families conduct backroom negotiations."

As Etienne unbuckled his belt and unzipped his fly, Anton dropped heavily to his knees. When Etienne pulled his cock out of his briefs, a howl threatened to burst from Christophe's throat, but Trent clutched him more tightly.

"Hands behind your back," Etienne growled. "And open."

Anton obeyed, and Etienne grabbed his hair and thrust into his mouth. While Anton trembled and groaned, Etienne bared his teeth at the dancing flames.

Trent couldn't look. While he appreciated porn as much as the next guy, the live sex show with humiliation sauce on the side was more than he could handle. Besides, this was Christophe's *brother*, for fuck's sake. Although he'd just confessed to hating Christophe enough to do something dire to him—not that Trent was sure of the details—nobody deserved to have their privacy violated like this.

Judging by the tension in Christophe's body, he wasn't exactly a fan either. If Trent released him, he wasn't sure who Christophe would go for first: his brother, or the guy who was face-fucking him. Either way, if he killed one of them, it wouldn't be good for anybody.

So he held tight, pulled Christophe's head against his chest, and buried his face in the rough fur.

After what felt like forever, Etienne shouted, followed by a choking sound from Anton. *Guess backroom negotiators aren't polite enough to pull out.*

Trent peeked through the foliage, but kept Christophe's head against his chest because no way did he need to see any of this. Etienne was buckling his belt while Anton was still kneeling at his feet, wiping his mouth.

"You're sure about the ranchers' routine?" He didn't offer to help Anton rise, and obviously hadn't allowed the guy to come—Anton's trousers were bulging at the front. *Douche bag.* Anton had agreed to the deal though, and must have gotten into it a little, considering said bulge.

"Yes." Anton pushed himself to his feet. "They never arrive at the north pastures until well into the morning."

"It won't do for me to arrive too early, then. We want to make sure they get the full effect, and know exactly who—or what—to blame for their poor, slaughtered sheep. In the meantime . . ." He grabbed Anton by the back of the neck. "Your next lesson will help pass the time."

They returned inside, Etienne pushing Anton ahead of him.

Christophe lunged, almost escaping Trent's grasp. Trent grabbed him in a nearly full-body tackle because, Jesus *fuck*, wolves were big— holding him until the door closed behind the two men.

Christophe growled, but his gaze was fixed on the door, so Trent knew who the anger was for. *Disaster in the making, right here.* He got up and hauled Christophe farther into the trees, putting more distance between them and the danger zone.

"Look, dude, I know you want to rip this guy apart. Maybe both of them. But you can't. You need to *think*. That guy, Etienne, he's going to pretend to be a wolf, yeah? Frame you for killing stock?"

Christophe stared at him, and Trent was amazed at how much sarcasm could show on a furry face.

"So you can't *be* a wolf when it happens." If wolves could snort, this one did. *Canine disgust. Nice.* "And you can't do any other wolfy things in the meantime."

He sat down next to Christophe in their underbrush fortress and hoped like hell none of the bushes were poison oak. From this vantage point, at the side of the cabin, they could see if anyone left by either the front or rear doors. "At least you know their plan now. So change back and confront them."

Christophe huffed and laid his head on his paws, his snout pointedly turned away from Trent.

"I know it's obvious, but work with me here. Is this, like, a full-moon thing? Because if you could change whenever you wanted, you'd probably already have done it, right?" Christophe's ear twitched. "Do we wait until dawn? Will you change back then?" Another twitch, then a head shake that scattered fur in the air and all over the front of Trent's hoodie. "Come on, dude, give me something besides doggy snark."

Christophe raised his head—finally—and, God, his eyes were so . . . sad. Like in those commercials of dogs in cages at the pound, waiting to be put down. He sighed and rested his head on Trent's leg.

"Okay. I guess we wait and see what happens next." He put his arm around Christophe's neck, amazed all over again that he wasn't freaking out. *Maybe that'll come later. Delayed hysteria.* But unlike in the aftermath of his nightmares, he had no urge to run. Not from Christophe. Christophe wasn't like the implacable ghosts, or the hangman with his rope. He was a haven, a calm harbor, sheltering Trent regardless of fur quotient.

Yep, here I am. Cuddling with a werewolf. In his old legend-tripping days, this would have scored him major points with his group. If fact, they'd have probably crowned him their goddamn king. While those lame legend trippers in France had only *seen* a werewolf, Trent was hugging proof that the legend was real, and that proof currently wanted to take the head off his own brother. *No wonder there aren't many of them around.*

Trent leaned against Christophe and resigned himself to being bored. *Beats the hell out of being terrified.* But with a wolf beside him—with *Christophe* beside him—not even the forest could frighten him.

Trent jerked awake, disoriented. Above him, the pearling morning sky was visible through a canopy of fir branches, and beneath him was an extremely furry pillow. He bolted upright, heart racing. *Woods. Trees.* He checked behind him. *Wolf.* Oh. Right.

Wait. "Christophe? It's daylight. How come you're still a wolf?"

Christophe cocked one eyebrow, and Trent felt stupid. *Not like he can tell you the problem, idiot. He's a wolf, and you're not Dr. fricking Dolittle.*

He blinked the sleep out of his eyes, his mouth dry and foul-tasting. *God, what I wouldn't give for a glass of water and a toothbrush.* Shit, might as well wish for an airlift back to Portland—it was probably just as likely.

The forest seemed to have vomited on them overnight—twigs and brown fir needles were stuck to his jeans and hoodie, and more decorated Christophe's fur. Christophe sprang to his feet—well, paws—and shook himself, scattering the detritus.

Trent shielded his eyes. "Dude." *Too bad I can't clean up like that.* He brushed at his sweatshirt, but the damn needles clung like Velcro. He stood up and peered through the branches at the cabin. What had woken him? Voices? There didn't seem to be any activity going on. The windows were dark, the fire long dead.

Trent patted Christophe's back tentatively. "Just so you know, I'll help. Whatever it takes. I mean, I heard those guys plotting, so I can be a witness." Yeah, he had sooo much credibility. He could just imagine telling his good buddy Detective Bishop that two wealthy European dudes were plotting to slaughter a bunch of sheep to frame another wealthy European dude who could turn into a wolf, but apparently had some trouble turning back.

Trent regretted taunting Bishop with the ghost war story back at the airport now. He'd probably dismiss this story as more of Trent's smart-assery. *Talk about the boy who cried "wolf."*

"Well, maybe that won't work so great, but we'll think of something. First we need to figure out—"

The front door opened and Etienne emerged, jangling his keys. Christophe lurched forward, but Trent buried both hands in his neck fur and pulled him back.

"Chill," he whispered.

Etienne's head jerked up and Trent ducked. *Shit, did he hear that?* He eased all the way down next to Christophe and held his breath, peering through the veil of undergrowth. Etienne raised his nose in the air as if he were sniffing something. Anton stepped out of the door, and Etienne glanced at him irritably.

"I thought I—" He shook his head. "Never mind. Directions?"

"Go up to the main highway and head south for about ten miles. There's a forestry road on the left. Park there and head southeast for a couple of miles to the cave. You should be able to pick up his trail."

"As long as you aren't nearby to throw me off the scent. Is everything else in order?"

Anton nodded. "I'll contact my father shortly with the news."

"A few hours more and then we celebrate." Etienne grinned at Anton. "How do you propose we do that?"

"I want—" Anton licked his lips. "Your choice, Etienne."

Etienne clucked his tongue. "You almost slipped, Anton. You made a recovery, true, but a slip like that in negotiations could cost us dearly. Shall we discuss your punishment later, so that such a thing does not happen in the future?"

Anton pressed his lips together for an instant before inclining his head. "As you wish."

"You're learning. How satisfactory." He inhaled deeply. "Ah, the shame of a Clavret. You've no idea how sweet the smell." He gripped the back of Anton's neck—hard, to judge by Anton's grimace. "Meet me at the rendezvous. Don't be late."

Christophe vibrated against Trent's leg with a silent growl. Trent glanced down at him and mouthed, *What an asshole.*

Etienne strode off toward a Ferrari parked under a tree on the other side of the cabin. Anton watched him go, but once Etienne had climbed into the car, he turned, and the expression on his face was murderous. *Oho. So you don't altogether like playing the submissive bitch, Brother Anton. From what I've seen of the other dude, you'd better fucking get used to it.*

Anton slammed the cabin door, the sound masked by the Ferrari's engine as Etienne backed out and shot up the road in a shower of gravel.

Christophe bolted forward, and Trent lost his grip on the heavy fur. *Shit, is he about to confront his brother? Not good.* But instead, he bounded away in a wide circle around the cabin, then took off after Etienne.

Dude. Chasing cars? Seriously?

"Just fucking great." Trent eyed the woods behind him. *Not going in there by myself, no matter what last night was like.* But where else could he go? He had no fricking room at the inn. He couldn't just camp out here until Christophe came back.

If he comes back. Trent's hands turned cold, his stomach roiling. Christophe was heading right for the place these guys wanted him—into the crosshairs of a bunch of pissed-off ranchers. *The only person he's got on his side at the moment is me: Trent Pielmeyer, perpetual fuckup, who got his own ass handed to him by a forest full of ghosts.*

God, the poor guy didn't stand a chance.

Trent fought his way through the underbrush until he hit the road back to the lodge. With any luck, by the time he got there, he'd have come up with a plan. *There's always a first time, right?*

He broke into a run.

CHAPTER
TWENTY-ONE

Christophe-the-man knew the pursuit was fruitless. He couldn't hope to catch up to Etienne—the bastard drove like a bat out of hell, even on these substandard roads. But Christophe-the-wolf couldn't help it.

For his whole life, his belief in Anton's devotion to his father, to Christophe himself, had been absolute. Anton had been the rock Christophe had clung to when disgust at his mutation and despair over his destiny had overwhelmed him. To discover that devotion had been a sham, a mask concealing a secret agenda? He could no more fail to give chase than he could transform again without his clothes.

How had Christophe failed to see it? Anton's commitment to the success of the company had obviously never been simple loyalty. It was ambition—the desire to possess, to control, to *own*. A desire so great, that for the company, for *commerce*, Anton would condemn Christophe to death as a livestock-killing wolf, and overcome his own distaste for personal humiliation.

Christophe had seen Anton's face when Etienne had subjugated him. He had clearly been conflicted, yet he'd complied with Etienne's domination, the scent of his own thwarted arousal heavy in the air. Was this a secret desire Anton had never hinted at? Or had he only submitted because Etienne had demanded it of him as part of their plot?

Did Anton fondly imagine Etienne would honor his part of the bargain? If so, Anton was in for a rude awakening. Etienne Melion was nothing if not consistent. The way he treated Anton now—as a plaything whose wishes were of no importance—would be precisely how he'd treat him in the boardroom.

Clavret et Cie under the rule of a Melion? Christophe's father deposed or worse? Christophe condemned to life—or death—as a wolf? *Insupportable.* A howl burst from his throat. *He shall not succeed.*

Although one paw was hopelessly lame from last night's race to find Anton, Christophe managed to keep pace with the Ferrari on the hairpin turns up the hill, cutting a straight path through the woods while the car had to remain on the road. But once Etienne gained the highway and picked up speed, Christophe fell behind.

But he didn't need to follow the car directly. He knew where Etienne was headed—to the ranch beneath the cave where Christophe had transformed. Very well, then.

He plunged back into the woods. Despite his exhaustion from guarding Trent all night, despite his lame paw, if he was to prevent Etienne from killing innocent livestock—not to mention setting Christophe up to take the fall—he had to beat the bastard to the ranch.

Christophe didn't want to think about what would happen when they met. Etienne would be fresh, perhaps glutted from a new kill. But Christophe had one advantage.

He was in an absolute killing rage, and he knew of no better way to vent it than by ripping the holy shite out of Etienne Melion's wolf.

Trent wasn't blinded by any flashes of brilliance as he pelted along the bewildering—and fricking steep—mountain roads. Seven years as a ghost-equivalent hadn't given him the expertise to thwart a frame-up or figure out how to turn a wolf back into a man. He needed help, and if there were such a thing as a supernatural advice hotline, he'd never heard of it.

By the time he staggered into the parking lot, winded and holding his side where a stitch pierced him like an arrow, he'd come up with precisely one option: begging Logan for help.

Logan had said he was willing to resume their friendship—*and God knows he's had practice with weird shit*—but Trent hated the idea anyway. For one thing, he was sick of depending on other people to bail him out; for another, Logan was getting married today. Chasing down a wolf wouldn't exactly be high on his list of priorities.

But what else could Trent do? Run into the lobby and scream, "Help, I need to rescue a werewolf!"? If that got back to his father, he'd never see the outside of a psych ward again. No, Logan was his best shot at getting to Christophe before it was too late.

The sun cleared the trees as Trent skirted the parking lot and cars were trickling in as guests arrived for the wedding. What the hell time was the ceremony anyway? Morning? Noon? Midnight? Judging by the rate of the arrivals, it probably wasn't immediate, but it was definitely a complication.

Best get on with it. Christophe needs me.

Jesus, how twisted was it that Trent was able to accept the fact that he'd been dating a *fricking werewolf*? For a moment, the familiar panic clawed at his belly and his palms started to sweat. He dropped to his haunches between two Priuses, trying not to hyperventilate.

He'd just escaped after seven years in the supernatural hoosegow. Did he want to risk another sentence?

This was different, though. The ghosts had wanted to punish him. But Christophe . . . He was the first guy, including Logan, who seemed to *get* Trent. Of course, the werewolf thing explained a lot of Christophe's acceptance. A little involuntary vacation in a whacked-out alternate dimension was probably nothing to a guy who spent his leisure time as a completely different species.

Christophe, aside from being totally hot in his human form, had never done anything but make him feel secure. Loved? Maybe not that, but absolutely protected and cared for. And he'd turned to *Trent* for help. How cool was that? Terrifying, too, if he were to be honest with himself.

Nobody, not even Logan, had ever had that much faith in him. The least Trent could do was act like someone who knew his ass from an iPhone app.

Trent took a deep breath, huffed it out, and stood up. Man or wolf, Christophe was *so* worth fighting for, even if what Trent had to fight was his own fricking neuroses.

When he entered the lobby, the place was teeming with people in party clothes, shrieking with faux-delight whenever they spotted an acquaintance. Shit, didn't most of these people work together? How long could it have been since they saw each other last? He threaded his way through them, his filthy hoodie and grubby jeans in sharp contrast to their wedding finery, doing his best to look nonchalant. *Don't mind me, folks. I'm just your average guest returning from a night out with his wolf.*

A commotion started by the stairs that led to the second floor. *Oh shit.* Julie, the *Haunted to the Max* muckety-muck, and she had the cameraman with her, the guy who'd spotted Trent in the bar. How could he fly under the radar if someone from the show recognized him? Trent scuttled behind the giant chainsaw sculpture of a bear and peeked from behind its wooden ass, planning his escape strategy.

"Zack, film the crowd in the lobby. Meet-ups, conversations, greetings. I want lots of footage to cut."

"It's a fricking wedding, Julie, not the next Star Wars flick. Don't you think we should tone down the production values a little?"

She glared at him. "Absolutely not. This wedding is going viral if I have to break the internet to do it."

"Even you can't guarantee trending."

"Why does everyone doubt my superpowers? If I say it'll go viral, then it will."

"Are you sure that's what Logan and Riley want?"

Riley.

Logan had said that he was the one who'd figured out the ghost war. He knew about all this supernatural shit, so he was bound to know about werewolves, right? Or if he didn't, he'd know how to find out. This wasn't a great time, obviously, but if Trent didn't track him down now, it would be too late—Riley and Logan would leave on their honeymoon, and Christophe would get shot by ranchers as a livestock killer. *God.*

Trent started to shake again, crouched low behind the bear, as Julie and Zack patrolled the lobby, Julie pointing out shots she wanted and chivvying guests into restaging their arrivals for the camera. Trent balled his fists in the pocket of his hoodie and clenched his teeth so their clatter wouldn't give him away. *Come on, groupies. Tell me where Riley is. I don't have much time here.*

Just as Trent's nerves reached their snapping point, Riley himself trotted down the staircase. The instant Julie saw him, she abandoned Zack and the hapless guests, storming across the lobby like the Black Widow on an Avenger throw down.

"Hey, Jules, have you seen Logan? I need to ask him—"

"You are *not* allowed to see him before the ceremony. You're not supposed to be out of your room, doofus."

Riley rolled his eyes. "I'm not some Regency virgin. I think we can dispense with the traditional frills."

"No, we cannot. You put me in charge of this wedding—"

"Technically, I only asked you to stand up with me."

"It's the duty of the best person to make sure the wedding comes off right. You didn't hire a wedding planner—"

"Jules. We're two guys who just want to get married and get on with our lives. I'm surprised you were able to talk Logan into this big of an event in the first place."

"For a dickhead douche-canoe, Logan is a lot more sentimental than you. He would have gone for twice the spectacle if I'd let him."

"Then thanks for reining him in. I don't think I could stand any more fuss than we've already got. You should have seen him last night. He barely slept a wink. He—"

"What?" Julie shrieked, causing everyone in the lobby to duck and cover. "You *slept* with him? Last night?"

Riley winced, and Trent couldn't blame him. "Keep it down, will you? We live together. Why wouldn't we sleep together?"

"Because it was the night before your wedding. There are *rules.* There are *traditions.* You're the folklorist. You know these things carry weight. Do you really want to tempt fate at your own freaking wedding?"

Riley bit his lip. "When you put it like that . . ."

"Exactly. Get back in your room. You ought to be in your tux by now anyway."

"The ceremony's not until one. I can't sit around in the tux for hours. It'll look like I spent the night stuffed in a suitcase. Aren't you the one who's been harping on how important it is for the suit to look good from the rear for the video?"

"Then at least go to your room and get ready to put the tux on. Take a shower."

"Already did."

"Then do the crossword. Watch some porn. Meditate, for God's sake, anything. Just don't talk to Logan."

"Fine." Riley scowled. "If I didn't know you better, I'd suspect you were trying to kidnap him and scuttle the whole wedding."

"Are you kidding? I've put too much time and effort into producing it. Now go. Or do I have to walk you to your room?"

"No. I think I can find my own way."

"Good. Go. Or else."

"Okay, okay." Riley headed for the stairs. "Whose wedding is this anyway?"

Trent edged around the bear, keeping it between him and the camera crew. This was his chance to corner Riley; he couldn't blow it. If he didn't catch up with Riley soon, he'd lose him in the lodge maze. But how the hell was he supposed to sneak across a lobby with twenty-foot ceilings and up a floating staircase without anyone noticing him?

"Hello, everyone. Sorry I'm late."

A tall blond guy dressed like Indiana Jones posed in the entrance, blocking the path of three bellmen who were laden like pack mules.

"Max. Great to see you," Julie called, then grabbed Zack's elbow and towed him to within two feet of Trent's hideout. "I *still* can't believe Logan invited Max," she muttered.

"Believe it. Now what—"

"Zack." Max had already gathered a gaggle of guests around him by simply not letting them pass. "Great! Come on over, and we can film my entrance again. Maybe a tracking shot from the parking lot. Bucolic backdrops, and all that crap."

Julie sighed and the two of them followed Max out of the lobby along with most of the guests.

Trent had never been so thrilled to be upstaged. He strolled out from behind the bear and up the stairs without anyone paying attention to him at all.

CHAPTER
TWENTY-TWO

rent had no trouble tracking Riley; the guy was wandering along the hall like he had all fricking day. The corridor curved, so Trent was prepared to backpedal if Riley happened to turn around. Luckily for Trent, he was so oblivious that he didn't look back once, just made a more or less direct line for a room in the far corner of the second floor and went inside.

Okay, what's my best option here? He'd avoided being introduced to Riley when Logan had offered yesterday. Their only interaction had been that night at Stumptown Spirits, when Trent had shoved his foot past his tonsils. Somehow, after that little faux pas, he doubted he'd be Riley's favorite person, especially on his wedding day.

Hello there. I'm the guy who announced to the entire bar that I used to fuck your fiancé. How'd you like to help me out?

Yeah, that'd go over well.

But the longer he lurked in the hallway, searching for the perfect opening line, the more likely he'd be discovered. Considering how he looked—*really need a new hoodie and jeans without nonironic holes*—he'd probably be mistaken for someone tossing rooms for drug money and kicked out on his ass.

If that happened, Christophe's motherfucking brother and his asshole Dom might get their way, and Christophe could end up as a trophy on some rancher's wall. The dudes who shot him would never know they'd murdered a man who searched for the perfect rare hamburger in the most unusual places, who watched superhero movies as if they were documentaries, who'd held Trent in the night as if he was real and precious and worthy.

Shit, find your balls and do *it, Pielmeyer.* He took a deep breath, marched down the hall and knocked on Riley's door.

It opened almost immediately, Riley speaking before he saw who was there. "Logan, if Jules finds out you're— Oh. Uh . . . hello?"

"Yeah. Hi. Listen, can we talk?"

"This isn't the best time, Trent." *Yeah, Riley recognizes me all right.* "In case you didn't know, I'm getting married in a couple of hours and—"

"Yeah, I know. But this is important. It can't wait until you get back from wherever-the-fuck you're going on your honeymoon." Trent ran a hand through his hair and a few pine needles rained onto the carpet. Jesus, he must look like a deranged mountain man. "It can't even wait until after the ceremony."

"I'm not sure what you think is so dire, but—"

"Hey, what else are you gonna do for the next hour? It's not like Julie'll let Logan out of her sight to fuck you into the mattress before the wedding."

Riley's eyes widened. "How do you know she—"

"I caught that little scene in the lobby. Look, can we take this inside?" Trent glanced over his shoulder. "It's kind of, well, personal."

"If it's about you and Logan, you already announced that, thank you very much."

"No. It's not."

"Trent, I get that a shitty thing happened to you—truly, *unbelievably* horrible, and I can't imagine what it was like—but whatever the current issue, I don't think I can help you with it. Not now, anyway."

"But see, that's the thing. You're the only one who *can* help."

"Me?" Riley blinked his big brown eyes, and Trent could suddenly see the attraction. "I'm—"

"You're the folklore guy, right? You're the one who figured out how to bust me out of the ghost war."

"That was more of a joint effort."

"I don't care. You know about this shit. And I need someone with your chops."

"If you need a folklorist, I can give you the names of some others. In Portland or Eugene. Any of them could help you as well as I could." He glanced at his watch. "But I really don't have the time."

"Jesus *fuck*, dude. *I* don't have the time. This has to be now. Here. Before it's too late. If we—" Voices approached from down the hall again. "Fuck."

Trent glanced around wildly. Riley craned his neck to see who was coming and opened his mouth—to shout maybe? Trent didn't wait to find out. He had at least four inches on Riley, so he used them. He grabbed Riley's arm and spun him around, clapping a hand over his mouth. Riley struggled—Trent couldn't blame him. "I'm not gonna hurt you. We just need to *talk*."

He hustled Riley into the nearby ice machine room and shut the door, bracing his back against it in case the approaching parade was only in search of ice. But it seemed like the target was Riley's room.

Someone pounded on a door. "Riley." Julie's voice. Riley tensed in Trent's arms. "Don't sulk. Open the door."

"Be still." Trent whispered. "If you don't help me, I'll—I'll tell the cops that Logan was responsible for my disappearance."

Riley squawked, the angry sound muffled by Trent's hand, but he stopped struggling. *God, he believes I'd really do that? How big a dickhead does he think I am?*

Easy answer—the one who'd announce his fuck buddy status with Logan in a crowded bar three days before his wedding.

"Rile, come on." Julie's voice turned wheedling. "You know I'm only doing this for your own good. You'll thank me when you see the finished video. Videos." Her heavy sigh was clearly audible. "Fine. I need to have a little chat with Heather, but I'll be back later, okay?"

Julie passed by, muttering, "Wedding day divas."

After her steps died away, Trent took his hand off Riley's mouth. He didn't fight it when Riley wrenched away.

"Just freaking brilliant. Getting kidnapped on my wedding day was so not on my agenda."

Trent blinked. "I didn't kidnap you. I need your help."

"So you threaten Logan to get it? What are you, twelve?"

Fuck my impulse control. Why don't I ever think *first?* Self-disgust burrowed into Trent's gut like a sandworm. "No. I'm twenty-seven. Or twenty. You tell me." Although what twenty-year-old—who wasn't also a sociopath—would threaten his former best friend with police action? *God, I suck.*

Riley's eyebrows shot up. "I . . . Wow, I guess you do have the whole college-kid vibe. Even *I* look older than you, but I thought it was genetics."

"When you figure it out, let me know." *Because I seriously need a maturity upgrade.* Later, though. Right now he had no fucking time. "But in the meantime, this is a life-and-death matter. I'm serious. You're the only one who can help me, and I'll do whatever it takes to make sure you do."

Riley glared at him. "Exactly how much help do you think I can give you stuck in here with the ice machine? Need some rocks to go with your bourbon? Because I've got to say, this plan is worthy of someone who's had way too much to drink."

"What plan? I've got no plan. I haven't got a fucking *clue*. All I've got is you."

Riley crossed his arms. "That remains to be seen."

Trent growled and slammed the ice machine with one palm, causing a rain of ice cubes to rattle down onto the grate. "I have no idea how to help Christophe, and I'm afraid—"

"Wait. Christophe's in trouble?"

"Yeah. Didn't I say?"

"No, you jerk, you didn't. If you had, I probably would have helped you in the first place. He's my friend too."

"Oh." *Why didn't I think of that? Damn twenty-year-old brain strikes again.*

Riley rolled his eyes. "Yeah. *Oh.* So what's the matter?"

Trent eyed Riley. He definitely had the hot-nerd vibe going, and he'd totally sussed the ghost war, but would he think Trent was a nutcase like half the adult population of the planet? Still, who cared, as long as he helped Christophe.

"The thing is, it's sorta crazy."

"Thinking you could get away with abducting me is pretty crazy."

"I wasn't abducting you, and I mean like *really* crazy."

Riley tapped his foot. "If you're in such a hurry, maybe you should spit it out. What's wrong with Christophe?"

"Well." Trent rubbed the nape of his neck. "He's kind of a . . . a werewolf."

Riley's eyes widened, then he blinked rapidly. "Say what?"

"He's a werewolf. You know—man by day, wolf by night. Except that's not quite how it works because I've seen him at night and he's been fine, and it's daytime now and he can't shift back for some reason. And these two assholes are trying to frame him for killing sheep—wait, one of them's his brother, I think, and the other guy is one sick, twisted bastard—but his brother took his signet ring and—"

"Whoa, whoa, whoa." Riley made a T with his hands. "Timeout. Rewind to the main point here. He's a *werewolf*. An actual shape-shifter?"

"Dude. I just *said*."

"Oh my God." Riley tried to get by, but Trent blocked his way. "I'll help, of course I will, but I need my laptop."

Trent's eyebrows lifted. "You brought your laptop to your wedding?"

"I bring my laptop everywhere. You never know when you'll need it. Like now. Come on."

"Wait." Trent stopped him with a hand on his arm. "Julie said she'd be back to check on you. We need to go somewhere where we won't be disturbed by her or sixty-two other people with wedding on the brain, including Logan. *Especially* Logan."

Riley blushed and cleared his throat. "Okay then. We'll go to Julie's room. She's never there."

Trent ducked his head out the door. When he saw that the hallway was empty, he gave Riley a thumbs-up and they darted across to Riley's door.

"Good thing I always keep my key in my pocket, or your little abduction would have gotten more publicity than you want. I'd have had to ask Julie or Logan for a spare key."

Riley dipped his key card in the slot and let them both in. The room was sunny and spacious, a tux hanging in the open closet, a laptop on the desk under the window. He strode across the room and tucked the laptop into a messenger bag. Slinging the bag over his shoulder, he grabbed another key off the desk and held it up. "Julie's room. Let's go."

He led the way to the door and peeked out. "All clear. Her room's up one floor." Riley started down the hall but Trent stopped him.

"Not the elevators." He nodded at the emergency stairs next to their old friend, the ice-machine closet. "Stairwell."

Trent held the door for Riley, then eased it shut behind them. None too soon. Before they'd gotten two steps up the stairs, the familiar tromp of multiple feet approached. *Jesus, this guy has more visitors than Disney World on the Fourth of July.*

Trent urged Riley up the first half flight faster, breathing easier as soon as they'd rounded the landing.

When they got to the third-floor door, he caught Riley's arm again. Riley peered at him over the top of his glasses.

"Try using your words, Trent. You don't have to manhandle me. Just say 'wait' and I'll wait."

Trent let go. "Sorry. Words haven't worked so well for me for a while."

He poked his head out the door and when he was sure the corridor was empty, he beckoned to Riley, who scurried over and opened the door to Julie's room. The place was pretty much a mirror of Riley's, except that the closet held a rather severe dress instead of a tux.

"You still haven't told me how you know Christophe is a werewolf. I mean, did you see him shift?"

"No. But how many wolves do you know who carry around beer mats from Stumptown Spirits?"

Riley blinked at him. "Uh . . . none. That is, I don't know any wolves at all."

That's what you think, dude. I've seen how Logan acts around you.

Trent dropped into an overstuffed chair in the corner while Riley set his laptop up on the desk. "He was supposed to meet me last night at one of the cabins, but he didn't show. Then, when I was sitting outside on our patio, trying to figure how the hell to get back to Portland—"

"You weren't going to stay for the wedding?"

Trent smiled apologetically. "Yeah, sorry about that. Wasn't in my plans. After the last time I saw you, I didn't think I'd be particularly welcome."

"Um . . . well . . ."

"Logan said it'd be okay." Trent shrugged. "Didn't feel okay to me, although Christophe had hopes I'd change my mind. Hell, he bought me a fucking suit." Trent gestured to his clothes. "Guess he disapproved of my usual style."

"Uh-huh." Riley pulled a legal pad and a pen from his bag. "Okay, so you're on the patio. Go on."

"Yeah, and this wolf creeps out of the bushes, staring right at me."

"How do you know it wasn't a German shepherd or a malamute mix or something?"

"Have you ever stared down a wolf? Trust me. It was *so* not a dog. Anyway, he has this beer mat between his paws. Makes sure I see the Stumptown logo, then he flips it upside down. On purpose."

Riley stopped scribbling notes and tilted his head. "And this is significant . . . why?"

"On the night we met, I did the same thing at the bar. Christophe matched it. So I knew it was him, and when I put my hand on his back—"

"You *touched* a wolf? Because of a freaking *beer mat*? Jeez, I don't think you're *twelve*, let alone twenty. More like three. Your prefrontal cortex is nonexistent."

"Look, he wasn't threatening, okay? But he wanted me to come with him, so I did."

"He— You— Do you even— Augh!" Riley clutched his hair.

"Hey, take it easy. You'll give yourself an aneurism."

Riley let go of his hair and stared at Trent. "Logan said that very same thing to me after he told me you'd displaced Danford Balch."

"Then I guess you'd better make sure you never go off your blood pressure meds. Forget about judging me for what I did or didn't do. The point is, he led me to this other cabin. His brother was there, and another guy who had the same Eurosexual vibe that Christophe has, only his was creepy and sleazy. Christophe's is—"

"Hot," they said together.

Trent grinned. "I promise not to tell Logan you said that."

Riley turned to his laptop, but shot Trent a sly sideways glance. "Tell him. It does him good to remember he's not the only wolf in the pack." He tapped the table with one finger. "'Wolf in the pack.' Hunh. That explains so much."

"If you say so. Anyway, we were out there overnight. I figured he'd, you know, change back at dawn or some shit, but he didn't.

Then that sleazy guy takes off in his fucking Ferrari and Christophe chases it up the mountain."

"I think you're leaving out a few significant details here."

"We'll get to those. Why didn't he change back? Isn't that how it works? I mean, full moon, blah, blah, blah."

"Not all werewolf or shifter stories are the same. The legends vary about why they might shift and what the triggers could be, as well as what the remedy is. Go on."

"When we got there, Christophe's brother—Anton, his name is—had this roaring blaze going in the fire pit on the patio of his cabin. He had a bundle of Christophe's clothes with him and he burned them. The whole lot, although he took a little too much satisfaction out of ripping the shit out of some of them first. Oh, and he kept Christophe's signet ring. Put it on his own hand."

Riley's eyes narrowed. "Clothing. There are stories about werewolves whose shifting is controlled by clothing." He typed furiously. "More than one. I think—yes. Two are connected with the Arthurian cycle, but there's a Breton story. Marie de France wrote of it in the thirteenth century. Bisclavret." He met Trent's eyes and they both goggled. "Clavret. Bisclavret. Why didn't I ever see the connection before?"

"Maybe because you don't normally wonder whether any guy you meet is secretly a werewolf?"

"Did they say anything else?"

Suddenly unable to sit still, Trent stood up and paced across the room. "Anton and the sleazy guy . . ." He snapped his fingers. "Etienne. They talked about killing some livestock and making it seem like a wolf had done it."

"These guys were speaking English?"

"No. French."

"But you understood them?"

"Hey, I squandered the best prep school education money can buy. Just ask my father." Trent peered out the window. Jesus, the sun was almost right overhead. The *hurry, hurry* alarm in his head stepped up its game. "Afterward, the sleazy guy—"

"Etienne."

"Yeah, he makes Anton blow him."

"Oookay. TMI."

Trent snorted. "Tell me about it."

Riley swiveled the laptop and Trent sat on the bed so he could see the screen. "This is the story. This baron, Bizuneh, is the Bisclavret, which means werewolf in Breton. He has to transform into a wolf for three days out of every seven. Could that be it?"

"You tell me. When you were dating him, did he disappear three days a week?"

Riley blushed. "We weren't that serious, but I don't remember him being missing for long periods at regular intervals."

Trent narrowed his eyes, wondering whether Logan would notice if his fiancé was missing chunks of hair at the wedding. "Uh-huh."

"You know," Riley drawled, "if we're going to get anything done, we need to let go of the fact that each of us screwed the other one's—"

"You said you weren't that serious."

"We weren't serious, I didn't say we were celibate." He held Trent's gaze. "Nor were you and Logan."

Trent told his inner jealous asshole to stand down. For now. "Point taken. Go ahead."

"The baron's wife didn't know about his nature, and when he told her, she freaked. The big dope even told her the secret to changing back, which was that he needed to put on the clothes he'd been wearing when he shifted."

"How the fuck can a wolf put on clothes? Wouldn't the lack of opposable thumbs be a roadblock?"

"Obviously he can't, not literally." Riley squinted at the laptop. "But he has to be in possession of them. And the baroness, being a resourceful sort of person, stole the clothes. The baron ended up trapped as a wolf for seven years."

"Seven years," Trent muttered. "Why is it always seven years?"

Riley scrolled down the page. "Bisclavret managed to ingratiate himself with the king and accompanied him everywhere. One day they visit the baron's old home, and Bisclavret attacks the wife, bites off her nose."

"Ouch."

"I know, right?" Riley peered at the screen. "The king tortures her to get the full story, which encourages her to produce the baron's clothes."

"No shit."

"Even then, he wouldn't shift until they put the clothes into another room and granted him privacy."

Trent tapped his lip with one finger. "I don't get it. Why the hell did the wife keep the clothes? That's just begging for a bitch-slap from fate. Why not . . ." he met Riley's gaze ". . . destroy them?"

"Maybe that's why Anton and Etienne are being so thorough. They want to prevent the possibility." Riley's eyebrows drew together. "Wait. Etienne. Christophe ranted a lot about a guy who'd been at school with him, who was the heir to this other import-export business. I got the impression that their families were rivals socially and professionally, but that they were closely connected. The family was called Melion. Which—" He checked his computer screen again. "Is the name of another werewolf whose shifting was controlled by clothing. Melion's story was one of two werewolf tales associated with King Arthur. The other was Sir Marrok."

"So they're descendants of the werewolf dudes? Then why couldn't Anton shift and do his own dirty work?"

"Maybe he can't. Legends don't always tell the whole story." He shrugged. "Maybe not all of the werewolves' male descendants can shift, or maybe there are factors we don't know about."

Trent blinked. "But if Etienne is a werewolf too, then he doesn't have to make the livestock deaths *appear* to be a wolf attack. He can actually do it. And if he can shift back and Christophe can't—"

"Then Christophe will be the only wolf in the area when the ranchers go gunning for the predator."

Trent shot off the bed. "We've got to do something."

"How? You said Anton destroyed his clothes."

"The ones he must have been wearing, yeah." Trent slapped his palm with his fist. *Think, think.* "He bought me a suit. Does that count?"

Riley shook his head. "He may have purchased it, but that doesn't make it his. He intended it for you."

"Why the hell does that matter? Clothes are clothes, and it's not like I ever wore it."

"We're talking about tradition. Myth. Legend. These things have rules. You should know. Logan said you were into legend tripping, and that's how you ended up—"

"Let's not go into that. I learned my lesson."

"From everything I've read about this type of werewolf, if we can't find the clothes he was wearing when he changed, we need a garment that's touched his skin—an *intact* garment that's in good shape. You were at his cabin. Did he have any other clothes there?"

Trent guffawed. "A metric fuck-ton. This *is* Christophe we're talking about."

Riley sat up straighter. "That's good. There's bound to be something there that he's worn, something unwashed. He is a guy, after all."

"Yeah, but he's super picky about his clothes. I can't see him packing anything dirty on purpose. Anton mentioned the clothes being clean, but maybe Christophe changed and he didn't know about it. I'll go check, just in case. I left my duffel and backpack under a chair on the patio anyway." Trent froze behind Riley's chair. "Shit. Anton said he was going to clear out the cabin. I better hurry." *If I'm not already too late.*

"Do you still have a key?"

"No. I left it inside. But if I have to, I'll break one of the damn windows. They can fucking bill me for it."

CHAPTER
TWENTY-THREE

When Christophe finally made it to the hillside above the ranch, the morning was well advanced. He'd made poor time, limping heavily, exhausted, and ravenous as he was from the exertion.

Etienne's wolf scent was strong. He'd obviously marked as many rocks and trees as he could, probably to taunt Christophe with his presence. Perhaps, if Christophe's wolf were in charge, it might madden him to the point of foolishness. But his human logic prevailed over his wolf instincts. He cared nothing about staking claim to this territory.

However, he cared very much about revenge: for Etienne's treatment of Anton, for the threat to his father, and for the plot against Christophe's life.

He limped through the last of the trees at the edge of the pasture, and his heart sank.

Too late.

A half dozen or more pitiful carcasses littered the field, one or two adult sheep, but mostly lambs, their throats torn out. Christophe crept forward and nosed one pathetic little corpse. The scent of its terror hadn't yet faded, nor had the traces of Etienne's vicious delight in that terror. *Malice. Killing for the love of suffering.* Etienne had dragged the body off to the side and eviscerated the poor thing. *So he's fed.*

Despite his hunger, Christophe had no desire whatsoever to take so much as a morsel from these poor creatures. *If not for me, they would still be alive.* His head was suddenly too heavy to hold up, his chest hollow and raw as if he too had been eviscerated.

"There it is! Get it!"

The baying of hounds followed the shout. Christophe crouched, gaze darting around the field to assess the threat. Three men armed with long-bore weapons zoomed across the field toward him on ATVs, several hounds racing in front of them.

Must get away. Now. Livestock killers were fair game. As the only wolf at the scene of the massacre, Christophe was the obvious culprit. *Just as Etienne intended.*

He took off, his lame front paw impeding his speed, imagining the dogs' breath on his heels at every step, until he could dodge through the underbrush and into the trees.

Was he back on the forest lands? Would the men follow him here? They weren't supposed to, but would they abide by government rules when they'd just lost so many of their flock?

Christophe pelted around a boulder and—*shite, where had that ravine come from?* He skidded to a stop, falling to his haunches. Below, a river glinted between rocky banks. *Trapped.* There must be a way across. But where? He dropped his nose to the ground, seeking his own scent.

A sharp report rang out behind him, and a bullet struck the tree next to his head. The bark exploded outward, splinters catching in his fur. Yelping, he flinched away from the impact toward the edge of the precipice. *Mistake!* The ground gave way under his hindquarters. He scrabbled for purchase, but his injured paw had no strength, and one of his rear paws caught nothing but air.

The more he struggled to find a toehold, the faster he lost ground, until he slid over the edge and down the steep slope, tumbling head over arse, brambles tearing at his fur, rocks smashing into his ribs.

Dizzy. Hurts.

The slope disappeared suddenly, and he toppled out into the air. Down, down. He howled, but it was cut off when he hit the water, jarring his left hind leg against a boulder. The water, frigid from spring runoff, began to numb him even through his fur as he tried to paddle to the shore. Hampered as he was by two injured legs, the current swept him away. Then his head slammed against deadfall, and he knew no more.

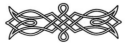

Trent left Riley poring through online research about werewolves and sneaked down the stairs to the lodge's side exit. He peered around the corner of the building—the quickest way to the cabin was through the parking lot or the lobby, but the place was teeming with wedding guests. *Too risky.* Jesus, what if he ran into Logan? *Damn it, it's the fucking woods again.* Sucking in a breath, he dove into the forest, fighting his way through the underbrush beneath the trees. He kept expecting the panic to strike, but it wasn't too bad. The daylight was filtering through the thick canopy. Was that what made the difference?

The idea made him pause for a moment. He'd freaked the fuck out the other day just driving by Forest Park in the middle of the day, in a car, with two other men. Now he could bushwhack his way through the Mount Hood National Forest on his own. Sure, the resort had a few more amenities than the Witch's Castle, but maybe he was finally getting better.

He stayed under cover of the trees until he reached the rear of Christophe's cabin. His backpack, duffel, and garment bag were still barricaded behind the Adirondack chairs where he'd left them, and his phone charger was still plugged into the outside outlet.

Why wouldn't they be? It wasn't as if some tech-savvy squirrel had designs on his laptop, or a fashion-forward deer was eyeing his suit. And it'd be a damn desperate bear who'd want a duffel full of dirty clothes. Trent didn't really want them himself, but they might be the only clothes he'd be able to afford for a while. *Two birds. One stone.* He'd haul it all back too, but Christophe came first.

As he crept onto the patio, a movement from inside caught his eye. *Shit.* He plastered his back against the cabin wall. Could it be housekeeping? What time was it anyway? Staying out of range of the vast expanse of glass in the French doors, he sidled over until he could peek into the living room.

Nothing there. But he could have sworn he'd seen movement. Could it have been a reflection in the glass? Just to check, he circled to the other side of the cabin by going back into the trees again, and peered through the bedroom window.

Anton. God damn *it.* He was too late.

The bastard took an armful of Christophe's jackets from the closet and tossed them into the open suitcase on the bed in a jumble that rivaled Trent's packing techniques. *That's so wrong. Christophe would* never *treat his clothes like that.* That lack of regard for something so important to Christophe sent a spike of anger through Trent's chest. And when Anton yanked open a drawer and scooped out a careless armful of Christophe's meticulously folded undershirts and socks? Trent couldn't watch any more or he'd be in danger of punching the wall.

He ducked down and pulled out his phone, speed-dialing Riley, who answered on the first ring. "Did you find anything?"

"Yeah, unfortunately. Anton."

"Crap."

"Tell me about it. What now?"

"Do you think there's any chance he'll leave something behind?"

"I don't know. He's being sloppy." *The asshole.* Trent inched up and peered over the window ledge. "Hurrying. But I don't know if—" A dead branch under Trent's foot cracked like a rifle, and Anton's head shot up.

For an endless moment, their gazes locked. Then Anton threw down the underwear and strode back to the living room.

Trent stumbled toward the front of the cabin. "Shit-shit-shit."

"What's the matter? What happened?"

"He saw me."

"Oh no," Riley moaned. "This is not good."

"You think?" Trent had no illusions about Anton's scruples. The guy had been willing to get his ass reamed so he could frame his brother for murder. And now Trent was a witness. In the middle of nowhere where it would be way too easy to hide a body. "Listen. Play along, okay?"

Trent made it to the porch as Anton yanked open the door.

"The next time you send me on assignment in the middle of fucking *nowhere*, boss, you can at least verify the *rendezvous*." Trent put on his best sulky twink voice, with a little whine thrown in. *Don't oversell it.* But he was pleased that Anton had winced slightly at the word *rendezvous*. *Guilty much, asshole?* "Hold on. Here he is." He smiled, the wide, charming smile that had guaranteed a drink, if not a hookup, in the past. "Hey. I'm . . . Logan. From the service." Riley squawked, and Trent muffled the phone against his chest. "Sorry I'm late. The cab driver got lost in the Gorge."

Anton frowned. "You have the wrong destination. Go away." Trent pouted. "No way. You're Mister . . . Mister . . ." He put his phone back to his ear. "Boss, what's the client's name again?" Riley spluttered. "Got it." He beamed at Anton. "Mister Cavalry. Or do you prefer Chris?"

"I tell you, you have the wrong—"

"Oh I don't think so." He pointed above the trees. "Big-ass mountain? Secluded cabin in the woods? Hot guy with a killer accent? This is definitely the place." Trent buried his revulsion for the bastard and sashayed forward to drape his arms around Anton's neck and press against him. *If I can sell this, I deserve the Tony right fucking now.* "It's okay. You're nervous. I get it. Giving up control is hard. But I'll make it good for you, I promise. I've serviced *dozens* of satisfied bottoms."

Anton wrenched himself out of Trent's grasp, his face taking on an alarming purple hue. "Don't touch me."

"Don't be ashamed, sugar. You wouldn't believe how many of our 'clients' have second thoughts after they book something a bit naughty. We can do everything you asked for—the handcuffs, the blindfold, even the ball gag—and nobody but you and me will ever know."

Anton gritted his teeth. He pulled out his wallet and tossed a couple of Benjamins at Trent. "Here. Now leave."

Trent would have dearly loved to spit on Anton's fucking money, but he was flat broke. And he couldn't think of anyone he'd rather fleece than Anton, unless it was Etienne.

He turned and bent over to pick up the money, giving Anton a deliberate ass-shot. "This is a nice tip, you know, but we've got your credit card on the site." He popped back up, lifting his chin in his best haughty club-boy imitation. "You'll be charged for the full service anyway. That's in the contract."

"Whatever. Just go." Anton slammed the door in Trent's face.

Holy fucking shit. He bought it. Hook, line, and ass-play. Maybe a career in theater wasn't totally out of the question.

Trent high-tailed it into the woods and around the cabin again. "Did you hear that?"

Riley snorted. "I think that particular rainbow snow-job was visible from the International Space Station."

"Yeah, well, nuance would be lost on this guy. But since he'd seen me, I needed to make sure he wasn't the *last* one who saw me, if you get my drift."

Riley sucked in a breath. "He's . . . ah . . . not exactly a boy scout, I guess."

"Understatement much? And what are we gonna do without Christophe's clothes?"

"I don't know. Yet. But we'll figure something out."

"Okay. Be right there. Just have to get my stuff before brother dearest decides to burn it too. Later."

CHAPTER
TWENTY-FOUR

(hristophe floated. His fur, soaked and heavy, dragged at him, but
he was caught in the branches of a deadfall across the swollen
creek. He blinked at the sky through the tangle of branches. *There is
something... I must do... if only—*

Anton. Etienne. The betrayal.

Christophe fought free of the clutching branches. The creek,
though swift, wasn't particularly deep at this point, so he could stand.
He made his way to the bank and shook himself, spraying water in all
directions, startling the crows from the trees, and setting the squirrels
chittering at him in protest.

He assessed his condition—his front right paw and left rear leg
were still painful. His ribs hurt when he breathed and his head felt as
if someone had taken a mallet to it. For a moment, he was tempted
to simply lie down here and be done. He'd been too late to prevent
Etienne's massacre, and had no chance of escaping his wolf form when
the one who usually abetted his transformation had decided instead
to prevent it.

What hope did he have? In his ancestor's day, wolves had had
power, a fair chance in a fight against any man. But now? He was
virtually helpless. All the power lay now with the men with the guns,
or almost worse, with the authorities who would do near as much
damage to him in the name of preservation. To be collared and
monitored as if he were no more than the animal he appeared? How
could he deal with such humiliation?

He had few illusions about his ability to survive in the wild. A
man with the spirit of a wolf might dominate in the boardroom, but
a wolf with the spirit of a man had no such advantage in the primal
savagery of the forest. He could barely force himself to hunt as it

was; it made him feel less than human. If he were forced to remain in this state for long—as long as his ancestor had been—would he even remember how to be a man? Or would the wolf take over completely, turning him into the beast he resembled?

And what of his father? He didn't know Anton's plans, but he had no more faith in Etienne Melion's professional ethics than in his personal morals. Between the two of them, his father's odds of survival after the merger were as slim as his own.

So ironic that he'd been brought to this state just as he'd found a true partner at last, one who wouldn't betray him for power or prestige or money. Yet the first Bisclavret's wife had betrayed him, just as Anton had done. What guarantee had he that Trent wouldn't tire of him and do the same?

Because if Trent tired of you, condemning you to a supernatural prison would be the last thing he would ever do. Not after enduring a similar fate himself.

Christophe had taken his measure that day in the park, when Trent had confessed his ordeal. If he'd admired the man before, his respect had increased tenfold then, hearing of Trent's ability to reassimilate after seven years of being *other.*

Trent knew what he was now. If nothing else, perhaps if he could get to Trent, they could find a way to shield Christophe from the authorities. *And do what? Put you in a private zoo?* Would he be able to stand being around Trent if he was nothing more than a pet dog?

Better that than the wilderness. Better that than death.

He limped away from the water, and as he took the path through the trees, the wind shifted and he caught it.

Etienne's scent.

Christophe growled, tempted to howl, but if he did that, he'd reveal himself to his pursuers and his prey. No, he intended to take Etienne unaware, as unaware as the poor sheep had been to their fate.

Etienne would pay for what he had done. One way or another, Christophe would see to it.

He took off into the trees at an awkward, uneven run. *Pray God I'm able to stand when I meet him, because I couldn't live knowing that Etienne Melion killed me.*

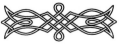

Getting back to Riley's room was trickier than getting out of it had been. Judging by the number of people in clothes too fashionable for mountain climbing, or white water rafting, or horseback riding, or whatever the fuck people did out here, wedding zero-hour must be close.

After two near-misses, he legged it up the stairs, calling Riley on the way. "I'm almost there. Open the door for me."

"Yeah, about that—"

"Hurry. We don't want anyone to catch on." Trent cleared the last curve of the hallway. "We don't want Logan," the door swung open, "or Jul—" He skidded to a halt. *Shit.* "Uh . . . hi, Julie."

She crossed her arms. "Nice to see you too, *Mister* Pielmeyer."

Riley grimaced at him from the desk. "Sorry. I forgot she'd have to come back here to get dressed."

"Yes. Dressed for *your wedding*, and yet I wonder why *you* aren't making a similar effort."

"Well, see, there's this thing." Riley fidgeted with the drawstring of his sweatpants.

"A thing. Really." Julie's narrow gaze flicked between Trent, hovering in the open doorway, and Riley. "What, are you two comparing Logan's dick size or something?"

"Jules!" Riley jumped up. "It's not like that."

"No? Then I suggest you get your ass back to your room and put on your tux before Logan decides you've gotten a better offer from his old fuck buddy."

"Hey." Trent stepped inside and let the door close behind him. "A little out of line, don't you think?"

"No. What I *think* is that Riley's getting married in less than half an hour and he looks like he just rolled out of bed."

"I don't. I've been up for ages. Showered. Used that stupid hair product."

"Then you've gotten sidetracked by some folklore shit. Your front hair's doing that thing where it sticks up and sideways.

Riley clapped his hand on his head. "My— What?"

"It's a total tell, Rile. You clutch it while you make notes." She'd been edging toward the desk as she spoke, and on the word "notes" she lunged and grabbed the legal pad off the desk. "Aha! You *have* been making notes. Seriously, Rile? I know folklore is your passion, but it's your wedding day and . . ."

Her eyes grew rounder as she read. Riley shared an *oh fuck* glance with Trent.

"You have got to be shitting me. A *werewolf*?"

"I know it sounds crazy." Trent unloaded his backpack and duffel onto the floor and tossed the garment bag on the bed.

"Are you kidding? This is *amazing*! Forget the Witch's Castle reunion episode. An honest-to-God werewolf? The ratings will be off the charts!"

"Jules, you can't—"

"It's a damn good thing Zack's already here with the camera. We can take the van. Where is he?"

Trent stalked over to Julie and blocked her path. "You can't exploit Christophe like that. We need to help him. He's either about to get blamed for a sheep-killing and offed by a bunch of pissed-off ranchers, or else he's gonna murder his own brother *and* another guy."

Julie stared him down. "How are you going to get to him?"

Trent blinked first. "I thought—" Except he hadn't thought The cave Anton had told Etienne about was over ten miles away. They'd never get there on foot, and once they were there, then what? They still had no way of turning Christophe back.

Wait. *François*. "Christophe has a driver. He's the one that brought me here. I'll bet he could check out Christophe's condo. Bring him some clothes."

"Where is this alleged condo and this alleged driver?"

"The Pearl."

"It takes a minimum of ninety minutes to get here from Portland. You think you have that much time?"

Riley shoved his glasses up his nose with his knuckle. "That's assuming there are any clothes there that haven't already been laundered."

"Hell." Trent smacked the wall. "I just remembered. Anton said he'd sent everything to the cleaners before he left town."

"Damn it," Riley muttered.

Julie smirked at them. "If you guys want to get there, you'll have to do it my way. We'll film it as a legend trip."

"Jules, you can't expose Christophe like that. It'll ruin his life."

"If he kills someone, or gets killed himself, do you think that won't put a slight crimp in it? Come on, Rile. It's a win-win for everyone."

"Except Logan. He'll never go for it. Don't you think he might notice if half the wedding party is missing, including the other groom?"

Julie waved a hand. "So he gets married a couple of hours later. He can deal."

"We can't delay the ceremony." Riley clutched his bangs, sending them even more cock-eyed. "We only have the chapel from one till two."

"So pay the officiant extra and have the ceremony at the reception." Julie picked up a clipboard from the bedside table. "Send the guests in there first. I've always thought weddings would be way better if the guests were allowed to get sloshed before the ceremony. Especially those excruciatingly long Eastern Orthodox ones like my cousins had. Lord." She pulled a pen out of her vest pocket and scribbled a note. "I'll call Heather once we're in the van. She'll take care of everything and calm Logan down."

"Guys." Trent was fairly bouncing on his toes by now, the *hurry hurry* klaxon in his brain nearly deafening. "We don't have time for goddamn wedding planning. Can we please just fucking *go*?"

Julie eyed him. "We can only pull this off if we're unobtrusive about absconding with one of the grooms. Hate to point it out, but you're not exactly dressed in wedding attire."

"Dude. We're heading into the woods. Hiking. Muddy trails." He flecked a pine needle off his sweatshirt. "Tree boogers. You really want to wear your good clothes?"

"If we expect to sell it, yes. As it is, it'll look suspicious when we all pile into the van." She strode back to the door. "I'm getting your tux, Rile."

Riley frowned at her. "You wouldn't let me put the damn thing on for fear I'd wrinkle it and ruin the shot from the back. Now you want me to wear it on a wilderness hike?"

She paused with her hand on the doorknob and widened her eyes at him. "Hello? *Werewolf*? You do the fricking math." She zipped out the door.

Trent studied Riley, huddled in the desk chair. "Hey. I'm sorry for fucking up your wedding day."

"If you think I'm leaving Christophe twisting in the wind, you're delusional."

"Dude. If I told anyone else what I told you? Delusional is the least they'd think me."

"Anyway, if the wedding went perfectly, we'd be tempting fate, especially since Logan and I never manage to do anything the easy way." Riley's smile was wistful. "Maybe this is our best shot at appeasing fate from the get-go."

"You could always stay here. You and Logan could go through with the ceremony. I mean, there's not a lot you can do that you haven't already done."

"You think Julie will let me stay behind if she's got her eye on a ratings bonanza? That'll trump wedding planning any day, and she wants me on-camera. She wants Logan too, but if we tell him about this, I don't think he'll react well."

"Understatement."

Riley nodded at Trent's garment bag. "So better do what she says. Put on your suit."

"Yeah. I guess." Trent unzipped the garment bag and pulled out the jacket and one of the shirts.

Riley whistled. "Nice."

"I know, right? First time I'll have it on, and I'm about to subject it to cruel and unusual tree punishment." He pulled out the narrow trousers. *Okay. Commando ain't gonna fly in these.* What were the odds he had clean underwear?

He unzipped the duffel, with the usual explosion of clothes.

Riley chuckled. "That's like a giant milkweed pod."

"More like an IED." He pawed through the tangle, scattering his mangy T-shirts and holey jeans across Julie's floor. *She has no one to blame but herself.*

Jeans, shorts, T-shirt, T-shirt, T-shirt, socks—*ewww*, sweats, undershirt—

I don't wear undershirts.

He fell back on his ass, the wisp of white jersey clutched in his hand. *The first night. I ripped this off him and threw it in the corner.*

"Riley?" His voice trembled as much as his hand. "I think we've got it." He held up the undershirt. "Wolf's clothing."

CHAPTER
TWENTY-FIVE

Trent had to hand it to Julie. She didn't shit around when she wanted something. Within ten minutes, all of them—her, Riley, Trent, Zack—with his camera—were out the side door and trying to be nonchalant about speed-walking through the parking lot.

Riley stumbled, and when Trent reached out to steady him, Julie and Zack kept going, heading for the van at the far end of the lot.

Trent held on to Riley's arm. "Do you think this will work?"

"I . . . I think so. All the pieces fit. But I don't know if one undershirt will be enough."

Trent shook his elbow. "Don't say that. It's gotta be. Otherwise he's never coming back."

"Who's never coming back?"

Trent whirled, sending Riley skittering on the gravel, free arm flailing, in his slick-soled dress shoes. Trent steadied him as Detective Bishop stepped out from behind a pickup truck.

"Bishop. Jesus *fuck*, dude, your timing sucks."

"I'd say my timing is perfect. What the fuck are you doing, Pielmeyer? Kidnapping a guy from the middle of his wedding?"

Riley blinked. "I'm not being kidnapped. At least not at the moment."

Bishop stared pointedly at where Trent was still clutching Riley's elbow. "That's what victims always say if they're being coerced."

"Dude, what is it with you? You've got kidnapping on the fricking brain. You seriously need to get a life." Trent let go of Riley and glanced at the van. Zack was already behind the wheel, but Julie was standing next to the shotgun door, frowning at the lodge. *Come on, Julie, now's when we could really use your butt-in-ingness.*

But she wasn't paying attention, instead staring across the parking lot in the other direction.

Trent held up his hands. "Fine, Bishop, you got me, okay? I'll confess to anything you fucking want, but *not now.*"

Bishop scowled. "I don't want you to confess to some random act. I want the truth. If you'd behave like a rational person—"

"I'm not rational. I have it on good authority that I have the instincts of a three-year-old and my prefrontal cortex is nonexistent, but we don't have time to discuss it now. We—"

"Damn straight we don't have time for this." Logan loomed behind Bishop's shoulder, his expression a combination of thunderous and hurt. *How the hell is he pulling that one off?* "Where the fuck are you going, Riley? Did Trent tell you anything that—"

Riley rushed over to Logan. "No. No, of course not. But something's come up and we need to take care of it."

Riley cuddled up and stroked Logan's face, teasing a smile out of him as the tension left his jaw. He wrapped an arm around Riley and rested his cheek against the top of Riley's head.

That. Right there. That's what I feel like when I'm with Christophe. If Christophe was willing to put up with Trent's bullshit, the least Trent could do was return the favor. Trent couldn't deny that the werewolf thing was an issue—especially if their current lame plan didn't work. But when he poked that tender place in his mind, the one that shied away from the supernatural—*it's not a deal-breaker.* Besides, hadn't Christophe mentioned sharing each other's burdens the night they'd met? *I could do that. I think. For him.*

Logan lifted his head but still held Riley close. "Can't it wait until after the wedding? Everyone's getting in place. Even my father has stopped trying to schmooze the constituency and is ready for his grand entrance as father of the groom."

"It really can't. It's . . ." Riley took a deep breath. "It's a folklore thing." He peered over his glasses. "You know. A *folklore* thing?" He jerked his head at Trent, as Bishop's gaze bounced between them, a frown knitting his forehead.

For Logan, however, the light had apparently dawned. His eyebrows made a break for his hairline. "No shit? You mean a . . ." He wiggled his fingers in the universal sign for woo-woo shit. Riley nodded. "No way am I letting you do it on your own. Just a second."

He turned and beckoned to a silver fox who stood by the loading zone, tapping his watch significantly. He scowled, but strode over.

Shit. William Conner, Logan's father.

William Conner's eyes narrowed as he took in their happy little group. Uh-oh. *Here it comes.* Logan's dad had never liked Trent, and considering the guy had lied like a wall-to-wall to keep Logan off the cops' radar, this could get awkward. Especially with the lead cop looming at Trent's shoulder.

"Logan, you realize what time it is? Riley, shouldn't you be inside? Where's the other attendant? I thought you had this better organized."

Trent squared his shoulders, ready to improv the shit out of this, depending on what line William decided to take.

But William paid no attention to Trent. "Mr. Bishop."

Huh?

Bishop winced and rubbed the back of his neck. "Commissioner."

"What business do you have at my son's wedding?"

"He's the detective who was following Trent's case," Logan said.

"He *was* the detective. He was suspended six months ago."

Trent glared at Bishop. "Suspension? You're fucking kidding me. Didn't you think to mention that any of the times you popped up like a freaking jack-in-the-box?"

"You didn't ask."

"Jesus *fuck*."

William raised his eyebrows. "A kidnapping case, wasn't it? Excessive force against the alleged perpetrator?"

"Alleged my ass. The guy was guilty as sin."

"Nevertheless, I believe there's a restraining order."

Bishop glowered. "Doesn't apply. The guy isn't here."

"I doubt it will help your case that you appear to be harassing Mr. Pielmeyer. How exactly are you managing that? Unauthorized use of department resources?"

"No! I wouldn't. My cousin . . . he's a PI. I'm . . . working with him."

William closed in on Bishop, like a shark scenting five-star chum. "If you think—"

"Dad. Give it a rest. This isn't City Hall." Logan took his father's arm and drew him a couple of steps away. "Listen, something's come up."

"Something more important than starting the ceremony on time?"

"Yeah. I can't go into it now, but I need you to go in there and stall."

"Stall? You mean, the guests? All of them?"

"Yeah."

"For how long?"

Logan glanced at Riley, who shrugged. "As long as it takes. Listen. Find Heather. Tell her to break open some of the champagne and give everyone a glass. Then you can, I don't know, practice your next stump speech. A captive audience of registered voters—what more could you ask for?"

Logan's father's eyes gleamed with the fanatical light of a true politician. He straightened his tie. "Very well. But I expect a full explanation when you return." He strode off toward the lobby doors.

"Not likely," Logan muttered. He turned and hooked his arm around Riley's waist. "All right. Let's get this circus on the road."

Bishop blocked their path. "I'm coming with you."

"Seriously?" Trent carded his hand through his hair. "What the fuck do you want from me, Bishop?"

Bishop held Trent's gaze with his interrogator's stare. "You're the key, so I'm sticking with you until you give me some answers."

"Jesus, you act like this is personal. Can't you let it go?"

"It *is* personal."

"What did I ever do to you?"

"Nothing. But if you could come back, then maybe *he* could too."

"He who?" *I have zero time to fall down this freaky rabbit hole.* "Never mind. But if you tag along, Mr. Ex-detective, you'll need to make yourself useful. Then I might be inclined to be more cooperative."

Bishop's eyes narrowed, then he nodded sharply. "Right. I'll hold you to that. What do you want me to do?"

Logan grabbed Trent's arm. "Are you nuts?"

"Maybe." Trent shook off Logan's grip. "But, dude, check it out. The guy's the size of the Portland Building. We could use some muscle, and I'm so in the mood for excessive force."

They marched to the van. Julie glared at Logan, but then frowned at Bishop. "Who the hell are you?"

Bishop glanced at Trent. "Apparently I'm extra muscle."

She looked him up and down. "Not bad. You can drive. Trent, you ride shotgun and give him directions." She shooed Logan and Riley toward the van's open panel door. "The two of you are going to make nice with the camera on the way."

"Christ," Logan muttered as he climbed in, "I said it was a circus, but I didn't expect a fucking clown car."

Riley followed him, wincing. "Don't mention clowns. Too creepy."

"Sorry, Riley. Sit here by me."

Julie followed him in. "Think of it this way, Logan: at least you're both dressed right. You'll class up the show."

"Hey, wait up." Max Stone, complete with his Indy Jones hat and jacket, raced up and hung on the open door. "There you are, Zack. I've been waiting for you by that bear statue for twenty minutes. Did you forget about reshooting my entrance?"

"Sorry, Max. Something came up."

"But . . ." A grin broke out on Max's face. "Oh, I get it. Road trip! I'm totally in. We can shoot my arrival from the highway."

"Just what we need," Logan muttered. "Another clown."

After miles of grueling pursuit, Christophe's stamina was fading rapidly, but he refused to give up. He suspected Etienne was toying with him—not only attempting to run him to exhaustion, but to direct the chase back to the killing field, remaining always out of reach.

Christophe had his own goal, however: keep Etienne away from the cave. If he could prevent the rendezvous with Anton, Etienne would be unable to shift as well. Then, should they encounter the ranchers, there would be two targets instead of one.

A rabbit darted onto the path and froze. Christophe's belly was beyond empty, but he couldn't make himself see the poor frightened thing as prey. He yipped once and the rabbit bounded into the brush. *I make a truly lamentable wolf.* Anton and Etienne didn't have to go to the extreme of slaughtering livestock to ensure Christophe's demise—he'd starve to death if he was forced to live in the wild.

He lifted his nose in the air, scenting for Etienne's direction, and froze. Another scent, achingly familiar, mingled with Etienne's, and Christophe's protective instincts kicked in with a vengeance.

Trent.

Trent was in the woods near Etienne. If Etienne got close to him, he'd be able to scent Christophe on him—both man and wolf—since there was scant chance that Trent would have shed his regrettable sweatshirt. If Etienne believed harming Trent would injure Christophe, he would show no compunction.

Christophe growled. *That bastard shall not go anywhere near Trent.* In an adrenaline-charged burst of speed, he sprinted down the path.

Etienne's trail led toward the cave now—had he tired of the chase? Was his time to meet Anton near, or—fear lanced through Christophe and he stumbled—had Etienne detected Trent?

No time to waste.

While Etienne circled the hill to the more gradual incline, Christophe crashed his way directly up the steeper slope, heedless of the brambles that tore at his fur and tangled around his legs. He staggered onto the ledge just as Etienne reached the top of the path, putting Christophe in front of the cave.

Exactly where I want to be.

He crouched low, hackles raised, teeth bared. Etienne mirrored him, then made a quick feint to the side. Christophe snarled, but didn't move. *You think to trick me into leaving you a way inside. I am not so foolish.*

If he allowed Etienne inside, Christophe stood no chance. With access to his clothing, Etienne could shift.

But he'd be vulnerable. I could kill him then. His throat in my jaws, his blood on my tongue.

Saliva flooded his mouth as a savage, alien joy coursed through him. Is this how a true wolf felt when closing in for a kill? *You can't even kill a rabbit, yet you think you can kill a man?*

Etienne was not just any man though—he was the man who had suborned Anton, the man who'd planned to murder Christophe. *And my father? Will he allow my father to live after deposing him from the company he loves more than anything?*

Would his father *want* to live?

Then, subtle and seductive and familiar, Trent's scent reached him, borne on the breeze that quickened across the hillside. Christophe's last reservations crumbled as another jolt of adrenaline surged through his veins. His vision shifted, everything suddenly tinted red. *Some things—some people—are too precious to risk. I may not be able to kill the man, but the wolf? Let it end here. Now.*

Etienne lunged for the cave mouth, and Christophe leaped to intercept, only to have Etienne scuttle to a safe distance, tail down. Once at the brink of the ledge, he turned and assumed his aggressive stance.

What?

Then the truth dawned. *Etienne Melion, terror of the Old Families, scourge of schoolboys, bully of the boardroom, is afraid of a fair fight.*

Christophe wanted to laugh, but in his wolf form it emerged as a howl. *Of course.* With all his needs catered to, even his shifts managed by the staff at the Melion estates, Etienne was little more than a pampered pet. No one had ever stood up to him before because no one had dared. The only person of their generation of equal status was Christophe, who'd never chosen confrontation.

Well, he chose it now.

He crept forward, a growl vibrating in his chest. Etienne backed up until he was poised on the edge of the drop-off. He attempted to dart sideways, but stumbled when he lost purchase with his rear paws. *My chance.* Christophe sprang, knocking Etienne to his side on the rocky ledge. Etienne yelped. *Hurts, does it? You'd best get accustomed to pain, because more is on the way.*

Etienne scrambled to his feet and Christophe charged again, this time snapping at an ear. Etienne jerked his head aside, sending him off-balance. This time, Christophe stayed with him as they rolled across the ledge in a tangle of teeth and claws and fur.

For every bite, every kick, every swipe of claws that Etienne managed to land, Christophe landed two. *You stand no chance. You want only to protect yourself, to return to your life of luxury. I am protecting my mate. And I have nothing left to lose.*

They fetched up hard against the mountainside, Etienne underneath. When he pawed the air, attempting to right himself, Christophe clamped his teeth on Etienne's foreleg.

Etienne yelped. *My advantage.* Christophe bit down harder and shook his head, feeling the bones snap beneath his teeth. *Yes!* His wounds were nothing in the hot surge of victory. Releasing his hold, Christophe howled while Etienne whimpered beneath him.

He glared down at Etienne, who held his injured leg crooked against his chest. *You have always underestimated me, you and my brother. You think me tame because I refused to fight. But until now, I had no need. Until now, I had nothing worth fighting for. Now, I do.*

He dove, grabbing Etienne's throat in his jaws, feeling the pulse of his life there, under his teeth. He could do it, he could snuff it out, rid the world of this—

"Back away, *mon frère.*"

Christophe froze. He needed only to bite down, a simple snap of his jaws. But not a foot from his face was the barrel of a shotgun, Anton at the trigger, with an unholy smile on his face.

"I said, back away." He jerked his head toward the ledge, but didn't alter his point-blank aim on Christophe's head. "You wonder at my choice of weapon? Not very elegant, I know, but it matches the arms of the ranchers whose poor flocks you savaged in your killing frenzy."

Christophe let go of Etienne and backed up one step, the growl rumbling in his chest, warring with his urge to whine. *His brother.* His rock through his turbulent childhood, his difficult adolescence, his rebellious early adulthood. He could almost understand how Anton might resent him enough to want to depose him, but to hate him enough to shoot him in cold blood?

The last vestiges of his victory euphoria drained away, leaving him empty, spent, and defeated.

But then he caught a whiff of a familiar scent on Anton's clothing. *Trent.* Anton had touched Trent. Had *dared* to touch Trent.

Shotgun or no shotgun, Christophe would not let such an outrage pass.

CHAPTER
TWENTY-SIX

"**D**id you hear that?" Trent whispered. "That was a wolf fight. We're close."

"Wolf fight?" Bishop grabbed Trent's elbow. "You said this was life or death."

"It is."

"The life or death of a wolf?"

"Jesus, Bishop. Just roll with it, okay? If everything goes well, you'll have a chance to play ex-cops and robbers, or ex-cops and kidnappers, or ex-cops and what-the-hell-ever. But for now, shut up. Everybody shut the fuck up." *Including me.*

"Zack, did you catch the sound of the struggle?" Julie scowled at the hillside that rose above them. "I don't think—"

"Stop trying to make this about the fucking video." *Screw tact. There's no time for that shit.* "We need to move, and now. Bishop, do you have your gun?"

"What? No. I'm suspended, remember?"

"Jesus fuck, what good is having my own stalker ex-cop if he can't even carry his own weight?"

"I didn't know I'd be going on a big-game hunt."

Trent grabbed his arm. "No. Do *not* shoot any animals. Or what you think are animals. Guns are only to help subdue the crazy men who're letting their kink get in the way of their sanity."

"Hey." Bishop held up his hands, palms out. "No gun. So no shooting."

Trent's panic receded. Slightly. "Okay. They must be on the other side of these rocks. We should split up: half go that way, half go this way."

"Riley, you're with me," Logan growled. "Max should take point."

Riley goggled at him. "Are you serious? For God's sake, Logan, he's not cannon fodder."

Max puffed out his chest. "Don't worry. They'd never attack a celebrity. Not on camera."

"I was thinking of him more as a distraction," Logan murmured, "but roll with that if it makes you happy, Max."

"I don't *care* who's with who, or who's on point, upside down, or backward," Trent ground out between his clenched teeth. "You figure it out and catch up when you can." He pushed past Bishop and ran toward the rocks. "Because I am fucking done."

Anton's smile was all the more horrifying because it was so familiar. "Do you know how many times I wanted to strangle you in your crib, you puling piece of shite. The little prince. The golden child. The new heir. They never even *looked* at me after you were born."

Etienne scrambled to his feet, any pretense of submission gone, although he yelped when he attempted to put weight on his front leg. *Good. I wish I'd ripped it off entirely.*

Keeping the gun trained on Christophe, Anton reached into the open satchel at his feet and pulled out a shirt. He spread it on the ground. Etienne hopped onto it, three-legged, and collapsed, panting.

"Etienne may have proposed the merger of Melion GmbH and Clavret et Cie, but it was my idea to get rid of *you.* Papa was ready to let everything go. The business that *I* built, despite your slacking, despite his pandering to your every whim. I knew I had to find someone strong enough to partner me. Whose belief in the old ways was as strong as Papa's but who had a more realistic view of running the company."

On the ground next to Anton, Etienne began to shift back, his limbs contorting, bones buckling, face distorting: a half-animal, half-human abomination. *Mother of God.* Christophe had only seen the transformation from the other side once—when his father had taken him to the woods for his first shift. He'd forgotten how hideous it truly was. How could he expect Trent to love a man who held this horror at his core?

Perhaps allowing Anton to go through with his plan would be best for them all.

Anton watched the transformation, a desperate longing on his face as, with every pop of realigning bone and snap of tortured tendon, Etienne was remade into a man.

Etienne stood up, naked, cradling his arm against his chest. He took two strides across the ledge and kicked Christophe in the side. "*Morceau de merde*. I won't be able to show my face in a meeting until this is healed." He kicked Christophe again, directly in his injured ribs and Christophe went over with a yelp. Etienne turned his back and walked over to Anton, snatching his pants out of the satchel. "Shoot him."

"With pleasure." Anton raised the gun to his shoulder. "Your whore showed up at the cabin today, so I know your dirty secret. You refuse to take control because you *can't*. You're not an alpha at all. You're nothing but a—"

"Hold it right there, cowboy." Trent stepped onto the ledge. "You weren't about to say 'bitch' were you? Because, *dude*. You've got no room to talk."

CHAPTER
TWENTY-SEVEN

Anton's brow knitted in confusion. "You."

Trent added a sashay to his stride—not easy, because *holy shit, they've got a fucking shotgun.* "Surprise."

The barrel of that fricking gun wasn't pointed at Christophe anymore, but, *hello*, now it was pointing at Trent. Sweat broke out on his forehead and his stomach dive-bombed his toes. *Jesus, now I know how poor Mortimer felt every night.* He edged closer to Christophe until the panic stopped battering at his brain.

Anton glared at Christophe. "This is what you prefer? Submitting to this rough-trade whore?"

"Don't knock it till you've tried it," Trent singsonged, amping up the bratitude to bolster his courage. "But check your facts before you start slinging insults."

Anton's gaze flicked to Etienne. If he was looking for orders, he got no help from Etienne, who was stepping into his trousers as if he were on the deck of a yacht. Zipping up seemed to give him some trouble, since his forearm was bent at an odd angle and oozed blood from a super-impressive bite.

Trent glanced down at Christophe. "That your work?" Christophe huffed, but kept his eyes trained on the two other men. "Good job. Too bad you didn't take off his dick." Christophe rumbled in that wolfish equivalent of an eye roll. "Yeah, excellent point. I wouldn't touch it either." He waggled his eyebrows at Anton. "Unlike some people I could name."

Anton pressed his lips together, and the gun barrel jerked. Trent flinched, then tried to cover it with a wink. *Time to dial it down a notch.* He wanted to distract the bad guys, not piss them off so much they'd pull the trigger. *I really hope everyone else is in place by now, because I'm running out of ad libs.*

Etienne picked up his shirt with his good hand, the picture of urbane sophistication despite an arm that looked like a chew toy. Shouldn't the guy show some sign that he was in pain? Maybe it was a werewolf thing.

Then he raised his head and glared at Trent. The hatred etched lines in his face, robbing it of any attractiveness. His eyes glowed— fricking *glowed*—like embers. Whenever Christophe's eyes had lit up, Trent had chalked it up to mood lighting. *Guess not.* But there was a shit-ton of difference between Etienne's red fury and Christophe's golden passion.

"This shirt will be ruined. You owe me a new one, Clavret."

"Of course." Anton reached out to take the shirt, but Etienne snatched it away.

"Not you, idiot. Your brother." Etienne turned his glowing eyes on Christophe, with a decidedly evil smile on his face. "A shirt made of a wolf's pelt. Perhaps I shall set a new fashion. Or bring back an old one."

"Dude. Did you threaten to *skin* him?" Trent dropped to his knees next to Christophe and wrapped an arm across his back. *Jesus, he's shivering like crazy. Where the hell is my backup?*

Etienne stared down his nose at Trent. "I never make threats, *whore.* I announce my intentions, and then I execute them." He shook out the shirt and thrust it at Anton without bothering to look at the other man. "Assist me."

Anton blinked, then seemed to remember his place. He tucked the gun stock under his arm, one hand still under the fore-end, and took the shirt by the collar. As he held it up, the gun swung toward Etienne.

"Watch out, you fool. Don't point that at me." Etienne shoved the barrel away, knocking the gun out of Anton's grip.

Oh shit! Trent flung himself across Christophe and tensed, waiting for the blast, for the shell to rip into his back the way it had shredded Mortimer's face and chest every night for seven years.

The gun clattered to the ledge and both Anton and Etienne swore, but—nothing. No blast. *Thank you, dancing baby Jesus.* Christophe whined, probably protesting Trent's chokehold.

Trent peeked up between Christophe's ears. Etienne's back was toward Anton, who had one foot on the gun stock as he slipped the shirt sleeve onto Etienne's good arm. Neither one of them was paying attention to Trent and Christophe.

Come on, Bishop. Now's your chance to ride to the rescue. But although Trent scanned the bushes, he couldn't detect any movement.

Etienne jerked, cradling his injured arm against his chest. "Careful, you clumsy oaf. Are you trying to add to your brother's damage?"

"Sorry, Etienne. If you'd just hold your arm out more, I could—"

"I can't hold my arm out. That is the whole point."

Anton adjusted his hold on the shirt, his balance clearly impaired by the gun under his foot. Damn it, one hit below his center of gravity and he'd go down. If Bishop would just—

I could do it. Trent gulped and blotted the sweat off his upper lip. *But it's a shotgun. I can't—*

Christophe shifted in Trent's embrace with a barely voiced whimper, and Trent's heart constricted. *If I don't get over myself, Christophe will die. For real. Forever.* He squinted at Anton, fussing with Etienne's buttons. *Not gonna happen, assholes.*

Giving Christophe one last squeeze, he took a deep breath. *On one, two, three—*

He launched himself across the ledge and drove his shoulder into Anton's side—a textbook-perfect stage-fighting tackle. But while Trent knew how to take a fall, Anton clearly didn't and sprawled onto the rocks with a grunt.

Trent scooped up the shotgun, the feel of it revoltingly familiar in his hands. Etienne lunged for him, but Trent dodged, sending the bastard staggering into the side of the hill as Anton climbed heavily to his feet.

"Surprise again." Trent backed toward Christophe, the gun trained on Anton's knees.

"Anton." Etienne's voice was laced with disgust. "Are you totally incompetent? Retrieve the weapon."

"Easy for you to say." Anton edged toward Etienne, never taking his gaze off the barrel of the shotgun. "He's not aiming at you."

"Him? He cannot possibly have the skill or fortitude to shoot a man." Etienne shooed Anton toward Trent. "Subdue him."

Trent raised the stock to his shoulder. "I'll have you know that I've shot someone in the face two thousand five hundred and fifty-five times. But who's counting?"

Etienne's lip curled. "You expect me to believe you have killed over two thousand men?"

"Technically it was always the same guy, and it's not like I wanted to do it. But the principle's the same. I may not aim for the face this time, but trust me, I have no problem pulling the trigger."

Bishop stepped out of the underbrush. "That won't be necessary."

About time, dude. "Bishop, for God's sake, take this fucking gun."

Trent handed it over, shaking out his hands and wiping them on his jeans as Logan appeared next to Bishop, the two of them forming a wall of muscle behind Anton and Etienne. *Guess the gang's all here. Finally.*

"How much of that did you get on film, guys?" Trent called.

Julie emerged from the bushes, holding branches aside for Zack to follow. "All of it, including the werewolf shift. The ratings on this are going to be *epic*. I mean, not one, but two werewolf transformations? We'll have to mask the naughty bits in postproduction. We're not that kind of show—yet. But I gotta say," she saluted Etienne, "nice butt."

Anton laughed, a pained sound. "You think anyone will believe this, even with your so-called evidence? Do you know who we are?"

Riley joined Trent next to Christophe. "Yes, actually. You're descended from Baron Bizuneh, the Bisclavret." He nodded at Etienne. "And you from Sir Melion. I'm sure your families have counted on the public's disbelief of the uncanny to hide your natures since the Age of Enlightenment."

Etienne sneered. "All conjecture. You'll prove nothing, regardless of anything you claim to have on film. Our influence reaches far beyond what you could imagine, you, with your paltry camera and ridiculous costumes."

Max bristled. "Hey. I'll have you know this hat is recognized worldwide."

"Perhaps. But not because of you." Etienne flicked his fingers as if Max was an annoying insect and faced Julie. "You, *mademoiselle*, won't be able to perpetrate your so-called werewolf hoax. I am clearly a man, the leader of my well-respected company . . . And this—" Etienne pointed at Christophe "—is nothing more than a wolf, now and always."

"Not so fast, asshole." Trent swung his backpack off and kneeled next to Christophe. He pulled out the undershirt. "Remember this? Will it be enough?"

Christophe sniffed at the undershirt, and the look in his eyes when he raised them to Trent's face . . . *Shit, who could ever think he was an animal?* Christophe rubbed his head along Trent's jaw.

"I take it that's a yes?" Riley said.

"Awesome!" Max rubbed his hands together. "Zack, be sure to get my good side. I'll stand behind him, so you can—"

"No." Trent stood up, shielding Christophe from the camera. "You can't."

Julie scowled at him. "Isn't getting video evidence of the legend the whole point of this trip?"

"The whole point of this trip, if you remember, was to rescue Christophe from these douche bags and help him change back into a man. All this other crap—the camera, the ex-police escort," Trent waved his hand at everyone crowding the ledge, "the extras. This was supposed to be me and Riley. The rest of you are only party-crashers. And I'm telling you, you can't do it. Not to him." Trent glanced down at Christophe, remembering their conversation about Mystique. "The cost is too great."

"But—but without the second shift the story will be—"

Riley stepped up. "Anyway, Jules, the de France Bisclavret story mentions specifically that the baron wouldn't transform until he was alone. Film the inside of the cave, show it's empty, then show the wolf going in. Have Max do commentary or something until a man comes out."

She frowned. "That's not nearly as dramatic."

"Too fucking bad. It's all you're gonna get." Trent laid his hand on Christophe's back. "So do it."

"Fine." She beckoned to Zack.

Max scuttled over to the cave mouth and faced the camera. "This is where the werewolf will transform into a man." He backed up, gesturing to the rock face. "This cave, this— Ow!" He rubbed his head where he'd smacked into a rock that jutted out over the entrance.

"Don't worry. I'm fine. We'll edit that in postproduction." He cleared his throat. "This primitive, barren cave in the Oregon wilderness, far from his home in Nanteez—"

"*Nantes*, you idiot," Logan muttered.

Riley chuckled and patted Trent's arm. "Once they're clear of the cave, you guys go ahead. I can keep Jules reined in and Max'll do anything Logan says, so don't worry. It'll be okay."

After the silly man in the Allan Quatermain outfit bumbled around in the cave for ten minutes, Christophe finally limped inside, still in shock from Trent's actions.

The fact Trent had figured out the problem, had found a *solution*, was but a secondary miracle. The true miracle was that Trent had stood up for him, had come back for him despite his fear of the forest, his mistrust of the supernatural, and his probable revulsion of Christophe's true nature.

But that Trent had realized how mortifying it would be for him to transform in public? That was beyond miraculous. He didn't know how Etienne could do it with others watching. Christophe had to be alone or he couldn't force the change to happen.

Christophe huddled against the wall as Trent spread the undershirt on the dirt floor. *But I could do it. I could change in front of him.* In fact, if Christophe wanted this relationship to go anywhere—and he did, now more than ever—he'd force himself to do it, to hide nothing. If Trent chose to stay with him, he must do so with full knowledge of Christophe's monstrous nature. Anything less would be unfair.

Trent pulled a pair of gray sweatpants and a crumpled Henley out of his backpack and set them on the floor next to the undershirt. "These are mine. Not exactly daisy-fresh, but I guess it's a good thing I suck at laundry, huh?" He flashed an uncertain smile at Christophe.

Why was he uncertain? Surely he didn't imagine Christophe would object to wearing his lover's clothing? Cold settled in his belly as Trent backed up several steps. Perhaps Trent's fear of the uncanny was reasserting itself, now that the moment of unfortunate truth had arrived.

"Anyway, I figured wandering around the mountains in nothing but a wifebeater wouldn't do much for your image with camera-happy Julie stomping around. Although . . ." His smile changed to impish. "If you wanted to give me a private show later, I wouldn't object."

Thank God. Perhaps Trent hadn't been so repulsed by the truth that, having staged the rescue, he planned to say good-bye.

Christophe limped over to the undershirt and lay down on it with a pained grunt. *This is going to hurt more than usual.* How could Anton think this a blessing? It was a curse, plain and simple, a darkness that could twist any soul. *Although Etienne would have been evil, mutation or no.*

Trent laid a tentative hand on Christophe's back and stroked him. "Hey. I saw that Etienne guy shift. I know this isn't gonna be easy. But whatever you need, I'm here, okay? Well, everything except, you know, doggy sex, because that would be gross."

Christophe huffed, the only way he could laugh in wolf form, and his injured ribs protested. Trust Trent to defuse the direst situation with the ridiculous.

"I won't watch. I know it's private. But I'll guard the door, make sure no one tries to sneak in. I—" Trent sucked in a breath and let it out on a low chuckle. "I'll be here when you're done."

Christophe raised his head as Trent walked to the mouth of the cave and took a wide stance, blocking the interior with his body. *He was about to say something else.* Christophe could only hope it was what he felt himself, bone-deep and irrevocable.

I love you.

He needed to talk with Trent, confess his own feelings, beg for their return. And for that, he must transform.

Time to get this over with.

Christophe lowered his head with a sigh. When the undershirt had last touched his body, he'd been aroused to the point of pain, his mating instincts at the fore. That was imprinted here, in this shirt. His wish—to find a true mate, the kind his ancestors never had, a mate who would stand by him, protect him, love him—all of that was here. His hopes, his dreams, his fears. The true essence of himself as a man.

He let it take him, and for perhaps the first time in his life, he welcomed the pain. Because it would return him to the one person he could call home.

CHAPTER
TWENTY-EIGHT

Trent tried to ignore the crunches, cracks, and squelches that accompanied Christophe's moans of pain. *Jesus fuck, that must hurt.* He faced the group on the ledge, arms crossed, feet planted, daring any of them to come close.

None of them did. In fact, everyone looked a little alarmed. *Guess I can play intimidating as well as slutty. Good to know.*

Well, maybe not all of them were intimidated. Max appeared to border on bewildered, as if wondering when he'd get called for his close-up, and Etienne still smirked as if beurre blanc wouldn't melt in his mouth, the prick.

Bishop, though. Bishop seemed uncertain, as if the confidence he wore like he'd worn his imaginary badge had been stripped away. If the guy hadn't hounded Trent since he'd landed in Portland, he might almost feel sorry for him.

Nobody spoke. Zack hadn't stopped filming, so he had to be picking up Christophe's whimpers and yelps from inside the cave. Trent ground his molars together with every whine and abortive howl. Christophe had called it—nobody was entitled to intrude on something this personal, the public's right to know be damned.

The sudden silence was broken by a hesitant *cheep* from some enterprising bird.

"Trent?" Christophe's gravelly voice was a bare thread of his usual smooth baritone.

Trent half turned, but didn't look inside the cave. *Not yet. Not until Christophe says it's okay.* "Yeah?"

"Could you please . . . I need you."

"Abso-fucking-lutely." He aimed a panoramic glare at the group on the ledge, punctuating it with a finger-point. "You stay put. Get it?"

"Got it," Logan said, with a grin at Riley.

Trent nodded. "Good." For some reason, that made Riley laugh. *I'll figure that out later.*

He ducked into the cave.

Christophe was huddling on top of the sweatpants, naked, the undershirt held against the side of his face with one hand. Jesus *fuck*, he looked like freaking hell. A long gash on his thigh, the fingers of his other hand swollen, and huge bruises blooming across his ribs.

Yet the sight of him, human once more, made Trent's heart catch and release in his chest. He had never seen anything so beautiful in his life.

He strode across the cave and dropped to his knees. "Hey, hey, hey." He took Christophe in his arms, and dropped a kiss on his tangled hair. "It's okay now."

Christophe choked out a laugh. "It can never be okay. Not ever again. My own brother wanted to kill me. Our family shame, a secret kept for centuries, is in danger of becoming the next viral video." He lifted his head and gazed into Trent's eyes, his own shadowed and haunted. "And you—you know the truth. I am far more broken than you could ever be. But while you will get better—are already better—I never shall. I will always be a monster."

"Fuck that." Trent cupped Christophe's jaw. "You're no monster. Your brother and his buddy out there? The ones that hatched this whole fucked-up plot? Those are the monsters, whatever their shape, however slick their clothes, however fancy their cars. They're monsters on the inside. You're so not."

"But you find the supernatural distasteful."

Trent shrugged. "What can I say? Your level of weird makes me seem almost normal. I think I kinda like it."

"This?" Christophe gestured to himself with his swollen hand. "This...otherness? There is no cure, you realize. It's fixed in my DNA."

"Exactly." Trent dug some wipes out of his backpack and dabbed at the scrapes and the grime on Christophe's face. Christophe accepted the attention docilely. "You're a mutant. Like Mystique or Wolverine."

"A monster."

"Nah. A superhero." He kissed Christophe's temple, which now smelled of oil of bergamot. "You found a way to communicate with me. The important stuff anyway. Who you were. What we needed to do. But dude . . ." Trent smoothed Christophe's hair back from his forehead. "We gotta work on that chasing-cars thing."

Christophe's rusty laugh wobbled a bit. "You . . . are a revelation to me."

"Me? I'm nothing special." Trent concentrated on cleaning Christophe's swollen hand. "Just a twenty or twenty-seven-year-old theater geek who can't figure out how to work an iPhone."

"You are the superhero, *mon amour.*"

He glanced up. "Uh . . . so, that's different. Usually you call me *cher*, like a generic endearment. This time—"

"My love. It was intentional, I assure you. You are by far the strongest, bravest, sexiest, most remarkable twenty or twenty-seven-year-old it has ever been my privilege to meet."

Trent wanted to say it back. That was what he felt, wasn't it? But how could he be sure? He'd jumped into shit before without thinking it through, and he'd ended up in the middle of hell's own nightmare. Besides, there was the asshole brother, the dickhead rival, and a domineering father somewhere in the wings.

Hell, between the two of them, the weight of their emotional baggage could ground a 747.

"Come on." He wiped down Christophe's other hand. "Let's get you dressed. I don't want you flashing the entourage." He could at least admit this much. "Your ass and its attendant equipment are all mine."

Christophe smiled crookedly. "Always."

Yeah, say that after the adrenaline has worn off and you've had a rare burger or two. No other partner had ever found him compelling enough to stick with. Even Logan's loyalty was a friend's, not a lover's. *We'll sort it out later.*

He stood and, out of consideration for Christophe's swollen fingers, put a hand under his elbow to help him rise. When Christophe put weight on his injured leg, he winced and nearly fell. Trent wrapped an arm around his waist.

"Steady. Let me help you with that." He reached for the undershirt, but Christophe snatched it away with more energy than Trent had thought he possessed.

"No. I—" He swallowed. "Forgive me, but I must do it myself."

"Sure. No problem."

"But if you could . . . support me as you are, I would be grateful."

"You got it." Trent tightened his hold as Christophe almost reverently eased his arms into the undershirt and pulled it over his head. He smoothed it over his chest as if he were petting a cat. Or maybe a wolf.

Christophe took a deep breath and straightened a bit in Trent's embrace. "That is . . . better. Much better."

Despite the words, though, there was a hint of sadness, maybe resignation, in Christophe's tone. He probably hadn't missed the fact that Trent hadn't returned his avowal of love. *Working on that. Really. Just give me time.*

"Ready to face your adoring fans?"

"Perhaps I should put on some pants first."

"Oh. Heh. Right. Can you stand on your own?"

"Well enough."

"Awesome." Trent snagged the sweats off the floor and handed them to Christophe, then steadied him while he put them on. The Henley was next. "Sorry I didn't have another sweatshirt. You can have this one—"

"No. Thank you, but I will be fine with this. It is far more than I ever expected." He took a step forward and winced. "Shite. Walking barefoot back to the road will be a challenge. My feet are not as suited to this terrain as my paws."

"Gotcha. No worries." Trent dug in the backpack and pulled out a pair of flip-flops. "Not exactly handmade Italian leather—"

"They are perfect." He slipped them on. "Shall we?"

"After you, Marshmont, old bean."

Trent helped Christophe limp out of the cave. When they emerged, Riley rushed over.

"God, Christophe, are you okay?"

"I will be."

Riley put a hand on Christophe's arm and Trent was tempted to brush it off, but remembered his pact with Riley—they needed to get over their parallel pasts with each other's partners.

Partner. He couldn't deny that's what he wanted. But what he wanted and what he could have were two different things. Seven years of desperately wishing to undo his own stupidity had taught him that.

Logan left Bishop to guard both Etienne and Anton and stalked over to put a possessive arm around Riley. Apparently, that constituted a threat for Christophe. He took a halting step sideways, putting himself between Logan and Trent.

Trent met Riley's amused gaze over Christophe's shoulder. They shared an eye roll.

"Dude." Trent turned Christophe until they faced one another. "The two of you need to stop playing Don't Steal My Bone, yeah?"

"Mmmphm," Logan grunted.

"I will if he will," Christophe growled.

"He doesn't want me, and you don't want Riley. Right?" Both of them nodded grudgingly. "Okay then. Back off, because we've got other shit to deal with."

"In a moment." Christophe stood on both feet, although from the pinch of pain around his lips, it wasn't easy. "Trent Pielmeyer, I owe you my life and more. So much more." He took Trent's face between his bergamot-scented, fifty percent swollen hands. "I love you."

He pressed his lips to Trent's, softly at first, then with increasing heat, and Trent's own libido rose to meet it. The kiss turned hotter, tongues meeting and mating, and Trent felt Christophe's erection hard against his own.

Oops. Not exactly SFW, let alone a family TV show, not with Christophe going commando. Trent pulled back, breathing heavily, a smile blooming on his face.

A public declaration. Wasn't that what he'd wanted? Someone who wasn't ashamed to own him to the world. Yeah. Maybe their damn baggage wasn't so heavy after all. Hell, they could hire a frigging bellman, if it came to that.

"For God's sake, Trent," Riley said, "don't leave the man hanging."

Trent glanced around at the audience, some of them smiling, some frowning, some (Max) oblivious. *And the camera. Let's not forget the fucking camera.* He swallowed and met Christophe's gaze from under his lashes. "Yeah. Well, I guess I—"

"No!" Anton lunged forward, but Bishop hauled him back by an elbow. "You'd choose this—this *whore* over your family?"

Christophe growled low in his throat. *Perhaps my transformation was not as complete as I wished.* Because despite his injuries, only Trent's hand on his arm prevented him from going for his brother's throat.

"Chill, babe. I'll handle this." Trent tossed his bangs out of his eyes and stared Anton down. "I'm not a real whore, dude. I just play one on TV." He gestured to the camera.

Anton ignored Trent and bared his teeth at Christophe, as if he were the wolf. "You give him money for sex. How is that—"

Trent whistled and waved his hands like a semaphore. "Yo, bro. Eyes on me. First off, he didn't give me money for sex. You did." Trent tapped his chin with one finger. "Although, technically, you gave me money for *not* having sex, which was a nice touch, because seriously, dude? *I'd* have paid to not have sex with you, but I'm not sure there's enough money in the whole state of Rhode Island to meet that price."

"You—"

"That was an act. I was trying to keep you from stealing Christophe's clothes and murdering me for your little fuck-master there."

Anton scowled, trying to step away from Etienne, but not able to move with Bishop's huge hand clutching his arm. "Look at him. He's clearly not in our class. No better than a beggar. He may not charge you by the hour, but money is on the table nonetheless."

Christophe met his brother's desperate gaze and felt no shred of sympathy. "You know nothing of the matter."

"Don't I? Tell me how this is different from a marriage contract with one of the Merrick women. Or one of Etienne's sisters?"

"Hello?" Trent pointed to his groin. "I think the dick would be a big giveaway there."

"So flippant." Anton sneered. "Will you feel the same when he's no longer such a rich prize? When he's disinherited? Stripped of family and prospects?"

"Hey, no big." Trent draped an arm across Christophe's shoulders and gave him a squeeze. "I'm an expert at dealing with that kind of shit. Besides, if *you're* the family and Melion's the prospect? That's not a drawback, sugar. That's a fourteen-carat solid gold goddamn fricking *bonus.*"

"You see?" *Thank you,* cher. *Pray God you truly mean that.* "A relationship grounded in affection and loyalty can weather such trials, unlike one based on outmoded tradition and corporate law. Our curse has outlived its usefulness, if it ever had one. It's time to let it die."

"You aren't worthy of the gift." Anton spit on the ground. "It should have been me. It ought to have been me."

Christophe stared at his brother, whose face had gone from red to paler than new milk. "Even after what you have done, after your willingness to kill me, after you conspired against our father and our business, I couldn't wish this fate on you." He turned to Etienne. "You, however, deserve the burden."

Etienne raised an eyebrow. "You assume I believe it a burden. But I consider it the manifestation of a time-honored noble prerogative."

"Not anymore. The world has changed, and we must change with it."

"Please, brother—"

Christophe whirled on Anton and would have collapsed on his weak leg without Trent's support. "You have lost the right to call me that. Do you imagine that by pleading when threats have failed, you will change my mind?"

"Think of what this will do to our family. To our father."

"I prefer to think of what it would do to my son. Besides, what consideration did you have for our father when you conspired to wrest the company from him and kill his heir?" He held out his hand. "My ring, if you don't mind."

Bishop, who still held the gun at the ready, nodded his permission. Anton removed the signet and handed it over. "You don't deserve it."

"Perhaps not. But neither does Etienne Melion. How long do you think it would have been before he took control of both companies?"

Anton glanced at Etienne, who merely maintained his urbane half smile. "I— He wouldn't. We have a partnership."

"Do you? Equal, is it? You must forgive me. I didn't see him sucking *your* cock."

Anton stared at the ground. "That's different."

"Only if you do it of your own volition, Anton, because *you* desire it. If you comply only because it's what *he* desires, and succumbing is the only way for you to get the payout you want?" Christophe injected steel into his tone. "That, my erstwhile brother, is the very definition of a whore."

Anton lunged at him, but Bishop caught him, twisting his arm up behind his back. "You've got enough on your rap sheet, pal. Don't add to it. I may not be on the force at the moment, but anyone can report a crime, and I'm calling in both of you."

Etienne brushed a stray pine needle off his shirt. "For what?"

"For destruction of livestock. Assault. Conspiracy to commit murder."

"Really? But as I understand it, those poor sheep were slaughtered by a rogue wolf." He gestured to the group on the ledge. "I see no wolf here. Do you?"

Bishop pointed to the camera. "We have your threats on tape. Your attack on Christophe."

"I threatened a wolf. Attacked a wolf, who probably was responsible for the death of half a dozen poor little lambs. Surely that isn't grounds for arrest, not now that wolves are no longer a protected species in this state."

"You held a gun on Trent."

"Technically, Anton held the gun. I was merely a bystander." Etienne tapped his lips with a finger. "Ah yes. Then *Trent* held a gun on *us*. We quite feared for our lives, I assure you, since he freely confessed to shooting an astonishingly large number of men."

"It was only one guy," Trent muttered. "And he was already a ghost."

Bishop's eyebrows bunched together over his nose. "Trent, you've got no reason to stick to that bullshit story. You—" He broke off, his gaze darting from Christophe to Etienne. "Aw, fuck me sideways. You mean that's true too?"

"I *told* you." Trent scratched the side of his neck, where his scars were only partially hidden under his sweatshirt. "But I'd kinda prefer not to have to explain that to a judge. Know what I'm saying?"

"So." Etienne smirked. "Stalemate, I believe."

"No, damn it," Bishop growled. "Somebody give me another reason to report these assholes." He gave Christophe the side-eye. "One that won't make me look like a lunatic."

Christophe nodded at Anton, who was glowering in Bishop's grasp. "Mr. Bishop, my brother's greatest offenses are against my family and me, and we won't press charges in an American court. I suggest, therefore, that you remand him into my father's custody."

"I don't like it. They both deserve—"

"I assure you, he will be punished. Severely. But in accordance with our own laws, and in our own country. If you would be so good as to restrain him, however?"

"That I can do." He pulled handcuffs out of his pocket and slapped them on Anton.

Trent blinked. "I thought you were suspended."

"Pays to be prepared."

"And you, Etienne," Christophe said. "The boards of our companies may have something to say about your methods."

"Who will tell them? You? You have no clout. The boards would scarcely recognize your face. And with no true Clavret to follow him, your father will have no choice but to agree to our terms, which, I might add, will be far more favorable to us than to him."

Anton blanched. "Etienne? You swore that the company would remain in my hands."

Etienne shrugged. "I lied." He slung his jacket over his shoulder. "Why would I ally myself with an incompetent fool who can't even shift? Now, if you don't mind, this gathering has turned tedious, and I am a very busy man."

"Not so fast." Julie beckoned Zack over. "Don't forget, we've got your transformation on tape, along with these lovely confessions."

"You have nothing. My company knows what I am. It's what we've built both our partnerships and our rivalries on since the Middle Ages."

Christophe clenched his fists. "True. So your directors will know the transformation is fact, not fiction, as will those of Clavret et Cie and Merrick Industries. How do you think they'll respond to your methods of hostile takeover by way of murder? I doubt you'll retain their confidence, or your position."

Etienne's gaze slid to the side, and he swallowed convulsively. "I'm the only remaining shifter. Our traditions—"

"Are less important to shareholders these days than profits." It was time for all three of the Old Families' companies to change their antiquated leadership model. *Let it begin here.*

Etienne scowled. "What is it you want?"

"Step down."

"What? Preposterous."

"If you do not, I will make sure all three of the Old Families know that while your bluster and cruelty may be true, your strength is nothing but a sham. When asked to risk yourself, you turn tail like the most craven of betas."

Etienne's face lost all color. "You— No one would believe you."

"No? Your arm injury is testament to your lack of prowess in battle. But if that is not enough . . ." Christophe turned to Julie. "Ms. Ainsworth? Will you make your footage available to me?"

Julie grinned. "Whenever you say the word."

"Thank you." Christophe called up his full alpha power, battered and weary though it might be, and stared down Etienne. "Resign voluntarily and bask in your glory as the last cursed werewolf of your line, or be forced out, disgraced, and shunned. Your choice."

Etienne drew himself up, although his dignity was rather marred by his injured arm. "I concede nothing. This is not over, Clavret." He stalked across the ledge. Bishop blocked his path. "Do you mind? I have a plane to catch."

Bishop growled, but let him pass. "Christ on a soda cracker," he muttered as Etienne strode down the hill. "It chaps my hide to let him go."

"Don't worry. He won't get away with this either. I promise."

"You got that right," Trent said, "because no way can he drive that fricking Ferrari with only one hand."

Julie watched Etienne disappear into the trees, bouncing on her toes. "Did you see that? How he backed off? *That's* the power of the media."

"Yeah." Trent leaned close to Christophe and murmured into his ear, "You know we don't have the wolf throw down on camera, right?"

"Yes. But Etienne does not. I suggest we keep it that way."

"Got it. But—" Christophe's knees buckled, and Trent caught him around the waist. "Whoa. Hey, come on, let's sit you down."

Julie hugged herself, apparently oblivious to Christophe's distress. "Zack, you got it all, right? Everything?" Zack gave her a thumbs-up. "Excellent. When we air this—"

"You can't." Jesus fuck, this woman could give Bishop serious competition in the one-track-mind department. He eased Christophe onto a flattish rock.

"What do you mean?"

"I mean, you can't air this footage. Any of it. For one thing, we'll lose some of the leverage we've got over Etienne." He looked at Christophe, whose face had gone nearly gray now that he didn't have to play the Big Bad for Etienne. "And you can't expose Christophe this way. It's wrong."

"But—but—" She slapped an overhanging fir branch. "Shit." Then she glanced up at Riley and Logan, her expression turning sly. "I can cut out Etienne's *name*. Christophe's too, and we can mask faces. We've got that footage of the road trip and the search through the woods."

"Lots of great shots of me," Max said. "But we'll need to cut out the part where I hit my head. And when my jacket got tangled in those brambles."

Riley glared at her. "Jules. What are you plotting?"

She widened her eyes at him, like that animated cat in the *Shrek* movies. Trent would bet his last dollar that she was twice as deadly. "I need something to pitch to the money people, Rile, you know that. This is perfect. They'll see the potential and then—"

Riley narrowed his eyes. "What's your price for not airing any of it?"

"Well . . . I'd need something to replace it. Something good. Leads with proven audience appeal."

Max preened. "Say no more, Julie, I accept." Julie ignored him, smirking at Logan.

Logan sighed. "How many?"

"Six legend-tripping specials."

"One."

"Five."

"One."

"Three."

"One."

"Fine, I'll use this footage."

"Logan," Trent and Riley warned simultaneously.

"Fine," he muttered. "Three."

Julie punched the air. "*Yes!*" She turned to Trent. "And you. Oh my God, you were awesome! Just what my new show needs. I mean, we've got Riley for earnest, Logan for surly, and Max for . . . well . . . Max. But your flash and moxie could put us over the top. What's on your near-term agenda? Think you might be up for sharing the screen with these bozos?"

Trent's mouth dropped open. Jesus, she was offering him a job? Acting? Hell, *legend tripping*? He waited for terror to knot his gut, for sweat to break out on his forehead.

And waited. And waited.

"Trent?" Julie's normally confident tone was hesitant.

Joy bubbled up under his sternum. *Holy shit. I'm an actor again. And the supernatural can kiss my ass.* "Hell yeah. Where do I sign?"

"Ms. Ainsworth?" Christophe struggled to his feet, and Trent steadied him with an arm around his waist. "Does your production company accept investors?"

"Sure, when we can get them."

"When we arrange a private showing of your uncut footage for the Clavrets and Merricks, I'm sure both families will be quite interested."

"Seriously? But you told Etienne we'd keep everything under wraps as long as he behaved."

Christophe smiled, flashing his canines for the first time since he'd shifted back. "I lied. And in return for your evidence of Etienne's machinations, the other families will no doubt express their appreciation in a suitably lucrative manner."

Julie dropped her gaze to her feet. "I wouldn't really have outed you, you know."

"I do. You have ethics, although you may need to be reminded of them at times, and a skill in negotiation that sharks would envy. That is something the Old Families respect."

Julie's head popped up, her smile blooming. "Wow. *Thank* you."

Christophe smiled wryly. "You're welcome. Now, could we please get off this bloody mountain?"

CHAPTER
TWENTY-NINE

Christophe leaned heavily on Trent. Truly, he had reached the limits of his stamina.

Logan strode to the center of the ledge. "That's right. In case everyone has forgotten, there's a wedding waiting for us back at the resort. Assuming the guests haven't given up and gone home by now."

Riley took his hand. "Don't worry. Even if there's nobody there but the two of us, I'm still marrying you today."

"Damn straight."

Riley grinned. "Damn gay, don't you mean?"

"Whatever. You're not getting away from me, Riley Morrel."

Riley looped his arms around Logan's neck. "Who says I want to?"

This time, Riley initiated the kiss, and Christophe was surprised that Logan didn't melt into a puddle at Riley's feet.

Christophe tugged the hem of the crumpled Henley Trent had provided for him. *This may well be my favorite shirt now, other than the undershirt beneath it.* "Then let us depart." He cast a disgusted glance at the cave mouth. "I, for one, never wish to see this spot again."

Everyone straggled down the hill, Bishop hauling the cowed Anton at the head of the line, followed by Logan and Riley, their hands laced together. Zack, who'd never stopped his camera rolling, brought up the rear with Julie and Max.

"You gonna be okay on this hike?" Trent murmured. "Flip-flops aren't exactly wilderness-friendly."

Christophe chuckled, grateful for the support of Trent's shoulder. "*Cher*, I would gladly trek barefoot over broken glass to leave this place."

"Let's hope it's not that bad. I can't carry you, but I'll help."

"Thank you." They followed the parade through the woods. "I am so proud of you, *mon amour*. You, with your fear of the woods, withstood it without showing any weakness in front of the conspirators. And I guarantee, they would have exploited it, had they known."

Trent helped Christophe across a tangle of exposed tree roots. "You know, it's a funny thing. It doesn't bother me so much anymore. It did a bit, when we were on our way, but now that you're here . . ." He grinned. "Guess you keep my ghosts away."

"I am more than happy to do so."

They were silent as they negotiated a rough bit of terrain. "I've been wondering. You and that prick, Etienne, are the last of the line, right?"

"That is correct. The mutation only manifests in the male line, and then only if the mother carries the dosage-dependent gene. Etienne has only sisters. The Merricks of this generation are both female, as are our Clavret cousins. Anton carries the gene, but it's not expressed."

"So how come there aren't more of you?"

"Because women aren't idiots."

Trent grinned. "Non sequitur much?"

"The mutation carries with it a high rate of maternal mortality. The babies are born with vestigial claws. That's how they're identified at birth. No matter what precautions we take, the outcome is never certain."

Trent winced. "Ouch."

"Indeed. When I was born, my family had planned so carefully. My father had contracted with a discreet private hospital, attempting to cover every contingency, reduce the risk as much as possible. But he hadn't counted on early onset labor coinciding with a blizzard. So despite his best laid plans, my first act in the world was to kill my mother."

"Listen, you know you can't blame yourself for that anymore, don't you?"

"Perhaps. But I can blame my father. And I would certainly blame myself were I to subject any woman to such a fate."

"Would you? I mean, if there weren't any danger? Marry a woman?"

Christophe stopped Trent on the path. "*Cher*, Trent, werewolves may be bisexual by nature, but although I've had liaisons with women in the past, my inclinations have always skewed more toward men. Yet another reason I could never accede to my father's wishes. I harbor secrets enough. I could not bear to live another lie."

Trent thought about Christophe's words. "Can I ask you something?"

"Of course."

He swallowed against a suddenly dry mouth. "For a minute, did you believe him? Anton, I mean. That I'm only with you for your money. Because the penthouse is awesome, sure. François is a totally kick-ass Alfred or Bunter or whatever. And your clothes—before Anton burned them anyway—were to die for." *Jesus, I'm babbling. Focus, Pielmeyer.* "It sucks that you'll lose all that, but just so you know, it won't make any difference to how I feel about you."

"Trent—"

"And when it comes to making do on a budget—hey, I'm your go-to guy. I'll take you to my favorite thrift stores. You could make even this sweatshirt look good."

"Shhh." Christophe laid a finger across Trent's lips. "I never believed him. Not even for an instant."

"Why?" It wasn't like his rocking grunge-style gave away his silver-spoon roots.

"No one who only wanted money would sit with a wolf overnight. Or risk his own dear, foolish neck on the off-chance of a rescue."

"Dear, huh?"

Christophe kissed him softly on the lips, then again on the forehead. "Adored."

"If it meant reconciling with your dad, though—if he allowed you to study genetics, revamp the company structure, forget the arranged marriage, blah, blah, blah—would you . . . would you go back? To Europe?"

Christophe shook his head. "It is not my father's place to *allow* me to live my life. I shall *choose* to do so on my own terms. That includes remaining here in America. In Portland. The genetics program at OHSU is exemplary. I need look no further. That is . . ." Christophe held Trent's gaze. "If *you* plan to remain."

Trent grinned. "Well, I've kind of got a job now, don't I? I may have to travel with the show a little, and there are some things I need to take care of, but—"

"Guys!" Julie hollered from where the van was parked on the verge above them. "Come on. Wedding, remember?"

"Keep your skirt on," Trent shouted. "We'll be right there."

"Trent?" Christophe's voice was tentative, maybe a little fearful.

Trent urged him up the last slope. "I—"

Logan stormed over. "*Now*, guys." He fairly hauled Christophe out of Trent's arms and into the van before he climbed into the driver's seat.

"I guess we'll talk later," Trent muttered. With Riley riding shotgun, the only seat left was next to Bishop.

Fucking great.

Trent slumped down, arms crossed, prepared to sulk in silence all the way back to the resort. He managed several minutes of moping before Bishop cleared his throat.

"So. What you said back there. You really weren't kidnapped? You were—shit, I don't know—haunting Forest Park for seven years?"

"Yep."

Bishop ran his hand over his head. "So there are other places, other . . . what . . . dimensions?"

"Call 'em whatever you want. They're real, dude, just like werewolves. There's probably a bunch of other supernatural shit out there too. Better get used to the idea."

Julie turned around and grinned at them. "Don't worry. You can hear all about them on my legend-tripping specials."

"Christ on a carousel," Bishop muttered. "And I thought kidnapping was the worst that could have happened to—" He clenched his jaw shut, throat working, and stared out the window.

The worst that could have happened to whom? Trent opened his mouth to ask, but at that moment, they pulled up to the resort, and

Logan hustled them all out of the van so fast that Trent checked his seat for skid marks.

Chalk up one more thing to talk about later. My to-do list is seriously out of control.

Ahead of him, Christophe caught his flip-flop on the edge of the lodge stairs and stumbled. Trent rushed forward and caught him around the waist before he could fall, earning one of Christophe's sharp-toothed smiles. *God, I love that smile.* Trent leaned in and captured it in a kiss.

Yep. Kissing was so going on that list—right at the very top.

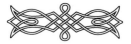

Jesus *fuck.* The wedding. Was. Awesome.

Yeah, the guests were a bit glassy-eyed, maybe from the champagne, which Heather had apparently been quite generous with. But Trent put his money on the fact that Logan's father had *talked* at them for the whole hour and a half of the werewolf-hunt delay.

Who knew you could filibuster a wedding?

William had even convinced the resort to allow them to hold the ceremony in the chapel despite the postponement. Trent sat at the back of the crowd, next to Christophe, who was still in Trent's grubby sweats. Logan had offered to let them check Anton's cabin in case he'd left any of Christophe's clothing intact. The instant Christophe declined, Logan practically frog-marched Riley down the aisle.

It was a nice gesture on Christophe's part—given how meticulous he was—although it may have been simple self-preservation. If Logan had had to wait another instant, he might have detonated, and then everyone would have been caught in the blast zone.

Logan and Riley stood at the front of the hall, their fingers intertwined. Sure, there might be mud on their shoes and the hems of their tux pants, but—

Trent squinted at the back of Riley's coat. He turned to Christophe. "Dude," he murmured, mindful of the crowd hanging on the officiant's words, "is that a *paw print* on Riley's ass? You want to explain to me how that got there?"

"No," Christophe murmured with a sly smile, his gaze never leaving the ceremony.

Zack was downstage left, filming the whole thing, panning across the wedding party, getting what had to be a perfect shot of Julie, in her best-person dress and Doc Martens, fighting tears and glaring at Logan for all she was worth.

Logan—God, had anyone *ever* in the history of the world looked that fucking *happy*? If joy were helium, he'd be halfway to Mars by now. Riley was serious and intent as usual. He fumbled Logan's ring, and it rolled halfway down the aisle before Julie—who had clearly lost the not-gonna-cry battle—managed to catch it.

Trent couldn't blame her for the sentiment. When the officiant—a woman with a blue fauxhawk and two full tattoo sleeves—pronounced Riley and Logan husbands together for life, Trent choked up a little himself. Even Bishop—lurking at the back of the chapel with a handcuffed Anton—knuckled his eyes as if he was wiping away a tear.

Yeah, true love'll do that to you, especially if you're afraid you'll never get it yourself.

He glanced sidelong at Christophe. *On the other hand . . .*

Christophe sagged in his chair, a plate of half-eaten wedding cake on the table in front of him. If he had to sit here much longer, he might slide *under* the table from sheer exhaustion.

Considering that the reception had gotten such an early start—at least from the perspective of alcohol consumption—it had lasted an inordinately long time. Long past Logan and Riley's departure for their honeymoon, destination undisclosed.

Logan had stopped by their table while Riley was bidding Julie good-bye. "If I tell anyone where we're going, Ainsworth'll be there with her camera crew and Max fucking Stone. That's not my idea of a honeymoon." He'd pulled a key out of his pocket and handed it to Trent. "My old apartment. I told 'em to hold off on the renovation, so you can stay as long as you need. See you in three weeks."

As Trent had grinned and tucked the key in his pocket, Christophe's heart sank to his unfortunately grubby toes. In those first bewildering moments after Trent had recognized Christophe as a wolf, he'd revealed he had nowhere to go. Christophe hadn't forgotten—he had hoped to capitalize on the confession and convince Trent to move into the penthouse immediately. How disturbing was it that he actually wished for Trent to have no choice but to allow Christophe to save him?

Ludicrous. How could he demand the right to make his own choices, yet wish to deprive choice from the man he loved?

If only I can convince him to stay with me. Prove that together we could build something as strong as the relationship Logan and Riley enjoy.

He'd simply have to depend on his powers of persuasion. He knew how to woo a man, or he had once. Pray God he hadn't lost the knack, now, when it mattered the most.

As Christophe slumped in his chair, watching the wedding guests snake across the floor in a sloppy conga line, Trent put an arm around his shoulders. "Hey. You look beat. Ready to call it a day? Since Logan and Riley have taken off, I don't think anyone will blame you."

Christophe smiled at him and gave him a gentle kiss. "I didn't want to say anything. You seemed to be having fun."

Trent waved his hand. "Nah. Just sending Logan and Riley off in style. They deserve it. They've got . . ." He heaved a sigh and took his arm away. "Listen. We need to talk."

"Oh dear. That sounds ominous."

Trent shrugged. "Maybe not. Should we go somewhere quiet?"

"No. If I need to recover, I want access to alcohol. Lots of it, in company with people sufficiently inebriated that when I make a maudlin fool of myself, nobody will remember it tomorrow."

Trent's eyes widened. "What do you need to recover from? Is there something—" He ducked as someone's stiletto flew overhead. "Jesus *fuck*, things are getting out of control," he muttered as he tossed the shoe back to its owner. "I want to tell you—"

Max Stone plopped down in the chair next to Trent and slapped him on the shoulder. "Hey, buddy. These gay guys know how to throw a party, am I right?"

Trent scooted away, closer to Christophe. "I'm pretty sure Julie and Heather are the ones who staged this shindig."

"Really? Maybe I should—"

"Pardon me, Max." Christophe pointed to the dancers gyrating in the middle of the room. "Isn't this the—what do you call it?—the Macarena?"

"Yes! Got to get in on this action. Later, dudes." He dashed off, scattering other guests in his rush to the middle of the dance floor.

Trent chuckled. "It's a good thing Riley and Logan are already gone. I don't think either of them would survive hearing the Macarena at their wedding reception. So. As I was saying..." He took Christophe's hands in both of his, so careful with Christophe's swollen fingers.

Suddenly, Christophe couldn't bear to hear it. If Trent was about to leave him behind, he wanted to delay that moment as long as possible. "I can help you get your trust fund back," he blurted.

"What?"

"Your father's legal stonewalling. I may no longer be the CEO-in-waiting of Clavret et Cie, but I nonetheless have access to the finest lawyers ever to rip an opponent to shreds."

"That's very... feudal of you."

"What can I say? It's in my blood."

"But you're broke now. Same as me."

"Anton overstated his case. I inherited money from my mother, so even without the company backing, I am far from destitute."

"So I guess the thrift store shopping trip is off the table, huh?"

"Perhaps. But I appreciated the offer nonetheless. Allow me to assist you in this small way." *Please,* cher, *let me be* necessary *to you.*

Trent ran a hand over the back of his head. "Thing is, it's a little more than a trust fund. I always called it that because that was the part that mattered when I was nineteen."

"You mean last week?"

Trent grinned at him. "No, you jerk. Seven years ago. And it wasn't only a trust *fund.* It was a whole freaking trust. My grandfather left his estate to me."

"What, you mean the house?"

"No, I mean everything. The house, the money, the yacht, although that didn't make it through some hurricane or other. He left it in trust for me until I turned twenty-five. My father is one of the trustees. His asshole lawyer is another one. There was a third one, Grandfather's lawyer, but he died while I was checked out of reality. A new one has to be appointed, I guess. I'm not really sure how it works."

Christophe's heart sank. "So you're wealthy."

"Theoretically, yeah. I mean my family is. Whether any of it'll get to me remains to be seen."

"So everything I gave you was superfluous. Laughable, even."

"Dude. At the moment, the only money I've got on me is the two hundred bucks I got for not having sex with your brother."

He doesn't need me at all.

"I see."

"Anyway, can we get back to the point? I wanted to tell you that I want this." He gestured at the crowd gyrating on the dance floor.

"The Macarena?"

"No. God, I'm fucking this up. I want what Riley and Logan have. That connection. That commitment. That knowledge that someone always has their back, no matter what. I want to look at someone with that same giant freaking joy that Logan had leaking out his ears when he made his vows."

"I . . . see. Well, I suppose if you—"

"No, idiot. I want that *with you.* I know it's early days yet, but—" Trent scooted forward and put his hands on Christophe's knees. "When I thought you'd get killed by those ranchers, or by your own damn brother—Jesus fuck, Christophe. I'd rather volunteer for another seven years in the ghost war than let anything like that happen to you again. I mean, sure, you take care of me, keep my shadows away. But the thing is—" He swallowed, ducking his head so that his hair fell over his eyes. "You need someone to keep *you* safe. To chase *your* shadows. And I . . . I want to be that person. I'm not sure I can be—I mean, fuckup is my middle name, but . . ."

Christophe's chest filled with light. He brushed his fingers over Trent's lips. When Trent raised his chin, his impossibly blue eyes were filled with doubt. *No more of that. Not if I can help it.* "You saved me, *mon amour.* Despite the odds against us, despite my inability to communicate, despite the shock of discovering my true nature. You are smart, resourceful, brave, and without a doubt the most remarkable man it has ever been my privilege to meet. I could ask for no one better."

Trent's smile was uncertain. "Um . . . that first night, you said burdens could be lighter if they're shared. I've practically buried you in mine. Let me share yours. Please?"

"What is it you say? Abso-fucking-lutely."

Trent exhaled, as if he'd been holding his breath. "Oh thank God." Then he laughed and pulled Christophe into his lap. He laced his fingers through Christophe's tangled hair and angled his face for a kiss, moaning as their tongues met and danced to a beat far more sensual and primitive than the Macarena.

Suddenly, a light shone on them.

"Hey, guys, we're doing a video guest book." Julie's face appeared over Trent's shoulder, wearing a decided smirk. "Care to say something to help Logan and Riley remember the day?"

"I don't think they'll have any trouble remembering it. It was . . . eventful." Christophe smiled for the camera, but wished he didn't appear at such a disadvantage. Forever now, he would be the savage at the feast—which, when he thought about it, was exactly what he'd always been. But with Trent beside him, it scarcely mattered. *He's seen the beast, yet loves me anyway.*

"If Logan and Riley can't remember *this* day, they need more help than video footage," Trent said, his hot gaze never leaving Christophe's face. "And as for you guys—fuck off. I'm busy."

To Christophe's great and utter joy, Trent dove back into the kiss.

EPILOGUE

Two months later

The sun hadn't yet cleared the trees when Trent threw open the French doors of their cabin—the same one he and Christophe had shared back in May. He wore only his running shorts and a tank top, and the morning air was cool against his skin. If yesterday was any indication, though, the day would turn hella hot before noon. All the more reason to get Christophe on the trail quickly.

After moving into Christophe's Pearl District condo when they'd returned from Riley and Logan's wedding, Trent had discovered that Christophe was not exactly a morning person. *Hello, understatement?* And on days when he had to do the werewolf thing, he dragged his feet three times as much.

"Hey, babe. It's time."

Christophe, in nothing but boxer briefs and a scowl, stalked out of the bedroom. "You're far too chipper for this early in the morning."

"That's because I slept really well again last night." Trent stretched, taking a deep breath of the clear air. "Of course, it helped that you fucked me into the mattress first."

"Yes. You retain that regrettable habit of dropping off after sex."

Trent sauntered over and pressed up against Christophe, tucking his thumbs inside the waistband of Christophe's briefs. "You know you love that. It gives you a chance to get all wolfy and protective."

A smile quivered on Christophe's lips. "Perhaps."

"My scars have even started to fade. See?" Trent tilted his head, exposing his neck, something he'd never have done two months ago.

Christophe nuzzled beneath Trent's ear, sending a shiver from the base of his skull to his heels. "I've noticed."

"My therapist says it's because I'm finally coming to terms with my captivity."

"We know the truth, however." Christophe's grin was positively feral. "No nightmare would dare challenge a wolf."

Trent chuckled. "You talk about nightmares as if they're sentient."

"Are they not?"

"Uh..." Trent really didn't want to think about *that* possibility. He was already getting a little creeped out by the work he and Riley were doing to prep the first of Julie's legend-tripping specials. Sure, having someone he could depend on absolutely, like he did Christophe, had done wonders for his PTSD, but recovery was about the journey, not the finish line.

"Did you hear from your lawyer yet?"

"Yeah, she texted me this morning." He kissed Christophe. Twice. "She is so fucking awesome. She thinks she'll have at least the interest available to me soon, so I won't be dependent on you forever."

"What's mine is yours, *mon amour*. I've told you many times."

"Yeah, but somebody has to keep the lights on, and you're gonna be a starving student this fall, same as Logan."

"Hardly starving, as you are well aware. Once the merger of Clavret et Cie and Merrick Industries is complete, and Gemma takes over as CEO, I'll be on the payroll as a consultant."

"'Starving' has nothing to do with money—it's a frame of mind. You need to get with the program here or your degree won't mean shit. Eat ramen. Drink only on dollar-beer night. Tailgate." He threw his arms wide. "Embrace the beauty of the true academic experience."

Christophe chuckled. "As you will?"

"I'm working on it." His job with Julie's company was rebuilding his confidence—on-camera work fired fewer of his emotional triggers, enabling him to work up to audition-readiness. "I'll be good to go once the trust fund's back online."

"Does she think that will happen soon?

Trent shrugged. "Soon enough. I told her Dad and Mom could have the house, so that's a giant bargaining chip for her. Although I'm having that damn memorial taken down. That's nonnegotiable."

"It's about time."

"No shit." Trent's cell phone vibrated in the pocket of his shorts. "Hold on. Maybe this is her." He pulled out the iPhone—which was finally as familiar as his old Nokia—and barked a laugh when he read the text.

"Your lawyer makes jokes?"

"It's not from her." He stowed the phone back in his pocket. "It's from Petersen, this guy from my old PSU legend-tripping group."

Christophe's eyebrows shot up. "I thought you had lost contact with them."

"Got back in touch for Julie's show. You'll love this. Know who their newest recruit is?"

"Mystique."

"No, smart-ass. Bishop."

"Your detective?"

"Ex-detective. Apparently he's left the force to be a PI or something." Trent bumped Christophe's shoulder with his fist. "But he's into the supernatural now. Guess you made a believer out of him."

The morning sun highlighted the pinch of Christophe's lips. "One does one's poor best."

"Hey." Trent laced his fingers behind Christophe's neck and dropped a kiss on his forehead. "I know you hate the whole shifting thing, and it fricking sucks that you've gotta do it. But if you don't, you'll feel like shit."

Christophe sighed. "I know."

After Trent had found out what Christophe went through with that damn suppressant, he'd insisted that Christophe cut way back. Plus, Riley had put them in touch with this new-age shaman or witch or whatever—although she called herself a psychic counselor—and she'd come up with a much better potion than that Middle Ages crap. It didn't have nearly the side effects—nothing worse than a few hours' worth of mild headache.

But she warned them not to overdo, and gave them some other ideas about how to extend the time between shifts. The answer was to keep the wolf happy without provoking him to come out and prowl.

Sex was one way to do that. Lots of sex, and Trent was more than happy to oblige.

With a little—okay, a lot—of experimentation, they'd found the optimum schedule: a couple of wolfy hours every two or three weeks did the trick, although Christophe still groused about it.

"Ready to do the deed then?"

Christophe's scowl returned. "No."

"Come on. Don't be a baby. Or should I say pup?"

"Don't push it, *cher.*"

Trent snapped his fingers. "Oops. Almost forgot. Hold on."

He trotted into the bedroom and dug one of Christophe's undershirts out of his own jumbled drawer. Trent always kept several pieces of Christophe's clothing—worn and not laundered—amongst his own things, just in case. Undershirts were definitely his favorite.

He returned to the living room. As soon as Christophe spotted what Trent carried, his eyes glowed gold with possessiveness. Trent grinned and waved the undershirt as if it were a cape and he a matador.

"You like it when I hold your clothes, don't you?"

"Yes," Christophe growled. "Come here."

Trent backed toward the door, waving the shirt like a handkerchief this time. "Oh no. You have to catch me first."

He bolted out the door—to tease, yes, but to give Christophe privacy too. Behind him, he heard the now-familiar sounds of Christophe's transformation. Jesus, they both hated that part, and Christophe was still uncomfortable shifting with an audience. Trent granted him privacy for that, but for everything else? Trent intended to be there always, helping in whatever way Christophe needed.

He'd gotten a mile down the path when the beat of wolf paws sounded behind him and Christophe appeared at his side. Trent grinned down at him and buried his hand in the fur at Christophe's neck, adjusting his pace so they were loping along together.

Together. Hell yeah.

Legend tripping be damned. Trent had a sexy wolf-man in his life and in his bed. Nothing could ever be more badass—or more thrilling—than that.

AUTHOR'S NOTE

When I heard about the legend of Bisclavret—a werewolf whose shifts were controlled by access to his clothing—on the *Fakelore* podcast, I immediately thought of it as the source of another legend-tripping adventure. While researching the original story, I discovered two other werewolf references with similar tropes: Sir Marrok, mentioned briefly by Sir Thomas Malory in *Le Morte d'Arthur*, and Melion, the subject of an anonymous French lay from the early fifteenth century.

I've used these clothing-dependent werewolves as the progenitors of the three Old Families in *Wolf's Clothing*, updating "Marrok" to "Merrick" and "Bisclavret" to "Clavret."

Naturally, I've taken some liberties with the stories. For instance, in the original lay, Melion's shifts were controlled by the stones in a ring. Sir Marrok was apparently trapped by sorcery, although Malory's reference to him was extremely brief: "Sir Marrok, the good knight that was betrayed with his wife, for she made him seven year a wer-wolf."

Each man, however, was betrayed by the person he trusted most, and trapped in his wolf form until he was able to convince someone else of his identity.

Explore more of the *Legend Tripping* universe:
riptidepublishing.com/titles/universe/legend-tripping

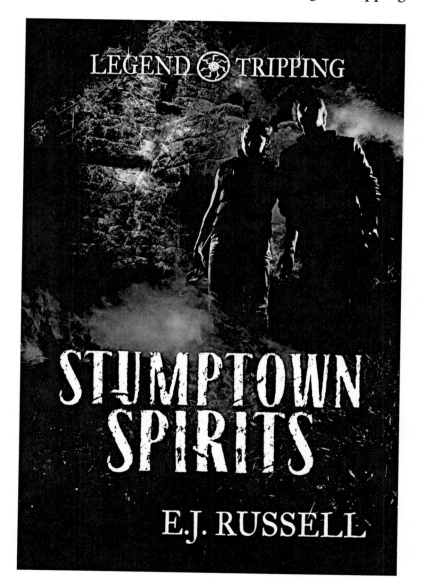

Dear Reader,

Thank you for reading E.J. Russell's *Wolf's Clothing*!

We know your time is precious and you have many, many entertainment options, so it means a lot that you've chosen to spend your time reading. We really hope you enjoyed it.

We'd be honored if you'd consider posting a review—good or bad—on sites like **Amazon, Barnes & Noble, Kobo, Goodreads, Twitter, Facebook, Tumblr,** and your blog or website. We'd also be honored if you told your friends and family about this book. Word of mouth is a book's lifeblood!

For more information on upcoming releases, author interviews, blog tours, contests, giveaways, and more, please sign up for our weekly, spam-free newsletter and visit us around the web:

Newsletter: tinyurl.com/RiptideSignup
Twitter: twitter.com/RiptideBooks
Facebook: facebook.com/RiptidePublishing
Goodreads: tinyurl.com/RiptideOnGoodreads
Tumblr: riptidepublishing.tumblr.com

Thank you so much for Reading the Rainbow!

RiptidePublishing.com

ACKNOWLEDGMENTS

As always, I owe enormous thanks to the wonderful folks at Riptide—especially to Sarah Lyons, for believing Trent deserved his own story; to Carole-ann Galloway, for editing kung fu and for not getting annoyed with me for my continued obtuseness about past progressive tense (and for my tendency to write long sentences—like this one); to Amelia Vaughn, for preventing me from plotzing about publicity; and to L.C. Chase, for the awesome cover art.

Sincere appreciation to Caitlyn Paxon and Magill Foote from the *Fakelore* podcast, whose "Sexy Wolf Men" episode introduced me to the legend of the Bisclavret.

Thanks also to Anne Tenino and Gina Fluharty, for beta reads; to C. Morgan Kennedy, Ravenne Law, and E.W. Chang Gibson, for hand-holding and/or butt-kicking as required—and to all five of you for friendship, brunch, and wine, whether real or virtual.

Finally, thank you to my family, who understand (or at least accept) my compulsion to commune with my computer for hours at a time, and for not expecting me to do housework.

ALSO BY
E.J. RUSSELL

Legend Tripping series
Stumptown Spirits

Lost in Geeklandia
Northern Light

Coming Soon
Clickbait

ABOUT
THE AUTHOR

E.J. Russell holds a BA and an MFA in theater, so naturally she's spent the last three decades as a financial manager, database designer, and business intelligence consultant. Several years ago, she realized Darling Sons A and B would be heading off to college soon and she'd no longer need to spend half her waking hours ferrying them to dance class.

What to do with all that free time?

A lucky encounter with Jim Butcher's craft blog posts caused her to revisit her childhood dream of writing fiction, and now she wonders why she ever thought an empty nest meant leisure.

Her daily commute consists of walking from one side of her office to the other, from left-brain day job to right-brain writer's cave, where she's learned to type with a dog attached to her hip and a cat draped across her wrists.

E.J. is married to Curmudgeonly Husband, a man who cares even less about sports than she does. Luckily, C.H. also loves to cook, or all three of their children (Lovely Daughter and Darling Sons A and B) would have survived on nothing but Cheerios, beef jerky, and satsuma mandarins (the extent of E.J.'s culinary skill set).

E.J. lives in rural Oregon, enjoys visits from her wonderful adult children, and indulges in good books, red wine, and the occasional hyperbole.

Find E.J. at ejrussell.com, on Twitter at twitter.com/ej_russell, and on Facebook at facebook.com/E.J.Russell.author.

Enjoy more stories like
Wolf's Clothing
at RiptidePublishing.com!

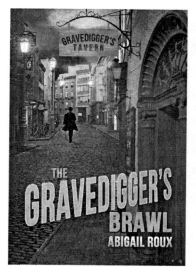

The Gravedigger's Brawl
ISBN: 978-1-937551-53-7

The Secret of Hunter's Bog
ISBN: 978-1-62649-374-2

Earn Bonus Bucks!

Earn 1 Bonus Buck for each dollar you spend. Find out how at
RiptidePublishing.com/news/bonus-bucks.

Win Free Ebooks for a Year!

Pre-order coming soon titles directly through our site and you'll
receive one entry into a drawing for a chance to win free books for
a year! Get the details at RiptidePublishing.com/contests.

CPSIA information can be obtained
at www.ICGtesting.com
Printed in the USA
FSOW01n0053031216
28100FS